Journey to Wizards' Keep

Sara Cole
K.C. Cowan   Nancy Danner

Here's to
your journey!
KC Cowan

Sara Cole

Enjoy the journey!
Nancy D

JOURNEY TO WIZARDS' KEEP

by

K.C. Cowan, Sara Cole & Nancy Danner

Copyright © K.C. Cowan 2016
Cover Copyright © Shanon Playford 2016
Website: http://www.shanonplayford.com/
Published by Chimera
(An Imprint of Ravenswood Publishing)

CHIMERA

Ravenswood Publishing
1275 Baptist Chapel Rd.
Autryville, NC 28318
http://www.ravenswoodpublishing.com

Printed in the U.S.A.

ISBN-13: 978-0692762301
ISBN-10: 0692762302

K.C. Cowan: To my mother, who never denied me a book, and to my husband, Glenn, who supports me in all things.

Sara Cole: To my father, who encouraged me to read, and to my mother, who encouraged me to dream.

Nancy Danner: To my mother. And in gratitude to my dear friends, K.C. and Sara, for including me in this endeavor.

PROLOGUE

Irene ran swiftly, blindly, and more frightened than she'd ever been in her life. Tree branches slapped into her face. She tried to keep from stumbling on the narrow, rough path as the daylight faded. From behind, she could hear her best friend, Nan, panting as she struggled to keep up.

Hatred echoed in the distance. Eerie war chants of the mysterious army that had attacked their town without warning called through the valley.

Irene had no idea who the soldiers were, or why they had chosen to wage war on her peaceful community.

She only knew she and Nan had to get to safety.

I can't believe this is happening!

My day started out so…

Normal!

PART ONE:
ATTACK OF THE SECRET VALLEY

CHAPTER 1

Irene, Princess of Cabbage, pulled the thread tight in the tapestry, set her needle down, and studied her work with a critical eye.

It was far from ready to hang with the many other tapestries in her suite. However, she didn't want to continue working on the scene, which depicted mountains and meadow flowers.

She moved across the sunny room to make herself a cup of tea. After putting the kettle on the fire, Irene looked around and considered her options for the afternoon.

She could practice her harpsichord. She could finish the dress she was sewing. Or, perhaps, she could take a walk in the village outside the castle.

None of these possibilities seemed appealing at the moment.

Irene sighed, wishing Nan was here.

But her friend was studying with the famed dance instructor, Gene the Ewe (so called because with her pale, pink skin and tall bouffant of white hair she rather resembled a sheep). After moving to a new school, many miles south of the Valley, Nan's visits home had been rare.

Irene reached up and twirled a lock of her long, brown hair. As she did so, her eyes fell on the most recent letter from her brother, King Jeo II. She picked it up and read it for what felt like the hundredth time.

It is time you came back to Cabbage, my dearest sister, and take up your royal duties. When I sent you to live in the Valley of William Etté with the family of our father's former servant, I never intended that you reside there for so long. Now that you are sixteen, it is high time you accept the responsibilities of your position and come home to prepare for marriage. I have several appropriate prospects in mind.

Irene dropped the letter on the table.

The thought of an arranged marriage filled her with despair. She well remembered the first match her parents had agreed to when she was but eight. When that man had arrived, a year ago, the match had proven to be disastrous. Fortunately, Irene had managed to find a way out of the wedding.

Now, she poured her tea and sat by the window, leaning on the cool stone ledge and gazing out at the lush, green valley and the range of snow-capped mountains that lay beyond.

Even the warm spring day didn't lighten her mood.

I want to marry someone I love. Not someone my brother chooses for me.

If only Michael and I could have married.

Of course, Jeo would never permit a match so far below my station...

She glared at the letter, contemplating her brother's demands. A surge of panic washed over her.

I can't do it. I can't go back.

I...

I don't even want to be a princess any longer!

Irene rushed over to her desk, pulled out a fresh sheet of paper, a sharp quill and her inkstand. Once she had her tools in hand, she took a deep breath and began to write.

My dear brother, my heart is heavy as I write to tell you I will not be returning to Cabbage...

Lost in the composition of her letter, the knock at the door made Irene jump. When she opened the door, she was stunned to find Nan on the other side, smiling. She rushed forward to wrap the girl in a warm embrace.

"Surprise!" Nan cried.

Irene gave a startled laugh and returned the hug before pulling back. "Nan! I can't believe you're here! Why? Is the dance school closed for some reason?"

"No, but I'm home for good. I've learned all I can at the school, so I left. I just left!" Nan bounced up and down on her toes in excitement, making her curly, red hair bounce as well. Her green eyes sparkled within her sweet face, which was sprinkled with freckles. "I've been riding since before daylight," she added, as she entered. She twirled around the room. "I didn't even take time to flirt with the cute soldiers I passed along the way." She giggled.

Irene smiled at her friend's enthusiasm. "But, Nan, are you sure you want to leave? You might become a famous dancer if you continue your studies."

Nan stopped twirling and shrugged. "Maybe. But I missed everyone too much. I care more about being with my family and friends than about becoming famous."

She resumed her dancing, twirling her way over to the kitchen area.

"May I?" she asked, pointing to the tea. At Irene's nod, she poured herself a cup.

"Are you hungry?" Irene asked, smiling. "Sit down and I'll fix you something to eat."

"Oh, no. I really would love a walk. It's such a long ride to here on horseback, you know. Why don't we go up to the forest like we used to? We can take supper....?" Nan broke off, a stricken expression on her face. "That is...if you don't mind...or have other plans. Oh, dear, I should have sent a message ahead—I'm so sorry!"

Irene shook her head. "Nan, you always worry too much about other people's feelings. A picnic sounds perfect," she assured her friend. "I'm so glad you've come home."

Nan looked relieved. "I'm glad to *be* home."

Irene began to pack bread, cheese, fruit, and a bottle of cider in a wicker basket. "Why don't you move in with me here at the castle? King Neil won't mind. There's plenty of room. And we'll have so much fun. It will be like when I lived with your family."

"I was hoping you would ask me! In fact," Nan paused, looking a bit sheepish, "I already ordered my things be sent here. They should arrive tomorrow. I've been envious of your living on your own since King Neil let you take a room in the castle after I left for dance academy. Quite a change from our little home. I'll tell my parents, later, that I'm not moving back in with them. After all, I am sixteen now! Papa might be upset, but mother will be fine—one less mouth to feed."

The two exited the castle and walked through the courtyard to the main gate and onto the cobblestone street leading though town. They swung their basket of food between them as they passed village shops and homes.

"Princess Irene," a shopkeeper called, coming out of his store. "The new sheet of music you requested is here."

"Oh, thank you, Ephraim. I will pick it up on our way back."

A plump woman sweeping the stoop of her shop glanced up and smiled broadly at the two girls. "Nan, bless my soul! How lovely to see you! Have you come home, then?"

"Yes, I..."

"Tell your mother I've got fresh strawberries today—first of the season."

"Oh, I'm sure she..."

"You won't find fresher anywhere in the village!"

"Of course, but I..."

"Wait until I tell my Jeffrey you've come home. You can expect him to call on you very soon, I'm certain!"

"Oh, uh...that is..." Nan stammered.

"Yes, thank you, Madame Bouchette," Irene called as she dragged Nan away. The girls exchanged amused glances. When they reached the end of the town, they turned to climb a hill and hike through the forest to a favorite clearing. They set up their supper in the field near a solitary apple tree filled with pink blossoms.

"So what do you think you'll do now you're home?" Irene asked, between bites.

"I suppose I will dance at King Neil's court. He's as much as told me I have a standing invitation," Nan mused. "Beyond that, I don't know."

"You could accept the marriage proposal from Jeffrey," Irene teased. "After all, Madame Bouchette already has you engaged in her mind."

Nan rolled her eyes. "I can't imagine why she would think that! I never did the least little thing to encourage him. At least, I don't think I did. Besides...I'm not...well...I don't really *feel* anything for Jeffrey beyond affection. We played together as children and I like him well enough. But that's no reason to wed. I want a real romance."

"I understand. Only the truest love would ever make me happy."

Nan reached over and took her hand. "You still miss him, don't you?" she asked softly.

"I think I always will. Although I am *determined* to put my love for Michael behind me. There's no point continuing to pine for him. Someday I may meet someone who will make me feel the same way he did. But if not, I would be content to never marry at all. Though, I fear my brother will have something to say about that."

Nan nodded. "Yes, I noticed a letter from him on the table."

Irene sighed. "Jeo insists I return to Cabbage."

"Well, we knew this day would come. But imagine if my father had never worked for your father. Jeo wouldn't have thought to send you here after your parents died. We might never have met. And with *six* brothers, I needed you for a sister!" She threw her arms around Irene. "I can't imagine my life without you nearby!"

Irene returned the hug. "Me either. I was only meant to stay with your family for a year or two until Jeo felt more comfortable as the new king. But I was happy, so he let me be. And now I feel like the Valley of William Etté is my real home. I know I should go back, but I don't want Jeo picking out my husband. What if he finds someone like my first fiancé, Jean de la Grande Pomme?"

"I'm sure Jeo would choose better. Still, I'd hate for you to move away." She leaned back onto the grass. "When I marry, I hope I have

8

a half dozen children and live a quiet, happy life right here in the Valley."

"You have no idea how much I envy you, Nan. You will never worry about always being on your best behavior at stuffy royal events or making a marriage to improve relations between kingdoms. You can do as you please." She shook her head with determination. "No. I can't face it. I've decided I won't go back. In fact, I was writing my brother a letter telling him so when you arrived."

Nan sat up, her eyes wide. "But what will you do? Can you truly just...give up being a princess?"

"I honestly don't know. But I can't live the life my brother has planned for me. I need to make my own choices and decisions. I won't be anyone's puppet!"

"But don't you have a duty? I mean, isn't that what being a princess is all about?"

"A duty to do what? It's not like I'll ever rule on my own. Even if I do marry some prince and he becomes king, there's no guarantee he'll ever let me do anything except look pretty at balls and give him lots of sons."

"It might not be...*quite* so awful," Nan said hesitantly.

"Oh, Nan, you don't know what a royal marriage can be like! My parents had a true love match, but sometimes a king and queen can't abide each other. Then the king takes mistresses and ignores his wife and she has nothing to do all day but drink wine and play cards with sycophants from the court. I'd go mad!"

"So, you'll run away?"

Irene moaned and put her head on her knees. "I don't know. I'm afraid to send Jeo that letter, but I'm even more afraid not to."

The girls were lost in conversation, unaware of the chittering of the birds above them. The birds became excited and chirped more loudly, hopping from branch to branch, flying a short distance away, and returning to the tree.

The girls looked up and watched the birds take to the air, circle and fly away. Once they left, the forest seemed strangely quiet. There was no wind, and no sound from any other birds or animals.

Irene turned to Nan. "We'd better go back to the castle. It's getting dark."

"Yes, I hadn't noticed it was so late."

They quickly packed the remains of their meal and half ran, half walked, anxious to get out of the silent forest.

Irene pointed to the sky. "Is that smoke? Or clouds?"

Nan shook her head, uncertain, and they hurried on.

"Watch out!" Irene shoved Nan aside as three deer came bounding from the brush, narrowly missing them.

Frightened, the girls began to run.

Near the edge of the woods, they were startled by a flock of blackbirds that flew, cawing loudly, into the woods, as if they were being chased.

The girls exited the woods at the top of a hill and looked down in shock to see the castle prepared for battle. The flags of the army were raised on the twin towers, flanking the main gate, which, now, appeared secured. Glancing to the west, Irene realized the smoke she noticed was coming from hundreds of torches carried by a massive army in the distance.

"Irene, what is all this?" Nan's voice trembled.

"I don't know." Irene said, frowning. "Wait. Didn't you say you saw some soldiers on the road on your way home?"

"Yes."

"Were they from the Valley's regiments?"

"I don't...no. No, they weren't. Their leggings were black. Our soldiers wear white. I'm sure they weren't from the Valley."

"They must have been enemy scouts. We're going to be attacked. Come on!"

They raced down the hill and through the now deserted village to the castle. Once there, they stood before the gate, trying to attract someone's attention.

"Please, let us in! It is Nan and Irene!"

No one responded; the army was inside, listening to their general shout orders for the approaching battle. Nan and Irene grabbed stones and sticks—anything they could get their hands on—and threw them at the gate, hoping someone would hear them. They looked back at the huge army steadily moving closer.

At last, a young lieutenant waved to them from the watchtower.

"Open the gate! It is Nan and Irene," the girls shouted.

"We can't. 'Tis already secured," he called back. "Even if we let you in, ye'd probably die within the walls. We're no match for this army. Run for your lives! Go to yer brother in Cabbage, Irene. It's yer only chance. Warn him about the army!"

"But who are they? Where are they from?"

"We don't know. They sent a message earlier and all it said was: 'Be ready this evening at dusk to fight an army larger than any ye have ever seen.' Go—run! Stick to the back roads!"

"Irene, we can't leave. My family!"

"We must." Irene grabbed Nan's arm. "Look!"

The army was now close enough for Nan and Irene to read the banners they carried. Battle trumpets sounded and the soldiers roared as they charged the castle. A hail of arrows flew through the air, some falling close to Nan and Irene as they ran along the south side of the fortress. They rounded the corner only to find more soldiers moving forward to secure the back.

Nan screamed in terror while Irene frantically looked for an escape route. Spying a narrow, overgrown path to the left, she grabbed Nan's arm, and pulled her towards it. They fled up the path, tearing their dresses, scratching their hands and faces on undergrowth. The sounds of battle followed them. They finally stopped running at the top of a far hill.

"I can't run anymore," Nan gasped, holding her sides.

"Nor can I," Irene whispered.

From where they stopped, the valley was in full view below them. It was hard to pick out details as the darkness grew, but the army set fire to the village. Flames lit scenes of horror. Irene and Nan heard a low thudding noise from a battering ram being pushed into the main gate again and again. Soldiers placed four tall ladders against the walls of the castle and were rapidly scaling them.

The defenders of the Valley of William Etté did their best, but the attacking army was large and organized. The enormous battering log finally crashed through the castle gate, and the enemy soldiers poured inside. Irene and Nan sank to their knees, holding each other as they listened to the distant clang of steel against steel and the cries of fighting men. The screams! Would they never end? After two hours, the battle seemed over. Nan and Irene, huddled together on the ground, heard only an occasional whoop from a member of the victorious army.

Holding hands, they stood and peered down, trying to see through the gloom. The castle was charred black in places and many fires still burned. Celebratory noises floated up from men breaking into the castle's store and picking the pockets of the dead. The Valley's army barely made a dent in the huge number of enemy soldiers. The girls stood in shocked silence, too stunned and angry to even cry. The home they loved so much was gone.

"We must warn my brother," Irene said abruptly, turning away. Nan took one last tearful glance at the town before rushing to catch up with Irene. They began walking southeast over the hills towards Cabbage. It was late and they were tired, but they knew they must hurry lest Cabbage be the army's next victim.

After a while, they came to a stream, where they stopped to quench their thirst and wash the blood off their scratched hands and faces. As they rested, they heard rustling in some nearby bushes.

"We've been followed," Nan cried. "Hide!"

Irene pointed to a dead log. They ran over and ducked behind it. The rustling continued for a few minutes until, finally, someone burst through the bushes. The person (or was it two?) walked towards the stream, each step landing heavily on the ground. The footsteps stopped and a noisy slurping began. Nan peered over the log and let out a yelp of surprise.

"It's only a horse!" There was a white stallion. He bore no saddle but wore the coat of arms of the Valley's regiment.

"Whoa, boy, whoa." Nan slowly walked towards him. "We won't hurt you." She snatched the reins and the horse reared back, his eyes rolling. He whinnied with fear, but Nan held tight. As Irene and Nan talked softly to him, he calmed down.

"He must have run away from the battle after he lost his rider," Irene said.

"He's as scared as we are."

"Do you think he's calm enough, now, to let us ride him?"

"We'll find out. Help me up."

Irene boosted Nan up and then, with Nan's help, climbed behind.

◆

By late morning, Nan and Irene were almost at the kingdom of Cabbage. The mountains were behind them and her brother's province was at the river's bend. As she saw the familiar homes and landscape, Irene had a sudden pang of longing. She realized how much she missed Cabbage.

Once we get to the palace and see my brother, all will be well.

They galloped towards the safety of the village. Suddenly, Nan pulled back on the reins to stop the horse.

"Why did you stop? Is there a problem with the horse?" Irene asked.

"No. I...hope I'm wrong, but...see the house on the right? And the one behind it? They're burned."

"No, not Cabbage, too! The army must have come here first. Jeo!"

Nan nudged the horse and they moved into the town square. There was a child's shoe abandoned in the road. Nearby, a basket of vegetables spilled into the dirt. Then, they began to see bodies in blood-soaked clothing lying in awkward positions, flies buzzing around.

Horrified, Nan whispered, "They never had a chance. Irene, let's leave. There's nothing we can do."

"No, there is a chance Jeo is still alive. Let's go to the palace."

"But, I don't think..."

"Please, let's go."

Nan kicked the horse and they cantered through the streets, trying not to look at the carnage. When they reached the palace, they came across a brown horse tethered to a post. It was the first living thing they had seen since entering the village. Its coat was rough and uncurried, and every blade of grass within circumference of its tether was gone.

"Perhaps it's my brother's horse. In fact, I'm sure it is. He's probably inside right now."

"I don't know, Irene. The horse looks abandoned. He clearly hasn't been cared for in days."

"Maybe Jeo is hurt and hasn't been able to tend to him." Irene slid off the horse and dashed over the green lawn towards the front doors, which stood open.

"Irene, wait!" Nan dismounted and chased after her friend.

Irene ran from room to room, calling for her brother. Finding no one on the main level, she climbed the stairway to the second floor and went to her brother's bedchamber, with Nan close behind. The grand stone room, which bore high ceilings, was ransacked and the bed appeared as if it had been slept in.

Irene turned to Nan. "He's here; I know it. There is a secret room behind the bed. My father showed it to me once. He told me if I were ever in any danger I should hide there. My brother is probably in there now. All I need to do is push a lever under the bed and a panel between the bedposts will slide open." Irene stooped down and reached for the lever to push. "Help me; it's stuck."

Nan crouched on the floor beside Irene and tried the lever, but it was too stiff.

"Get that log," Irene said. Nan ran over to the fireplace and brought it back. Bracing themselves, the two girls pressed the log with their feet until the lever slowly moved forward. It finally clicked into position, sending the panel sliding freely. A huge bear of a man came from behind it. Before Nan and Irene could react, he grabbed them both.

"Surprised my darlins'? I bet it weren't me ye was lookin' fer," he bellowed in a gruff voice. "Well, whoever it was ye wanted, I'm sure ye'll agree I'm a much better prize, eh?"

Irene struggled to get away and slapped at the beast's wrist, but he only held her tighter.

"Did ye think ye'd be leavin' now?" he laughed. "Naw, I'll be pleased if ye would consent to stay a while. The colonel might look on me more kindly if I was to bring him two prisoners, especially ones as pretty as ye be. Yeh, I made a grave mistake when I deserted the army, but I might be forgiven if ye two ladies would help me out a bit. I'm really a nice man once ye git to know me, as ye soon will."

Nan and Irene stared at each other in horror.

What now?

CHAPTER 2

Good Heavens, Nan thought. *What can he mean by 'if we're 'nice to him?' We've found Irene's home devastated and her brother missing. Irene and I shall be less than nice! Of course, I'm not sure if that is possible for a Princess...*

"Ladies—yes—ye be true ladies, I can see that," the man spoke again. "Per'aps my commander will even give me a commission fer such a pretty prize."

Irene recovered somewhat from the shock the man had given them. "You brute! Do you think we would allow you to present us to some ancient cretin whose only purpose in life is to wage war? We *are* ladies and won't be treated as if we were common doxies to be passed around like a salt shaker at the table!"

She tried to wrench her slender wrist from his grip as she stormed on, "Let us go at once. And if you took the life of my only brother, you may take my own as well before I allow you to insult me further with your foul breath!"

"M'lady, I fear you have no choice," a firm, masculine voice spoke from behind. The three whirled around to see a dark-haired man of perhaps thirty years. His features were handsome, but the tilt of his eyebrows, combined with his twisted smile, gave him a sardonic appearance, which somewhat countered the effect of his good looks. He nodded at the soldier.

"Thank you, my good man, for a catch worthy to present to Lord William, Son of Dob." His eyes roamed over Irene and Nan. "You two lovelies will become members of the entourage in the wake of his Majesty's victories."

The foul man shouted at the stranger. "Naw! 'Tisn't fair, Sir Richard! I needs these girls to get back in the colonel's good graces— ye can't take 'em!"

The man laughed shortly. "You stupid fool—as if two common wenches will serve as recompense for what you did. Desertion is punishable by death, as you well know." He strolled casually over to the three. "You might as well hand them over to me now."

The man cried "No!" and, flinging away the two girls, reached for his weapon, but Sir Richard's hand was quicker. As Nan and Irene watched in horror, the dark-haired man's blade found a home under the ribs of the deserter. The wretch gasped and stumbled backward onto the bed. Coughing blood, his eyes bulging, he made an unsuccessful attempt to pull out the knife. At last, he fell back, dead.

Richard coolly walked over to the body. "Stupid fool," he muttered as he pulled his blade out of the dead man and carefully wiped it off on the sheets before sticking it back in the sheath on his belt. He turned to the girls, who sat in shock on the floor. "Now my fair ones, will you not be pleased to come with me to my Lord William?"

Irene spoke with what little spunk she had left. "We...we shall not be pleased to go *anywhere* with you! We are searching for my brother, and anyone who tries to keep us from our search may only fear for his life!" The princess scrambled up and marched over to Richard. "So I advise you to be on your merry way and leave us alone!"

Richard didn't bat an eye as he slapped Irene across the face. She fell with a cry to the floor. Instantly, Nan was upon Richard, beating him with all of her remaining strength. He seemed unaffected by her blows and, with another slap, Nan found herself by her friend.

"Now if you are through with your temper tantrums, we will continue. Two ladies would be a fine catch, but please believe me when I say I have absolutely no qualms about reducing that number by half if necessary. Now come with me."

Holding hands for courage, the stunned girls followed him downstairs and outside.

"I only brought one horse with me, and this other is too exhausted to continue." He motioned to the horse Nan and Irene had ridden all night. "You will ride together on this nag." He pointed to the brown horse.

Irene climbed on the horse and helped Nan up behind her. Richard had already mounted his black steed. He came alongside the girls and tied the reins from their horse to the back of his saddle.

"Just in case you get any ideas of trying to escape." He smirked. He rode off with Irene and Nan in tow.

◆

Hours later, Irene's anger had barely cooled. Never, in all of her life, had she been so mishandled! They had traveled all day, heading northeast. Sir Richard granted few breaks for the poor girls to stretch their legs or sip water from his metal flask. As dusk came and he searched for a suitable spot to camp, Irene realized with dismay they might be traveling for some time.

After halting for the day, and letting them off their horse, Richard reached into his saddlebag and threw them each a little cold meat and dried fruit.

"Sorry the portions are small." He laughed. "I didn't expect to feed extra people."

He tied them securely and gave them the horse blanket to wrap themselves in for the night. He barely spoke to the girls, and bedded down nearby. When he was snoring, Nan and Irene tried, without success, to wriggle out of their ropes. Finally, they fell asleep.

The next two days were similar—riding most of the day, minimal food to eat, and sleeping on the ground. By now, the girls' clothes were filthy, their hair a mess and they were emotionally spent. They avoided all towns and villages, staying for the most part on paths in the nearby forests. But on the third day, Richard began to lead them into the mountains.

Nan whispered, "Irene, do you know this path? Where are we going?"

"I'm not certain. I think...I think he may be going over the Hooded Mountains."

They climbed for hours, higher into the mountains. Nan and Irene shivered. Finally, Irene called out, "Sir Richard, what are you thinking taking us over the Hooded Mountains without proper attire? We shall surely perish from the cold!"

Sir Richard shot them an expression even colder than the air on the poor girls' legs. "Fear not, girl, I'll not be delivering damaged goods to my Lord William. Now keep still—we'll soon be at our destination." He turned away from them again to study the landscape, searching for something. After a bit, Sir Richard directed his horse deeper into the woods.

"This really *is* too much," Irene cried. "Now we can't even stay on the main path!"

"One more word out of you, wench, and you'll regret it."

"Irene, be careful—remember what he did to that brute in your brother's room," Nan's voice cut through Irene's anger.

Sir Richard overheard and laughed. "Your friend's got more sense than you, girl. Best take her advice."

Irene fumed.

Tree branches brushed against her and Nan's faces, and bushes scratched their already scraped and bruised legs. Just when Irene thought she would scream from frustration, Richard brought his horse to a stop and dismounted. He motioned for the two girls to follow.

16

Irene slipped off the horse and helped Nan, who sagged against her, exhausted. Richard went to a sheer rock wall and began to feel along the bottom edge.

"What's he doing?" Nan whispered.

"Shh. Watch him carefully."

After a moment, Richard found a catch of some sort. There was a loud click and he pushed hard on one side of the wall. To the girls' amazement, it pivoted as if there was a hinge in the middle, revealing the entrance to a cavern.

Two large and well-armed men came out to greet Richard. He spoke to them in a low voice. They nodded to Richard and separated, one returning deep into the cavern and the other walking with Richard to the girls. He barely glanced at them, but took the two horses and led them away. Richard motioned the girls to come with him and entered the cave.

Nan and Irene followed Richard into the cool darkness. The rock wall swung shut behind them. At last their eyes adjusted to the dim light shed by wall torches. They realized they were in a tunnel that stretched a great distance. Sir Richard walked so briskly that the tired girls were hard pressed to keep up with him. After a while, the torches became less frequent as the tunnel was becoming increasingly brighter. Ahead of them, Irene saw daylight. "We must have gone clear through the mountain," she spoke her thoughts aloud.

"Correct." Richard's voice startled her. "We are approaching the Secret Valley. Only its inhabitants know of its existence. We are nestled between two of the peaks of the Hooded Mountains and are unobservable from the trail that leads over them."

Irene studied their captor. He seemed excited to be home, and his face shone with an anticipation that made his boyish face more handsome. They continued to the end of the tunnel and stood, blinking in the late afternoon sunlight.

"Who found this place?" Nan asked.

"Our King, Lord William, stumbled onto the valley while lost on a hunting expedition. He persuaded his father, Dob, to bring their kingdom here. We have flourished over the years and grown to become the mightiest conquerors of the land. Behold! The land of William, Son of Dob!" He extended a hand dramatically over the valley, which lay below them. There was a castle, town center, homes, and fields, all surrounded by thick forests. Richard began to walk down the wide path and Nan and Irene followed.

"Why, 'tis far too large not to be seen by anyone from above!" Irene exclaimed, gazing in amazement at the thriving community.

"We suspect some ancient enchantment keeps it from being seen." Sir Richard shrugged. "Not for nothing is it called the Secret Valley.

It allows us to attack our enemies and retreat to safety. No one can find us. But enough gawking. You'll soon get to learn the place. After all, this is your new home. Follow me." Richard continued down the path.

ZZZZZZIP!

An arrow landed directly at Richard's feet. He jumped back, but made no move for his own weapons.

"Kay!" he called, looking around him. "I recognize that arrow. Come out at once, or I'll tell his Lordship you've been neglecting your duties again!"

The three of them whirled about as laughter rang from above them. Out of a nearby tree a young girl jumped down, smiling brightly. She was dressed all in soft doeskin from her shockingly short skirt to her knee-high moccasin boots. On her boyish, blond curls, she wore a garland of spring wildflowers. She carried a bow; upon her back hung her quiver of arrows. She laughed again, showing two deep dimples on either side of her smiling mouth, and spoke in a light, musical voice as she mockingly bowed to the man.

"Not neglecting my duties at all, Sir Richard, not at all. Merely looking for a bit of excitement and possibly a choice piece of venison or grouse to present to his Lordship." She paused, her gaze falling on Nan and Irene. "Looks like you've had fair hunting." She walked over to the trio and retrieved her arrow.

"Just a pair of wenches I picked up for his Lordship."

"Oh? Her Ladyship will *love* that, Richard. Or have you forgotten her? She'll not stand for two wenches in the palace."

"I'm...I mean *we're* not wenches!" Irene burst out in anger. "Nan is an accomplished dancer from the Academy of Gene the Ewe."

"And Irene is of royal blood!" added Nan.

The blond girl cocked her head, impressed. "I think you've made an error, Sir Richard. Now, surely, you're not going to hand them over as mere bed warmers, are you?"

Richard scowled. "Why didn't ye tell me, girl?"

"You didn't give me a chance!" Irene replied icily.

"Bravo!" The girl laughed. "She's got some spirit. Come, let me take them to my chambers and fix 'em up. Then we can decide what's to be done with them. You can't present them to anyone now, Richard. Truly, they look like a dog's dinner."

Sir Richard started to protest, but Kay was already leading the two girls down the path to the town below.

◆

18

"Well, here we are. Sit down and relax. You look to be on your last legs." Kay gestured to a large pit in the middle of the cool, stone room. It was filled with furs and large, soft pillows. Irene and Nan sank onto them gratefully, examining the pleasant room. Tall windows with leaded panes along one side of the room let in the afternoon light. Across the room, Irene noticed a workbench with tools where the strange girl apparently made her own arrows. Otherwise, the room was surprisingly spare, with little in the way of decoration or feminine touch. On one wall hung a long banner depicting a hawk clutching arrows against a field of flames.

"I 'spect you'll be wanting to rest a bit." She leaned in and sniffed. "And perhaps clean up. I'll have Beth draw you a bath." She turned away, "Beth!"

Through a pair of silky curtains came a petite girl. She was hardly more than a child. She had long golden hair and a lovely heart-shaped face.

"Yes, my lady Kay?"

"Beth, prepare a bath for these two ladies. I am going to visit My lady Ruth."

"Her Ruthlessness?" Beth giggled.

"Lady Ruth to you, girl!" Kay snapped. "Now do as I say. Oh, and get them something to eat as well."

"No! 'Tis not my job. Food's to be prepared by Zeelah, not me."

"Beth, what is the first rule of being a lady in waiting?" Kay asked sharply.

"To do as you're told," the girl mumbled.

"Exactly! So, do as you are told. I want as few people as possible to know about our...guests. Just say you're preparing it especially for me. Go."

"As you wish, m'lady." Beth bowed before leaving; her face impassive, but her eyes narrowed. Kay watched after her for a moment.

"I won't be long," she said to Nan and Irene, and left the room.

◆

Kay hurried down the corridor to her Ladyship's rooms. Even from a distance, the sound of angry cries filled the hall.

Ah me, 'tis not for nothing she be known as her Ruthlessness!

Kay rapped on the door. A crash of glass against the wall was the answer. Kay sighed. It wasn't going to be easy calming her out of this mood. She knocked again, and called through the door.

"Lady Ruthless...uh, Lady Ruth! 'Tis I, Lady Kay. May I enter?"
After a pause, the door flew open revealing her Ladyship in complete

disarray. Her long, uncombed, chestnut hair tumbled about her shoulders. Her dressing gown was loosely tied and misbuttoned around her plump body. She grasped Kay's arm and yanked her into the room, shutting the door behind them.

"Oh, Kay, what am I going to do?" Lady Ruth wailed as she paced the room. "My husband would have me dead, I know it!"

A shocked Kay hurried over to comfort her mistress. "My lady, calm yourself! Why should your good Lord William wish you dead? What a wicked thought! He loves you as life itself."

Lady Ruth laughed wildly through her tears and the sound sent chills down Kay's spine. She broke away from Kay and paced again, wringing her hands.

"Then why...why is he trying to poison me?"

"Poison! My lady, I..."

"Only he failed. Failed! Because I was not hungry and gave my soup to Ginger, my dear little dog. Look at him!" She pointed to the corner where a small brown dog lay. "My poor Ginger gave his life for me!" She broke down again.

"But my lady, how can you be sure it was Lord William? Anyone could have added poison." Kay saw a look of shock on her mistress' face. "If, indeed, Ginger was poisoned, and did not die of natural causes," she hastily added. "Which I'm sure he did."

"No. William brought my lunch to me himself. He encouraged me to eat so...so I would recover from this cursed grippe. Recover! He wishes me dead, I tell you!" Lady Ruth threw herself on the bed, moaning. "Leave me, Kay—and take poor Ginger with you. Tell not a soul. We must think...think what to do!"

Kay picked up the stiff dog, wrapped a shawl around it and hurried out of the room.

"Ho there, Kay! I would speak with you!" Kay turned to see the redheaded, handsome knight, Sir Fitzgerald, coming down the hall. She wanted to run and hide the dog, but it was too late. Fitzgerald was by her side, his freckled face grinning. Kay smiled back. She felt a deep affection for him. And she knew he felt the same. The entire court was just waiting for him to declare himself formally to Kay. Then the wedding plans would begin.

"Is her Lady's temper tantrum over with? Are you free for a walk in the garden?"

"Oh, Fitzy, I cannot. I...have many things to attend to just now." Kay turned to go, but Fitzgerald caught her arm. The shawl fell open, revealing the dead pet.

"What's wrong with Ginger?" He took the dog from the protesting girl. "Why, he's dead! What happened?"

"Natural causes, I'm sure. I'm to bury him, may I please have him back?"

"Natural causes? It was but a pup! What is going on here, Kay? You can tell me," he coaxed.

"I'm sure I don't know, Fitzy," Kay stammered. "Now, I must bury the dog..."

"Such work is not fitting for a lady such as yourself. I'll bury the poor thing."

"Really, Fitzy, that is most generous of you, but—"

"Not at all, Kay. Not at all. I'll talk with you soon."

Fitzgerald was already moving down the hall. Kay looked after him with exasperation. "Men!"

As Kay walked back to her rooms, she thought of Lady Ruth with more than a little pity. Lord William had been content with his bride early on, but lately his attention wandered. His wife had given him an heir, Alex, and now he seemed to no longer need her. In her despair, her Ladyship had let a once lovely figure get plump, and she often neglected her toilette. If Kay did not attend her—comb her hair and choose her clothes for the day—she was like as not to wander around disheveled and half-dressed.

Kay opened her door to find the two strangers asleep. A tray of food lay nearby, she saw with some satisfaction. Choosing an apple, she sat down and surveyed the girls carefully, thinking.

CHAPTER 3

As Kay crunched on the apple, Irene's eyes fluttered and then flew open. She appeared startled for an instant, and then relaxed as she recognized Kay.

"Sorry. I didn't mean to disturb your sleep," Kay said.

"Oh no, I was hoping we could talk." Irene glanced over at Nan, who was still deep in slumber. "Your name is Kay?" she continued softly.

"That's what they call me."

"And we are in a valley hidden somewhere in the Hooded Mountains?"

"That's right."

"Are we prisoners?"

"Prisoners? I should say not!" Kay paused, frowning. "Well, not exactly, anyway. It will depend on what Sir Richard decides. His word is law around here unless Lord William overrules him. But, usually, he supports Richard's wishes."

"Lord William is the ruler here?" Irene asked.

"Yes. He is the one you ladies were bought here for. But he won't get near you if I have any say. My lady Ruth wouldn't like it. I don't need another thing for her to throw a temper tantrum over. Besides, it seems you two have been through enough already. What in the name of Mirn happened to you?"

Irene eyed Kay. "How do I know you weren't asked to find out about us?"

"Well, you don't. But I give you my word I ask only out of my own curiosity and I promise not to breathe a word of your story."

Irene considered for a moment. "You've been kind to us so far, and I do need to tell someone."

Irene described what she and Nan endured in the past few days. Kay listened, shocked at the story. The army that waged war on Nan and Irene's people was from her home, but she couldn't believe the soldiers were so cruel. She also couldn't see how Nan and Irene could be construed as the "enemy." Kay had been told the people in the

Valley of William Etté were ruthless murdering tribes with plans to attack them. Now she felt unsure. She shook her head when Irene finished.

"Well, I don't know what your fate will be here, but I will try to protect you if I can. I want to keep your presence here a secret, too. You are the first strangers to enter our Valley in a very long time. Tell me more about the attack on your home."

While Irene and Kay talked, Beth returned to prepare a bath for the two girls, but paused just outside the door. She stood listening to Irene's story, and then slipped away.

An hour or so later, Nan woke up and the three girls ate some supper and bathed before bed. Kay drew the water herself, as Beth was still gone.

Irene and Nan slept well that night. They were exhausted from their ordeal. Kay, however, sat up for some time, thinking about Irene's story.

Were Nan and Irene the enemy? Could she trust them?

When Beth showed up, she explained her absence saying she was at the home of a friend who was ill. *A feeble excuse*, Kay thought. *Where had that girl been?*

Finally, Kay retired for the night in the pit near Irene and Nan.

◆

Kay rose at first light, put on her best doeskin garments and grabbed her bow and arrows to get a little practice in before breakfast. When she stepped outside, Sir Richard galloped up on his horse.

"Kay. I trust the two ladies are a'right."

"Oh, yes. They ate well and seem improved in spirits. They're still asleep."

"I haven't quite decided what's to be done with them yet, but I don't want them leaving the valley. I'm holding you responsible for them while I'm gone."

"You're off again so soon?"

"Yes, I'm going to scout for more enemy tribes."

"You mean you're going to search for Demetrius, don't you? Why don't you give up? He's been missing for three weeks. He would come back if he were alive."

Richard's eyes flashed with anger and, for a moment, welled with tears. "Do not speak to me again of Demetrius!" he said through gritted teeth. "You have no right." He regained his composure. "I will expect the ladies to be here when I return in a fortnight. Farewell." He rode off.

Irene and Nan, roused by the voices, came out of Kay's quarters. "Was that Sir Richard?" Nan asked, sleepily. "What did he want?"

"He wants me to take care of you while he's away."

"Is he leaving to abduct more girls?" Irene asked scornfully.

"No." Kay laughed. "He's gone to scout for enemy tribes—or so he says. He's really looking for a friend of his named Demetrius Keats, Son of Thom. He was Richard's right-hand man and...uh...companion until a few weeks ago. A battle was fought against a town south of the Hooded Mountains. Richard led the right flank and Demetrius the left. Demetrius pushed forth to attack the center of the village while Richard circled around. A battalion of soldiers hiding in the forest ambushed the left flank. Many of our soldiers died. Richard searched for Demetrius' body, but it was never found.

"The soldiers came home, but Richard stayed on for days thinking, perhaps, Demetrius was only hurt and somehow managed to crawl away and hide from the enemy. He still insists Demetrius is alive."

"So that accounts for his rude behavior," Irene said.

"Oh, 'fraid not," Kay replied, grinning. "He's always been a bit on the brusque side. Especially with women. He's not particularly fond of our kind."

"Why do you put up with him?" Nan asked.

"Sir Richard is the best knight here. There's not a man alive who can beat him at swords, arrows or spears. He's a genius about strategy, and, besides, he's truly concerned with the welfare of the inhabitants of the Secret Valley. He possesses a good heart, though he keeps it well hidden." Kay sighed. "We'd best go inside. I'd rather no one saw you at present and we've already been standing here for some time."

Kay scrounged up two of her dresses that fit Nan and Irene decently and got them something to eat. Then she went to assist Lady Ruth. After she returned, the three girls sat together and talked about their lives—how they'd grown up and their differing customs. Kay explained how, in the Secret Valley, every man, woman and child devoted much of their time to practicing the use of weapons and studying war strategy. She said Lord William wanted their kingdom to be the largest and strongest in existence.

"My specialty is archery. And, not to brag, but I am considered one of the best in the whole valley."

Kay didn't want Nan and Irene to go out, so the three spent all day inside, talking until Kay went to get supper for them.

"I'll be right back," she assured them. When she was gone, Nan turned to Irene.

"I like Kay," she said. "She's rather a tomboy, but she's so lively. I've never met anyone quite like her."

"Yes, and she's funny too. I hope she can protect us like she says. Maybe she can even help us escape."

Kay soon returned with their dinner, and set it up on a small table for them to eat.

Kay's rooms opened into an interior corridor for easy access to Lady Ruth's suite. There was also a door, which exited to the courtyard garden. After they ate, the trio heard footsteps along the path leading to the outside door and, at the same time, in the corridor.

"Quick, hide!" Kay whispered to Nan and Irene. She motioned to the pit, and the girls dove under the many furs and pillows seconds before a rap sounded loudly on the door.

"Who is it?" Kay called nonchalantly, covering the girls with fur rugs.

"It's Fitzgerald, Kay. We're here on Lord William's business."

"And what might that be?"

"Open up and I'll tell you."

Several guards stood outside in the garden.

Drat, no way out.

"Beth!" she called loudly, stalling for time. "Beth, let Fitzgerald in. Oh, where *is* that girl when you need her?" Kay leaned down and whispered, "Don't make a sound or move a muscle!" She went and unlatched the door.

Fitzgerald came in with three members of the royal guards. "Good evening, Kay."

"Good evening," she replied with a curtsy. "Now, what's this all about, Fitzy?"

"Lord William sent us to fetch the two ladies."

"Whatever do you mean? I'm the only lady here, as you can plainly see."

"Come now, Kay, I know that you're watching them for Sir Richard, so you may as well hand them over."

Kay found it difficult to deceive Fitzgerald, but she was afraid of what might happen to Nan and Irene if they fell into the clutches of the King.

"Really, I don't know what you're talking about," she insisted, blinking her blue eyes innocently at Fitzgerald. As the two talked, one of the guards walked to the pit. He poked at the fur rugs with his spear.

Fitzgerald sighed. "Kay, someone saw you with them earlier today. I understand you are trying to carry out Richard's orders, but be assured Lord William will set things straight. Now, where are they?"

Kay glanced at the guard, who continued to poke and inspect the furs. She turned back to Fitzgerald and smiled. "Actually, Fitzy, they were here, but they left a while ago to walk around the town. I'm sure I can find them. After all, they can't possibly escape the Valley. I'll bring them to you tomorrow. You'll want them to be well rested before they're presented to Lord William, after all."

Fitzgerald searched Kay's face. "You *really* know where they are?"

"Oh, I swear."

"And you'll deliver them tomorrow morning?"

"On my honor."

"All right. By the way, I'd like a word with you soon about Lady Ruth's pup. I've discovered something which might interest you."

"Really? We must discuss it, yes." Kay took Fitzgerald by the arm and steered him towards the door. "I'll meet you in the garden tomorrow at noon. Until then..."

"Ouch!"

Kay and Fitzgerald turned to the pit from which the muffled cry came. The startled guard jumped back as a hand grabbed the spear from him and a redheaded girl popped up and hit him on the head with the blunt end of the rod.

"Stop pricking me, if you please!" Nan cried.

"Oh, horse pizzle!" Kay blurted, trying to avoid Fitzgerald's stare. "I'm sorry, Fitzy. I didn't want to lie to you, but I had my reasons."

"I'm sure you did," Fitzgerald replied gruffly.

"Irene, you may as well come out, too."

Irene stood up. "Nan, how could you?" she whispered harshly.

"She was going to turn us over tomorrow. Besides, it hurt."

"You ninny! She was going to try and get us away from here."

"Oh!" Nan said. It was clear she now fully understood the situation. She glanced over at Kay, abashed.

"Guards, escort these ladies to Lord William," Fitzgerald ordered.

Two guards took Nan and Irene by the arms and pulled them into the corridor. The other guard followed, still rubbing the bump on his head. Fitzgerald shook his head at Kay. She could not meet his eyes and fixed her own on a crack in the floor. "I'd still like a word with you on the morrow," he said softly.

"Of course," she mumbled, managing to look up for an instant.

Fitzgerald followed the others out and Kay closed the door and sighed.

I'm in the soup now!

◆

26

The guards escorted Irene and Nan along several hallways and staircases and deposited them just inside the throne room. The room was long and narrow with thirty-foot high ceilings and polished wooden floors. Ornate tapestries and tall mirrors shaped like arches hung on the walls. Intricate stone carvings embellished the room.

A series of wall torches lessened the evening gloom. At the far end of the room, a red velvet throne sat on a raised platform. On it lounged a slender man in his 40's who was of medium height, with black, thinning hair slicked back over his head. He had brown eyes, a neatly groomed beard, a long narrow nose and an imperious expression. He wore a blue tunic embroidered with the same hawk Irene had seen in Kay's room. He sat with both legs thrown over one arm of the throne and was stroking his beard, his eyes dancing in amusement.

"At last. So glad you could join me," he said, in a deep baritone voice. "Come closer, ladies, so I can see you...oh, you can walk faster than that."

When the girls reached the foot of the dais, the man stood. "Allow me to introduce myself. I am King William, Son of Dob. You will address me as my lord, Your Grace or Your Majesty. I'm told you are from the Valley of William Etté. As such, I should order you burned at the stake or imprisoned for life because you are enemies of my people. But, perhaps, if you can be of some use to me, you will live." William rocked back and forth on his heels studying the two. Then he pointed at Nan.

"You—with the red hair. You are the dancer. Is that true?"

"Yes," Nan replied meekly.

William raised his eyebrows and leaned forward. "Yes...what?"

"Oh! Yes, my lord," Nan said, and bobbed a curtsy.

"That's better. You learn fast, and I like the curtsy; that was nice. Yes, well, anyway...the other claims to be a princess." He studied Irene. "Princess of Cabbage. That would make you Princess of nothing! My soldiers didn't leave much standing in that worthless little kingdom. Hardly worth the trouble to attack."

Lord William leaned towards Irene and, cupping her chin in his hand, lifted her defiant face to his own. "What would your name be?"

Irene silently glared at him.

"Your new ruler is addressing you—don't be contrary. It is hardly fitting behavior for a princess," he mocked.

In reply, Irene spat in his face. He grabbed her by the wrist and hoisted her onto the platform. "No one treats me disrespectfully!" He struck her across the face.

Irene held her hands up for protection and leaned away from him until she was sure he wouldn't strike again.

He left her standing as he paced back and forth. "What were you thinking? Are you unaware I hold your very life in my hands? You don't appear to care," he mused. "As for the red-haired maiden, we could use the diversion of a dancer. My people don't enjoy much of the artistic pleasures of life. It's been a long time since I saw a dancer who was really good at her craft. In her day, my Ruth used to dance...but that's all past now."

He sighed before turning to Irene.

"As for you, little princess, you deserve a flogging. But my innate, gracious nature makes me realize your ill manners may be the result of the recent strain you've been through." He chuckled. "Perhaps some time in my dungeon will make you appreciate me more. I'll have you brought forth again in a few days and, if you seem more agreeable, we'll see about more suitable accommodations. Guards!"

Two men stepped from a corner of the room and put shackles on Irene's wrists. Irene continued to stare coldly at Lord William.

"Oh, no, please, sir! You mustn't do this to Irene," Nan blurted in a panic. "She's a princess, after all, and isn't used to such places as dungeons. She's truly very sweet and kind. Please let her go." William ignored her. "At least let me go with her. *Please,* my lord." Nan curtseyed again for good measure.

"Shh! I'll be fine," Irene said. "It won't do us any good to both be in the dungeon."

"Ah, so you found your tongue at last. Pity you didn't speak sooner. You might have avoided punishment. Take her away," Lord William said in a bored voice.

Nan watched her childhood friend pulled from the room. Lord William slouched again on his throne and devoured Nan with his eyes. He smiled. "And now, shall you dance for me?" He paused, considering. "I think not. We shall save that for another time." He stepped off the platform and came closer to Nan. "What color are your eyes?"

"Green, my lord," Nan answered shakily.

"So they are, so they are," he chuckled. Then he went to the side of the platform and rang a gong. Four large, masculine-looking women appeared and bowed. "Prepare her. I have meetings with my council tonight, but tomorrow I shall visit her. Emerald would be a good color, I think," he added with a grin.

The women took Nan away. William assumed his original pose on the throne and a young girl came towards him from out of the shadows. She gently coughed to get his attention.

"Oh, yes. I'd almost forgotten," William said when he noticed her. He untied a small leather pouch of gold coins from around his waist, pulled one out and handed it to her.

"Good work, Beth."

◆

Kay paced back and forth in her room, anxious about her new friends.
There must be some way I can help them. If only Demetrius were here—he'd know what to do.

CHAPTER 4

Demetrius Keats wandered in a haze of pain and shame. Pain, from his wounded shoulder, which, despite treatment, still refused to heal. Shame, because he was running away from the Secret Valley. And now he was lost.

He climbed a small mountain to get his bearings and found, to his surprise, there was no top to the mountain. It was actually the lip of a large crater, formed by an extinct volcano. At the bottom of the crater lay a crystal-clear blue lake with an island in the center. The banks of the crater were steep and Demetrius half-walked, half-slid to the crater floor.

This is as good a place as any to die.

He walked to a sandy beach by the lake and collapsed.

◆

"Tell me your name!"

A piercing voice dragged Demetrius from unconsciousness. He slowly opened his eyes a fraction to see a wizened old man leaning over him. Again, the voice yelled, "Tell me your name!"

Demetrius winced and stared at the man but didn't speak. The stranger became impatient. "Your name, name, name, name, name!"

In an attempt to quiet the odd man, Demetrius waved his arm and croaked. "My name...my name is Demetri..." He closed his eyes and swallowed hard.

"Demi-what? Speak up! I can't hear you!"

"Demetrius Keats, Son of Thom," he said in a slightly louder voice.

"Demetrius Keats? A fancy name, that! My name is Ben de Blanc. What are you doing here? You're trespassing on my land."

Demetrius tried to raise himself on an elbow. "I'm running away from my people. I'm trying to forget, to sort things out in my mind. I want to...to...ah! My arm!" He fell back, clutching his shoulder.

Ben spotted blood seeping through Demetrius' clothing near the right shoulder. He tore back the fabric of the shirt to reveal a festering wound. He nodded and pulled a small pouch from under his shirt. From this he removed an egg-sized ball that glowed in changing colors. He closed his eyes and concentrated.

"Bring me my raft!" Ben commanded.

The lake water responded, lifting the raft from down the beach and moving it to Ben and Demetrius. Ben helped Demetrius onto the raft, and with the glowing orb, ordered the raft to take them across the lake to the island. When they arrived, he lugged the semi-conscious man onto the beach and climbed a rope ladder to a cave to get supplies.

When Ben returned, he fashioned a primitive bandage, made Demetrius as comfortable as possible on the beach, lit a fire and quietly sat with him.

◆

Demetrius woke as the morning sun rose over the crater to light the beach. He managed to sit up and look about him. He didn't remember much of the previous day except for a dim recollection of an odd old man with sandy hair tinged with gray and a half-crazed expression in his eyes.

Demetrius inspected his shoulder and found it had been bandaged rather amateurishly, but the crudely wrapped fabric had proved its worth as the bleeding had stopped. He heard singing and turned to see the strange man descending a rope ladder from a cave a hundred feet or so above.

When Ben reached the ground, he came strolling towards Demetrius and said, "It's awake, the Demetrius thing. I can't remember the rest of its name."

"Demetrius Keats, Son of Thom, sir. Are you the one who brought me here and ministered to my wounds?"

"Yes, I suspect I am. No one else lives here, so it must have been me." He plopped down beside Demetrius. "I am Ben de Blanc."

"I humbly thank you, sir. I am not well yet, but when I regain my strength, if there is anything I can do for you, it is yours for the asking."

"Do you realize you are trespassing? This is my land; I don't like anyone on it. No one has set foot within a day's walk of here for dozens of years."

"I'm sorry, I didn't realize. I became lost trying to escape from something."

"Escape from what?"

"From myself, actually. From...from something I couldn't face. I was a coward to run. I deserve to die."

"Be more specific, man. What do you mean? What happened?"

"You see, I am a soldier, a knight in Lord William's army from the Secret Valley. I was proud to be in his Majesty's army and dedicated to making my homeland safe. Lord William told us of the cruel tribes surrounding our valley. He said they would stop at nothing to find our homeland and destroy us. Our only chance was to strike them first."

Demetrius sighed. "My trusted friend, Sir Richard, and I took a battalion of soldiers to fight an enemy village. Since we outnumbered them nearly three-to-one, we expected no trouble. They fought hard, however, and, unfortunately, a spear struck me down.

"I fell off my horse and thought my life was over. The skirmish was all around me, but I must have passed out. When the battle ended, I was too weak from blood loss to move. A large man came over and, seeing I still lived, picked me up and heaved me over his shoulder. He carried me a long distance, perhaps two or three miles. He took me to a camp where I stayed a week. The people there showed me nothing but kindness. I tried not to believe the enemy could be so good-hearted, but I could not deny these were humane people.

"They didn't keep me bound, or try to obtain information from me. They seemed only concerned with my well-being. I lived in torment those days. I waited for them to interrogate or torture me, but they treated me as an honored guest. I was free to go if I wanted, or to stay if I chose.

"I didn't know what to do. These people were enemies of my country. I couldn't stay with them. Nor could I go home. My duty would be to tell Lord William where the enemy was, but I could not betray their goodness. I decided to leave the camp, but not go back home.

"I traveled south for ten days, but I was without a means to hunt. I survived on what I could find in the forest. My wound kept breaking open and, between that and the lack of food, I fainted. That is apparently when you found me," Demetrius finished.

There was a long pause.

"Ha, ha!" Ben exclaimed, clapping his hands. "A good story, very good! Tell me another. My mummy used to tell me one about the bunny who couldn't hop. Do you know that one?"

Demetrius realized with dismay the old man was quite addled. He vowed to leave that night. He also realized that recalling his story aloud had made him change his mind about running away. He would return to the Secret Valley after all, and try to persuade Lord William to stop his senseless killing.

That night, they slept on the beach because Demetrius was unable to climb the ladder to the cave with his bad shoulder. When Ben had been snoring for a long while, Demetrius walked to the lake and quietly pushed the raft away from the shore. He boarded and paddled his way across the lake with a full moon to guide him. He had reached the far shore when the weather suddenly grew quite windy and cold, and billowing clouds roiled across the sky.

The gales grew stronger, making it hard for Demetrius to climb up the bank towards the top of the crater. Large raindrops and hail started to fall, turning the ground to sloppy mud. His clothing was soaked through in a matter of minutes. He finally made it to the lip of the crater and peered back down. He saw an eerie, violet light from the beach where he had left Ben.

A flash of light, followed by a loud crack sounded behind him. A thunderbolt had struck a tree only twenty feet from him. Seconds later, another struck ten feet away and yet another even closer. Demetrius ran away, sliding down the muddy hill towards the lake. More bolts struck the ground next to him.

Could they be following me? Surely, it's impossible!

He kept running and, as he reached the water, three thunderbolts hit in a semi-circle around him. Frantic to escape, Demetrius dove into the lake. He began to swim to the island as the stormed raged.

He finally reached the island and dragged himself out of the water. He collapsed a little ways from Ben who was kneeling with his eyes shut tight and grasping a small, glowing object.

Ben opened his eyes and the thunder stopped abruptly, the wind died down, and the evening was as warm as it had been an hour before. The shoulder wound had torn open again and Ben tended to it. Demetrius lay on his back, staring at Ben with astonishment, and a growing hatred, as his shoulder was repaired once more.

CHAPTER 5

Kay paced on the gravel path in the secluded garden where she had promised to meet Fitzgerald. Already it was half past the appointed hour and Kay was worried. It was not like her friend to be late.

Hearing the sound of light footsteps, Kay swung around. The sight of Beth's pinched face stifled the welcome cry on her lips.

"Yes, Beth—what is it?" Kay snapped at the girl.

Beth ducked her head and swallowed a great breath of air before she replied, "Lady Kay, I have a message for you from Lord Fitzgerald. M'lady, he asks you to await him in your chambers. He was unavoidably detained by some important matters and would like to delay his audience with you 'til later this afternoon."

"Thank you, Beth. That will be all." As she watched Beth's furtive movements away she said to herself, "Damn! Well, there is not much I can do until I speak with Fitzy. I've some mending to do for my lady, and now will be as good a time as any to do it."

She plucked a small, yellow flower from a vine clinging to the archway to the garden. She tucked it into her yellow hair as she walked back to her chamber, thinking of her new friends. Kay had always been a bit of a loner, without close friendships with other girls. It surprised her that she cared so much about these two strangers. She had heard Irene was locked in the dungeon for offending Lord William, but could not learn Nan's fate. She had hoped Fitzgerald might be able to tell her where her new friend was, but now she would have to wait. Frustrated, she busied herself with some work and hoped it wouldn't be long.

◆

Nan sat nervously on a bed in a grand sleeping chamber. Her eyes darted to the locked door every time she heard a sound. She'd spent a fitful night's sleep in a tiny room before the same four women who had locked her in appeared. They gave her breakfast and took her to a bathing chamber, washed and anointed her with oils and perfumes.

They brushed her long, red hair and dressed her in a long, flowing, silken gown of emerald green.

Then the women escorted Nan up a flight of stairs and down a hallway to a grand room, which Nan guessed was that of her captor, Lord William. The women put her on the bed and arranged her until they were satisfied. She was told to wait. Then they left.

Alone and afraid, Nan now sat and stared about herself in dismay.

Better I should have perished with my family in the attack than to face this man as if I were his chattel to do with as he pleases.

Nan examined the beautiful garment fitting so close and low at the bodice, but floating around her legs with gentle gathers designed for freedom of movement. The designer of this article of clothing certainly knew the needs of a dancer, yet had also made the garment so enticing that even the smallest gesture could be interpreted as an invitation to sweeter moments.

Tears welled in Nan's eyes.

I fear my virtue will soon be lost. If that is his intention, he won't take it without a fight!

Nan moved off the bed and marched to the door with determination. At that moment, it swung open and she found herself staring full into the eyes of Lord William. Even his fastidious tastes seemed to be pleased by the sight of her.

"My dear, you give me great pleasure," he murmured as he came nearer. Nan tensed as he approached. He pulled her to him, his hands roaming over her hips as he took in every inch of her beauty with his eyes. His voice was low and mesmerizing and Nan fought to keep from trembling.

"Those eyes of yours, what do they say to me? I wonder; they flash dark lights though they are the color of a sparkling green pool in the forest." His hands lingered a moment as if considering, then abruptly pushed her back and laughed. "Time enough for fun later. Anticipation will make the prize that much more delicious. For now, I shall see you put your other talents to use. Dance for me, Nan the Dancer. Let us see if you are deserving of your name."

Nan felt a sudden urge to slap his arrogant face. *He toys with me as if I were a mouse in a box!*

"I have danced in the finest courts of the land, sir. I am sure you will find my talents are adequate," she said coolly.

"That remains to be seen." He chuckled as he went and hopped on the bed.

Nan prepared herself to dance. She hummed a tune softly and moved in time with the melody. Soon, she was caught up in a spell and abandoned herself to the music. Every movement became an extension of that inner force. The dance was an expression of her terror and loss at finding her family gone, her love for Irene and her deepening sense of friendship with Kay. Out of this trance-like state came her voice, deep with sorrow, yet sweet as a nightingale, singing to accompany her graceful movements.

Sitting on his bed, William became lost in Nan's world, transfixed by her grace and beauty. Finally, Nan reached an end to her deep feelings and her dance. She lay crumpled on the floor like a doll carelessly flung away. Neither William nor Nan moved—each silent and deep in thought.

A screaming voice shattered the mood. From the outer corridor Lady Ruth's strident soprano could be heard. "You are a mere guard—if I demand an audience with my husband, I shall have it!"

The door flung open and Ruth sailed into her husband's room. She took in the situation at a glance and strode to Nan's side, examining her. "Hmm, no marks or bruises—good," she murmured. She turned to her husband.

"William, what is this girl doing here?" she asked sweetly through gritted teeth. "You must realize this places her in a most compromising position."

"Ruth, my dear," William drawled from his perch on the bed. "You missed the finest performance I have ever beheld. Meet our new court dancer, Nan. When I am ruler over all the nearby lands and kingdoms, she will be our finest showpiece of entertainment."

Ruth shot a look of hatred at Nan before smiling at her husband.

"Ah, so it is thus, William. Then, I shall take her to my chambers and outfit her with the finest from my own dancing apparel. As you know, I have not worn it since giving you your son and heir."

William opened his mouth to protest, but thought better of it. After all, there was plenty of time to take the girl at his leisure and Ruth was frightened enough not to attempt anything after the lesson with Ginger.

Oh yes, Beth was a useful child.

He smiled as Ruth pulled Nan to her feet and dragged her out of the room. Nan looked back at Lord William, wondering if she had escaped one problem only to land in another.

◆

After she finished letting the seams out on another gown for Lady Ruth, Kay's thoughts returned to Irene, who was in the dungeon deep under the castle. How could she get the poor girl out when there was only one entrance? Kay looked up from her needlework to find Sir Richard staring at her intently. Before she could open her mouth, he spoke.

"Well, Kay, you've managed to get yourself into a fine mess. I've orders to escort you to the dungeon and join the little princess."

"Sir Richard—I thought you went in search of Demetrius, I mean, you were scouting for enemy...that is...what are you doing back so soon?"

He shot her a withering glance. "My schedule is no concern of yours. Now get up. I'm taking you to join Princess Irene."

"To help you question her?"

"No. You have fallen from the good graces of Lady Ruth and she has ordered you shall suffer a while. Let us go."

◆

Irene looked up in astonishment to see Kay roughly handed into the cell in which she herself had struggled to pass a comfortable night.

"Kay—in the name of Mirn—why are you here?"

"Funny, that's what I asked Richard when he announced he was bringing me down here. Actually, the better question is, how will we get out?"

Both girls sat in pensive silence. Finally, Kay moved to the door and said, "Well, maybe I can pry these old bars apart enough to slip through or something..."

Irene sat down and watched Kay labor in silence, doubtful that a man, much less a girl, could pull the iron bars apart. Soon Kay gave up and stood, peering in the dim light down the hall to the other cells.

Suddenly she gasped. "What? Ho, there! Fitzy, is that you?"

"Kay! I should have expected you would be here, too. Actually, it's your fault I'm here. I took Ginger to the animal physician to find out about his death and I fear I discovered too much. Now I am in a cell big enough to store my uniforms in and that's all!"

Kay stifled a laugh, for Fitzgerald was well known as a man who loved his clothes. "Fitzy, what did you discover about Lady Ruth's dog?"

Sir Fitzgerald dropped his voice. "Ginger was indeed poisoned. A rare poison made from the roots of the Maja plant. The black tongue was the tip off. Where whoever did this came by the Maja I'm not sure, it is only found..."

"...on the higher regions of the Hooded Mountains," Kay finished. "I know. I picked some when I was hunting the other week. Correctly prepared, Maja has great medicinal properties. But who could have taken it? I kept it stored away where only..."

"Beth of Coombs had access?" Fitzgerald interrupted. "Now the pieces all fit. She must have taken the plant, put it in Lady Ruth's food hoping to make her ill and have the blame fall on you. When

Ginger ate it instead, the dose was too strong for the pup, poor thing. But before I could speak to Lady Ruth, Beth likely told her you were responsible."

"Lady Ruth thinks I am trying to murder her? No wonder I was sent to this dreadful place. But Fitzy, why are *you* here? You didn't pick the Maja or put it in her food."

"Ah, but I was found burying the dog's body you were supposed to deal with. And..." Sir Fitzgerald blushed. "Knowing of our...friendship, they naturally assumed the worst. We were in it together."

Kay peered through the gloom of the dungeon at her sweetheart. "Oh, Fitzy. You have always been the court's favorite knight. What now?"

"Oh, I expect I shall lose my place at Lord William's table. At worst, they might torture us...I mean *me*," he finished in a rush.

Kay gasped. "Do you really think they will torture you? I'm so sorry!"

"So am I," Irene spoke for the first time. "It's all Nan's and my fault any of this happened."

"You couldn't help it, Irene. You were brought here by force, remember?" Kay said, smiling at her new friend. "However, none of this is getting us out of here! We'd best put our energy into finding an escape."

The three began to explore their cells, looking for a trap door, a removable stone, anything. After some time, Kay and Irene sat back in disgust.

"Nothing," Kay said.

"Nothing but filth," Irene added, wiping her dirty hands on the worn blanket on the cot.

"Did you find anything, Fitzy?" There was no response. "Fitzy?" Kay rushed to the door and saw a now empty cell. "He's gone! Irene, Fitzy found a way out!"

"Well, why didn't he say something?" Irene said irritably.

"I don't know, but I'm sure he'll be back for us soon."

"Well, I hope it's before evening. I can't bear the thought of another night in this cold, damp place." Irene said in a huff.

Kay smiled in sympathy. Undoubtedly, Princess Irene was used to better accommodations. She sat next to her.

"You think this is bad, you should have been with me when I lived with a tribe of gypsies. Sometimes I couldn't bathe for days on end! One time..." and she went on to entertain Irene with tales of her adventures to help pass the time.

◆

Sir Fitzgerald certainly would have told Kay and Irene of his discovery, had he had the time. The trap door opened so swiftly, and he fell down into the passageway so immediately, he didn't even have time to cry out, much less tell them about it. Even now, as he made his way through the dank passage, he was not sure how he had tripped the secret whatever-it-was that opened the floor beneath him and sent him sliding down into darkness, where he landed in a pile of musty straw.

Fitzgerald estimated he dropped about ten or twelve feet. Already, the dungeon was two floors beneath the courtyard of the castle, so he thought he was now perhaps 30 feet beneath ground level. He also guessed that the passageway had not been used in many years, judging by the cobwebs he kept spitting out of his mouth.

If only I had a torch! He stumbled for the umpteenth time, this time falling flat.

"Curse it!" He said aloud. "Ho, what's this?"

Fitzgerald felt something cold and metal. He fingered it and realized it was a key. It was good sized and heavy, with a great deal of design around the base.

I wonder what it could be for—a door, perhaps? It's certainly heavy enough. Or, it could belong to a large chest. Maybe it's the key out of here. Putting it in his pocket, he picked himself up and began to feel his way along the passage once more. After some time, Fitzgerald tripped again, this time on a staircase.

At last! A way out, surely. He groped his way up the stairs.

◆

"So. You are a dancer, are you?" Lady Ruth said as she dragged Nan down the hall.

"Yes, m'lady," Nan gasped, trying to keep up with the large woman.

"Well, as long as *all* you do is dance!"

Nan huffed indignantly. "M'lady, I was taken there against my will! I..." Before Nan could finish, Lady Ruth whirled around and slapped her.

"You dare to presume...you...dare to even suggest my husband would have...have done anything with a wretch like you? He has me! And he loves *me!*" She broke off, breathing heavily, tears shining in her eyes. Nan shrank under the wild expression upon the woman's face.

My heavens, is she sane? I had best keep my mouth shut on the subject of her husband! Oh, why isn't Kay here?

She sputtered an explanation to the woman. "Oh no, m'lady...I never meant any such thing...it...it was as your lord and husband said. I merely danced for him."

"But if I hadn't come in? What then, eh? No! I refuse to think about it. Come!" She dragged Nan into her room.

Nan gawked at the splendors. Rich tapestries hung on every wall. Dark mahogany furniture filled the room and plush carpets covered every inch of the floor. It was beautiful, but somehow too much, as if the pieces of the room didn't fit together. Nan continued to gaze about the room and finally her eyes rested on none other than Beth of Coombs. Nan gasped.

"This is Beth, my new lady in waiting," Ruth said with a gesture towards the girl. "Kay has been...indisposed."

From her cushion in the corner where she sat, Beth smiled coolly.

CHAPTER 6

Demetrius Keats lay on the sandy beach by the lapping water of the lake. It was a mild afternoon, and it would have been pleasant if it weren't for his current situation.

Demetrius eyed Ben de Blanc with a cold hatred. After his first failed escape attempt, Demetrius tried reasoning with the man, explaining why he needed to go back to the Secret Valley. Ben had simply replied that no, he liked Demetrius' company and would keep him, thank you very much.

As if I were a pet of some kind. Demetrius glanced over at the snoring Ben with disgust.

Ben smiled in his sleep, holding the glowing orb tightly. Demetrius had learned that this was the source of power that caused the storm the night of his attempted escape. Ben told him the orb had the power to change the weather and more. Three times in the past few days, Demetrius attempted to steal the orb while Ben slept, so he could escape without Ben using it against him. But each time, before Demetrius laid hands on it, the ball turned bright red and made strange noises, waking Ben and spoiling Demetrius' escape plan.

If the orb responds to Ben's moods, why does it turn red when I approach? He can't turn it red—he's asleep. Demetrius rolled over on his stomach and frowned.

Perhaps it is my mood! Maybe the orb feels my fear of being discovered and reacts to that. If I could control my emotions, I might be able to get it and escape. When I do, I will try to convince Richard and Lord William to cease their senseless slaughter.

Demetrius stared at the orb, tight in Ben de Blanc's grasp. He began to concentrate on his home...on the beautiful valley and green trees and clear streams. He slowly approached. The orb continued to glow a soft peachy-pink. Demetrius came within a foot of it when a loon flew overhead crying loudly. It startled Demetrius and he lost his concentration. The orb turned red and made squawking noises. Ben's eyes flew open and he sat up, clutching his treasure fiercely.

He laughed at Demetrius. "Fool! You should know better! Trying to steal it again?"

"Not at all, Monsieur de Blanc. I merely wanted to tell you I am going fishing for tonight's meal," Demetrius quickly lied.

"Good idea! I'll join you," Ben said, putting the glowing ball back into its leather pouch. "Did I ever tell you about the time I caught a sea serpent twenty feet long?"

◆

Twilight was falling and the coals of the small campfire glowed in the dimming light.

"A good meal!" Ben de Blanc spoke, breaking the silence. "Lake trout is always a good meal, don't you think?"

"A fortunate thing you like it, since it's about all there is to eat on this blasted island," Demetrius said. "Don't you ever get tired of fish?"

"Oh, never!"

"Well, I am heartily sick of it. I long for a venison steak as only Kay can prepare."

"Who's Kay?" Ben asked as he idly tossed the orb in his hands.

"A friend."

"A friend. Hmm. I once had friends...I think. I'm not sure now."

"Not sure they were friends, or not sure you had any?"

"What?"

"Skip it." Demetrius stood and stretched. "I'm tired...I'm going to bed."

"I will, too." Ben kicked sand over the fire and began to sing a little goodnight song.

"Goodnight, dear Ben, goodnight.
I hope you sleep all right.
So say a prayer and comb your hair,
And goodnight, dear Ben, good night."

"Do you like my song? I made it up myself!" Ben said with pride.

"Could have fooled me," Demetrius said dryly. Sarcasm, however, was lost on Ben de Blanc.

"No, really. I once aspired to be a great singer."

"What happened?" Demetrius asked, too curious to ignore him.

"I found I had no talent!" Ben sang his goodnight ditty again as he climbed the rope ladder to the cave above.

Demetrius hardly noticed, for he was practicing on controlling his emotions. Tonight, he would try again to steal the orb. Then, he could get away from Ben and his crazy little songs! He followed Ben up the ladder.

Demetrius waited to hear the even breathing that told him Ben de Blanc was asleep, and then waited further still. He would take no chances on spoiling this attempt. Carefully, when the time was right, he got up from his bedding and looked at Ben, who clutched the orb as usual.

Staring at the glowing ball, Demetrius concentrated on beautiful and peaceful images. Slowly, he approached the sleeping old man until he stood above him. Demetrius willed himself to remain calm. He knelt beside Ben and slowly reached for the orb.

Wonder of wonders, the orb's color did not change. Nor did it make any noise as Demetrius carefully slipped it out of Ben's hands and picked up its pouch which lay on the ground. Demetrius rose and slowly backed out of the cave. With one final look at the crazy man, Demetrius climbed down the ladder and then headed to the beach and the waiting raft. The orb continued to glow in the night, lighting his way.

CHAPTER 7

After what felt like a hundred steps, Fitzgerald reached a landing at the top of the stairs. But he found no door; only a dead end.

Impossible! Who would build a staircase leading to nowhere? There must be a trapdoor.

Fitzgerald began to examine the rough stonewalls and the wooden ceiling. He stopped when he heard steps above and a muffled voice, which he recognized as Lord William's. He picked out a second voice too, softer and female, but he could not place it. She seemed to be protesting, but Fitzgerald could not catch the words.

More than likely, some poor serving wench lured to his Lordship's bedchamber for a bit of fun. Fitzgerald's heart went out to the poor girl, for he did not approve of such behavior.

While he waited in the dark for Lord William to have done with the girl, he continued to feel the ceiling and finally was rewarded. He discovered what he thought was the outline of a door above him.

Good. If I can force this open, I can get the key to the dungeon, free Kay, and we can make our escape.

Fitzgerald sat down on a step to wait. Finally, he heard Lord William take his leave of the room, leaving a weeping girl on the bed. Fitzgerald waited until he was certain the girl had left as well.

"Now!" he said to himself and began to shove with all his strength against the door. For some time, it resisted all force, but just when Fitzgerald was about to give up, it shifted. He lifted the panel slightly and peeked into the room. The entry was in a far corner of the enormous bedroom. A quick glance told him he was alone. He pushed it wider to climb out when a sudden crash stopped him. A small table on the top of the trap door fell over, sending a vase to the floor.

Curses! But no time to stop now.

Fitzgerald climbed out, closed the trap door, put the table back in place and surveyed the room, trying to guess where Lord William kept his keys. He spotted a large desk across the room and moved over to it. Carefully, so as to not overly disturb anything, he searched through it, but found no keys.

Now if I were Lord William, I should probably keep my keys in...the pocket of my trousers. Fitzgerald rushed over and rifled through the discarded trousers lying next to the bed, finding a set of keys. Not knowing which key he needed, he took them all.

I had best not go back through the passage, for how would I set the table back on the trap door? Or get back into my cell? I shall have to sneak back as best I can.

Fitzgerald checked the hallway and, finding it empty, slipped out. Since it was now rather late, no one was around. He ducked into Kay's room to pick up a few items—her best bow and quiver of arrows, and some extra clothes. He put these into a sack and hurried over to his own room. He added some personal items into the bag. He looked for his bag of gold, but couldn't find it.

Confiscated, no doubt, by my good Lord William. Fitzgerald turned to leave, but stopped in front of his large wardrobe. *I certainly could use a change of clothing after being in that dank dungeon. And it won't take long—'tis still plenty of time before dawn.*

He put the bundle down and opened the doors to his wardrobe. He was halfway through changing when he noticed a movement inside the wardrobe. He grabbed his dagger.

"All right! I see you—come out slowly."

Much to his surprise, a beautiful redhead stepped out. He stared at the girl and she stared at him. "Aren't you Kay's friend?" he asked at last, breaking the silence.

"I hope I may call her my friend, though I have known her but a short time," she said shyly. "My name is Nan. "

"I am Sir Fitzgerald, my lady."

"Yes. Aren't you the one who had Irene and me arrested?"

Fitzgerald blushed slightly—*had he ever seen such lovely green eyes?* —and stammered, "Well, uh, yes...I was responsible, but I regret it greatly. In fact, I am now on my way to rescue your friend and Kay from their imprisonment. So, if you come with me, we shall all make our escape."

"What? Kay is in prison, too? How so?" Nan asked, stepping a little closer to the knight.

What a darling face. And freckles, too!

"It would take too long to explain, my lady. And, speaking of explanations, what are you doing in my closet?"

"I ran away from Lady Ruth and her handmaiden, Beth, while they slept. I tried to find Kay's room, but came in here by mistake. When I heard you entering, I hid in the wardrobe."

"Well, I am glad you did...I mean...well, uh...hadn't we better get going?" Fitzgerald finished in a stammering rush.

"Hadn't you better finish dressing first?" Nan smiled sweetly.

Fitzgerald felt his face burn and hurriedly dressed.

◆

Nan and Fitzgerald moved through the castle passages towards the dungeon stairs.

"Won't there be guards?" Nan whispered.

Fitzgerald stopped short. In his haste, he had forgotten. "Curses. Perhaps we should have gone back through the secret passageway."

"The what?"

"Never mind. Too late now. Come on." Taking Nan's hand, he pulled her on. At the next corner, he stopped and peered cautiously around. There was the entrance to the lower levels and, as Nan had suspected, a guard. The guard had his back turned to them, but Fitzgerald saw him clearly and his heart began to pound when he recognized Sir Richard, head of Lord William's army!

He drew back, his mind racing. *Why would Richard be pulling guard duty? Unless...*

"You can come out Fitzgerald. I know you're there. Yes, and bring the redheaded trollop as well," Richard's voice called. Gripping Nan firmly by the hand, Fitzgerald turned the corner. Richard stood smiling at him.

"Sir Richard, I..."

"I hoped you would come back," Richard interrupted. "I counted on it, in fact. I figured you were too much of a gentleman to leave Kay and the princess behind. And I see you've found this one as well. How cozy. All planning to just slip off in the night?"

"Where's the regular duty guard?" Fitzgerald stalled for time.

"I offered to relieve him for an hour or so while he visits a lady friend. Most thoughtful of me, don't you think?"

"Most thoughtful."

"I decided to pay you a little visit to see how you were all doing in your, uh...new accommodations. Imagine my surprise to find you missing. So I waited. I didn't want you to go without saying goodbye."

"Except that you have no intention of letting us leave, correct?"

"Correct!" Richard drew out his dagger. "Now, if you will be good enough to lead the way to his Lordship's chambers, I'm sure he'll be most pleased to receive us. Even at this indecent hour."

Nan, who had remained silent and half-hidden behind Fitzgerald, suddenly leaped out and, with her strong legs, kicked the knife out of

Sir Richard's hand. Fitzgerald seized the opportunity and struck Richard with two quick blows leaving him a crumpled heap on the floor.

"Good work, Nan, but you might have been hurt."

"I'm so sorry, there wasn't time to ask. Come on, let's hurry."

Grabbing a torch, the pair ran down the stairs to the cells.

"Fitzy! I knew you'd be back!" Kay cried in delight.

"And Nan! Are you all right?" Irene asked.

"Perfectly fine, except I want to get out of here—oh, do hurry, Sir Fitzgerald!"

Fitzgerald fumbled with the keys and finally found the correct one, releasing Kay and Irene from their cell. "Hurry!" he said.

The four sped up the steps, pausing only briefly where Richard still lay unconscious.

"Richard?" Kay asked in surprise. "Fitzy, is he dead?"

"Not now, but he may be when Lord William gets through with him. Come on!"

◆

By dawn the four were high in the hills overlooking the Secret Valley.

"I wish we had stolen some horses," Nan complained about the long walk.

"Never mind. At least we're out of that dreadful place," Irene said.

"We can likely take a horse or two from inside the tunnel leading out of the valley," Fitzgerald said. "There are usually a few kept in reserve."

"Aren't there guards, too?" Nan asked, remembering the ones she and Irene saw when they were first brought to the Valley.

"Yes," Kay said, "but most likely asleep on the job. Quiet, now— this way." She was right. They skirted easily past two slumbering guards and, before long, the small party stood outside in the midst of the Hooded Mountains.

"Well, now what?" Fitzgerald asked.

"We can't go west. Our homes have been destroyed," Irene said.

"Then let us go east and all the way over the Hooded Mountains," Kay said. "I always wanted to know what lay beyond them. I started out once to learn, but found the Secret Valley instead and made it my home."

"Well, it's no longer our home, that's for sure." Fitzgerald sighed, digging into his sack. "Here. Put on these warm clothes. It's over the Hooded Mountains for us all."

CHAPTER 8

Nan slipped out of the sheer, green gown and put on a blouse and skirt that Fitzgerald had packed from Kay's chambers. Irene donned a fine muslin shirt, leather vest and a pair of pants, which all belonged to Fitzgerald. She cinched up the pants with a belt and pushed her hair up into a cap.

"Oh, Irene, you look like a young boy," Nan exclaimed.

Kay put a clean blouse and vest over her doeskin skirt, and then the four discarded Nan and Irene's lighter garments in a deep ravine. They rode the horses they had stolen from the tunnel by twos—Kay and Irene took a small brown horse, while Nan clung closely to Fitzgerald on a black charger.

Fitzgerald led the way over the Hooded Mountains. The rocky trail was hard to navigate and, several times, the horses balked.

"Fitzy," Kay called. "This is terribly slow going. If Richard has recovered himself, he's likely sent soldiers after us. We've got to get away faster than this."

"Yes, I know, but I have an idea. It shouldn't be much farther."

Soon, the quartet became aware of the sound of rushing water. They came upon the mountain river, churning with muddy run-off from the melting snow of the high peaks.

Fitzgerald jumped down from his horse and helped Nan dismount. He moved to a rock outcropping along the side of the river. He ran knee-deep into the water and waded up to a large boulder jutting out over the river. Fitzgerald crouched down and went into a sort of opening. After a bit, he emerged, victoriously pulling an old, battered dory, which, clearly, had seen better days.

"I used to go fishing here as a boy." Fitzgerald pulled the boat to shore. "Climb aboard. She may not seem too sturdy, but she's as sound as she ever was, believe me."

Kay slapped the horses to make them run away and the girls got into the boat. The current was swift, but Fitzgerald guided them well away from any rocks or shallows.

"You should sleep," he told the others. "If Sir Richard catches up with us, you'll need to be alert."

"Wake me up when you get tired," Kay said, yawning. "I'm pretty handy with a boat." She made herself as comfortable as possible in the front of the dinghy.

"Thank you, Kay, I will." Fitzgerald kept a steady hand on the rudder. Irene curled up next to Kay. Although the sun was bright, the two had no trouble falling into a deep slumber.

"Won't you try to rest, too?" Fitzgerald looked at Nan seated beside him.

"Not yet. I wanted to talk to you," Nan said. She bit her lip and lowered her eyes.

"What is it?" Fitzgerald asked gently.

"Well, I... I just wanted to thank you for rescuing us. You were so brave. And if you hadn't helped us, who knows what would become of us?" Nan leaned closer. "You are very gallant, and I, for one, will be eternally grateful. Truly, you saved our lives!"

"Oh, I wouldn't go so far as to say..."

"No, really! Even if they had spared us, our existence would have been worse than death." Nan scooted closer. "I had to tell you how much I... how much I...I..." She quickly pressed her lips hard against Fitzgerald's for a few seconds, then pulled away and settled into the bottom of the boat at the knight's feet. Shocked by Nan's bold kiss, Fitzgerald's face burned and a broad smile spread across his face. As he steered the boat, he reached out and stroked her thick, red hair.

◆

"How did this happen?" William screamed at Sir Richard and Lady Ruth. "Can I trust no one? You'll never redeem yourself for this, Richard! And Ruth, tsk, tsk. How could you let that dancer get away? Why did you leave her unattended? No. No, I see it now. You *wanted* her to get away. You probably aided her escape!"

"No, dearest, I would never—"

"Silence!" William roared. He paced back and forth for a few moments, deep in thought. His eyes met Richard's hard gaze and he said, "Bring those four back to me and I might find my way to forgive you. I don't care what condition they are in, but spare the dancer. I have plans for her."

"Yes, my lord. They will be yours." Richard bowed, and departed to dispatch some soldiers.

Ruth remained, trembling before her husband. William grasped her chin, hard, in his hand and tipped her head back, studying her. He smiled.

"My dearest Ruth," he drawled. "I think it's time you took a little break from court life. There are some hot springs to the east. I think you would enjoy them. Warm air, sunshine, change of scenery—just what my Ruthie needs."

"Please don't send me away, William. I don't wish to be parted from you or our son. I promise I'll—"

He cut her off. "Now Ruth, let's not make a fuss. It's only for a short time—a few weeks at most. The nursemaids can care for Alex."

"Don't you love me anymore? There was a time when you and I used to talk over such things."

"Darling wife, don't misunderstand me. I'm not trying to get rid of you. I simply think you and I need to be apart for a while. We'll have a long talk when you return. Now, be a good girl. Go pack your things and I'll arrange a caravan to escort you." He kissed Ruth condescendingly on the forehead and pushed her away from him.

"Goodbye, William," Ruth said, her eyes filling with tears.

"Yes, yes, goodbye. Have a nice trip," William replied in a bored voice.

Ruth went to her rooms and ran Beth ragged packing dozens of her dresses, jewelry, perfumes, and other things for the journey. Meanwhile William arranged for a caravan with plenty of provisions, twenty escort soldiers, and an ornate carriage for his wife.

"Captain, I will give you your orders," William said to the officer of the caravan.

"Yes, sir!" the man replied stiffly.

"You are to travel east for five to six days. When you reach a suitably deserted area, you are to kill my wife and her servants. No survivors. Understood? We'll say you were attacked by bandits and hold a lavish funeral for my poor wife."

"All, sir?" the man asked, unable to keep the astonishment off his face.

"If you are squeamish, I'll find someone else to carry out my orders. Of course," William continued smoothly, "you realize now you know this plan, I could not afford to let you live, should you decide not to undertake it. You see, Ruth is no longer an appropriate wife to one as exalted as I, and she would rather die than live without me. So..." He continued to glare at the soldier, who nodded.

"I understand perfectly, my lord. All will be as you say."

William smiled. "You will be generously compensated, of course. As will your men. You may take your leave."

CHAPTER 9

Kay yawned as she held the rudder. The sun beat down, and her head throbbed. She had taken over for Fitzgerald two hours ago and needed a reprieve. She was about to wake him up when she heard the sound of horses on the shore. She looked up and saw two men riding along a crest above the beach. Then one aimed his bow and arrow at her. Kay ducked just in time to avoid being pierced. She peered at the soldiers over the edge of the boat and recognized Lord William's colors.

"Fitzy, wake up—soldiers!"

Nan and Irene stayed low in the boat as Fitzgerald crept towards the back. Two more arrows flew over their heads.

"Take the rudder!" Kay called to Fitzgerald, pulling an arrow out of her quiver. Her first shot missed the mark because of the unsteady boat. Another arrow came at them, this time dangerously close to Kay and Fitzgerald. Kay returned an arrow, which found its mark in the chest of one of the soldiers, felling him.

"Kay, be careful!" Nan cried, as one more arrow flew by.

The second soldier and Kay both fired at each other, unsuccessfully. Kay took aim again when the dory began to pitch wildly. Kay lost her balance and fell down, but immediately scrambled back up.

"Hold on," Fitzgerald yelled. "We've hit some rapids!"

The archer raced ahead about four hundred yards to a calm place in the river.

"Damn! He'll have his back to the sun, I won't be able to see," Kay said.

"And the current's slowing down—we'll be sitting ducks," Fitzgerald said grimly. "Nan, Irene, stay down!"

Kay bit her lip and knelt down to ready her bow and arrow. The dory slid into the sluggish part of the river. Kay popped up, aimed at the silhouette on the hill and didn't hesitate. Before the solider could release his arrow, Kay's arrow struck him and he tumbled off his horse.

"Got him!"

"Well done, Kay," Fitzgerald said. "I don't see any more soldiers. Those were probably the advance scouts. We'd better stick to the river 'til nightfall and gain some distance." Fitzgerald took hand of the rudder again as the others tried to rest.

Kay and Irene soon fell asleep. Nan smiled at Fitzgerald, but her expression changed to one of shock.

"Oh, Sir Fitzgerald, you're hurt!" She pointed to a long red mark along Fitzgerald's check where an arrow grazed him. She dipped a kerchief in the water to wash away the blood.

"It's nothing—really," Fitzgerald protested.

"Hold still."

"You are very kind."

The sun went behind some clouds and the wind came up. Nan shivered.

"Are you cold?" Fitzgerald asked.

"A little."

"Perhaps if you sat next to me we might be warmer."

"Yes, we might." Nan scooted closer and pulled his arm around her shoulders. She snuggled against him and they remained that way as the sun fell below the horizon. Smiling, Nan turned her face up to Fitzgerald's. He returned the smile, then bent his head and pressed his lips against hers.

Nan had never really been kissed before, but she responded to Fitzgerald's attentions eagerly. She felt excited and a strange sensation came over her. At first she thought it must be love, but then she realized the sensation was the boat swaying. While they kissed, they had drifted into a series of rapids. Kay and Irene instantly awoke.

"Fitzy," Kay cried. "What's going on?"

"Hold on!" he yelled, trying to gain control.

"Waterfall!" Irene screamed, pointing ahead of them.

When they went over the small waterfall, Nan pitched backward and Fitzgerald just barely kept her from spilling overboard. They landed with an enormous splash and headed into more rapids. Irene, Nan and Kay screamed and grabbed onto the boat as they headed to another waterfall and more rough water. The rocky ride became an out-of-control blur of white, roaring water with the craft narrowly missing jagged rocks jutting above the water's surface. Finally, the dory was pitched over yet another, much larger waterfall. Everyone was thrown out of the craft as it landed in a deep, calm pool at the base of the falls.

"Swim to the boat!" Fitzgerald yelled, when he surfaced. Kay was the first to reach the capsized dory, followed by Nan, who was assisted by Fitzgerald. They clung, gasping, to the side of the battered boat, drifting farther downstream. It was several seconds before they realized Irene was nowhere to be seen.

"Irene! Where is Irene?" Nan asked, frantically looking around.

"She may have been pulled under by the current. I'll go look for her," Fitzgerald said.

"No," Kay gasped. "I saw her. She fell out of the boat after the second waterfall."

The three swam to the shore and dragged themselves on land. Keeping their eyes on the river as much as possible, they hurried upstream to the waterfall. But they could find no sign of the princess. They searched the banks of the river, calling Irene's name, but heard no reply. As the last of daylight slipped away, Kay managed to make a fire. Nan sobbed as Fitzgerald cradled her in his arms. After some time, the three finally fell into a fitful sleep.

◆

Irene had hit her head against a rock after she was jostled out of the boat. She was stunned for a moment, but her instinct to survive kicked in and she managed to grab onto a boulder above the surface before she was swept farther down river. She was only twenty feet from the bank, but the strong current made getting to the shore dangerous. She moved slowly from boulder to boulder until she reached shallower water and finally stumbled to shore. Her head throbbed, but she fought to stay alert. Once she caught her breath, she headed downriver to find her friends.

Had she stayed in view of the river, Irene would have seen the others on the opposite shore. But at one waterfall, the bank dropped off, forcing Irene to climb a hill and negotiate deeper into the woods to get around. The roar of the water drowned out any voices she might have heard.

She reached the pool at the bottom of the larger waterfall but saw no survivors. Irene finally curled up under a tree and cried herself to sleep, supposing her friends to have been swept away with the boat.

CHAPTER 10

In the morning, Irene awoke to the sound of someone singing. It was a strong, powerful tenor voice with incredible brilliance and tone. At first, she thought she must be in Heaven, but then one of her human senses made her realize she was indeed alive. She smelled something delicious and her stomach growled. She tucked her hair securely under the cap and headed towards the singing.

Irene crept closer and peered through the shrubbery to see the source of the beautiful voice. She saw a smallish man with short, red-brown hair and a well-trimmed beard. Near him, a larger, dark-haired man knelt by the fire cooking two rabbits. Moving closer, Irene stepped on a twig and snapped it. She froze in fear, but neither of the men seemed to hear.

Finally, the smaller man said in a loud voice, "I must go down to the river to fetch some water. Will you follow me?"

The larger man replied, "Indeed, I shall." The two men left the encampment. Irene waited a moment, then raced over and pulled one of the rabbits off the fire. She was about to sink her teeth into the seared flesh when a strong hand grabbed her from behind and spun her around so that she was facing the smaller man.

"Ho there, boy, I wouldn't do that if I were you," he said, holding a knife up to Irene's throat.

"You tricked me!" Irene protested.

"That I did. Do thieves deserve better treatment?"

"Well...I was hungry."

"Then why didn't you ask us if we would share our food with you?"

"You would have?"

"Of course not. Catch your own food!"

"I can't. I don't know how."

"A fine, strapping boy like you? I find that hard to believe. What is your name?"

"Remove the knife from my throat and I'll tell you."

"All right, but don't try anything."

Irene nodded to indicate she would make no move. "I am called Ir... uh...Isaac."

"Isaac, eh? Permit me to introduce myself. I am David, kin to the Hebraice. I am a vagabond; a cohort of the earth and sky. I live for a song, a laugh, and a profitable existence! This good humored fellow"—he indicated the large man—"is my faithful servant and business companion, Stephon."

Stephon nodded at Irene.

"Who are the Hebraice? I've never heard of them."

"A tribe of skilled musicians and artisans who live quite far from here. I left several years ago to see what the world could offer. I met Stephon a year or so ago and we have been working together ever since." He sat down by the fire. "So, Isaac, what are you doing in this region? Speak the truth, boy. If I find you're lying, I'll tear the tongue from your head."

"I... was traveling with friends on a boat. We came to some rapids and I fell out. I searched for them, but I fear they drowned." Tears slipped down her cheeks.

"You're in a bad way, aren't you, lad? There, now, stop your crying. 'Tis no way for a man to behave," David said, handing Irene a red handkerchief. She sat next to him and dabbed at her eyes as Stephon brought her a plate of food and a mug of wine drawn from a small cask.

"Where will you be going from here?" David asked gently.

"I don't know." Irene said as she shook her head and blew her nose.

"Where's your family?"

"Dead."

"No friends?"

"Gone."

Stephon and David exchanged glances.

"You could join up with us if you like. That is, provided you won't be dead weight. Any special skills? Archery? Swords?"

Irene again shook her head. "I can sew and do tapestry," she offered lamely.

"Tapestry?" David asked. "Isn't that rather a feminine art?"

"Oh! Well, I, uh...I only depict great battle scenes, you see," Irene said, attempting a gruff voice. "Very violent."

David nodded. "We have little use for tapestry, but our clothes could do with some mending."

"Can you cook?" Stephon asked eagerly.

Irene nodded. "A little."

"He can tend the camp for us and take care of the horses, too."

"Good idea," David responded.

Irene nodded. "Yes, I'd like that." *With a little luck, I can be on my way before they find out I am really a girl.*

Irene stayed in camp for a few days, learning how to light and cook over a fire and feed and curry the horses. She also repaired small rips and loose buttons on the men's clothing. Daily, she washed her arms and face, but didn't dare to bathe completely, for fear of being discovered.

Three days later, Irene and David sat by the fire while Stephon was out hunting.

"David," Irene began, "if you don't mind my asking, how do you live? Do you have some means of earning money?"

"I do, actually. I save ladies in distress."

"You're joking," Irene said, bemused.

"No. You see, I only save wealthy ladies, and after they're rescued, they are so grateful they always give me a nice token of gratitude. It can be surprisingly rewarding."

"You must have long waits between plighted, wealthy women."

"Oh, no, not really, my lad. You'd be surprised."

Irene laughed, taking it as a joke.

Then, Stephon came racing down towards them. "David! A caravan is approaching. Traveling on the road just the other side of the hill."

"What's the set up?" David was suddenly all business.

"About twenty men, a few women, extra horses and a carriage, lavishly decorated. The spoils should be quite prosperous."

"Let's go. Isaac, come with me. Stick close and don't interfere."

David ducked into his tent and came out wearing a black cape. He grabbed a sword, tossed a dagger and mask to Stephon and climbed aboard his horse, pulling Irene up behind him. Stephon mounted his horse and they galloped off.

They caught up with the caravan and followed out of sight until it came to a halt. Stephon pulled a spyglass from under his coat to watch the assemblage.

"They're stopping to water the horses," Stephon said. He looked on before continuing, "Ah! Someone is getting out of the carriage."

"Male or female?" David asked.

"Just a moment. I believe...yes, it's a large woman; richly dressed. She's talking to a girl. Perhaps her handmaiden? The girl's rather pretty. The woman is pointing towards the river and trying to hand the girl a jug. The girl's shaking her head 'no' and is leaving her. Now the woman is going to the river with the jug. She's unhappy."

"Quick, now's our chance. Rendezvous at the small waterfall we passed a few minutes ago."

"Right. Good luck to you."

"And to you."

Stephon dismounted, put on his mask and ran down the hill. David and Irene took both horses back up the trail to the waterfall and tied them up out of sight, then returned to watch Stephon through the spyglass.

As the woman bent clumsily to fill the jug, Stephon grabbed her throat and thrust a knife in front of her face.

"Don't say a word, or I'll put this knife to good use!" Stephon said. The woman whimpered as he bound her hands behind her and prodded her to walk with him.

"Good, no one saw him. Isaac, stay put until you hear this." David sounded a five-note whistle and made her repeat it. Then he moved closer to the waterfall. Irene waited for a while, but curiosity got the better of her. She slipped quietly through the trees for a closer look at Stephon and the woman.

"Would you care to know what I'm planning to do with you?" he was saying. "The gypsies need hardy wenches like you to take care of their cows and chickens. And to satisfy their men's desires," he added suggestively. "They'll pay a nice sum for you!"

The woman began sobbing. "Please sir, not that. Have pity!" she blubbered.

"Pity? Never!"

"Oh, I beg of you, sir. Release me and my husband will give you riches beyond your wildest dreams."

"Bah! I've heard such promises before and they always come to nothing."

"No, truly — my carriage at the caravan is filled with jewelry! You may take it. All of it! Only let me go!"

"No more of this idle chatter!" Stephon moved to strike her across the face.

"Unhand that maiden!" Irene heard David's voice. She followed it to see him by the waterfall posing elegantly on a rock. Stephon snarled at David.

"I said...let her go!" David repeated.

"I'll not!" Stephon retorted dramatically.

David jumped down from the rock and held his sword out. "Release her, I say!"

"Not without a fight!"

"As you wish. Fear not, fair one," David told the woman. "I've never been beaten."

Irene watched in amazement as the two men performed a convincing mock battle. The woman cowered, too frightened to flee.

At one point, Stephon disarmed David, knocked him to the ground and was about to pierce him through the heart with his dagger. David rolled away in the nick of time, leaped to his feet and flung himself at Stephon. The two grappled over the knife. Finally, David caught Stephon off balance and sent him flying. He dropped the dagger, which David quickly retrieved and held to Stephon's throat.

"Prepare to die!" he said dramatically.

"No sir, please. I don't want to die. Mercy!"

"Why should I show you any mercy? You were not so kind to this beautiful maiden." David pointed at the large woman who, just then, was looking far from beautiful.

"Oh, please spare me! I never wanted to become a rogue," Stephon babbled. "You see, my parents beat me as a child. I ran away from home when I was eleven. Some gypsies took me as their slave. They whipped me every night. I came to hate them and everyone I met. It's only my circumstances that made me so uncaring and despicable. No one has ever shown me kindness. Have pity!"

"My lady," David said, "you shall decide his fate. After all, it is your honor that has been insulted. What say you?"

The woman's face was filled with compassion. "Let him go. He can't help himself. Perhaps mercy will now put him on the right path in life. And give him this." She took a ruby ring from a plump finger. "It is worth a great deal and he won't need money for some time."

"Let this be a lesson to you, rogue," David pronounced, handing Stephon the ring. "All people are not so heartless. Go, now, and cease your wicked ways. If I hear you have not, I'll take it upon myself to seek you out and finish that which I started today."

"Thank you, sir," Stephon said. "Kind lady, I am most grateful." He bowed and ran into the woods.

David graciously helped the woman to her feet and offered her his arm. He led her back to the caravan, Stephon and Irene following at a distance. When they arrived, the woman revealed herself to be Lady Ruth. She told the soldiers and her servants what had transpired, while David stood modestly to one side. Of course, no one had even noticed her disappearance. After she had finished her account, she motioned for David to follow her to her carriage.

"I wish to reward you for your bravery." She pulled a large, jeweled box from the carriage.

"Oh no, m'lady, I cannot accept. I merely wanted to defend your honor. Knowing you are safe is reward enough for me."

Irene thought David was laying it on a bit thick. The woman, however, seemed to believe it. Stephon nudged Irene and the two crept away to wait for David.

"But I insist!" Ruth continued. "You must take it. It is but a small recompense for placing your own life in peril." Ruth opened the box, displaying a diamond necklace, several jeweled bracelets, many rings, a bag of silver coins, and one of gold coins. David's eyes fairly popped at the sight of it all. "You may take this box and all it contains. Please. I want you to!"

"Well, I wouldn't wish to offend your ladyship. I am a gentleman, after all. I, of course, am not concerned with personal gain. But since you insist, I graciously accept your gift."

♦

Irene and Stephon were waiting for David about two hundred yards up the road from the caravan when they heard someone talking.

"Quick, hide!" Stephon whispered. "That's not David."

They ducked behind trees as the captain and one of his men from the caravan approached, speaking in low voices.

"I think tomorrow evening would be the best time," the captain growled. "There is a fork in the road several leagues from here which we should reach tomorrow morning. To the left, the way is little traveled and it takes us to the Wallowing Mountains. There are no villages there that I know of, so it should be the perfect spot."

"Will we wait until they're asleep?" the soldier asked.

"Correct. You are all equipped with daggers, aren't you?"

"Yes, sir."

"Good."

"Sir, is no one to be spared?"

"No one."

The two men turned and walked back to the caravan. In a little while, Irene heard the five-note whistle from David. She and Stephon came out of hiding and the three returned to their camp. Irene was silent on the trip back, but Stephon and David were so ecstatic about their treasures that they didn't notice.

Later, as they sat around the fire, Irene, who had been deep in thought, finally spoke. "I am most grateful for the kindness you have shown me, but I think it's time I moved on."

"Why, boy?" Stephon asked. "We were just growing used to you."

"There is something I must do. If you'll be good enough to give me provisions to last me a week or so, I'd be most appreciative."

"You're welcome to stay with us, you know," David said. "You'll not last more than three days alone in those woods. Why, you can't even hunt."

"I'll take my chances," Irene replied.

"But, Isaac, why do you decide this so suddenly? You're no burden to us, if that's what you're thinking. This camp is as clean and neat as I've ever seen it since you came. The horses are well cared for and our clothes have no more rips or loose buttons. You're doing your share, lad. As for some money, we'll give you some of today's haul. We'll not want for money for some time to come."

"Indeed, *you'll* not," Irene said sarcastically.

"Ah, that's it," David nodded. "You don't approve of the way we come by our wherewithal."

"Of course not. Did you think I would? There are other, honest ways to make your livelihood!"

"Though not as profitable." David grinned.

Irene stood up and pointed at David. "You, sir, are a rotter; a scoundrel! No good to anyone, even yourself! I'll have no more of you!"

David shrugged. "As you wish, boy, but don't forget that, though I may be a reprobate, I offered you the hospitality of my camp when you had no others to help you."

"Yes, but why do you make a fraud of helping people? There are those who truly need your help. Why, the woman you pretended to save earlier today is in grave danger. Her guards plan to kill her!"

"Sad, but 'tis no concern of mine."

"More's the pity," Irene retorted. She grabbed a knapsack and began filling it with dried meat, bread and cheese. "I'll reimburse you for these things as soon as I am able, but as you know, I am without any money or anything of value at present."

"No matter, you may take them."

"Oh no, I insist! I want no more favors from you. I'll return to pay you in a week or so."

"But you see, you won't be able to find us. We're moving the camp soon to...greener pastures."

Irene sighed. "Very well. I can do without the food."

"Oh, just take it," David said, in exasperation. "Small bit of good it will do you, but accept it in trade for all your work."

"No," Irene said flatly.

"Damn, you're a stubborn lad; I'm glad you're going! Why is it so important you leave right now? Stay a few days and think things over. There's no need for you to be rushing off."

Irene gave David a dark look. "There *is* a reason for me go."

"Mirn help me! You're not going to do anything foolish, are you, boy? If you think you're going to save that Lady Ruth, you can't possibly! There are twenty soldiers guarding the caravan. They'll cut you into a hundred pieces and they'll have no qualms about it, I assure you."

"I have to try."

"Isaac, why? Surely she means nothing to you. Why risk your life for her?"

"Because no one else will," she said, looking pointedly at David. "Goodbye. Thank you for allowing me to share your camp." Irene turned and walked into the woods in the direction of the caravan.

"Fine! Goodbye and good riddance to you!" David shouted after the retreating figure. He stood watching for a minute, and then turned back to Stephon. "What are you gawking at?" he yelled.

"Nothing...not a thing," he shrugged.

"Well...well, fix us some supper or something. I'm hungry."

"What would you like?"

"What? Oh, uh, anything." David paced around the camp.

"Cabbage and beef stew?" Stephon inquired politely.

"Fine, fine."

"Or maybe braised rabbit...or quail?"

"Yes, that would be good," he muttered.

"Or perhaps mud pies? Or I could cut off your toes and pickle them?"

"Anything you want will be all right with me." David seemed to be staring into oblivion.

Finally, Stephon spoke, "You'd better hurry if you're going to catch him."

David grinned at Stephon. He jumped on his horse, bareback, and took off.

◆

When Irene saw David approaching she began to run, although she knew it was pointless. David hopped off his horse to pursue Irene on foot. Irene tried her best, but in a flash, David caught up to her and grabbed her.

"You're coming back with me."

"No!" Irene said, struggling to escape.

"I'll not have you throwing your life away for nothing!"

"Let me go!" Irene broke away but David grabbed her by the arm and the two fell to the ground, wrestling. Irene kicked and screamed and bit David on the wrist. As she tried to get up again, Irene's cap fell off and her long dark tresses tumbled around her shoulders. David, who had a hold of Irene again, stopped short and stared at her in astonishment.

"A girl?" he whispered. "A *girl?*"

He released Irene's arm and stood up. He looked at her a moment more and then walked a short distance away, shaking his head. There was a silence for some time and then David began to chuckle softly. The chuckling grew louder, eventually turning into raucous laughter.

CHAPTER 11

Kay sat by the fire as Nan fell asleep, yet again in the arms of Fitzgerald, as she had every night since losing Irene. Fitzgerald tried to catch Kay's attention to talk, but she stared stubbornly into the dying flames. After a while, he drifted off to sleep.

Two tears slid down Kay's cheeks. *I don't even know if I'm crying because we lost Irene, or because I seem to have lost Fitzy. I guess I can't blame him. Nan is so pretty.*

She couldn't remember the last time she'd cried, especially over a man. *Except for the time Demetrius told me about him and...*

She sniffed a little as another tear fell. She thought of how happy she had always been in the Secret Valley. A secure job of a high position, good friends and a match with Fitzgerald. Of course, nothing official had been announced yet, but everyone in the Valley knew it was only a matter of time before the betrothal feast would take place. Even Lord William had hinted his approval.

Now, Lord William is my enemy. I have lost my home, my friends, Fitzy's love, and everything is changed. But if I had to do it again, would I betray Nan and Irene and hand them over to Lord William? No. Whatever may lie in the future for us, there is no regretting what I did.

Kay sniffed a final time and wiped her eyes with the back of her hand. *Enough feeling sorry for myself. I'll go hunt some night game for breakfast.* She picked up her bow and arrows and walked silently into the forest.

After several hours, Kay was still empty handed. She sat down on a log to rest. *Horse pizzle! At this rate, we'll never eat.*

"You happen to be on private land. And, in case you didn't know, the penalty for poaching is not a pleasant one," a voice from behind her said.

Kay gasped and wheeled around to see a tall, handsome man staring intently at her. "As you can easily see, I have not caught anything. You cannot prosecute without some evidence, m'lord," Kay snapped, too tired and irritated to be even a little frightened. "I'm sorry to have trespassed. I lost my way."

Kay stood and tried to walk past the man, but he blocked her way. Kay hesitated, and glared at him. Swallowing the rude words she longed to say, she smiled tightly. "So, if you'll give me your leave, good sir, I'll depart these woods and go back to my friends." She swiftly brushed by the man.

"Hey, wait! I'm only joking!" He caught Kay by the arm and turned her back to him. "I'm no groundskeeper—I've been following you. You've had little luck tonight."

"No thanks to you, I'm sure—you likely scared away all the game!" Kay shot back.

The man laughed. "If an expert hunter like yourself didn't notice me, I'll warrant the woodland creatures didn't either. You simply didn't pick a good part of the forest to go searching for your dinner."

"Breakfast," Kay replied, with a gesture towards the sun, which was now beginning to show itself over the mountains. "Would you mind terribly letting go of my arm?"

"If you tell me your name."

"My name is of no concern to you," Kay said testily, "as I shall be leaving now, and will never see you again."

"Oh, but it is my concern," he said dramatically. "For I have fallen so deeply in love with you, I must at least know your name, that I may speak it to every flower in the woods, so they will know there is one fairer than they." He smiled mockingly at her, but his eyes were kind.

Kay stared at him for an instant and then burst into laughter.

"There! I thought I could get you to smile. Although, usually I need not go to such lengths. My name is Christian."

"Just...Christian? Not Lord of this or that, or Duke somebody of something?

"No. Just Christian. And now, you must please tell me who you are and how you came to this place."

"Very well. I am called Kay, of late from the Secret Valley. I am fleeing Lord William, Son of Dob, who, I now realize, is a tyrant and murderer. I was with three other friends but, while traveling down the river, our boat got into trouble and we lost Irene, Princess of Cabbage. Nan and Sir Fitzgerald, who was once a knight in Lord William's service, are back at our camp, asleep."

"So they sent you to hunt their breakfast?" Christian asked.

"No. I... I couldn't sleep."

"Thinking about your friend, no doubt. Are you certain she was swept downstream?"

"We can't be sure of anything, as we didn't find her body. But we've been searching for days. I suppose we will try again today."

"Then you must let me help you! I grew up near these woods and know them well. If she's alive, and hasn't traveled far, we'll locate her."

Kay smiled at Christian. "Thank you, sir. We would welcome your assistance."

"Good. Let us return to your friends."

The two strolled back to the campsite. On the way, Kay told Christian more about Lord William and his powerful army. Kay, now she had gotten over her initial anger, took time to study Christian. He was tall, at least six foot, with brown, curly hair which was cut fashionably long. His eyes were the most intense she had ever seen — so dark brown in color as to almost appear black, but with flecks of gold in them. His facial features were firm, yet there was a mischievous boyishness about him when he smiled, which brought out a small cleft in his chin. He was well built, and quite the handsomest man Kay had seen in some time. Over his shoulder, he carried a pack, his bow, and a quiver of arrows.

He told Kay he was in service to the king of a community called Tondlepen, although he didn't say how large the kingdom was, or its exact location. Nor did he explain his position. Kay attempted to question him about his occupation, but he kept sidestepping the queries and turning the conversation back to her. Before she realized it, Kay divulged a great deal about herself to this man.

When they reached the clearing, Nan and Fitzgerald were still asleep.

"Are they betrothed?" Christian asked, noting Nan lay in Fitzgerald's arms. A pained expression crossed Kay's face.

"No. He...he was comforting her over the loss of Irene."

"And you had no need of such comfort?"

Kay sharply examined Christian's impassive face. Were his eyes mocking her?

"Irene was Nan's lifelong friend," she said defensively. "I just met her." All at once, Kay sighed, exhausted. Christian took note and suggested she lie down.

"Your friends will probably sleep on for a while yet. Meanwhile, I will attempt to succeed where you did not in catching our breakfast."

Kay placed a couple of sticks on the embers of the fire, lay down and watched Christian disappear into the forest.

She soon fell asleep.

◆

A few hours later, Kay awoke to the tantalizing aroma of roasted quail. She glanced over and noticed Nan and Fitzgerald were both awake and talking softly with Christian.

"Ah! You're awake," Christian said, smiling at her.

"And I see you had good luck—the bird smells delicious," Kay answered.

"I'm so glad you met Christian, Kay," Nan said. "Else we might have had to go hungry!"

Kay scowled. "I would have caught us something."

"Well, it really doesn't matter who caught our breakfast, does it?" Fitzgerald said. "Let's hurry and eat and be on our way. With Christian, we are certain to find Irene if she's alive."

The mention of Irene made everyone forget about their own strife. They quickly ate and gathered their things.

"It's so kind of you to help us, Christian," Nan commented. "How is it you know this area so well?"

"Christian is in high position with the king of whose land we are near," Kay explained. "What was his name, did you say, Christian?"

"I didn't," smiled the man. Abruptly changing the subject, he went on, "You say you lost your friend by those large rocks? Let us search downstream first." He walked off, Nan and Fitzgerald following. Kay looked after them for a moment, frowning, and then hurried to join them.

◆

Demetrius Keats had traveled for many days after escaping Ben de Blanc and the tiny island. Without a bow and arrows, he had not been successful in finding food, except for some not quite ripe berries. His wound had become inflamed again and was red and tender. He was feverish and hungry.

I could almost long for some of that cursed lake trout.

He rested on a log, took the orb out of the pouch he kept around his neck and gazed into it. It glowed a deep green. Demetrius was beginning to understand a bit of the orb's magical powers. So far, he could make the wind blow a little and gather dark clouds.

I wish I knew how to make it bring me a good meal. His stomach ached. *Or find the way back home for me. Everyone must surely think me dead after so long an absence.*

He sat on the log for a long time, thinking. Finally, he decided he wouldn't get any dinner just sitting, and began walking again. After a time, Demetrius heard the sound of rushing water. He headed towards it and thought he heard voices.

At last! Where there are people, there's sure to be food and help.

He hurried his pace. When Demetrius stepped into a clearing, he was shocked to see a familiar face. "Lady Ruth!" he cried out in astonishment.

"Demetrius! Long-lost friend—we gave you up for dead!" Lady Ruth cried in equal amazement. Demetrius rushed to her and fell to his knees, kissing her hand.

"My lady, you are like a vision after what I have been through."

"My dear Demetrius, pray get off your knees. We are not at court," Lady Ruth simpered. "Although, it is lovely to be treated with such respect, even here in the wilderness."

Demetrius rose, wincing in pain. He placed his hand over his shoulder and took a deep breath.

"You're hurt! Demetrius, what happened?"

"I would need days and nights to tell you the story of my travels and the people I met, m'lady."

"Days and nights we *have* aplenty. My lord and husband is displeased with me and has sent me away for a time." Lady Ruth led Demetrius over to the makeshift table. "Beth, tell the cook to prepare some hot food at once." She pulled back Demetrius' shirt and began to examine his wound. Beth gaped in amazement at the handsome man before running off towards the kitchen area.

"Why is my Lord William displeased with you?" Demetrius asked, wincing as she probed his injury.

"Because I allowed a girl he was interested in—as a dancer, mind you, nothing more—to escape the Secret Valley with Kay and Fitzgerald."

"What? Kay and Fitz are gone?"

Ruth smiled sadly. "As you see, there have been many changes in the valley since you rode off to battle." She sighed. "Your wound is infected. I do not have all of the tools or medicine I need, but we can at least start with a good cleaning."

Beth returned with a plate of food and wine. Lady Ruth sent her back to fetch some clean linens and hot water and soap.

"Eat, Demetrius, and I will tell you all I know," she said.

◆

Word spread through the camp that the almost-forgotten Demetrius was alive.

"I tell you, it's a sign. A sign from above we shouldn't kill 'er," one of the guards said.

"Sign or no sign, if we kill her, now we've got to kill him as well!"

"Remember, no survivors, no witnesses," another added.

"But if Richard finds out about it—him, I mean—we could get into big trouble. Demetrius was his...well, *you* know."

"Yeah, Richard might even reward us for bringing him back!" another spoke hopefully.

"But what about our orders?"

◆

"I am nearly ready to give up," Fitzgerald said as they sat by the river after another day of searching.

"Oh, don't say that!" Nan exclaimed and began to sob. Fitzgerald hurried over to comfort her.

Abruptly, Kay rose and stomped away. Christian stared after her for a moment, then followed. He found her by a tall fir tree, her back turned to him.

"I gather that in the past you and Fitzgerald were more than...friends?" he said.

"It's none of your affair!" Kay said curtly, her voice choked with emotion.

"Forget him, Kay. What do you want with a mere lad when you can have a man?"

Kay wheeled around, eyes flashing angrily. "What do you know about it, anyway? And don't you dare insult him!"

Careful, Christian, don't mess it up now, after you've come so far. His Majesty wouldn't like it. Aloud, he said, "Forgive me. I only said that because he had hurt you. Fitzgerald's a fine man, I'm sure."

"The finest!" Kay said in a quavering voice. "He's the...finest knight I've..." She broke off crying. "Oh, damn him! Damn all men!"

Christian stepped to Kay and pulled the crying girl into his arms. Slowly, he caressed her hair all the while making soft, crooning sounds.

"Don't cry, Kay. Please don't cry, my sweet," he whispered over and over. He began to kiss Kay, softly on the brow and down her face, now wet with tears. Kay lifted her face to his as he kissed her on the mouth. She tightened her grip around Christian.

Christian repeated her name as he continued to kiss her. His arms around her were so strong. His hands stroked her so gently. Kay felt dizzy and weak. She wanted to surrender to this strange sensation. Christian pulled her closer and suddenly she felt his arousal below. Her eyes flew wide open and she pushed herself out of Christian's arms.

"No!" she cried. For a moment they stood staring at one another. Then Kay broke away and ran back to camp. Christian watched her. Slowly a smile crossed his face.

CHAPTER 12

After David finally stopped laughing, he sat and stared at Irene for a long while. Irene became a bit uncomfortable with his gaze. At length, he spoke, "I *felt* there was something odd about you, but I couldn't put my finger on it. Why the deception?"

"I thought it would be better to travel as a lad—a lady might not be safe alone."

"I would come to your rescue anytime."

"Even without any riches in recompense?" Irene smiled.

"I'm sure we could find a suitable reward." David grinned in return. He stroked his beard thoughtfully. "Now, Isaac—no—what *is* your name?"

"Irene, Princess of Cabbage."

"Cabbage! Stephon and I passed through there many years ago—a pleasant enough place."

"Alas, little remains now. Lord William and his army left my home a burned-out ruin." Irene sighed, tears coming to her beautiful eyes at the memory.

"Lord who?" David asked.

"Lord William—the ruthless ruler of the Secret Valley. He killed my family and friends. Unless we do something, he will continue to kill defenseless people. He must be stopped!"

"And just how do you propose to stop him?"

Irene shook her head. "I don't know. My friends and I were escaping when I fell out of the boat. We didn't even have a plan. But, surely Sir Fitzgerald would have thought of something."

"Boat? Fitzgerald? What is all that about?"

Irene smiled. "I forgot. You really don't know anything about me, do you?"

"Why don't you tell me on the way back to camp?" David said, standing and offering his hand to Irene. She took his hand and stood. They smiled at each other. Still holding hands, they strolled back to Stephon.

◆

"I mean to find them, and find them I will!" Sir Richard paced back and forth in front of the fire. He eyed his men carefully. They sat silent with their gazes lowered.

"I cannot believe you let them escape!" Richard stormed on. "Two of my best men killed, and by a mere slip of a girl. You call yourself soldiers!"

"You always thought her a fine marksman before," muttered one of the men.

"What did you say?" Richard barked.

"Nothing, sir," the man replied with a gulp.

Richard glared at the man for a moment before he continued pacing. Speaking almost to himself, he said, "Never fear. I shall catch up with Kay and her little band of friends. And when I do—'twill be sweet revenge. She always tried to come between me and Demetri..." he broke off. "Get to sleep!" he shouted at the men. "We've a long day ahead of us tomorrow."

◆

After their evening meal of roasted quail, Fitzgerald, Nan, Kay and Christian sat by the fire, deep in their own thoughts.

Finally, Fitzgerald spoke, "I... I think we must assume Irene is...lost to us. We've searched hard for many days now and there is no trace."

Nan began to weep for her childhood friend.

"I agree, sadly," Kay said. "The question is: where do we go from here?"

"We can't return to the Valley of William Etté or Cabbage...we have no place to go," Nan whispered. "No place at all."

Christian cleared his throat. "I think the best possible solution would be for you to return with me to Tondlepen. His Majesty would want to learn all about this Lord William so he may prepare for battle, if necessary. I'm sure you would all find places in court with no trouble."

After a moment, the others nodded in agreement.

"I believe you are right, Christian," Kay said. "We have nowhere else to go...and people must be warned of Lord William."

"Yes. I agree," Fitzgerald said.

Nan nodded, her green eyes shining with tears.

"Then, let us go to sleep and start afresh tomorrow," Christian said.

Soon they were all asleep except Kay, who stared up at the stars, questioning if this was the right move. *Or...are we headed for more trouble?* Finally, she fell asleep.

The next day found the four more cheerful, because at least they had some sense of purpose. Irene was still not far from their minds, but they accepted she was dead and tried to put it behind them. After all, they reasoned, life does go on.

As they traveled, Kay could hardly turn around without finding Christian nearby. He was very attentive and Kay was touched by his thoughtfulness. He made no reference to the earlier episode, but every now and then, Kay would catch him looking at her with a strange expression. It was almost wistful, and his mocking eyes were no longer teasing her, but soft and kind. The expression would last only a moment before he was his old, teasing self.

But behind his joshing banter, Christian was struggling with his feelings.

Should I tell her the truth—that I was sent to find her? Or could I pass it all off as mere coincidence, as his Majesty suggested?

◆

For six days and nights the four walked to Christian's homeland.

"How much farther, Christian?" Nan asked. "I'm tired of walking, sleeping on the ground and eating nothing but game. I don't mean to complain—you've been so kind—but what I wouldn't give for a nice, juicy apple tart."

Christian gave her an encouraging smile. "Not much farther now, Nan. In fact, over the next rise, we should be able to see our kingdom."

They hurried to the top of the hill. Below them lay a lovely green valley dotted with many farms, homes and a large central town. Two buildings stood out. One was a stone church with a tall steeple, and the other, a stone castle with four towers.

"This place seems familiar. I am sure I have never been here, yet it reminds me of some place. I can't think what," Kay said.

"Probably a coincidence, Kay," Fitzgerald said. "Come on—let's hurry!" He grabbed Nan's hand to run down the path. Nan laughed for the first time since losing Irene.

"Shall we?" Christian held out his hand to Kay. She smiled back at him and took it in her own. They began to chase after Nan and Fitzgerald.

"Ouch!" Kay cried. She let go of Christian's hand and fell down.

"What is it?" Christian asked, very alarmed. He knelt beside Kay, who was moaning and rubbing her left ankle.

"Oh, my bad ankle," she said. "It does this every now and then. Don't worry, I'll be all right."

"Can you stand?"

"I think so...help me up, please."

Christian lifted Kay up, but she crumpled into his arms. "No good," she said, wincing in pain. "I think I hurt it good this time!"

"I shouldn't have made you run on this narrow path."

"Don't blame yourself. Can you still see Nan and Fitzgerald?"

"No. They're too far down the path by now. Come on—I'll carry you."

"Oh, Christian, no—you can't possibly!" Kay protested, but he lifted her up.

"I rather like this." He smiled at her. "Now, I have you where I want you!" He tossed her up and caught her again. Kay laughed, before wincing again. "Sorry," Christian said as he headed carefully down the trail.

◆

Nan and Fitzgerald soon reached the town square, and what they came upon made them pale with shock. On top of a platform, which was located in the middle of the square, stood a regally dressed, large, bearded man. A row of people were lined before him, bent at the waist. To the couple's horror, they realized that the man was methodically chopping off their heads!

None of the people were bound in any way—they simply stood calmly while the man took careful aim and severed head after head with a long, sharp blade.

"Mirn preserve us, Nan!" Fitzgerald gasped. "What has Christian led us to?"

Nan stood transfixed as the man took aim again. When he swung the blade backwards once more, Nan cried out, "STOP!"

The man dropped the sword in surprise and the entire crowd turned as one to stare at the strangers. All was silent. The regal man slowly walked off the platform and came over to Nan. When he was within inches of her, he stopped and stared. He cocked an eyebrow and asked, "Stop?"

Nan gulped. She almost ran, but instead she summoned up every ounce of courage she had and said boldly, "Yes. Yes, stop! What on earth are you doing? How can you slaughter these people like so many sheep?"

A murmur ran through the crowd. The stern expression on the man's face turned to one of amazement, then to anger, and finally petulance.

"I'm bored," he said simply.

Nan stared in disbelief. "Bored?"

"Yes." And he began to sing:

"When I'm bored and feeling sad and lonely,
I can do just one thing only.
I go down where the peasants are so lowly,
And chop off a dozen heads.
Tiri-tumba, tiri-tumba, tiri-tumba,
Killing peasants is such fun!
Tiri-tumba, tiri-tumba,
Killing peasants is such fun!
There is nothing that cheers me up so quickly,
Tho' it may make you quite sickly.
And the blood tends to make things very sticky.
Still, I love to chop those heads!
Tiri-tumba, tiri-tumba, tiri-tumba,
Killing peasants is such fun.
Tiri-tumba, tiri-tumba,
Killing peasants is such fun!
Now you may say, 'How simply dreadful of you!
What about the God above you?'
Well, I'm sure if he knew them quite as *I* do,
He would go and chop some heads!
Tiri-tumba, tiri-tumba, tiri-tumba,
Killing peasants is such fun.
Tiri-tumba, tiri-tumba,
Killing peasants is such fun!"

He ended his song with a flourish and a high C. The crowd applauded. Nan continued to stare at the man before saying, weakly, "Have you ever thought of taking up backgammon?"

The crowd of townspeople stood with expressions of fear, but then the man laughed and they quickly joined in. Abruptly, the man stopped laughing and strained to see past Nan and Fitzgerald. They turned as well to find Christian approaching with Kay in his arms. Kay smiled at her two friends, but her expression turned to one of astonishment as she recognized the man behind them. Christian walked up to the royal man and stood, waiting. There was silence.

Then Kay whispered, "Luciano?"

The man smiled broadly. "My little Principessa! You have returned to me at last!" He held out his arms. Christian transferred Kay into the King's grasp. She looked from Christian to the King, and fainted.

CHAPTER 13

When Kay came to, she found herself on a soft bed with silk sheets. She gazed around at the large, round room, with red velvet curtains and dark mahogany furniture. Rich tapestries hung on the stone walls.

Kay sat up, noticing for the first time she was naked. *Who removed my clothing? And how long did I sleep?*

She wrapped the sheet around her and crossed over to the window. She was in one of the towers overlooking the same large courtyard where she had last seen Luciano, but she saw no sign of any activity below her.

Kay sat at the table, where a plate of food had been placed for her. She hugged herself and shivered as her mind flashed back to her first meeting with Luciano, six years ago.

◆

Ten-year old Kay stowed away on a cargo ship in Fools Bay. She needed to get out of town quickly, because the authorities had noticed she was young and without family. Fearful of being placed in an orphans' home, or worse, a workhouse, Kay managed to sneak aboard a ship heading up the coast. She hid among the many boxes and barrels in the hold.

That first night, afraid of being discovered, she barely slept. But the next morning, seeing the light spilling down a narrow stairwell, she began to take stock of her situation. The space, filled with cargo, was in the front half of the ship. The back half, with a larger stairway, consisted of the captain's quarters, the mess, first mate's cabin, and the crew's sleeping compartment. Kay hoped the crew would mostly use the other stairway, lessening the chance of her being discovered. There was also a small cubicle nearby on the starboard side, which appeared to be the brig.

The sailors were preparing to get underway. The girl listened to the hustle of the men's feet as they adjusted and secured the rigging, and unfolded the sails. They sang songs unfamiliar to Kay as they worked.

Then, Kay heard the raised voices of some dispute. The argument seemed to be between the captain and one of his men. All work ceased, and it was quiet enough for her to make out some reference to the brig. Kay ducked behind a barrel of salted fish. Footsteps and voices came down the stairs.

"It is not fair. I cannot sing wit a cold in de throat! De captain is a man without a heart! Tell me; is this any way to treat the first mate? Wait! I am almost starving. I have been working all morning. Please be so kind to bring me something to eat. I'm sure the captain would not want a corpse on his hands!"

The heavy iron door of the brig creaked as the wrongdoer was placed in the cell, then it clanged shut and the footsteps retreated. After a while, Kay became anxious. She could not move about without being discovered by the prisoner, so there was only thing left to do. She came out from her hiding place and crept over to the brig. She waited a moment, then cleared her throat.

"What is that?" the man inside asked. "Speak! Who is there?"

"Lower your voice, I beg of you," Kay pleaded. The brig's door was solid iron except for a small window large enough to view a face through, and another space nearer the bottom, through which food could be passed.

"Who are you? Did you stow away on this ship?"

"Yes. But please don't give me away!"

"You are only a child. What is your name?"

"Kay."

"I am pleased to meet you. I would kiss your hand, but it is impossible under these circumstances. My name is Luciano. I call myself King of the High Seas—ha!"

Kay could not see all of the man behind the door, but his face was very good looking. She spied deep-set, dark eyes, black wavy hair, a beard, and a devilishly handsome and expressive face. Kay stood silent, so completely entranced with this handsome man that she could not speak.

He chuckled. "Do not worry, my little angel. I will not give you away."

"Oh, thank you, sir."

"Luciano, please."

"Thank you, Luciano."

"You know, Kay, you are much too pretty a girl for such a plain name. You should be called something like Tatiana, or Esmeralda, perhaps Angelina; yes, Angelina suits you with your yellow hair and blue eyes. Yes. I give you this name! You are an angel sent to keep me company while I rot down here."

Kay fell in love with Luciano at that moment. As the ship sailed up the coast, Luciano and Kay spent hours in each other's company. He told her stories of his childhood, they played word games and shared their dreams and, fortunately for Kay, food. Large meals were sent down to the brig three times a day. Luciano shared them with Kay and, despite the damp air and the lack of light, she slowly began to assume a healthy glow to her face again.

After several days, Luciano proposed an idea. "Angelina, I was thinking. I grow tired of a sailor's life. It is time for me to go home. Since you no longer have a Mama and Papa, if you like, you come with me, yes?"

"Nothing would make me happier, Luciano. Thank you!"

"Alright, then. We leave when the ship makes port and I get out of this stinking brig."

Bad weather prevented the ship from sailing as fast as the captain would have liked. It took four days for them to get to the Biaumcol River and they nearly ran aground on a sand bar. The captain wanted to continue to the William Etté River and make port in the Valley by nightfall, but thick fog rolled in making it dangerous to navigate. They anchored near the mouth of the Biaumcol to wait for the fog to lift, but the thick mist lingered all day. The next morning, the fog was still present and the captain, at an end to his patience, elected to move slowly and cautiously up the river.

The ship proceeded near blindly up the river. It was still impossible to see more than thirty feet in front of bow and the captain could not be sure if he had missed the place where the William Etté River meets the Biaumcol. The wind changed directions, bringing rain with it and the fog began to dissipate. The vessel gained speed as a strong gust filled its sails, and the captain sought to determine his location. He could now make out the shoreline on either side and observed a barren and almost treeless terrain on the left shore. The land only looked like that well east of the river of William Etté. The captain cursed; they had gone too far. As he consulted his charts, he failed to notice a high, arched bridge ahead of him, stretching the entire span of the wide Biaumcol. When he finally looked up from his work, he recognized it immediately as the "Bridge of Doom."

The captain and his crew had heard tales of the "Bridge of Doom" since they were children. They knew it only appears once a year, and all who pass under it disappear to some dreadful land to become slaves to someone called the Black Lord. Unable to turn the ship around, everyone on ship panicked as they sailed closer to the bridge. An invisible choir of voices began singing:

"Bridge of Doom, Bridge of Doom, looming under angry skies.
Bridge of Doom, Bridge of Doom, there your ship forever lies.
Let the world grow cold around us. Let the demons cry below.
Bridge of Doom, Bridge of Doom, where your soul forever cries."

"Abandon ship!" the captain ordered. "All hands abandon ship! To stay on board is to give your life to a fate worse than death. Jump overboard, all of you!"

The men dove in the cold water and began to swim to shore. The captain was ready to dive in, when Kay rushed up from the hold.

"Please! You can't leave him! Luciano is still in the brig. The key. Give me the key!"

"It is too late, little one!"

"No, we must save him!"

"You don't know what you're saying!" The captain picked Kay up and threw her in the river, diving in after her.

"Luciano!" Kay screamed when she surfaced.

"Stay back!" she heard him call. "Do not follow me. Perhaps one day, you will find a way to release me from the Black Lord!"

"I'll find a way," Kay cried. "I promise I'll find some way to free you!"

"Good bye, my darling Angelina!"

"Good bye Luciano! I love you! I love you!"

Kay watched as the ship sailed under the bridge and as it passed the arch, slowly faded from sight. She swam to the riverbank, and collapsed on the shore.

"I'll save you, Luciano. I swear some day I'll find a way to get you back."

◆

In her castle room, Kay shuddered. Although she had tried for years to find a way to help Luciano, no one she had ever approached knew of a way to bring people back from wherever the Bridge of Doom sent them.

Yet, Luciano did find a way.

She tried the door to her room again, but it was still locked. Since there was nothing else to do, she had something to eat, went back to the bed, and soon fell asleep again.

CHAPTER 14

Kay woke to the sound of a piper and drums playing in the courtyard below. She went to the window and looked down on a band playing military music as soldiers performed a regimental display. She crossed the room to the heavy wood door and tried it, but found it was still locked. Frustrated, she returned to the bed and sat on the edge to await her fate and to ponder the strange appearance of Luciano.

Not only had he somehow returned from the land of the Bridge of Doom, but now he was also, apparently, a king. She was happy he had survived, but was troubled by the change in his personality. The Luciano she had known as a girl would never hurt anyone, much less slaughter entire groups in the streets!

The band music stopped and Kay heard the gentle sounds of a mandolin, followed by Luciano's voice. She looked out the window and saw him below, singing an Italian love song.

> *"O del mio dolce ardor bramato oggetto,*
> *bramato oggetto, L'aura che tu respiri,*
> *alfin respiro, alfin respiro."*

At the completion of his song, Luciano called up to Kay's window. "My Angelinetta, at last you are returned to me! I am glad to see you have indeed grown into a beautiful woman."

A pang of the old affection she had felt for him long ago tugged at her heart. She waved from her window.

"My lovely little Principessa, I can stand it no longer! I am coming to you!"

"You cannot!" Kay shrieked. "They took my clothes!"

"Yes, I know!" he called back, grinning. Luciano entered the base of the tower and bounded up the circular stairway. Kay wrapped the silk sheet tighter around her body and sat in a large chair next to the fire. The key rattled in the lock for a moment and in stepped Luciano, dressed in royal splendor. He rushed towards Kay and dropped on one knee to kiss her hand. As he stared up at her with his expressive black eyes, her heart melted.

"I have missed you, my little angel," he said.

"And I, you, Luciano. Very much."

Luciano kissed her hand once more and pulled her down to sit with him on the rug in front of the fire. He smiled at her, taking in every detail of her face.

"Luciano," Kay ventured, "how did you manage to escape from the land of the Black Lord? I tried many times to discover some means to..."

"Shh, it is not important." He stroked her hair.

"But how did you escape? No one has ever succeeded before, and if you told everyone how you escaped, perhaps many more lives..."

"Hush, my little one. You are much too pretty to bother with such things."

Kay grabbed Luciano's hands. "Luciano, please. At least tell me this. Did you order me brought here? Was Christian acting at your behest?"

"Of course! You see, when I learned where you were, I knew I must find you again. I told Christian to use whatever means necessary to convince you to follow him back here."

"I'm not so sure his methods were all that necessary," Kay murmured, remembering the man's attentions to her on their journey.

"Well, now we are together and nothing can separate us. My sweet, I have a wonderful story to tell you. When you met me, I was only a simple sailor. Now, I am a king!"

"Yes, I see, but how?"

"I will tell you. The former ruler of this kingdom was an eccentric old bachelor who died leaving no heirs. Or so everyone thought! When he was a young man, he met a beautiful girl and fell in love with her. As she was not of royal blood, he was not permitted to marry her, but he took her as a willing mistress. She stayed with him for two years, during which time she gave birth to a child. She called the child Luciano. Ah, you see? It is I! Only I never knew I was the son of a king! My mother told me this as she lay dying, and gave me a ring with a royal crest on it as proof.

"After I escaped from the land of the Black Lord, I came here to seek out my real father, but found he had died several years before. The kingdom had been taken over by a council of inept men, so when the villagers learned I was the son of the late king, they were happy to make me king, despite the fact I was a...how do you say? A bastard." He smiled broadly. "That is why it was so important to find you, my Principessa. You see, I wish to make you my queen."

"You mean you want to marry me? But...this is all rather sudden, don't you think? After all, it has been, what?—six or so years since we last saw one another? Wouldn't it be better if we got to know one another a little better, first?'

"You are wise beyond your years, my dear one. You are right. Absolutely! I was going to suggest we marry on the morrow, but now we will postpone the wedding until next week!"

"But, Luciano," Kay stammered, a bit panicked, "I have not yet consented to be your wife! What I meant is, after a few months' time perhaps we can speak again about the possibility of marrying, and until then, we could spend time together socially—in the presence of attendants, of course."

"You mistake my meaning, Kay. I am not asking for your hand; I am taking you as my wife. Because I am King Luciano, and whatever I want becomes mine. Your needs and wants are of no matter. We *will* be wed!"

The abrupt change in Luciano's manner shocked and frightened Kay. All at once there was an angry tyrant in front of her.

"We will be married in one week's time," Luciano said firmly as he rose and stepped towards the door. "So, I advise you to try and recover some of the feelings of tenderness you once had for me. It will go easier for you. I like affectionate wives."

Luciano left the room, locking the door behind him. Kay was confused. This man seemed so hard and cruel.

What did he mean when he said he liked 'affectionate wives?' Have there been others? Where are Fitzy and Nan—what has Luciano done with them? Have they abandoned me?

A feeling of dread washed over her.

During the next five days, Kay remained in the high tower, seeing no one except an old woman who came daily with fresh water and food. Kay was finally given a rough woolen dress to wear, but no one would answer her many questions.

◆

Nan and Fitzgerald had been seized immediately after Kay fainted in Luciano's arms. They were taken to a large compound outside Tondlepen, and put in shackles. The guards took them to separate rooms, each filled with other prisoners in chains. They spent three days in the compound, but on the fourth day, all the prisoners were bound together and driven from the city like cattle. There were more than a hundred people, and Nan learned some of the victims had been imprisoned for almost a year.

Nan and Fitzgerald tried to communicate with each other, but they were at opposite ends of the line of bound prisoners, so there was no hope of them talking. All Nan could do was pray she and Fitzgerald might end up together, wherever they were being taken.

The company made slow progress. Rain fell constantly from the moment they left Tondlepen. The soldiers wore long capes with hoods to keep them dry, but the prisoners had no protection and became soaked to the skin. At night, the guards herded everyone into barns, which seemed to be constructed for the sole purpose of holding them for the night. Then the next day, they were back on the road. With little food and not enough rest, many became ill.

They trudged along for three more days when two men approached on horseback. The men asked to speak to someone in charge. A guard pointed to the senior officer, a tall man with a somewhat dimwitted expression, and the two men rode up to him.

"Excuse me, my good man," one of them asked, "could you tell me if it would be possible to purchase one or two of these slaves?"

"I'm afraid not," the officer answered. "Ye see, these are not slaves. They are prisoners, actually."

"Ah, I see. Well, you couldn't be persuaded to sell one or two?"

"I wouldn't mind, actually, but ye see, a lot of them are dangerous. They'd like te' stab ye in the back as much as look at ye."

"Well, most of them seem as if they're too weak to harm a gnat. I'd be willing to take my chances."

"Oh, don't be deceived, sir. They look meek as lambs now, but that's only 'cause I discipline 'em with a heavy hand."

"I'm sure you do. I am a believer of strict discipline myself. I'm certain I could handle them."

"Mebbe so, but ye see, I could get in trouble back home for selling prisoners, actually, so the answer is still no."

"Well, there must be a solution to benefit us both," the man said. "Tell me, do prisoners often die when you transport them?"

"Yeah, sometimes. Just yesterday, an old woman caught a fever and died, actually."

"And how would anyone know whether or not a couple more people hadn't also 'caught a fever' and died?" the man said with a grin.

"Oh, I see what yer saying!" he nodded sagely, and then shook his head again. "But the answer is still no. It's the principle of the thing."

"I truly hate to encroach upon a man's principles, but I wonder if you could possibly be prevailed upon to...uh...*alter* them temporarily. I'll make it worth your while."

The man on the horse gestured to his friend who passed him a beautiful jeweled box. The man extracted a sapphire ring from the box and handed it down to the officer, whose eyes widened at the sight of it.

"Oh my, that's a pretty piece, ain't it? Whoo! It's awfully tempting...but I don't know."

"What is your favorite gem?"

"I'm partial to diamonds, actually."

The man on horseback handed over another ring with a large diamond in it. "Both those rings are yours if I can have my choice of two of your prisoners."

"Ye must want 'em awful bad." He hesitated a moment, and shrugged. "Alright—take yer pick."

Nan, who overheard most of this conversation, was stunned when the man on horseback pointed to her. She was even more surprised when he next chose Fitzgerald. The guard removed their shackles and the strange man tied Nan and Fitzgerald to his party's horses.

"Don't even think of trying to make a break for it," he warned. "Though I think you'll find your fate is better with me than with the rest of those poor souls."

All Nan could think was at least she and Fitzgerald were still together. They followed the men into the woods for about half a mile and came to a small campsite. As they approached, a girl in man's clothing came running to Nan, calling her name. In a flash, Nan recognized her.

"Irene! You're alive!" Nan shouted.

"Nan! Thank Mirn!" Irene said as she untied the girl and hugged her.

Soon, Irene, Nan, Fitzgerald, David, and Stephon sat around the fire relating all their adventures during the two weeks. Irene explained they were at their camp when they heard the sound of the prisoner transport. Upon investigating, Irene spotted Nan and Fitzgerald, and David had the idea to try and buy them. Irene sent David and Stephon to "purchase" them, because she was afraid if Nan saw her, her reaction might spoil the plan.

"But what happened to Kay?" Irene asked. "She wasn't among the prisoners, was she?"

"No," Fitzgerald answered. "As far as we know she is still in Tondlepen with King Luciano."

"We must go back and get her," Nan said. "Who knows what Luciano may have in mind? I don't think he'll chop off her head or anything, but I don't think he is the nicest person, if you'll forgive me for saying so."

"I thought you wanted to rescue that other lady we met before—the one you said the guards were going to kill," David said to Irene.

"Perhaps we can try and save her later, but rescuing Kay comes first," Irene said firmly. "We return to Tondlepen in the morning."

◆

Lord William's soldiers were still in a quandary as to their orders to kill Lady Ruth since the reappearance of Demetrius Keats. The decision was taken out of their hands when Sir Richard, who was still tracking Kay, Fitzgerald, Irene and Nan, stumbled upon Lady Ruth's caravan. He greeted Lady Ruth, and would have kept on, but when he learned Demetrius was now among the party, he decided to stay.

Richard moved his friend into his own tent, using Demetrius' still weakened condition as an excuse to spend many hours alone with him. Demetrius was still feverish and slept much of the time, but Richard didn't mind.

When he was ready to get back to hunting Kay and the others, Richard wanted to enlist the assistance of the caravan's soldiers, but they told him of their secret mission from Lord William. Richard agreed that, with Demetrius present, it would be impossible to kill Lady Ruth.

"Not to worry. I have another idea how to dispose of her," he said. "We'll head north tomorrow to the Biaumcol River. I'll inform Lady Ruth the remainder of the trip will be taken by boat."

The caravan arrived at the river's edge within a couple of days and traveled along its banks. Soon, Richard caught sight of a merchant vessel. After much bickering, combined with a few threats, Richard persuaded the owner to part with the ship for a reasonable sum. Richard dispatched a couple of soldiers to guide the ship upstream the next day, and told them exactly when they should jump overboard to save themselves. Then the rest of the soldiers, with Richard at the lead, left Lady Ruth's caravan and continued the search for the escaped prisoners.

◆

Early on her wedding day, two handmaidens entered Kay's chamber and prepared a bath for her. When she was finished, they dressed her in a flowing white gown of silk. They placed white slippers embroidered with seed pearls on her feet and set a long, white veil on her head.

It took several hours for the maidens to prepare Kay, and by the time they were finished, the sun was high overhead. Four soldiers led Kay out of the castle and through the streets of the town, which now appeared deserted. When she asked a soldier about it, he replied that it was forbidden for the townspeople to gaze upon the King's betrothed until after the wedding vows.

The soldiers escorted Kay past the large church and into the woods. They walked until they arrived at a tiny stone chapel. One soldier pushed the door open and gestured Kay to enter, closing the door behind her. There were two murals on the walls and Kay was stunned to see one depicted Lord William, standing on a hill overlooking the Secret Valley. The other picture was of the Bridge of Doom!

Luciano must be a comrade of Lord William's! Damn that Christian!

A man in religious robes stood at the head of the chapel. His hood was pulled so far forward over his head that Kay could not see his face. He beckoned her to come forward, and she did.

"Please, can you help me? I must escape this marriage!" Kay begged the holy man.

Before he could answer, the chapel door flung open and Luciano entered. He was dressed in a golden suit of armor, but in place of a headpiece, he wore his crown. He closed the door behind him. There were to be no witnesses to the wedding. Luciano strode up to Kay and motioned for her to kneel with him in front of the holy man.

"Luciano, please, can we talk first?"

"Kneel!" Luciano commanded.

"But Luciano, I only want a brief word with you."

"I said, kneel!"

"No! I won't marry you, Luciano!"

"You *will* marry me. Now, kneel!" He pulled Kay down next to him. Kay's heart sank. There seemed no way to avoid marrying Luciano. The holy man waved his hand over the two as he recited some words in an ancient language. Then he handed Luciano a goblet from which to drink. Luciano took several large gulps before passing the goblet to Kay. She was about to take a sip from it when the holy man snatched it away from her. At first, she thought she had done something not in keeping with the marriage rites, but she could see by Luciano's startled expression that something was amiss. The King began to protest, but the words seemed to catch in his throat. All that came out was a garbled moan before he fell forward in a clanking heap.

"My lady, make haste, we've no time to lose!" Kay looked up as the man flung back his hood and Christian unmasked himself.

"Christian! I'm so glad to see you! If you can get me out of this mess, I'll forgive you for all the awful things I'd been thinking about you!"

"Yes, yes...now put this on, we must hurry!" Christian pulled out a second religious robe from behind the altar. Kay tore off her wedding dress and slipped on the robe while Christian yanked some loose stones out of the back wall of the chapel. The two scrambled through the hole. On the other side, Kay noticed a holy man bound and gagged, lying in a ditch. She followed Christian into the woods to a pair of horses hitched to a cart full of melons.

"Christian," she asked as they jumped on the cart, "what did you do to the wine? Is Luciano dead?"

"That was not really Luciano. It was his 'mirror image.' But no, he's only drugged. A mirror image cannot be killed."

"The real Luciano, then..."

"He's still in the Black Lord's domain." Christian laid leather on the horses' backs and the cart lurched forward.

"What? Luciano is still a prisoner? Can't we find a way to save him?"

"Right now I think we'd better concentrate on saving ourselves, don't you? Besides, you'd need to exchange him with his mirror image."

"What do you mean?"

"You would have to take him to the Land of the Black Lord," Christian answered grimly. "And I don't think you want to go there."

"No, Christian, go back. We must take Luciano with us."

"Kay, you're insane! We'd never make it."

"Stop the cart."

"Why?"

"I'll go back myself," Kay declared.

"No! Do you think I put my own life in danger so you could go running back there to be captured again?"

"I'm sorry, but I'm going with or without you. I have to save Luciano. I made a vow and I intend to stick to it." She prepared to jump off the wagon.

Christian made an exasperated moan. "All right, I'll help you. But when this is all over, I just may kill you!"

Christian turned the cart around and they raced back to the little stone building. Luciano was still on the floor, unconscious, and the soldiers waiting out front had not yet discovered their disappearance. Kay and Christian managed to lug Luciano through the hole in the wall and drag him to the cart. They removed his suit of armor, rolled his still sleeping form onto the top of the melons and hastily tied him down. As they set off in the cart for the second time, they heard shouts from the soldiers, who had now discovered the empty chapel. The soldiers ran to the town for horses to chase after their king.

Despite their head start, they soon heard hoof beats coming up behind them.

"The load's too heavy, Kay. Push some of those melons off the back."

Kay shoved hard on the melons and they spilled off in rapid succession. The soldiers behind them were traveling too fast to slow down before they reached the fallen, rolling fruit and several horses fell, along with their riders. Two riders remained mounted, but their progress had been slowed.

Christian, taking advantage of their lead, pulled the cart off the path and behind a large grove of aspen trees. He grabbed a rope and handed one end of it to Kay. He ran to the opposite side of the road with the other. He laid the rope flat and covered it with dead leaves and twigs. Kay and Christian hid behind trees holding opposite ends of the rope. Seconds later, they heard hoof-beats. The sound became louder and louder. On Christian's whistle, they both pulled the rope taut, lifting it about three feet high. The horses tumbled forward over the rope, crashing into each other and pitching their riders to the ground. Kay scrambled onto the cart and drove off. Christian ran to catch up and jumped up to the seat alongside her.

After a bit Christian said, "I don't see anyone. I think we've lost them."

After several more hours, Christian felt they had traveled a safe enough distance from Tondlepen, so they stopped the cart to rest the horses. Kay took the opportunity to ask Christian more about Luciano and what he had meant when he said the man she had almost married was a "mirror image."

"Somewhere in the Land of the Black Lord there is a chamber lined with mirrors. Anyone who enters and looks at his own reflection forfeits his soul to the mirror and must reside on the other side of the glass forever. The reflection trades places with the mirror's captive and, although the appearance of the reflection is the same, its actions are dictated by the will of the Black Lord. This is what happened with Luciano."

"I am so lucky to escape that marriage," Kay said.

"You don't know the half of it, Kay. You would have been wife number ten!"

"What?"

"He's had nine wives in the past five years. He soon tires of them and gets rid of them when he finds someone new. After Lord William alerted him you were on the run, he sent me to find you. Because the Mirror Image Luciano has the same body as the real Luciano, he also has his memories and feelings. But they are of a...distorted nature.

While the Luciano you knew felt a fondness for you, his mirror image seemed to feel only lust."

Kay shook her head. "I knew there had to be a reason Luciano changed. When I first met him, he was such a sweet man. I swore to help him escape when he first went under the Bridge of Doom and now I can."

"Well, your timing is good at any rate; the day the bridge appears is almost here. But I wish I could talk you out of this scheme."

"No, my mind is made up. And once he's changed back, perhaps I can get him to tell me what happened to Nan and Fitzgerald."

Christian thought it best to keep on the move through the night, since more soldiers may have been sent after them. They stole some hay from a nearby farm and covered the sleeping king with it. However, they realized Luciano might wake up soon.

Kay began to peer into the forest for a plant she knew would help. When she spotted it, she hopped off the cart and dug up some Dormitabis root. Throughout the night, Kay crushed the root, and gave Luciano a strong whiff of it anytime he began to wake up. He immediately lapsed back into a blissful sleep.

CHAPTER 15

The next morning, Christian and Kay were within half a day's ride of where the Bridge of Doom would appear. Christian was fairly certain the following day the fated bridge would materialize. Since neither of them had slept all night, and because they were so close to their destination, they decided they could afford to pull off to the side of the road and sleep for a short while. Kay put some pieces of Dormitabis root in Luciano's beard to ensure his continuous slumber. Kay and Christian pulled up the hoods on their religious robes, settled in on either side of the king and fell asleep. Doubting anyone would be traveling so early, they had not made an effort to hide themselves completely from view.

"Arise, monks! I would speak with you."

A commanding voice jarred Christian and Kay awake. Christian sat up and pushed the hood back from his face to see who was addressing them. Kay nearly followed suit, but something in the voice tugged at her memory. She kept the hood well over her face and peered cautiously out at the man. Her heart was in her throat when she saw the person attached to the voice was Sir Richard. At first, Kay thought she had been discovered, but she soon realized by Sir Richard's expression that he had no idea who she was. Several soldiers accompanied Richard and, among them, Kay recognized her old friend, Demetrius Keats. He was slumped over on his horse and appeared ill and in pain.

"Gentle monks," Richard spoke, "I am seeking four dangerous outlaws—one man and three women. Have you seen anyone like that?"

"No one fitting that description," Christian replied, groggily. "We were sleeping these last several hours."

"One or more of the women may be disguised as a boy."

"The only people we have seen were simple farm folk," Christian said. He was beginning to suspect Kay, who had said nothing and sat turned away from the soldiers, might be connected with this man.

"Very well. Sorry to interrupt your divine sleep. Tell me, monk, where are you going?"

"Uh...why, we are traveling back to our monastery after a week at the Grand Council of Monastics," Christian lied.

"Is your monastery far from here, and are there any healers among your order?"

"It is only a few hours from here, and there are a great many healers who..." Christian stopped short, realizing he may have taken his lie too far.

"I wonder then," Richard continued, "if you would mind seeing that one of my men receives medical attention? He has an old wound to his shoulder—a puncture from battle that is now infected. He is quite feverish."

"Oh...I would be happy to take him with us, but I am afraid today is our...uh...anniversary of the order's founding. Yes. And on holy days, our healers are not permitted to administer to the sick," Christian said, attempting to sound convincing.

Richard frowned. "Well, if your healers need to be *persuaded*, I can always send half a dozen men to impress upon them the urgency of this need. What a pity if your fellow monks met with...an unfortunate accident."

"Oh, no, it's not necessary! I'm sure the healers can make an exception in this case. We will take the man with us and see he is well cared for."

"I thought you might be reasonable. I shall return to your monastery in a fortnight to take him home. My business should be long since disposed of by then."

Christian made up direction to the imaginary monastery and helped load Demetrius on the back of the cart next to Luciano, who was still hidden under the hay. Sir Richard gave a longing glance at Demetrius before he and his soldiers departed. After they disappeared from view, Kay attempted to talk to her friend, but Demetrius' eyes were glazed and he showed no sign of recognizing her.

Although Demetrius was seriously unwell, they could not afford to waste time in search of a physician, so Kay did what she could to make him comfortable. They pressed on, towards the Bridge of Doom.

"Will Demetrius betray us, Kay?" Christian asked.

"No, I'm sure he will not. He and I are good friends. It is only Richard who hates me. At any rate, he's hardly in any position to be a threat now," Kay replied, looking at the feverish man.

◆

That same morning, Nan, Irene, David, Stephon and Fitzgerald started back on the main road to Tondlepen to rescue Kay. Nan rode behind Fitzgerald, Irene with David, and Stephon rode alone. They traveled as quickly as possible, and did not meet anyone until early afternoon, when they saw two monks racing at them in a horse-drawn cart. The two religious men showed no sign of stopping, passing them at a rapid clip. A moment later, however, it ground to a halt and one of the monks jumped down from the cart and began racing back towards them, yelling at them to stop. The monk's hood fell back, revealing Kay's blond curls.

"Kay!" Nan and Irene shouted together and jumped off their horses to meet her.

"Irene! I thought you drowned! What happened?"

"I fell from the boat, and went to look for you and got lost in the woods, and...oh, I can explain it all later."

Nan broke in, "We were on our way back to find you. How did you get away from Tondlepen?"

"That's a very long story. But I'm so glad we're all back together."

Over a hastily prepared meal, they all exchanged accounts of their various adventures. Kay told the others of her plan to save the real Luciano from the Land of the Black Lord, and they all tried to dissuade her. They pointed out it would be all but impossible for her to transport the still-sleeping Luciano to the Chamber of Mirrors by herself, not to mention find some way to come back, but Kay remained determined.

"How do you know what Christian told you is even true, Kay?" Fitzgerald asked. "After all, he did lead us to Tondlepen only to be captured!"

"I'm sure he was only acting under orders, Fitzy," Nan said. "Still, can we really trust you, Christian?"

"I understand your reluctance to believe in me, Nan," Christian replied. "And, yes, Sir Fitzgerald, I was ordered to bring Kay back. But I honestly had no idea Luciano would imprison you. Perhaps, if I explain a bit more about Luciano's history, you will understand my motives." He paused to gather his thoughts.

"I became an advisor to the King only a few years ago. At first, Luciano had seemed a most suitable ruler. He returned peace to the city, organized an army, secured more land by driving off squatters, repaired the church, and built a school, which was open to all. We lived a pleasant and harmonious life for a year or so. Then, some odd discrepancies crept into Luciano's behavior. He imprisoned his chef because one of his cakes gave him indigestion. Truth be told, the fault was Luciano's own for eating too much, too fast, but he blamed the chef and sent him to prison.

"Things continued to go downhill. Luciano began to make an annual list of people he deemed "unsuitable," and offer a reward of five gold coins to anyone who brought one of them to the prisoners' compound. Once a year, these poor folk were driven from the compound to some unknown destination. Everyone lived in fear of being put on his 'list.'

"This is why they cheer wildly when Luciano burns a wrongdoer at the stake, or laugh while he beheads others. They hate these displays, but they know he demands total adoration and loyalty—or else they might be next."

"How did you learn that Luciano is a mirror image?" Nan asked.

"Soon after you all came to town. I overheard a conversation between two of the King's closest advisors. That is when I decided to leave Tondlepen. But before I left, I wanted to undo some of the wrongs I had committed. It was too late to find you," he said, nodding at Nan and Fitzgerald, "but I knew I had to stop Kay's marriage if I could. I just wish I could talk her out of this idea of taking Luciano back under the Bridge of Doom."

The others nodded their heads and turned to Kay who merely shrugged and said, "I swore to help him and I will—with or without you. Now, come on. We need to get to the bridge."

◆

By evening, the group arrived at the Biaumcol River near where the bridge was predicted to appear the following day. They made camp for the night, caught some fish for dinner and fell, gratefully, to sleep.

Demetrius was still ill, but he looked a little better after Kay put some river clay on the wound to draw out the poisons. She had also applied cold, wet cloths to his forehead. Luciano slumbered on with the help of Dormitabis.

In the middle of the night, Fitzgerald shook Kay. "Kay, Kay, wake up. We need to talk," he whispered.

"Can't it wait until morning, Fitzy?"

"No, I'll never get a chance to speak with you alone before you leave."

"All right, but make it quick." Kay sat up, frowning.

"Well...I want to apologize. I know how it must seem. I mean, back home, we were practically engaged, and lately I...well, I hardly notice you. I guess I am feeling guilty about my affection for Nan."

"We don't have to talk about this, Fitzy," Kay said, avoiding his gaze.

"No, Kay, I must explain. After tomorrow it may be too late and I need you to understand. I know we were considered a match back home, and I did, I mean I *do* care for you. But you see...when I met Nan. I don't know what to tell you. I just…I mean…" He broke off in frustration. "She's just so...gentle and…feminine."

"Oh, I see. You mean I'm *not* feminine!" Kay hissed.

"No, no! I only meant, well, you're different than Nan. Stronger. You're able to take care of yourself and defend yourself. Nan can't. She needs someone."

"I think I understand," Kay said, biting her lip to keep from crying.

"That's good of you, Kay. I'm sorry it couldn't be different."

Afraid to trust her voice, Kay shrugged.

"Well, I'll let you get some sleep. I wish I could talk you out of going under the bridge tomorrow."

Kay's chin jutted forward. "My mind is made up, and as you say, I can take care of myself."

"Yes, well. Again, I'm sorry. Good night." He leaned forward and kissed Kay on the cheek.

"Oh, pardon me." Christian returned from keeping watch. "I wanted to speak with you Kay, but it can wait."

"You're not intruding, Christian," Kay said, pulling away from Fitzgerald.

"No, really, 'tis no matter." Christian headed to his bedroll and lay down. Slumber eluded him because he kept thinking about Kay. The things he planned to say to Kay were now best left unsaid. He was just glad he had discovered there was something between Kay and Fitzgerald before he placed her in an awkward position. Or, more importantly, embarrassed himself.

CHAPTER 16

The next morning, Kay stood on the bank of the river, staring at the bridge looming in the distance. She felt her resolve weakening, but she had come so far.

Besides which, what would they do with Luciano's mirror image if she *didn't* go to the Land of the Black Lord?

Using money David somewhat reluctantly gave her, Kay had bought a small boat and stocked it with a little bread, a flint, a bedroll (which she doubted she'd have occasion to use), a new quiver of arrows and a bow. She also bought a tunic and a pair of leggings to replace the monk's robe.

The men lugged Luciano, who was still sleeping, into the boat. She bid her friends goodbye and pushed off. Kay disappeared under the bridge as the choir of voices sang:

Bridge of Doom, Bridge of Doom,
Looming under angry skies.
Bridge of Doom, Bridge of Doom,
There your soul forever cries.

Kay was sick with apprehension as she and Luciano passed under the Bridge of Doom and into a thick fog. She also felt a little angry and disappointed that her friends had not joined her.

She could see their point, of course. All the same, she had hoped that at least Fitzgerald, whom she had known the longest, would come along. Instead, he stood clutching Nan's hand.

Once again, the conversation of the night before came to Kay's mind, and tears burned her eyes: "She's feminine," and "You are able to take care of yourself" played over and over in her mind.

Kay's thoughts were wrenched back to the present as the boat was abruptly pulled into a whirlpool and began to turn. The spinning became more violent, and Kay threw herself on top of Luciano, still tied to the boat, and held on for dear life.

Still circling, it felt as if the boat was going downward. A roaring sound filled Kay's ears.

Her stomach lurched again and she glanced over at Luciano. He remained blissfully unaware of the ordeal.

"Noooo!"

Kay cried out as her food stores and bedroll flew out of the spinning boat. They continued to go downward. Kay tilted her head up and saw a giant funnel of water.

She shut her eyes again and grabbed Luciano tightly.

Mirn, help me!

All became quiet. The spinning finally ceased. Kay lay with her eyes shut for several minutes, trying to regain control of her stomach. When she cautiously opened her eyes, she was in a large lake filled with debris from what appeared to be broken ships. As she turned her attention towards Luciano, she realized that he was showing signs of waking.

Damn! And all the Dormitabis is gone, too. Well, I couldn't possibly drag Luciano to the Chamber of Mirrors by myself anyway.

She grabbed a piece of floating wood and began to paddle towards the shore. She lugged the boat securely onto the bank and waited. When Luciano opened his eyes, a somewhat bedraggled-looking Kay smiled down on him.

"M'lord, you are well. I feared the worst from that imposter of a priest." Kay helped Luciano to sit up.

"Imposter?" he asked, attempting to clear his mind from the effects of the drug.

"None other than that beast, Christian. He drugged you during the wedding ceremony and abducted me! I was terrified, but managed to convince him I was willing to go along with him. At the first chance, I hit him on the head and came back to you." Kay prayed the King believed her. She was relieved when he grasped both her hands and kissed them passionately.

"My little Principessa, you are dearer to me than life itself, I..." He broke off suddenly as he became aware of his surroundings. A horrified expression came over his face and he pushed Kay back in shock.

"No! It cannot be! How...?" He turned back to Kay who was trying not to show her fear. "Do you know where we are? How in the name of Mirn did we get here?"

Kay had thought of blaming Christian for their presence here, but decided that would not lead her to the Chamber of Mirrors. Instead, she smiled again and said, "Dearest one, of *course* I know where we are, for it is I who brought us here."

"*You*? But why?"

"Because, my beloved—I wish to rule with you forever and only my mirror image can do that."

Luciano's eyes narrowed. "But how did you find out *I* am a mirror image, my sweet?"

Kay realized she had made a grave mistake. She forced herself to smile. "Why, my love, 'twas Christian who told me. Yes...yes, after he abducted me. He sought to turn me against you. Instead, I knew I had to get back to you at once. My true self is too soft, weak and easily swayed to be a proper consort to one such as you. After you take me to the Chamber of Mirrors, I will become strong and, together, we shall be invincible!"

Luciano stared at Kay for a moment. A smile crossed his face as he began to nod his head slowly. "Yes, my little one, I have achieved great power over myself since my transformation in the Chamber. You are right. We could be quite a team."

"Then let us hurry, dearest, and find the Chamber. For we must leave before the day is done." Kay stood up and helped Luciano to his feet.

"There is no need to rush. Mirror images can come and go at the will of the Black Lord. Only poor mortals stay here forever if they do not return in one day." Luciano smiled. "We have plenty of time."

That's what you think! Kay thought. She smiled at the King and took his hand.

◆

After Kay's boat disappeared, Nan burst into tears and the others turned away from the river to walk sadly back to their camp. They sat around chatting about nothing in particular, trying to keep their minds off Kay. Demetrius was alert, although shocked, to hear what Kay had done. Towards mid-day, they heard a noisy commotion near the river. They cautiously crept through the woods to see the remainder of the prisoners from Tondlepen being loaded onto a barge. It was apparent that they were to be sent under the bridge as well.

"I wish we could help them," Irene said. "Who knows what fate awaits them?"

"Any attempt at saving them would be foolhardy at best," David said. "I'm not taking a chance of being sent with them."

The soldiers guided the barge up the river. When it was almost beneath the fateful bridge, the men jumped into the river to swim to shore. As for the prisoners on the boat, they floated under the bridge and vanished from sight.

"Oh, Fitzy," Nan said. "That might have been us, too, if David hadn't bought us back." She gazed at him with sorrowful eyes and he put an arm around her waist, holding her close.

As they stood there, another vessel approached the Bridge. It was a sailing craft, with five women and two soldiers on deck. They were looking at the bridge curiously.

"Oh, great Mirn," Demetrius gasped. "There's my lady Ruth! We must save her!"

"You know her?" David asked. "She's the woman who gave me all her jewels after I rescued her."

"It wasn't exactly a rescue, David," Irene reminded him. "You set her up, you know."

"Details, details, Irene. I just hope she doesn't want her jewelry back." He patted his rucksack securely.

The group debated how to rescue her as the ship neared the bridge. They watched the soldiers jump from the deck and swim to safety. Watching them, it seemed that there would be no way to turn the boat around.

The women appeared a little dismayed at the soldiers' sudden leave-taking, but clearly did not realize their perilous position. However, without anyone manning the tiller, the ship drifted to the right and became caught on a small cluster of rocks jutting above the surface of the water not far from shore. David saw his chance and raced to the riverbank.

"Quick ladies! Abandon ship! The current will soon loose you from the rocks and there will be no chance for you!" he yelled.

"What?" Ruth called. "Don't be absurd, we cannot abandon ship!"

David tried again. "Pardon me, but you must realize that you about to go under the Bridge of Doom!"

Lady Ruth peered at David more closely. "Excuse me, but aren't you the gallant lad who saved me from that horrid beast of a man about a week ago? How lovely to see you again."

"Yes, quite, but please, dear lady, you must leave the ship at once!"

"Nonsense, but thank you for your concern. I am sure my husband's soldiers will return soon to right our vessel."

Demetrius came forward. "My lady, 'tis true! You are in the gravest of dangers! Once you pass under the bridge, you will become the Black Lord's slave!"

"Me? A slave? No one would dare! Are you quite sure, Demetrius?"

"Yes, yes! We will help you to shore."

"Very well, but I still think 'tis all folly."

David, Stephon, Fitzgerald, Nan and Irene swam to the ship and helped Lady Ruth, her handmaiden and servants onto the rocks and into the shallows of the river to swim to shore, where Demetrius waited. After some twenty minutes, everyone was on land except for Nan and Irene, who were still on the rocks, deep in conversation.

"Come ashore," Christian shouted.

"No," Irene called. "We have decided to follow Kay." She and Nan began pushing the vessel off the rocks. "She might need us."

"Don't be stupid," David cried. "There are only a few hours before dark. The bridge will vanish along with any chance for your escape. Think what you're doing!"

"We have to help Kay after all she's done for us," Nan called.

"Oh, for Mirn's sake—there is no changing your minds then?" Fitzgerald called.

"No," the girls answered together.

"Then I'm coming. We stand a better chance if more go." Fitzgerald dove into the water.

"Fitz, wait!" Christian called, following Fitzgerald into the water. Stephon also followed, assisting Demetrius.

That left only David, who stood with Lady Ruth and her attendants. He snorted in exasperation and gave a curt nod to Ruth before he dove in.

The men pushed the boat off of the rocks and clambered aboard as it floated away. It continued under the Bridge of Doom and into a dense fog. The group huddled closely together, trying to ascertain where they were headed, but the fog was too thick. The ship slowed and came to a dead stop. The friends waited for several minutes, but nothing happened.

"Can anyone see anything?" David asked.

"No," Christian replied, "and we haven't moved an inch for some time."

"Maybe someone ought to climb down the rope to the water and get a closer look," Fitzgerald suggested.

"Good idea," David approved. "Off you go then."

"Wait a minute," Irene said. "I think we should stay together."

"It's only a few feet down the hull of the ship," David said.

"We can't see a few *inches* away, David," Nan said. "I think it's silly to take unnecessary chances."

The ship lurched forward. Everyone grabbed on to something as the sailing vessel began moving downward. Then the ship began turning in circles as it dropped lower and lower. Fitzgerald shouted for everyone to move to the ship's center as it began to spin faster and faster as if caught in a huge drain. Everyone hung on to keep from being flung from the ship.

Irene clung desperately to a rope until she thought her arms would break. Above the roar of the water, she could hear Nan screaming. David cursed as he lost grip on his bag and his treasures flew away. The spinning became so fierce that the ship groaned under the strain and began to come apart. Boards flew from the hull and the mast broke off like a matchstick. To everyone's horror, the deck of the ship started to break loose from its frame. When all seemed lost, the spinning slowed and the descent stopped.

After it was still, they sat on what was left of the deck and looked around. They were in an immense cavern. On the shore, buildings were stacked on top of one another like a giant beehive. They appeared to be dwellings, but there were no signs of life. A gloomy light gave the whole place a dull, depressed atmosphere.

Christian and Fitzgerald grabbed loose boards and paddled the raft to shore. Once there, everyone disembarked.

"What now?" Nan asked. "Which direction do you suppose Kay went?"

"My guess is that way," Christian said, gesturing towards the buildings. "Maybe the heart of the city is close by."

They proceeded along the streets cautiously, but met not a soul. They passed under many arches, climbed or descended several staircases, and made so many twists and turns that they feared they'd never find their way out again. The buildings all appeared alike and there was a gray sameness to every path they took. Every now and then, they noticed a mirror attached to a wall. When Nan glanced into one as they passed by, she thought she caught a glimpse of a face with red eyes. When she looked deliberately into the mirror, there was only her own reflection.

"Did anyone else see that?" she asked. "A man's face in the mirror?"

The others shook their heads. Irene looked into the next mirror and saw only her bedraggled appearance. David peered into one and a cold chill spread over him. He said nothing about this to the others. They continued walking.

At last they came across another living creature—an old man, crouched with his back against a building. He was dressed in rags that might have once been a fine suit of clothes. The man's expressionless face was wrinkled and had a dull pallor. The group was about to approach him when they heard the sound of quick footsteps from many feet. They hurriedly ducked back into an alley and peered around the wall as ten marching figures entered the square. They were large, with broad shoulders. Hoods cloaked their faces, but their growls and grunts seemed unhuman. Hairy hands hung from their sleeves, holding spears.

The cloaked beasts caught sight of the old man and stomped towards him. The old man stared up in terror and tried to run away, but one of the beasts hit him with the back of its hairy hand. The smack sent the poor wretch careening into a wall. The old man's head met it with such a force that his skull was crushed and he fell, dead. The creatures howled their approval.

The hooded creatures dragged the limp body away, leaving a trail of blood behind it.

CHAPTER 17

"Luciano," Kay asked as they trudged along, "where is everyone?"

"They are all at work. Everyone here has duties to perform to aid the Black Lord's power. You will understand when you exchange yourself in the Chamber of Mirrors."

The two were moving along the main street of the community. *If there could be a street called "main,"* Kay thought. They all looked alike to her. Luciano, however, led the way with confidence.

"Tell me about the Chamber. Is it covered in mirrors, floor to ceiling?"

"Completely, my love."

"And does one need to look a long time to be exchanged—or—?"

"A mere glance does it."

"Is it painful?"

"You shall not feel a thing, dearest. In a moment you will be transformed. However, once you are, you must leave at once, lest you see into your own eyes again, and be changed back."

Kay nodded silently. A plan was hatching in her mind.

Presently, they arrived at a tall, stone building and Luciano was leading her up the stairs to a huge, oak door. He smiled at her broadly.

"Now, my little Principessa, when you return to me—after you exchange your soul with that of your mirror image—I shall take you to meet his most high—the Black Lord, himself."

Kay put her hand on the door handle and began to pull. Then she stopped and threw herself into Luciano's arms. "I cannot. I am so afraid! Oh, Luciano—come with me!"

Luciano gently disengaged Kay from around him. "My sweet girl, I told you. I cannot go with you. If I were to glance into my own eyes, I would be exchanged and one can only change twice."

Kay was sobbing and clinging to the King's arm. "Please, please, Luciano...come with me! You can keep your eyes shut and after I am changed I will lead you out. Oh, please!"

The King was almost ready to shout at Kay and push her through the door, but something in her voice made him hesitate. Despite his evil ways, a little part of him still loved Kay. He sighed. "Very well, I shall go with you."

"Oh, thank you. Thank you, Luciano!"

"Now, now. Enough crying. Dry your eyes and take my hand. Such foolishness."

"I'm sorry, Luciano. I'll be brave now that you are with me."

Kay took his hand and, after he had shut his eyes, pulled open the door and led him in. She tried to walk naturally, but it wasn't easy because her eyes were shut as well. She groped along a wall until she guessed they were well into the chamber. She positioned herself so that she faced Luciano and so that the tall man would look directly into the mirrors.

"Well?" he asked, "Have you done it?"

"No, m'lord. I... I am still afraid. Are you sure there is no pain?"

"Yes, I am sure. Now, my patience is quite at an end. Look into the mirror, Kay!"

"All right." Kay waited a moment and screamed with all her might. In surprise, Luciano's eyes flew open and he saw straight into his own image in the mirror. There was a long silence. Kay, still with her eyes shut, stood trembling, waiting.

"Luciano?" she whispered. In answer, she felt his arms wrap around her.

"My little angel—you have saved me."

"Oh, Luciano—it really *is* you! Quick, lead me out of here!"

"I'll do better than that." He picked her up and carried her out of the Chamber of Mirrors in his strong arms.

◆

"My stars, what are those dreadful things?" Nan asked in a horrified whisper.

"Whatever they are I don't want to meet them face to face. They killed that poor old man without batting an eye." Irene said.

"They must work for the Black Lord," Christian said. "We need to avoid them, or we'll be taken to the Black Lord himself."

"But if we met the Black Lord," David said, "we might find Kay."

"Are you suggesting we deliberately try to get caught?" Christian asked, aghast. "That's ridiculous—we don't even know that Kay's been captured!"

"Well, how do we know she hasn't?" David retorted.

"For that matter," Stephon said, "how do we know she hasn't already escaped? She obviously can't return the way we arrived." The others murmured their assent.

"Then precisely what do you suggest?" David hissed at Stephon.

"Will you all please stop bickering?" Irene broke in. "I think our best plan is to find the Hall of Mirrors."

"Chamber," Nan corrected gently.

"All right, *Chamber* of Mirrors! That's where Kay had to take Luciano, isn't it? And that's where they might yet be."

"Makes sense," Christian said. "All in favor say aye."

Nan, Fitzgerald, Stephon, and Irene all chorused "aye." A moment after, David muttered "aye" as well.

"Good, it's unanimous," Christian said.

"Wait! Demetrius didn't vote," Nan said. They all looked at the soldier, who was sitting on the ground, looking pale.

"I... I wish to find Kay, of course, for she is one of my truest friends. But, I am feeling rather weak again, and fear I shall only be a hindrance to you. You had best leave me behind."

"Never!" Nan, Fitzgerald, and Irene all cried. The others looked thoughtful.

"Well, 'tis true—he might be a problem," Christian said, gently.

"Christian, how could you?" Irene huffed. "You mean you would leave Demetrius to the mercy of those beasts?"

"I didn't say that, Irene. I propose we find a safe hiding place for Demetrius and return for him if...uh, *after* we locate Kay and Luciano."

"But how will we find Demetrius again?" Stephon asked. "All these streets and staircases look the same to me."

"We can mark spots along the way," David offered, pulling out a small knife. "Something we probably should have been doing all along. Who knows how many times already we may have backtracked."

"So what was stopping you?" Christian asked.

"Well, for your information, I..."

"Will you two stop?" Irene cried. "Now, let's find a safe place and go."

"I noticed an alleyway back there filled with all sorts of garbage and junk he could hide among," Stephon said.

"Good idea, Stephon, thank you," Fitzgerald said. He helped Demetrius to his feet and the seven of them headed down the road.

"Who will stay with Demetrius?" Nan asked. "I don't think he should be left alone."

"I agree, Nan. I will," Irene answered.

"A mere lass and a weakened lad—a fine combination should you be found," David said. "Better someone stay who could fight if necessary."

Irene was about to speak when Christian interrupted. "Much as I hate to admit it, Irene, David's probably right." He smiled. "Not that I wouldn't pity anyone who tried to tangle with you. No, I will remain with Demetrius."

"Heaven forbid, Christian. You are the only sensible man among us!" said Irene with a meaningful glance at David.

"Then *I* shall stay with Demetrius," Fitzgerald volunteered. "And let us put an end to this bickering."

"I'm staying, too," Nan said firmly as she took Fitzgerald's hand.

"Oh, Nan, I don't..." Irene broke off. "Well, I don't think it would do any harm," she finished with a sigh of exasperation.

By this time the group had arrived at the alleyway. The men carefully checked it out.

"Perfect," Christian said. "A dead end with lots of things to hide behind."

They built a makeshift shelter for Demetrius and tried to make him as comfortable as possible. Then they built a larger barrier of trash to hide the three and left.

"Do you think anyone saw us?" Irene asked.

"I doubt it. This place is like a tomb," David said.

Neither of them noticed a figure in the distance, which was moving slowly towards the alley.

◆

Safely outside the Chamber of Mirrors, Luciano kissed Kay on her forehead. "It's all right now, Kay, you may open your eyes."

Kay opened her eyes to see the King smiling down on her. "I am so glad," she murmured, "So very glad, Luciano."

"Not half so glad as I, my little one. For too long I was trapped behind those mirrors, helpless as my mirror image destroyed people."

"You were able to see everything he did?"

"In my mind's eye, yes. And when I saw him abduct you—take you to the altar by force—I shuddered to think of what lay ahead. I wished to die, I was so miserable." The King clutched Kay tighter to him.

"Uh...hadn't you better put me down now?" Kay asked softly.

"Oh—of course! Although I find this rather pleasant, too!" He set her down. "Now, we had best try to find a way out of here. Time grows short."

"Oh, dear. Don't you *know* the way out? Your mirror image did."

"Yes, but the only way a mirror image can get out is through the Black Lord. I don't think we wish to go that route."

"Certainly not! So, is there any other exit?"

"I have heard stories there is one other way...come!" Luciano took Kay's hand and began to walk briskly towards the center of the underground community.

◆

"This is hopeless," David grumbled. "We could easily spend a year searching for Kay, much less a day."

"Well, as long as we are here, we might as well keep on looking for her. I know of no way to get out, anyway," Christian said.

"Oh, fine!" David exploded. "Even if we do find her and the fat king, we may not be able to get out in time. Then we'll all be trapped here—that's just perfect!"

"How much time do you figure we have left, Christian?" Stephon asked, eager to head off another squabble.

"Hmm. Hard to tell. It isn't quite as light as day, nor as dark as dusk. I cannot even tell what the source of light is. 'Tis certain we are underground...so from where does this eerie light emit?"

No one had an answer, so they continued along the roads in silence. At every intersection, David would carve a small nick in the wall of one of the buildings. Presently, he spoke. "We should give up this folly. If Kay isn't already dead, she's likely exchanged herself in the mirrors and she and fatso are probably very happy together."

"For shame, David," Irene cried. "How can you speak so? Why, you hardly even know Kay. She saved my life—and Nan's! You just met her!"

"True, but she seems capable enough." David shrugged. "What good will it do if all of us get trapped here?"

"Fine. Leave us if you wish, but I will continue to hunt for her and Luciano. If you spent more time looking and less time complaining, we might be closer to our goal!" Irene retorted fiercely.

The others nodded in agreement. David only shrugged his shoulders. "I'll follow you—I have little choice. But 'tis all futile I'm sure."

CHAPTER 18

After the others left them hidden in the alley, Nan and Fitzgerald crouched near Demetrius, speaking in low voices.

"Do you think they'll be long?" Nan asked.

"Not too long, I hope. We don't have much time left to get out of here." He squeezed Nan's hand reassuringly.

"Well, I'm glad we're together, at least."

"Yes, I... I, uh..." He stopped and turned his gaze from Nan to the street. "Shh! I think I heard something."

The two listened to footsteps slowly approaching the alleyway. Fitzgerald pulled Nan down on the ground. They lay still as the steps came nearer.

"Nan. Where are you?" a voice called. "Nan, dear one. I saw you come this way. 'Tis I, your father."

Nan popped her head up.

"Pa—," she began. Fitzgerald clamped his hand over her mouth and pulled her back down.

"Please, daughter, show yourself. I have missed you so," the voice came again. "If you doubt my identity, who else but your father would know of the small scar above your left temple where you were dropped as a baby?"

"It's him, Fitzy. Let me go to him. Let me go!" Nan pulled away from the knight and clambered out of the alleyway to find her father smiling at her.

"Papa!" Nan cried, embracing the man.

"My daughter," the cobbler said, stroking her hair.

"I thought you died when the Valley was attacked."

"No, no. Only captured. Your mother and all your brothers are here, too."

"Oh, Papa, I'm so glad. I was certain you were all killed."

"And I thank the Black...uh, thank Mirn, you are well."

"But, how were you brought here? I thought the Bridge of Doom only appears once a year. You were not with the group of prisoners we saw."

"There is a backdoor, so to speak. We came through a large, magical mirror that the conquering army brings along. But what does it matter? We are all together again."

"Papa, we came here to rescue a friend of ours, and now you and our family must come back with us."

"Why would we leave, daughter? We are all quite happy here."

"Happy? Aren't you prisoners here?"

He laughed. "Quite the opposite. We are citizens in this kingdom. We are all well provided for."

"Truly?"

"Truly. We are safe and content here. All the Black Lord asks in return for our care is that we stay and work for him. We have no desire to leave."

"I...I had imagined it was different. The stories I was told..."

"Exactly. Only stories. Stay here with us. All your friends will be very welcome, too."

"I will be so happy to be with you all again. As for my friends, they can only speak for themselves. Oh! I nearly forgot. Papa, Irene is here. She's trying to find Kay, a new friend. Kay is looking for the Chamber of Mirrors. Do you know where that is?"

"Of course, daughter. Would you like me to take you there?"

"Yes, Papa. And on the way I'll tell you of my other new friends and all I've done in the past weeks. Oh!" she gasped. "Fitzy and Demetrius. I'd quite forgotten!"

Nan took her father into the alley and made brief introductions of Fitzgerald and Demetrius. Fitzgerald was reluctant to let Nan go with her father, but he had no recourse because Demetrius was still ill.

"I'll come back as soon as we find Kay and Luciano...then we'll find the others," Nan promised. She and her father left.

◆

"Luciano, we must hurry. I feel like we've been walking forever and everything looks the same! Where is the way out?"

"I'm not exactly sure, but there may be an exit through the sewer system. There is an abandoned temple not far from here with catacombs for burials. While I was still here, before the Black Lord sent me above to do his bidding, I overheard two servants say the lowest level of catacombs has an entrance to the sewer in case repairs are required. It is our best hope. Come."

Kay and Luciano hurried through the streets, keeping careful watch for guards. When they spotted two people in the distance, traveling towards them, they ducked into a side street. As the two walked by, Kay peeked out and gasped.

"Luciano—it's Nan," she whispered. "I don't know who she's with, but what on earth is she doing here?"

They followed at a safe distance, noting that Nan seemed to be on friendly terms with the stranger. Nan and the man stood before the Chamber of Mirrors, talking. Carefully, Kay and Luciano crept behind a wall to hear their conversation.

"The chamber is just behind that door," the old man was saying. "Is it safe to go in?"

"Oh, yes. You can go in and gaze in the mirrors for as long as ten seconds. But no longer or your mirror image will take your soul.

"Come with me to find Kay."

"I grow weary, daughter. I'll wait for you here."

"Very well, I'll be back in a moment." Nan walked to the door. Luciano shot up from behind the wall.

"Ho, there, lass! Go no farther!"

Nan, thinking Luciano was the evil mirror image, turned to her father in confusion.

"Go in, daughter, I can take care of him," the cobbler said, grimly.

Nan began to pull on the large oaken door to enter.

"Nan, no—wait!" Kay raced out from hiding. "Whoever that man is, he is deceiving you. Glance into a mirror even for a second and your soul is lost!"

"This man is my father!" Nan huffed.

"He may look like your father, but I'm sure I can unmask his true identity," Luciano said. "Come forth, Merle of Lots!"

Nan and Kay stood stunned as, before their eyes, the cobbler changed from a small, gentle-looking man into a towering wizard dressed in blue robes.

"A wizard can only hold his altered form until someone recognizes him and calls his name," Luciano explained, as Nan ran over to him and Kay. "I met him when I was here before. I thought it was you, Merle."

The wizard sneered. "So? You'll not escape. You were fools to come down here. We know Irene and the others are here, as well."

"I don't understand. Is my father alive, or is he dead? Please, Sir Wizard, at least tell me that much," Nan begged.

"Your father is alive—if can call it living—but you'll never see him again!" Laughing, Merle drew his cape in front of himself and became smaller and smaller. The cape took the shape of wings and then, Merle transformed himself into a moth. He began to fly away, but Nan ran forward, leaped in the air, and caught him in her cupped hands. Luciano pulled open the door to the Chamber of Mirrors and Nan, with her eyes firmly shut, deposited the stunned moth on the floor of the chamber. As soon as Nan dashed out, Luciano and Kay slammed the door shut.

The three stood with their backs against the door. Soon, banging noises came from inside as Merle attempted to escape. The thumping became louder and it became harder to keep the door shut. Soon, they could no longer hold the door. They fell flat as the door burst open behind them. A luminous blue cloud came out of the chamber, flew high and exploded, showering them with ash.

"We'd better run for it. That explosion is sure to attract someone's attention," Luciano said.

"Yes, but we have to find the others first," Nan said.

"The others?" Kay asked.

"Yes. Irene and Fitzy and everyone came to help you. I know where Fitzy and Demetrius are—let's go there first."

◆

Irene, David, Stephon and Christian were still wandering the maze of streets when an explosion filled the entire cavern with a shimmering blue light.

"What was that?" Stephon asked.

"Perhaps it has something to do with Kay," Irene said.

"Right. Let's go," Christian said.

"Wait a minute. Now, just hold on!" David protested. "I'm not going anywhere. If we don't get out of here soon—"

"It may be our last chance to find Kay," Christian interrupted.

"It may also be our last chance to get out of here alive," David shot back.

"And how do you propose we do that?" Irene asked. "We can hardly go back up the funnel of water we came down. Don't be an idiot, David, come on!"

Irene, Christian, and Stephon hurried towards the explosion. David stood watching them until they disappeared around a corner. Then, muttering an angry oath, he ran to catch up.

"If we are captured and killed," David grumbled, "just remember it wasn't my fault!"

CHAPTER 19

In the alley, Fitzgerald had also seen the blue light but remained hidden with Demetrius. After waiting so long, he was getting nervous for his friends. He was about to leave when he heard Nan's voice calling. He cautiously raised his head to see Nan, Kay, and Luciano.

"Kay! She found you!" Fitzgerald exclaimed.

"Well, it was kind of the other way around, actually, but it doesn't matter now," Kay grinned.

"And Luciano? Is he..." Fitzgerald asked.

"He's fine; he's his true self now."

"We'd better go," Luciano said. "Can this man be moved?"

"I am well rested," Demetrius said. "I can travel if it is not too far."

"The temple is fairly close. Let's go there first."

Luciano, Kay, Nan, Fitzgerald and Demetrius hurried through the streets. Before long, they came to a large, crumbling black structure. The front entrance had been sealed off, so the group went around to the back where they found a locked door. Luciano and Fitzgerald easily broke the lock and everyone entered, closing the door behind them. Little light came through the windows, so Fitzgerald groped around for some fallen wood and rags. From these, he hastily made two torches, which Kay lit with her flint. They looked around them. The building was falling apart from disuse and the wood interior was rotting away.

The walls were decorated with odd symbols and images of people being tortured in horrific ways. A long, narrow altar stood up front, covered in cloth. Its surface was littered with bones and what appeared to be dried blood.

"This way," said Luciano, leading them to the stairs near the altar. They walked down seven flights. The lowest floor had two long hallways, which formed a cross. They entered the catacombs at the far end of one hall and continued through a mass of cobwebs and dust until they reached the other end. A quick examination revealed no exit, only tombs filled with crumbling skeletons. They went back along the passage to the crux of the cross and moved down the corridor on the left. At the end of this passage was an ornate tomb with a marble statue.

Luciano was about to turn back to try the other hall, when he caught the sound of running water. He peered behind the tomb and discovered an iron gate, about three feet square.

"Here it is. The way out!" he exclaimed. The others crowded around. Above the door was a dirty bronze plaque with an inscription. Kay wiped off the dust and read aloud:

Herein lies the land of "Gar."
It's all uphill, but not too far.
Behind this door exists a sea,
That you must first unlock with key.
The key was lost in a dungeon dark,
Which never heard the song of lark.
One key only fits this lock,
We will not answer if you knock.
But if the key you hold does fit,
Prepare to meet some souls with wit.
We make merry, drink and sing,
And dance thrice daily with our King.
And if, by chance, you see us fly,
Please do not ask the reason why.
'Tis our secret, ours to know,
And if you ask us, back you'll go.

"Good heavens," Kay said. "Do you know what this poem means, Luciano?"

"No. I have never heard of this Gar."

"Well, this could be our escape, but how are we going to get the door open?" Fitzgerald asked.

"Kay and I will go back to find the others. While we're gone, try to figure some way to open the door," Luciano said. "We'll be back soon." He and Kay took one of the torches and hurried upstairs.

◆

"The light and noise came from about here," Christian said as the group approached the Chamber of Mirrors.

"Well, no one here," David said briskly. "Let's go."

"Not so hasty, David," Christian said. "We should look around a bit first."

The door to the Chamber stood open. The group slowly approached.

"Do you suppose this is the Chamber of Mirrors?" Irene asked. "It seems odd the door is open."

"I can't see well enough to tell," Christian said. "It's too dark in there."

"Kay may be in there," Irene said. "Let me go inside and explore."

"No, Irene. It's not safe," Christian said.

"Well, one of us should go," David said. "If it weren't for my darned near-sightedness..."

"I'll go," Christian volunteered.

"No argument from me," David commented.

"I believe the thing to do is to keep my eyes shut at all times. Once I'm well inside, I'll call for Kay and if I don't get a response, I'll come back out."

Christian withdrew his sword from its sheath and walked to the door. When he was about five feet away, he shut his eyes and groped forward into the chamber. Once he thought he was deep enough inside, he called Kay's name several times. Certain she was not there, he turned around to exit. As he did, he tripped and lost his balance. Startled, his eyes flew open for a split second. Then he slowly felt his way back to the door and came out.

"She's not there. We'd best move on."

The group walked down the street with David and Irene in front and Stephon and Christian in back. They walked a short distance when Christian suddenly tripped Stephon, kicked him flat, and held the point of his sword to his neck. He smiled sadistically, and seemed ready to slash his throat. David grabbed his own weapon and jumped in to save his friend.

"En Gardé!" he shouted.

The fight was on, but David soon found himself at a disadvantage. Besides being larger than David, Christian fought like a madman, disregarding the rules of good swordsmanship. He tried to back David into the Chamber of Mirrors.

"David, look out!" Irene tried to intervene, but Christian lashed out with his sword, cutting her upper arm.

Christian had nearly succeeded in forcing David into the Chamber when an arrow whizzed through the air, striking Christian in the back. Because he was a mirror image, the blow did not kill him. Instead, he turned around and glared at Kay standing with her bow in hand. He drew his dagger and was poised to throw it, when David, his wits recovered, grabbed Christian's shirt and yanked him violently off balance, sending him reeling back through the Chamber door. Christian rose immediately to come back out, but as he did, he caught a glimpse of himself in a mirror. Now a mortal again, and with the arrow still in his back, he collapsed to the ground.

"Oh, no. I fear that's not his mirror image," Luciano exclaimed.

"Christian!" Kay screamed, running to his side. "What have I done?"

"I opened my eyes," Christian gasped. "I didn't mean to."

"It's not your fault," Kay comforted.

"Is David...?"

"He's fine—we must get you help...I'm sorry I had to shoot you, Christian, I...I didn't know how to stop you. Please forgive me."

"No, Kay," Christian said. "Forgive me for tricking you and your friends into going to Tondlepen."

Irene, herself bleeding, inspected Christian's wound. She saw it was beyond any help. Christian shuddered and grasped Kay's hand.

"Kay, I want you to know something. The day I kissed you. That had nothing to do with my orders. I wanted to kiss you. I was falling in love with you, but I couldn't tell you because of Luciano."

"Yes, yes. I understand," Kay choked, tears spilling down her face.

Christian looked at Luciano and said, "Take care of her as I would have." He smiled at Kay and closed his eyes as if he were going to sleep. Irene felt for a pulse and turned to Kay, shaking her head. Kay dropped her head onto Christian's chest, weeping. The group stood awkwardly around them for a moment. Then Irene gently touched Kay's shoulder.

"Kay, we must go. It isn't safe here," she said softly.

"No, I can't leave him here!"

Luciano pulled Kay from Christian and held her close. "Come, my sweet. There is nothing to be done." He turned to the others. "Fitzgerald, Nan, and Demetrius are down in the catacombs of an old temple. Our escape route is there."

Everyone hurried towards the temple. Stephon took his handkerchief and wrapped Irene's bleeding arm. Everyone was so distressed they didn't notice they were being followed by a band of cloaked beasts. As the five made their way around to the back of the temple, David looked back and spotted them.

"The beasts!" he whispered. "Hurry!"

Everyone rushed through the temple's back door and used some fallen wood to jam the door shut. Afraid to light the torch, they tried to follow Luciano in the dark. They were halfway through the sanctuary when Irene, unable to see well and dizzy from her blood loss, ran into a bench and fell over. Alerted by the racket of the falling bench, the guards outside doubled their efforts to enter. Inside, the others were unclear of what had happened. David, who was at the rear, thought they were being attacked and rushed blindly forward, knocking everyone over. He didn't stop until he came into contact with the large altar. His hands touched some of the bones and he grabbed one for a weapon. After realizing, upon closer inspection, that it was a human bone, he screamed, threw it aside and ran directly into Luciano, knocking him down again. The sound of heavy footsteps sounded from above.

"They have found a way in through the second story," Luciano called. "Come on! Everyone—follow my voice!"

Luciano kept shouting "This way!" and "Follow me!" as he headed to the stairs. Tripping and stumbling, everyone followed, except Irene, who was disoriented.

"Help me!" she called. "Please, which way do I go?"

No one heard her over the noise of the beasts and Luciano's voice, except David, again at the rear of the group. He hesitated, afraid of being captured, but he knew if he didn't help Irene, she most certainly would be caught.

"Irene—here!" David raced back and groped in the darkness to offer his hand. She found it and the two stumbled forward.

Kay and Stephon caught up with Luciano at the stairwell, and the three began to race downstairs. The beasts were screaming in jubilation at having found a way down from the floor above. Heavy boot steps clamored down the wooden steps.

"Wait!" Kay cried, stopping. "Where are David and Irene?"

"We can't wait! Come on!" Luciano shouted, pulling her along.

The beasts were closing in on them rapidly. The three tore down the stairs with the beasts almost at their heels. Nan and Fitzgerald, who were still trying to pry the door open, turned at the approaching sound of the chase.

"Fitzy, is the door open?" Kay screamed as she ran towards him.

"No, it's stuck fast. What's that noise?"

"The guards. They'll be here in a moment!"

Luciano and Fitzgerald pounded on the door, in a vain attempt to force it open. Demetrius, who had been lying down, suddenly sat up and pulled a small round object out of the pouch he wore around his neck.

As the beasts rounded the corner of the corridor, the men pulled out their swords. Kay readied an arrow in her bow. They were about to rush into battle when a loud clap of thunder, accompanied by a bolt of lightning rang through the hall, halfway between the two sides. Everyone jumped back in surprise and stood silent. After several moments of uncertainty, the beasts cautiously moved forward. They had not gone three feet when another lightning bolt struck, this time a good deal closer to the beasts, driving them back again. After a longer pause the beasts advanced once more, only to be halted again by the mysterious underground lightning.

Demetrius, who had been in a trance, suddenly opened his eyes and spoke softly to Fitzgerald, "We must escape immediately. My concentration is gone. I can't do it again."

"Do what?" Fitzgerald asked, keeping his eyes on the creatures.

"The lightning. I used this to conjure it," Demetrius showed him the glowing orb in his hands. "But I've lost the magic."

"So, when they advance again, there will be nothing to stop them?"

"Exactly. I am sorry."

Fitzgerald looked sadly at the door—their only hope for escape. His eyes glanced over the poem and something jarred his memory.

A *key*? Hadn't he found one in the dungeon under Lord William's castle? Where had he put it? Fitzgerald searched his pockets and found the ornate key. Kneeling beside the door and saying a quick prayer, he tried the key and no sooner had he inserted it, then the locked clicked and the door swung open.

"It's open! Come on!"

No one asked questions, but dove one after the other through the small opening. Once the beasts realized what was happening, they began to advance, growling. The last one through the door was Luciano who, due to his large size, had to be pulled through by Fitzgerald and Stephon. In the nick of time, Fitzgerald slammed the door shut, locked it, and retrieved the key. The beasts reached the small door and stood on the other side, roaring their disapproval.

CHAPTER 20

Everyone moved farther away from the escape door and the still-snarling beasts. They stood on a wooden dock next to a sluggish river in a cave. The cave's ceiling was about ten feet high and an eerie light seemed to come from the river.

"Where are we?" Stephon asked.

"We are by the underground river, used for the sewage disposal," Luciano answered. "You will notice the aroma."

"Yes—horrible!" Kay said, making a face.

Nan suddenly gasped and asked, "Where is Irene?"

"We had to leave her and David behind," Kay answered.

"Oh, no, she's probably dead! Those horrible beasty things killed her. It's all my fault!"

"No, no, Nan," Kay comforted, "I'm sure she's alive. David and Irene may have been captured, but we'll go back and rescue them."

"Look over here," Fitzgerald said, pointing to a large dory by the dock. He read aloud the inscription:

All who travel in this boat,
To the land of "Gar" will float.

Everyone debated what to do next. They wanted to go back and find David and Irene, but without more weapons they would be little threat to the beasts. So without any other options, they boarded the dory.

When Fitzgerald untied the rope, the boat drifted into the middle of the river, seemingly under its own power. The river curved and curved again, and the boat gained momentum. The water became deep green-blue. Occasionally, large orange or yellow fish could be seen swimming up from the depths. They would often travel with the boat for a time before plunging again into deeper water.

They realized the fish were the source of light. The more fish that surrounded their boat, the brighter the cavern became. After a little time had passed, the river started to slant uphill, although the water continued to flow in the same direction. Gradually, the incline became steeper. As they continued, the fish deserted them and, soon, the boat moved in complete darkness. After a while there was a small point of light far above them.

Drawing closer, the light became larger and brighter until they saw it was the sun. The river did lead up to the surface! The exhausted group of travelers was finally out of the land of the Black Lord.

They leveled off and merged with a larger river that took them west. The landscape was picturesque with lush green grass covering gently sloping hills. Butterflies and graceful birds flitted among blooming trees and flowers. They saw a castle in the distance. It sparkled in the sunlight with a pink glow. It was clearly not meant to be a fortress, as it had no moat, and the walls surrounding it were low with several open gates.

The dory headed straight for the riverbank by the castle. It came to a stop, and everyone stared at each other.

"Well," Fitzgerald said, "I guess this is as good a place as any to get out."

Everyone disembarked and moved towards the nearest gate of the castle. Peering inside, they admired a beautiful courtyard, with many flowers and trees. A long, red carpet stretched from the garden to ornate silver doors in the palace.

The group cautiously entered the courtyard when a trumpet sounded, as if heralding their arrival. Startled, they turned to run back through the gate, but it had vanished, leaving only a wall. Panicked, everyone scattered; Nan and Fitzy climbed up into an apple tree, while Luciano and Kay took refuge under the cascading branches of a willow, and Stephon and Demetrius crouched behind a hedge.

The silver doors swung open and a grand procession began. First an orchestra came out. Flutes, piccolos, bells, and harps all floated through the air, playing music all by themselves. Next, in flew twenty slender nymph-like creatures with wings, and long, pale blond hair. They carried poles with colorful cloth banners, which they swept in lovely patterns.

Following them came more delicate beings with hair the color of the sky. They sang with the orchestra's music in delightful, lilting voices and carried baskets of flower petals, which they spread on the red carpet. Finally, a silver chariot pulled by two white deer appeared. On the chariot rode a handsome, burly man with a black beard and hair, and twinkling dark-brown eyes. Clad in a violet tunic and tights with a matching cape, he wore a circlet of silver on his head. As his chariot entered the courtyard, the trumpets sounded again and the winged beings applauded.

The procession stopped and, with it, so did the music. The man got off the chariot and walked to a large harp by a fountain. He sat down and began to play while the lovely creatures danced.

"Whatever are those things?" Nan whispered to Fitzgerald, who shook his head.

Even more winged beings appeared and joined the dance. It seemed quite complicated, but the creatures made it appear easy. Their feet barely touched the ground.

Nan became engrossed with the performance, as it was, after all, her art. But the tree leaves were blocking her view and she couldn't catch the steps. She crept farther out onto the branch, but the thin branch could not support her and broke, sending Nan crashing down onto rose bushes. Fitzgerald scrambled down and rushed over to her.

The celebration continued as if nothing had happened. Only the man at the harp seemed to have noticed. Kay and the others also rushed to aid Nan, but when they got there, they found Fitzgerald cradling her in his arms.

"She's dead!" he cried, holding Nan, limp and scratched from the thorns of the rose bushes.

"The fall must have broken her neck," Kay said, horrified.

The man interrupted his harp playing and made a gesture to three of the dancing creatures. The delicate beings flew to Nan and stood around her in a circle, beating their wings rapidly, while waving their arms in a strange fashion. They each took some silver dust out of pouches they wore at their waist and blew it off their palms onto Nan's prone form, before flying back to join the others.

Slowly, the scratches became lighter and shorter on Nan's skin until they disappeared completely. Nan's eyes fluttered, and she awoke with a smile on her face. She sat up and seemed quite unaware she had ever been hurt.

The dance ended and the three creatures came back to Nan. After observing her condition, they spoke in unison:

The lass appears to be a'right
Although she gave us quite a fright.
She'll be dizzy for a while,
And have a tendency to smile.
But her humor will only last
Until this spell is in the past.
She'll be normal very soon,
By tomorrow, right at noon.

"Thank you for saving her," Fitzgerald stammered. The lovely beings nodded and flew away.

The man at the harp came over to the group of friends and bowed. "Good day," he said in a booming baritone. "My name is Gar and I am king of this castle, ruler over the fairies you see here, as well as the inhabitants of all the surrounding lands, better known as Garsland. I bid you welcome!"

Nan giggled, but Kay came forward and said, "We are pleased to meet you, your Majesty. Please excuse us for trespassing, but we..."

"No need! No need!" he interrupted. "You're entirely welcome here—entirely welcome! Do you have any idea how long it's been since I heard someone speak without rhyming? My fairies are a great little bunch, but the damned pansies can't talk normally! I even held a contest a couple of years ago to see if any of the little bastards could...ah, but why am I rattling on like this? Come, you must dine with me!"

Gar ushered everyone into the castle dining room where they gratefully ate their fill. After the meal, fairies took them to luxurious rooms where they slept. Or, at least, the men slept. Kay, in the same room with Nan, was constantly awakened by Nan giggling in her sleep. The fairies' spell had put her in a very jovial mood.

◆

Seeing most of the beasts heading after Kay and the rest, David yanked Irene out the back of the temple, but three guards pursued them. Irene and David raced along the cobblestone streets, but the creatures were gaining on them. David pulled Irene down one side alley and bolted across the road to another street where they almost collided with a man holding a whip, driving thirty or more slaves home after their day's labors. As they screamed to a stop, the man quickly grabbed Irene's wrist and lashed his whip at David, catching him around the ankle.

Recognizing the man's face, Irene exclaimed: "Oh, no! Jean de la Grande Pomme!"

"Princess Irene, what a surprise!" the man smirked. He was short and barrel-chested, with a doughy face and thin, drab hair. He had an almost child-like appearance, despite his age.

The beasts caught up with them, and stood waiting for orders. Jean, still with a firm grasp on Irene's wrist, continued, "It seems this time the advantage is mine, Irene. You know I swore to get even with you for breaking off the arrangement our parents made for us."

"Jean, please, you're hurting me!"

"Well, you did the same to me once."

"Jean, how could you come here? Adopt the Black Lord's ways? It's not like you."

"Well, I've changed Irene, and so have you, apparently." He looked at her with thinly disguised disgust. "When did you decide men's clothing was more becoming to you than dresses? No matter. You are only an insignificant slave now."

"Please, Jean," Irene begged, "won't you help us? For old time's sake?"

"Help you? Why should I? You never allowed me to talk reasonably to you. You grew tired of me and ended our engagement."

"No, no—I was just not able to love you."

"Shut up!" he said, shoving Irene to the ground. He turned to the guards. "Take these two to my mansion and lock them in the cellar. I'll deal with them when my work is finished."

The beasts dragged Irene and David away, and the man turned back to his slaves.

◆

The guards deposited Irene and David in a cellar and put leg irons on them. They were too far apart to touch and, without any torch or candlelight, could not see.

David coughed a bit and cleared his throat. "This place is so damp—it cannot be good for my singing voice. I wish I had my scarf..."

"I hardly think your voice is our major concern at this moment, David!"

"Oh, of course, of course. I just...well, anyway..." There was a long pause before David spoke again. "How exactly are you acquainted with the man who threw us down here?"

Irene sighed. "I never thought I would see him again," she said. "We were once engaged to be married. Our parents made the match. I remember that day so clearly; I was eight years old. I had just come back into the castle with my arms full of tulips I had gathered when I overheard my father talking with a visitor. I realized they were speaking of me, so I crept up to the doorway to listen."

CHAPTER 21

"Oh, I do not think Irene will be ready to marry until she is at least seventeen," Irene heard her father, King Jeo, say. "Besides, I think it is wise for our children to know something of the world before they have to settle down. Don't you agree?"

"Yes, in theory," the guest, Monsieur Louis replied, "But I do not wish to give them a chance for their eyes to wander too much before they are married. That way, there will be no chance for them to fall in love with someone else, and therefore we avoid any potential heartbreaks."

"I see your point, Monsieur Louis. But, after all, what if Irene *were* to fall in love with a local boy? She knows her duty is to marry whomever her mother and I choose for her, in this case, your son, Jean Louis. Her heart may be 'broken', as you say, but only temporarily. After she is married to your son she will forget any others who came before him."

"But the thing that concerns me, your Majesty," persisted Monsieur Louis, "is that these two children will not even see each other until a few weeks prior to the actual ceremony. It would be different if they could visit one another sometimes as they grow up, but the distance is too great for that."

Irene saw her nurse was coming down the stairs to find her, so she scurried away from the doorway.

Later, Irene lay on her bed, unable to sleep. Hearing for the first time that there was a boy in La Grande Pomme whom her parents had already arranged for her to marry unsettled her greatly.

That evening, there was another discussion concerning the match, this time between her mother and father.

"Honestly, Jeo, I can't understand why you want to marry off our daughter to the son of a mere civil servant," Irene's mother said.

"You must realize time grows short for me. My physicians can promise me no longer than two or three seasons. What would happen if I were to die before the arrangements were made?"

"We'd find a match."

"But to whom? There seems to be a plethora of childless kings in this area. No, I want to be sure our daughter will be provided for. The Louis family may not be of royal blood, but there is no denying they have power and money. Irene should at least be very comfortable. Why, the bride price we settled on alone is quite a tidy sum!"

"But, what if Irene doesn't like the boy? There is no telling what kind of disposition such a lowborn sort would have. Now, if you ask me..."

"Now, now, my dear. Don't distress yourself," Jeo interrupted. "The father seems well enough. Give it a chance."

◆

Irene had only a short time more of family happiness before both her parents died. Her father passed away three days before Irene's ninth birthday and her mother died but a few months later. Irene's brother became King Jeo II at seventeen. Overwhelmed by his many responsibilities, King Jeo II felt ill equipped to look after his young sister. He also didn't want Irene to be raised by servants. A family life was what she needed, he reasoned.

Irene's brother sent his sister to live with a shoemaker in the Valley of William Etté. The shoemaker had been Jeo I's manservant while at school in the valley. As the two men were close to each other in age, they had really been more friends than prince and servant. When Jeo completed his studies, he returned to Cabbage without his manservant, who had expressed a wish to take a position as apprentice to the town's cobbler. Their parting was a sad one, but they always kept in touch. The shoemaker married and had a large family of six boys and one girl, Nan. As Nan was exactly Irene's age, Jeo II could imagine no better place to send Irene to live.

One day, when Irene was not quite fifteen, a stranger came to call. Irene answered the door when the bell rang. As it was washday, Irene, who helped with all the domestic duties, was wearing a simple work-dress and an apron, with her hair tied back under a handkerchief.

Irene opened the door to see a most gallant-looking gentleman with a charming face. He was more than six feet tall, slender, but with broad shoulders and wonderful bearing; he had wavy blond hair, wide-set blue eyes, a strong chin and beautiful nose, and a most disarming smile. Irene stood there, enraptured.

"May I help you?" she managed to ask.

"Yes. I seek Princess Irene of Cabbage. I was told she lives here."

"Uh, yes, that's correct," Irene stammered, a bit startled to hear her own name mentioned.

"At long last, I've found her! I should like to announce the arrival of her betrothed, Jean Louis de la Grande Pomme! Is she able to receive visitors?"

"Uh, yes. I think so. That is...I'll check. You may wait in the main room. I'll...go fetch my mistress."

"I thank you for your kindness."

Irene ran up the stairs to her bedroom, shut the door and leaned against it, her mind reeling. She was puzzled that her intended should arrive with so little notice and two years before the wedding was scheduled. But Irene was thrilled with her good fortune. She had often wondered what her betrothed was like, but this surpassed all her dreams. She'd never seen a more princely looking man! And to think she would someday be married to him!

Irene pulled her pink formal gown out of her wardrobe. Such a dress was entirely unsuitable for the middle of the day, but it made her appear more mature and was flattering to her slim figure. Then, she went over to her mirror and hastily undid the thick braid of hair and pulled her brush through it, letting it hang down in gentle waves. Hoping desperately that Jean Louis wouldn't recognize her as the "servant" girl at the door, Irene tried to think of witty things to say as she went downstairs, pinching her cheeks to make them rosy.

Irene entered the main room, and tried to assume the air of the self-assured hostess as she approached the high-backed chair in which her guest was sitting, with his back to her as he faced the fire.

"Monsieur Louis, how lovely that we meet at last. I've been so looking forward..." Irene stopped and stared at the man who stood to face her. This was *not* the gentleman who had been at the door!

"Excuse me," Irene continued, composing herself. "*You* are Monsieur Jean Louis?"

"Yes," he replied.

"From La Grande Pomme in La Nouvelle Yorkshire?"

"Mai oui! I am none other. Mademoiselle, I am so pleased," he said, kissing her hand. "You are even more beautiful than I imagined you would be."

"Thank you...you are so kind," Irene said weakly.

Irene could not return the compliment. The man who stood in front of her was short, a mere two inches taller than herself. He was a little on the fat side, with big shoulders and a barrel chest. His face was not bad looking, but his expression was somewhat childlike. He had a wide face with a pug nose and he wore an impish grin.

"Excuse me, sir," came a voice from the doorway.

Irene nearly jumped as she saw the handsome, blond man from before. She looked from him to Jean and back again.

"Should I take the horses to the stables, or will you be needing them anymore today?" the man asked Jean.

"I won't be needing them any further today," Jean answered. "But before you go, come here. I want you to meet your new mistress."

Irene could barely look up as the youth with the charming smile approached her.

"This is my bride-to-be, Princess Irene of Cabbage," Jean said. "My sweet, this is my servant, Michael from Yorkshire."

Michael raised his eyebrows in surprise as he recognized Irene as the girl he met earlier, but bowed gracefully and did not give her away.

◆

Jean Louis never really explained why he came earlier than the marriage agreement had stipulated, but from the moment he arrived in the Valley, he seemed most anxious to marry before Irene's seventeenth birthday. He said now that he had seen how beautiful Irene was he didn't want to wait any longer. Irene's brother was opposed, as his mother had stressed that Irene not be wed before she turned seventeen. Irene, however, saw no reason to put it off since it was inevitable. King Jeo II finally decided that the two could marry after six months of courtship. It was agreed that Irene would return to Cabbage and that Jean Louis would court her there. After saying goodbye to Nan's family and promising to have them all to the grand wedding in Cabbage, Irene left to go to her childhood home.

Irene tried to put the servant out of her mind and concentrate on her intended, Jean Louis, but it was not easy, because the handsome man was often with them on their outings. It was doubly difficult because she soon learned, to her dismay, that her fiancé was dull and tedious. Jean tried hard to please Irene; he made jokes, bought her little presents, wrote poetry to her which he recited, and was thoughtful in every way. Somehow, this only added to his dullness. The Princess of Cabbage tried very hard to find something about Jean she could love, but the more she tried, the more she discovered what was *not* to her liking. He was nice and sincere and quite amiable; he just wasn't a man Irene could fall in love with or imagine living with happily.

Irene found herself thinking about Michael more and more. As the months passed and the wedding day grew nearer, Irene began to feel quite desperate. She knew there was no way she could escape the arrangement, except by joining a religious order. She thought of running away, but that would bring disgrace on her family. Irene felt she had no choice but to stay and perform her duty, however distasteful. For the first time, Irene understood what it meant to have royal obligations.

◆

A few weeks prior to the wedding, Irene was in the home of her former music teacher, trying to teach Jean the steps to the dances that were customarily danced at weddings in Cabbage. While her teacher played the harpsichord, Irene went over the steps again and again. But Jean was not a fast learner and was awkward besides. His girth, combined with the heat of the day, also made him perspire rather heavily. Michael sat quietly by the harpsichord, observing.

After Jean stepped on Irene's foot for the eighth time, he said, "Why don't you try dancing with Michael for a while? He's a good dancer. I'm sure he'll pick up the steps, and it will probably help me to see someone do it right."

Irene looked directly at Michael for the first time since their initial meeting.

"May I have the pleasure of this dance?" Michael asked.

Irene nodded mutely in response and he took her in his arms. The two made a very good couple. Michael was an excellent dancer and the two glided across the floor. Irene tried not to enjoy herself too much, but it was such a relief to be dancing with a good partner—especially one as handsome as Michael—that she felt happy for the first time in weeks.

"My, you two look wonderful!" Jean said. "Pity *you're* not the groom, Michael. Ha ha! Oh, look at the time. I'm due for a fitting in a quarter of an hour." He gave them a quick wink. "Wedding clothes. I'll see you at dinner, Irene." Seeing that the pair had stopped dancing, he waved his hand in their direction. "Oh, don't stop, you two. It looks like fun."

Irene and Michael continued dancing for a couple of minutes after Jean left. Irene found that after Jean departed, it was very easy to look into her partner's eyes.

Michael smiled down at her. "You know, that first day I saw you, I thought you were a servant."

"I'm sure I must have given that impression the way I was dressed."

"I hoped you were one of Princess Irene's handmaidens, so that you would be coming back with us to La Grande Pomme. I thought you were very beautiful."

Irene abruptly broke away from Michael, crossed the room to a chair and sat down. She turned to her music teacher. "I think we have had enough dancing for now, Monsieur Serrat. Thank you."

The man bowed and left the room.

"Have I committed an indiscretion?" Michael asked. "I am sorry, your Highness, if I have angered you. Please forgive me."

"No, no. I'm just a little overheated. I felt…faint, but I'm alright now."

"How inconsiderate of me. I should have realized you have been dancing for nearly two hours. You must be fatigued in this heat. Are you sure you are alright?"

"Yes, I'm fine," Irene said.

"Just the same, I don't want to take any chances. Let me carry you to the carriage."

"Oh no! That is not at all necessary."

"Please, I insist."

Irene paused. "Well, alright," she said softly.

Michael scooped up Irene and carried her to the carriage. He seemed to hesitate before setting her in the carriage, as if he did not want to put her down. When he sat down next to the princess, he did not seem to want to start home, but appeared content to just sit there.

"My, how warm it is," Irene said. "This must be the warmest day we've had all summer."

"Yes."

"I hope it is still cool in the garden, under the elm trees."

Michael took the reins and moved the carriage into the street to head back to the palace.

"When I was little," Irene continued, "my nursemaid and I used to go into the woods on days like these. It was always cool under the canopy of fir trees."

"Can we get to the woods with a carriage?"

"Yes, but we can't go there now."

"Why not? It's hot, isn't it? And we aren't expected until dinner. That's hours away."

"Oh…but we shouldn't."

"Well, I can think of no reason we shouldn't. But if you'd rather not, I understand."

"No, I'd like to go—very much. It's just that…" Irene paused. "Oh, never mind. Yes," she said decisively. "Let's go."

Michael and Irene went deep into a dense part of the forest and stopped by a clear water stream, where it was cool, green and mossy. Michael placed his jacket on the ground for Irene to sit on. As they talked and laughed, Irene felt so much more at ease than she ever did with Jean. Michael was so easy to be with, so nice, so handsome. She knew she should suggest that they return home, but she wanted to be alone with him.

The two spent a wonderful, carefree afternoon together. She took off her shoes and stockings and showed Michael how she used to catch frogs when she was a young girl. This greatly amused Michael, and he insisted that Irene give him lessons. Neither took the lesson too seriously, and ended up splashing one another, scaring all the frogs away and getting one another quite wet.

"I'm sorry, your Highness," Michael said, laughing. "I shouldn't have gotten you all wet. Sometimes I forget you are a princess. Oh. I beg your pardon. I didn't mean that the way it sounded."

"It's alright. I know what you meant. I enjoy being able to forget royal protocol."

Michael smiled at Irene. "I've had a wonderful time this afternoon."

"So have I; more than I have in a long time." Her smile faded and she sighed. "Well, it must be nearly time for dinner. I suppose we should be going."

"We don't have to go back. We could stay here until they send soldiers out to look for us," Michael joked.

"Yes, we could hide in a tree and watch them scour the countryside. What fun that would be!"

"And when they give us up for dead and go back home, we could walk casually through the front gate, as if we were returning from a picnic. Can you imagine their faces?"

"Or, we could run away together. Jean would be furious!" Irene said, laughing.

"Yes. We *could* run away together. We could go to some country far away where no one knows us. Someplace where they wouldn't know that you're a princess and I'm only a servant."

"That sounds wonderful!" Irene sighed. "I would be able to go where I wanted—when I wanted—and to always do as I liked."

"And I! No more polishing another man's boots, currying another man's horse, seeing to another man's business, falling in love with another man's fiancé."

Irene turned and stared at Michael, not sure she had heard correctly.

"I would be free to tell her...that from the moment I saw her, I adored her. That I'd been thinking thoughts about her that only one's betrothed should think. I could say that I would not wish to live if it was without her smile, her laughter, her varied moods, and the many things unique to her. But, of course, these things are forbidden for me to voice." Michael paused. "I'm sorry, your Highness. I didn't intend to say anything, but I...I couldn't stop myself."

"If you hadn't said it, I would have," Irene said softly. "You see...I feel the same way."

Michael looked unbelievingly at Irene, and then rushed to embrace her. He laughed, and lifted her up and swung her around, and then kissed her before setting her back on the ground.

"Run away with me!" he entreated. "Now! Today! We can do it. We'll go back to the castle, get two fast horses, some clothes and food. I've saved some money. Say yes!"

"I would...I want to...but..."

"Of course, I'll marry you as soon as we reach a town far enough away from here that no one will recognize you."

"Michael, I—"

"It will be rough at first, but I'll find work."

"I want to marry you, but—"

"I'll build us a three-room cottage, with a vegetable garden in the back."

"Michael, please stop!" Irene cried, stepping back. "I *can't* marry you."

"Why? Is it the money? I know it would be a lot to ask you to give up the luxuries you're used to."

"No, that has nothing to do with it. I've lived a modest life with Nan's family. I can't marry you because I would disgrace my brother and Cabbage."

"And what about your feelings? Don't they count for anything?"

"My feelings don't enter into it. I don't love Jean, but I must marry him. It has been arranged since we were children. I must do my duty."

"No! How could you? And what about me? How could I remain Jean's servant with you there all the time? I'd go mad. I'd rather not see you at all, than to see you every day, knowing that I could never touch you!"

"Please, Michael, it can't be helped. But at least we had this one, perfect afternoon. I will treasure it forever."

"There must be some way I can make you see that you're making a mistake."

"No, Michael." Irene slowly shook her head. "It must be this way. Please accept it because if *you* don't, then *I* won't be able to. And if we ran away together, I would hate myself for turning my back on my duty. I don't want that between us. It would haunt me and make us both miserable." She blinked back tears.

For a moment they stared at each other. Then Michael sighed. "Very well."

"Thank you, Michael. Here, I want to give you something." She reached up and unfastened a chain around her neck, which held a ring of black onyx with a royal crest on it. "This ring belonged to my mother. Please take it. I want you to have it to remember this day by."

The ride back to the castle was silent. Irene arrived just in time to change her clothes before dinner. The evening was dull. Jean, sensing Irene's mood, tried especially hard to please her by telling her jokes and funny stories, but Irene was not receptive. Pleading a headache, she went up to her room before the evening meal was finished.

That night, Irene tossed and turned, wondering if she'd done the right thing. The next day, she remained in her room with the excuse that she was not feeling well. Irene realized she needed to ask Michael to pledge his silence about their feelings, so she asked one of the servants to have Michael pick some flowers and bring them to her room. She was, then, quite surprised when her fiancé entered her room, juggling five vases of flowers. Jean explained Michael was gone—he had departed in the middle of the night. Jean produced a note, which he allowed Irene to read:

To my Master and friend, Jean Louis,
It is with a heavy heart that I write this note. I find it impossible, after our long association, to confront you in person.
I must leave your service. Please understand it is not due to any feelings of ill will. You have shown me kindness and consideration, but these last several months I have been feeling restless. My life with you these last years has been pleasant, but has presented me with no challenges. I need to feel that my life counts for something while I'm still young. Perhaps I will join the militia. Do not try to find me, please. This is something I feel I must do.
I wish you and your new bride a long, happy life. You are to be envied. Peace be with you.
Your servant,
Michael

Irene began to cry as she handed the note back to Jean.

"Oh, my dear, do not distress yourself," Jean said. "Your concern touches me, but please do not worry about me. I will find another manservant."

"I'm sorry. I shouldn't be crying. It's just…well, it took me so by surprise, and I'm not feeling all that well."

"I am so sorry, my sweet. But truly, I did not expect you would feel so strongly about it. My bride must have a large heart, indeed, to feel such remorse over the loss of a servant! I believe your feelings on the subject exceed my own, and, after all, he was my servant! How tender would your feelings be if *I* were to disappear in the night? Ha ha! But do not concern yourself, my love. It will never happen."

"At least I have that to be thankful for," Irene blubbered.

"I think you had better rest," Jean said, awkwardly patting her shoulder.

"Yes. I'll try to sleep."

"Good! Our wedding is only two weeks away! I want my bride to be healthy and beautiful for the big day. Goodbye, my sweet."

Irene wept all the harder when she was alone. She should have guessed that Michael would leave. He had said he would not be able to stand working in the same house with her after she was married to Jean Louis.

Irene spent another fitful night trying unsuccessfully to sleep. Whenever she did manage to drop off, she had nightmares that jarred her awake, and then it was hours before she could sleep again.

Two days later, Irene was in the garden with Jean, half-listening to a poem he had composed that he wanted to recite at the wedding, when a letter arrived for Jean. As he read the letter carefully, his face drained of all color, as if he could not believe the words in front of him.

"What is it?" Irene asked. "Not bad news, I hope."

"Well…yes. I am afraid that it is."

"What? Tell me."

"I am afraid that it is about your settlement—the bride price. I was beginning to wonder about the delay. I am sorry, but it appears it won't be here before the wedding ceremony. My father assures me, however, that we will not have to wait too long."

"What went wrong?"

"It seems that…uh, our local government has temporarily possessed my father's estate. The estate, unfortunately, includes your settlement."

"How dreadful! Why would they do that?"

"Well," Jean seemed quite uncomfortable answering these questions. "It seems my father has a few…uh…debts, and until they are paid, the state is taking possession of our house and lands. It is undoubtedly just a misunderstanding. My father will pay his debts and then we will regain our property."

"When did he incur this debt?" Irene asked.

"Six months ago."

"And he hasn't paid it off yet? What will happen if he is unable to?"

"Then…the state will keep our house and land in payment. I am sure that won't happen, however. Not to worry, my love!" he finished with an attempt at a bright smile.

Irene knew at once that her prayers had been answered. Without the bride price from the groom, she was under no obligation to marry

Jean. She didn't care a whit for his money, but she wanted desperately to escape the marriage.

Later that day, Irene slipped away and met with her brother, King Jeo II. She told him about the money and he agreed it would not be wise to marry into a family suffering such financial setbacks.

The following day, Jeo II asked his sister's fiancé to come speak with him on a matter of utmost urgency. The discussion was short and as soon as Jeo dismissed him, Jean went to his guest quarters and began to pack. Then he found Irene in her room, working on a tapestry.

"Irene, may I speak with you?" Jean asked.

Irene put down her needle. "Yes, of course," she said, avoiding his gaze.

"I realize you are acting within your rights, but is there no way your brother can be swayed?"

"My brother?"

"Yes, it was he who insisted we adhere to the marital clause concerning the settlement. I'm sure if you appealed to him—told him how you felt about me, that he would…"

Irene took a deep breath. "Jean, I am sorry. But it was *I* who insisted upon adhering to the clause."

"You?"

"Yes. I am sorry."

"But, why? Things were going so well. Why did you do this to me? Is it the money? You don't have to worry. We're only suffering a slight setback. It will be resolved in a matter of weeks!"

"No, Jean, it is not the money."

"What then? Tell me."

"Please, Jean, I do not wish to hurt you."

"I must know! You must tell me the real reason you do not want to marry me!"

"Very well, then. It is simply this. I do not believe we are a good match."

"Why? I am good looking, intelligent, witty, and generous."

"Yes, you are…those things. But I believe we could not make each other happy. I am very sorry, Jean."

"Please, I appeal to you for the last time. Marry me! I need you, and I promise I'll make you happy. Please!"

"I cannot," Irene said, turning from him.

Jean slowly walked to the door and stood there, his back to her.

"You'll regret this, Irene," he said, fiercely. "You have ruined everything. I'll always hate you for this."

"Please try to understand, Jean. I didn't mean to hurt you."

But Irene's words were wasted. Jean stormed out of the room, slamming the door behind him.

◆

In the wine cellar, Irene shook her head. "I left Cabbage the next day, David. I said I was going to visit Nan for a while, but instead I searched for Michael. I traveled to every town and village for miles around, but no one had seen him. I even went to military camps, since he had said something about becoming a soldier, but could find no trace. After three weeks I returned to the Valley, discouraged and exhausted. Eventually, of course, my spirits improved and I got over the heartbreak. However, I never forgot Michael or that one perfect day when we revealed our love for one another."

"But what happened to Jean? Did you hear nothing of him before seeing him again today?" David asked.

"That's why I feel so guilty. I learned his life became a complete shambles—the family never recovered financially. I also heard he refused to work, and had become, well, quite a drinker. I don't know why or how he came to side with the Black Lord, though I suspect it was to gain back some of his former rank and glory."

"He seems...well...not entirely forgiving towards you."

"I will try to convince him to leave you out of this."

"It's you I'm concerned with. What do you think he'll do?"

"I wish I knew. He's not the same person I knew two years ago, clearly."

"I'll do my best to defend you."

"You've done enough. I'm so grateful you came back to help me today. Those beasts might have—well, you were so brave."

"Yes, I know. That's not like me," he said, smiling in the dark. "Being brave, I mean. I usually only help people when the odds are at least ten to one in my favor and there's some money in it."

The sound of footsteps coming down the stairs and a light on the walls interrupted Irene and David's talk.

"It's Jean!" said Irene, with a trembling voice.

"Never fear, I am with you," David replied, doing his best to sound courageous.

CHAPTER 22

The light became brighter as the steps approached, until Jean de La Grand Pomme stood at the foot of the stairs. In one hand he held a torch, in the other, a long sword, which caught the reflection from the flame and shimmered as he moved it back and forth. He stood staring at Irene. His eyes softened for a moment, and he seemed about to speak. Irene broke her gaze from Jean to look anxiously at David. At this, Jean's face became hard, and his eyes narrowed in anger. He set the torch in a sconce upon the wall and walked over to the two, standing between them.

"So," he said, addressing David, "who do we have here? Not a brother, surely, I remember Jeo well. Cousin? Companion? Or...lover!" Jean brought the tip of the sword inches from David's face.

"David and I just met a few days ago, Jean. We are not lovers," Irene said firmly.

"But you must be close, Irene," Jean replied softly, not taking his eyes off of David, "if you are on such a familiar name basis." He moved the sword closer until the tip touched David, beneath his left eye.

"Methinks the lady fancies your face more than mine, sir. Perhaps I could arrange...or" — he smirked — "re-arrange the circumstances to my favor." He gently brushed the edge of his weapon against David's cheek. David kept still and silent.

"Jean...have pity. Stop this," Irene implored.

"Careful, Irene. If you distract me...I...might...slip!" And he cut David sharply under the eye — a short wound which welled with blood. David drew his breath in sharply, and turned his face away.

"David, are you hurt?" Irene cried.

"I'm alright," David answered through clenched teeth.

Jean smiled in delight. He turned to Irene. His eyes were hard as steel as he walked closer to her. He stood silently before her, but she refused to meet his gaze. Slowly, he raised his sword and even more slowly ran it along the side of Irene's face. She shut her eyes, willing herself to not move.

"Shall I mark you similarly, Irene?" he murmured in a husky voice.

"I am helpless before you, Jean," she answered shakily. "You may do as you will."

"So I may." He chuckled. "So I may."

He withdrew the sword from Irene's cheek and brought it to the bottom of the lacings across her tunic. With a single stroke, he cut the lacing. Irene gasped and her eyes flew open. Jean methodically continued slicing, until all the lacings were cut. He hesitated...as if considering pulling aside the rest of the shirt that still covered Irene sufficiently to keep her decent.

Irene felt her face burn with shame. She glared at Jean before slowly raising her arms to pull the shirt closer around her breasts.

"Why so coy, Irene?" Jean asked. "I'm sure your lover, here, has seen your charms before. Surely he doesn't mind sharing you a bit?"

"Leave her be, you foul beast," David cried. "We are not lovers!"

In a flash, Jean stood above David, his sword raised and ready to strike. Then he paused. "No. I am not yet finished with you. Perhaps another time I will have the pleasure of running you through."

"On an equal battleground," David replied, pointing to the iron shackles binding his legs, "I would welcome the opportunity."

"You make me laugh—you really do!" Jean cried in delight. "No matter how equal a battle field, it would still be terribly one-sided, I'm afraid. No one can beat me in swordplay." Jean strode back to Irene, kneeled and unlocked her leg irons. He grabbed her arm, and hauled her to her feet. Irene, clutching her shirt together, stumbled after Jean up the stairs. She did not even have time to say anything to David, who soon sat alone in the darkness.

◆

Kay and Nan walked into the dining hall in Gar's castle for breakfast. Nan smiled brightly, still giggling a bit. Kay was bleary-eyed and yawning. Luciano, Fitzgerald, Demetrius, and Stephon sat at the huge, walnut table enjoying their meal. At the head of the table sat Gar, resplendent in a scarlet tunic with black tights, and an embroidered black cape. He nibbled a piece of toasted bread.

"Come sit by me, Kay. I saved you a place," Luciano called. In reply, Kay yawned again. Luciano liberally heaped her plate with eggs, meats, bread and cheeses. Kay stared at the food and shook her head. "I am not hungry, Luciano...I just want to sleep."

"Nonsense, my little angel. You haven't eaten in more than a day. That is why you are so tired, and have no energy. Eat, eat!"

"No," Kay replied. "That is why I am so tired!" She pointed at the bubbling Nan who was eating with gusto. "I did not get...a wink...of...of..." Kay leaned against Luciano and shut her eyes. Soon she was sound asleep. Everyone exchanged glances and smiled. Kay began to slip out of her chair...her head falling directly in Luciano's lap. He cleared his throat nervously.

"Uh...I think...I will take Kay where she will be more comfortable."

"She looks plenty comfortable right there, Luciano!" giggled Nan. The men laughed outright. Luciano's face reddened, but he smiled as he lifted Kay in his arms and left the room. The others returned to their breakfasts.

Fitzgerald spoke as he helped himself to more eggs. "Your Majesty, how is it you are King of the Fairies and not a fairy yourself?"

"Oh," Gar answered, "yes. It *is* rather odd. Well, you see in my youth, I was a bit of a ne'er-do-well, traveling the land, making my way as best I could. For a time, I worked in a traveling carnival as a gamesman, encouraging visitors to spend their money on games of chance, which, of course, they had no chance at all of winning!

"One day, the carnival came to this area. 'Twas a small village and we didn't expect much of a turnout, but nearly everyone in the community showed up so we made a tidy sum. Well. Our owner, Birnbach the Great, who was always looking for new acts, was walking around the woods and came across a band of dancing fairies. He tried his best to convince them to join our carnival, but they turned him down flat.

"Determined to get them, Birnbach confided he planned to abduct some fairies in the night, and cage them. Naturally, I was quite horrified at this and snuck away to warn them. They all went into hiding, foiling Birnbach's plan. The show moved on without any fairies, but also without me, as I had decided to leave the carnival. I stayed around for a while, trying to figure out what to do next.

"The fairies returned to their home, and in gratitude, asked me to become their ruler and protector. They built me this fine castle and have provided for all my needs, renaming the community Garsland. All they ask is that I watch over them and keep them safe. It's not a bad job at all, really, except for the constant rhyming."

When he finished his story, Gar stood up. "Well, my newly-found friends, what would you like to do today?"

"I would prefer something non-strenuous," Demetrius said. "I am almost myself again, but have not quite regained my full strength."

"I would love it if your fairies would teach me some of their dances!" Nan said with enthusiasm. "I have not danced since the Secret Valley, and I fear I am getting quite rusty."

Fitzgerald gazed at her with admiring eyes. "If you dance, Nan, I would like nothing better than to watch you, but I would also enjoy seeing more of our gracious host's kingdom."

The others quickly agreed with Fitzgerald that a tour would be the nicest thing.

"It shouldn't take too much of your time, for it's quite a small kingdom. Not even on the map." Gar said. "Only me, two-hundred or so fairies, some local people in the valley who farm, and a tiny town square with shops and such. Not all that impressive."

"You are being too modest, surely, your Majesty," Stephon said.

"You are probably right!" Gar said, smiling. He signaled to some of the fairies. They floated over to him and bowed.

"Make ready our royal carriage. We are going to make a tour of the kingdom," Gar commanded. The fairies twirled with excitement.

Hooray! Hooray! We're off for a ride!
We'll see the whole kingdom from in to outside.
It won't take too long, three hours at most.
It's the finest around, though we don't like to boast!

The fairies floated out of the room, singing.

"They are so clever, Gar," Nan said.

"True, but a pain in the royal you-know-what somctimes. Shall we?" Gar led the way to the courtyard. Soon a beautiful horse-drawn carriage pulled up.

"What about Luciano and Kay?" Demetrius asked.

"Well, let them stay behind this time," Gar said. "There won't be room enough for us all if everyone comes, anyway." So they all piled into the carriage for the tour.

◆

Jean de la Grande Pomme roughly pulled Irene along. He spoke not a word, and Irene feared his anger too much to ask where they were going. When he came to a large door, he stopped and looked at Irene...a wicked smile on his face. He pushed open the door and hauled Irene inside. A dozen or so young women jumped up from sofas and floor cushions and lined up before Jean. They knelt in reverence, their heads on the floor.

"We, thy unworthy servants, do humbly bid thee welcome, oh, Master. Thy every wish is our command," they recited in chorus.

"Arise, my lovelies, and meet your newest companion, Irene, Princess of Cabbage. Or should I say, former Princess of Cabbage." Jean brought Irene alongside of him so the girls could see her. Now standing, they eyed her carefully, dislike showing openly on each pretty face.

Irene realized with shock that this was some sort of harem. What struck her most was how all of the girls seemed like imitations of her. They were all young, with deep brown hair, and pretty with slender figures in scanty clothing. As the women stared at Irene, she felt their hostility. Each girl coolly sized her up...as if to see what on earth had possessed Jean to bring her into the harem.

"No... oh, no," Irene whimpered.

"Yes...oh, yes!" Jean cried as he flung Irene into the group. The women caught her in strong grips, causing her to cry aloud in pain.

"Clean the wretch up and tend to her wound," Jean ordered. "Then send her properly attired to my private chambers." Laughing, he left.

The others wasted not a second, but dragged Irene to the next room, tearing her already torn clothes from her. Irene lashed out and screamed, but she was outnumbered, and was soon stripped naked. The others formed a circle around her and eyed her critically. They poked and pinched her, and pulled her hair, all the while making deprecating noises. Irene, close to tears, tried to fend off the attacks and cover herself. At last, the others were satisfied with their inspection, and pushed Irene into a large bathing pool. She came up sputtering. One of them threw a bar of soap at her and they all left the room, laughing.

Irene sat in the pool, hurt and humiliated. Tears slowly rolled down her cheeks. She picked up the soap and began to wash.

After Irene finished bathing, she dried herself with one of the thick towels piled nearby, wrapping one about her body and another around her damp hair. The wound in her arm had broken open again and was bleeding. In the other room she could hear the girls laughing and talking.

Perhaps I could escape while they are preoccupied. But at that moment a tiny old woman carrying clothing and bandages entered. She was wearing a plain woolen dress with a long apron, and her hair pulled back under a scarf.

She went straight to Irene and led her gently to a bench, and made her sit. Carefully, she bandaged Irene's arm and unwrapped her head towel. She combed out the snarls until Irene's long hair lay smooth and sleek. Irene slowly relaxed under the gentle hands of this strange old woman.

"Thank you; you are very kind," Irene said, almost forgetting her earlier humiliation. "Tell me your name. I am Irene."

The woman smiled and shook her head. She pointed to her lips and shrugged her shoulders.

"Ah, you cannot speak, is that it?" Irene asked.

The small woman nodded. She rubbed perfumed oil into Irene's skin. Her hands were so gentle; Irene closed her eyes and began to drift off.

"Silent Susan!"

Irene wrenched back to alertness. One of the harem girls stood in the doorway.

"You are too slow, you old hag!" she scolded as she entered the room. "Dress the wretch; Jean Louis requests her. Though I can't for the life of me see why."

Susan gestured towards Irene's hair, still damp.

"I don't care if it's dry or not. Braid it and dress her. At once!" With one last sneer at Irene, the girl flounced out of the room.

Silent Susan started to braid Irene's long hair, sadly shaking her head. Irene's heart pounded with fear.

CHAPTER 23

Kay opened her eyes, yawned and stretched. She sat up, surprised to find herself in a garden alone with Luciano.

He smiled at her broadly. "Did you have a good sleep, Principessa?"

"It felt marvelous. How long was I asleep?"

"About three hours," the King replied.

"And you waited for me all that time? How boring for you."

"Oh no, not really. After all, I had a beautiful view."

Kay looked around. "Yes, the garden is lovely."

"I was not speaking of the garden, little one." Luciano took Kay's hand in his and kissed it gently. Kay blushed and smiled. As the two went into the castle they met the others returning from their tour of Gar's kingdom.

"Oh, Kay," Nan exclaimed, running up to her. "You should have come. It was all so beautiful; such green meadows, and majestic mountains, and a charming village. I haven't seen anything so nice since we left the Valley of William Etté."

"You haven't heard the best part, Kay," Fitzgerald said. "Gar says we may stay here always. There is plenty of land for us to farm. We can all live near one another; won't it be wonderful?"

Demetrius broke in. "Just think, Kay, a real home again."

Kay stared at the smiling faces before her. "Perhaps *you* had all better do some thinking!" she said angrily. "Fitzy, you trained for years to be a knight. Somehow I cannot imagine you mucking about in manure, trying to farm. Stephon—what of you? Have you already forgotten David, still in the Land of the Black Lord? And you, Nan? Are you giving up on finding Irene? And while you may have found a home, Demetrius, thousands of others will lose theirs and perhaps their lives if we don't find a way to stop Lord William and Sir Richard. How can any of you even *think* of staying here?"

Kay pushed past her astonished friends and ran upstairs. The jovial mood of the morning's ride had disappeared. Nan's eyes welled with tears. Demetrius and Stephon were shamefaced.

Gar leaned against a pillar, observing. "What *is* the matter with that one?" he finally said. "First she falls asleep at breakfast and now this! Really, I could become quite miffed with her."

"But she was right, you know," Nan sniffed. "We were so caught up in our own pleasures, we forgot all about Irene and David. I'm so ashamed."

"What's wrong with forgetting—for a while, anyway?" Stephon said. "We deserve a bit of pleasure after all we've been through. I have no illusions of saving the whole world from this Lord William-what's-his-name. I, for one, don't mind admitting I'm totally delighted by Gar's kingdom and would gladly stay here forever. I was getting rather tired of the life of a bandit—even a fake one."

The others stared in amazement at the large man. It was the longest speech he had made since they had come together.

Finally, Fitzgerald spoke. "Stay if you wish, Stephon. I, at least, choose to go back to the land of the Black Lord. Kay is right. Dead or alive, Irene and David must be brought out."

Demetrius and Nan nodded in agreement.

"I know I should return to my own kingdom, and try to correct some of the wrongs my mirror image committed," Luciano said, "but wherever Kay goes, so shall I."

"Then let me get her and we can begin planning at once," Nan said, running upstairs to their room.

She found Kay sitting by a widow, staring out at the countryside. "Kay!" Nan said, breathlessly.

"It is a beautiful place, Nan. I can't blame you for wanting to stay."

Nan rushed over and knelt beside Kay. "But we want to go! Oh, Kay—you were right. How could we possibly stay, knowing Irene and David are still in that dreadful place? And, maybe, my parents as well. We must go back!"

Kay turned to Nan. A smile lit her face and she embraced her friend.

◆

When Silent Susan had finished braiding Irene's hair, she handed the clothes to her and waited for her to get dressed. Irene stood still, the flimsy garments in her hands.

"I cannot...please," she whispered.

The old woman shook Irene's arm and gestured to the door, her face a mask of concern. Irene realized Silent Susan was afraid Jean, himself, would come for her. She began to dress.

She had been given a dress of sheerest silk that fit snugly about the hips and bust. The skirt had long slits, so every time Irene walked her shapely legs were exposed. Irene was even more uncomfortable because the bodice was low cut and she had no undergarments. She turned to the old woman in dismay.

Silent Susan nodded and took Irene out of the room and down a hallway. They walked up a flight of stairs and down another hall. Irene noticed there were no other rooms off the long passageway, just one large door at the end.

As if to be so isolated that no one could hear if one cried for help. Her heart was pounding again.

Susan led Irene to the door and knocked.

From within came the voice of Jean de la Grande Pomme. "Enter."

Silent Susan pushed the heavy door open and motioned for Irene to go in. Irene looked at the old woman with desperation, but Silent Susan refused to meet her eyes. Slowly, Irene entered the room. The door shut silently behind her.

The room was lit by wall torches, candles in beautiful chandeliers, and was exquisite in every detail. Large, airy and light, it was exactly suited to Irene's tastes, and reminded her of her parent's palace in Cabbage. Gazing about in wonder, she realized Jean Louis was nowhere to be seen.

"In here, Irene," Jean called from the next room. Irene walked across the plush rugs to the doorway. She gasped aloud at what she saw. In an enormous tub, set in the center of a marble bathing room, sat Jean! His back was to her, but somehow Irene was certain he was smiling.

"Well? Have you no tongue, girl? You must greet your master properly!"

"Good...Good evening, Jean," Irene said.

Jean slapped a fist into the tub, splashing water onto the floor. "No! No! No!" he cried in his high-pitched voice. "That is not at all correct! You must remember I am your master now, Irene. I *own* you. Kneel and place your head on the floor between your hands. Then say, 'Most gracious master, what is thy will?' Now try that."

Irene clenched her fists tightly. She wanted to scream, to run away from this horrid man, even to kill him. Slowly she began to back out of the room.

"Oh, I wouldn't do that if I were you, Irene." Jean's voice stopped her. "Not if you ever want to see your little friend in the cellar again. Now...why don't you try that greeting once more?"

Irene took a deep breath and knelt on the cold marble floor. Placing her head between her hands she said faintly: "Most gracious master, what is thy will?"

"What was that? I couldn't quite hear you," Jean smirked.

"Mostgraciousmaster,whatisthywill!" Irene shouted in a rush.

"Better. Now come over here and scrub my back."

Irene raised her head in dismay. Would her humiliation never end? She knew better than to disobey. She slowly crossed the room to the tub, while Jean de la Grande Pomme chuckled to himself.

CHAPTER 24

David, kin to the Hebraice, had little time to come up with any plan to rescue Irene. Not half an hour after Jean hauled Irene away, the hairy beasts removed David from the cellar. He knew it was useless to panic or fight. The beasts would only beat him unconscious and he wanted to be aware of where he was going. He vowed to somehow get back to Irene.

The guards took David through town to a holding pen for what he realized was to be a slave auction. Along with two dozen or so other wretched men and women, David waited his turn on the auction block. He tried to see any possible escape, but the great, hairy guards were everywhere and he feared it would be a waste of strength. David knew he would need all his strength in the coming days; he had a good idea of how slaves were treated in the land of the Black Lord.

Finally, David's turn came and he was roughly led to a wooden block in the middle of the room. About thirty foremen waited to inspect the new offerings. Unlike the slaves, these men were healthy, and appeared well fed. Each carried a heavy, black whip.

The beasts stripped David to the waist, so the foremen could better see his physical condition. Some appreciative murmurs came from the crowd as the beasts turned David this way and that before the bidding began. Bidding was quite spirited, as it had been some time since a specimen as fine as David was up for auction. Most of the people sent under the Bridge of Doom were weak and infirm.

After a few minutes, David sold for what seemed a high price. *Not that it matters,* he thought. *Whoever bought me will try and get his money's worth, I'm certain.*

The winning bidder was the foreman of the brick pits—one of the most loathsome, backbreaking jobs in the underground kingdom. Guards shackled David's feet and hands and put him with other slaves who had been purchased. Apparently the foreman now had all he needed, for he began to crack his whip and the slaves, fearful of the sharp sting, hurried away.

"Scrub a little harder, Irene. That's better," Jean said, as he sat smiling in the bathing tub.

Irene felt sick to her stomach as she thought about what was sure to follow Jean's bath.

"Fetch my robe. The blue one hanging on the wall," Jean ordered imperiously.

Irene obeyed. As he stood to put on the robe, Irene cast her eyes down and away from the man. She couldn't bear to be in the same room another minute, but escape seemed hopeless.

"Jean, couldn't we please just talk for a minute?" Irene begged, stalling for time.

"Seems to me we have done more than enough talking," he replied, briskly. "Now, go turn down the bed like a good lass."

Irene set to the task and when she finished, stood waiting for the inevitable. Jean prolonged her agony as long as possible by anointing himself with colognes and combing his hair. Finally, he emerged from the bathing room.

"Now, my love," he said sarcastically, "the long awaited moment is at hand."

Irene stiffened as Jean took her roughly by the shoulders and kissed her. She didn't respond to his repeated kisses, but he kept on. Irene was repulsed, and her wounded arm throbbed, but she was resigned to her fate. She fell backward onto the bed, refusing to meet Jean's eyes as he stood above her. He laughed softly, grabbed the low neckline of Irene's flimsy garment, and tore it down the front in one swift action. Irene gasped and attempted to hold the dress together while Jean gazed hungrily at her.

There was a knock at the door.

"Who is it?" Jean barked, but there was no answer. "Who comes to disturb me at this hour? Why, I'll have your hide, whomever you may be!" Jean crossed to the door and opened it.

No one stood in the hallway, but soft footsteps could be heard, running down a side corridor. Jean began to shut the door in disgust; then he noticed a note on the floor. He picked the paper up, read it, and frowned.

"I must away. An urgent meeting of the Black Lord's council has been called. I'll return shortly." Jean hastily dressed and departed, locking the door behind him.

Alone, the relieved Irene sat up and tried to discover some means for fixing the front of her gown. She went to Jean's closet and found a shirt to wear over the upper part of the torn dress.

Irene looked around. There was nothing to do but wait, and the longer she waited, the more desperate she became. She paced the room.

There must be some way I can prevent Jean from having his way with me.

Irene crossed to a small pedestal table with a decanter of wine on it. Although she seldom drank, Irene thought a little wine might calm her nerves, so she took the decanter and filled a glass to the rim with the rich, ruby liquid. She drained the contents in several gulps and then refilled it, downing that glass as well. She sat down to think. On an empty stomach, the wine went straight to her head. The chair was quite comfortable and soon Irene's head began to nod and she fell asleep. The heavy crystal goblet slipped from her hand and shattered on the floor, startling her awake. She stooped to pick up the pieces and noticed one shard still attached to the goblet stem was shaped very much like a knife.

A weapon! I'll hide this in the bed and when Jean returns and forces me there, I'll stab him!

The more Irene thought about it, however, the less confidant she became. Even if she succeeded in stabbing him, the chances of striking a fatal blow were slim and she most likely would only aggravate Jean. He might hurt her and David in retaliation.

Irene heard steps outside. She ran to the bed with the shard of glass and, despite her misgivings, hid it under the covers near the pillow on the left side, and ran back to the table to shove the other broken bits under a nearby bureau.

The door opened and Susan the Silent entered. She seemed nervous, and frowned at Irene as if she had an urgent message to convey. She pointed to a little bottle she had brought with her and led Irene to sit in a chair. Then she made Irene hold out her arms. Susan applied the fluid in the bottle to Irene's skin. It was a sticky substance smelling faintly of apricots. Irene began to rub it into her skin, but Susan stopped her. The process was repeated on Irene's other arm, both her legs, and down her neck. Susan held up a small mirror and Irene realized what purpose the sticky liquid had. Where the ointment dried, it appeared she had a horrid rash and peeling skin. It looked terribly contagious.

"Oh, thank you, Susan!" Irene said, realizing the woman's plan.

Susan bowed and smiled in response. She turned to leave the room.

"Tell me," Irene continued, "did you send the note? The one summoning Jean to a meeting?"

Susan hesitated, but finally nodded "yes" and departed. Irene heard the door lock again, and the fading footsteps of her friend.

◆

After fairies cleared away the evening meal, Kay, Nan, Fitzgerald, Luciano, Demetrius and Stephon remained around the table discussing the plan for Irene and David's rescue.

"First off," Kay said, "we'd better decide who will go."

"We will all go, of course," Nan said.

"I'm not sure that would be practical," Fitzgerald said. "Suppose we were captured by the Black Lord? Who would be left to rescue us?"

"A point well taken," Kay said. "Besides, it is much easier for two or three to sneak about than a group of six."

"I don't think we should be split up," Nan insisted. "At least if we are captured we will still be together, and what would happen if we ran into those dreadful beasty things? Six would stand better chance than two in a fight."

"I side with Nan," Demetrius said. "We must all go."

"Maybe some of us don't want to go," Stephon said. "I'm staying right here."

Nan stared at him in surprise. "How can you say that, Stephon? Why, your own master and friend is in great peril."

"Yes, and I am sorry for that. I'll miss him, but we were lucky to get out alive the first time. You can't expect me to go back and meet certain death. We are no match for the Black Lord and his foul beasts."

"Perhaps with the orb, we are," Demetrius said, thoughtfully. "I held off the beasts with lightning bolts and I am able to do other things. I can cause flooding rains, make it snow, and create thick fog."

"Demetrius," Fitzgerald said, "the orb saved us when we certainly would have died, but I recall the length of time you controlled it was...somewhat limited."

The handsome man tossed the glowing ball from hand to hand. "I only came upon it a couple of weeks ago. I am still learning how it works. Sometimes I can change the weather for as long as half an hour, and other times, nothing happens at all."

"Not completely dependable then. Although it may come in handy," Fitzgerald said. The others nodded in agreement.

After a pause, Nan spoke again. "I still can't understand how you can even think of staying here," she said to Stephon. "You have no heart!"

"I surely will have no heart, body, or anything else if I return to the land of the Black Lord!" Stephon retorted.

"He speaks the truth," came a voice from the corner of the room. Gar had returned from an evening stroll and had walked unnoticed into the room to overhear their plan. He ambled over. "Stephon is the only one of you who talks sense. You are madder than my fairies if you think you can go down there and come back alive with your friends. The portal you escaped through is surely being guarded by now. Those creatures are undoubtedly lying in wait for you to try a rescue."

"But we've got to try," Nan said. "Irene is my dearest friend. We must do something."

"Yes. Kay and her friends saved me," Luciano added. "The least I can do is... is..." he trailed off.

Gar shook his head. "Any attempt is beyond foolhardy. The Black Lord would take great pleasure in making you suffer. You see, you are the first to ever escape his kingdom!"

"There must be some way," Kay said. "Think! I won't let them stay down there."

"I'm afraid there is nothing for it," Gar said sadly. "If there were, my fairies and I would have released the Black Lord's prisoners long ago. You are all welcome to stay here. We have plenty of room, and life on the whole is quite pleasant, although I can't guarantee how long it will last. The Black Lord means to expand his kingdom above ground and this is probably one of the first places he will claim."

"You will fight him, of course," Fitzgerald said.

"Alas, no. The fairies and I will move on peacefully when the time comes. We cannot hope to defend ourselves."

"Wait!" Kay shouted. "Demetrius told us of a band of soldiers and citizens who were driven from their homes by Lord William. They now live in the woods. There must be more refugee groups throughout the Valley of William Etté and beyond. What if we were to bring them all here?"

"To what purpose?" Gar asked.

"Why, to build our own army to defeat Lord William's! And from there, perhaps the Black Lord himself. It would take some time, and perhaps we would be too late to rescue Irene and David, but we could at least defend your kingdom, Gar."

The others all began talking at once.

"Oh, Kay, you're so clever!" Nan said.

"Great idea. I'll leave tomorrow!" said Fitzgerald.

"Now, you're talking sense!" Stephon said, nodding.

"My Principessa! You are brilliant!" Luciano exclaimed.

"Yes, that's what we'll do!" Demetrius added.

"Now wait. Wait!" Gar interrupted. "I don't know how I'd like having my kingdom overrun with refugee soldiers!"

"It will only be temporary, Your Majesty," Kay said. "I'm sure they will leave to go back home as soon as the Black Lord is defeated. It is up to you, of course, but we'd stand a chance of saving your kingdom if we organized an army and no chance at all if we don't!"

Gar sighed. "I suppose you're right. Very well, you can organize your army, but absolutely no soldiers in the castle. Except for yourselves, of course. And everyone leaves the moment the Black Lord is gone."

"Oh, thank you, Gar!" Kay jumped up and kissed him on the cheek.

"You really are a trouble-maker, aren't you?" Gar muttered, but he smiled all the same.

◆

"Lock her in that room until the rash has disappeared!" Jean de la Grande Pomme screamed. "No one is to go near her until her skin is clear, especially my harem! It might be contagious. Silent Susan alone will attend her."

Two guards escorted Irene to a modest little room at the opposite end of the long corridor from Jean's room. Jean, his face red with anger, watched her go.

"What a night!" he ranted. "First, I am called away for a non-existent meeting of the council, and now this! If I ever find out who sent that note I'll...I'll...well, I don't know what I'll do, but they'll be sorry!"

Jean went back to his suite to change into more comfortable clothing. Then he went down to the kitchen, turning to food to soothe his nerves, as he always did. After he'd had a draught of ale, leftover lamb and three pieces of cake, Jean went to his harem to spend the night.

◆

Irene's room held just a bed, chair and small table. The only window was about two feet square with iron bars, which did not allow in much light. It was of little consequence anyway, since it always appeared to be twilight in the underground kingdom.

Twice a day, Silent Susan brought Irene her meals, accompanied by two guards under orders to see whether Irene's rash had gone away. Susan always hid a small vial of the apricot-scented liquid on the tray so Irene could maintain her rash.

146

This continued for several days. Aside from meals, Irene had nothing to do all day but sit and think or look out the window, from which she witnessed many distressing things. All of the Black Lord's slaves were expected to work—and work hard. Irene's heart ached as she watched old men and women struggle under heavy loads. Even the children were working. All of the prisoners looked pathetic. Their clothes were in shreds, their feet were bare or wrapped with scraps of cloth, and their ankles were bound in chains. And they were all so thin! Irene felt guilty each meal she ate.

By the tenth boring day, Irene began to think it would be better to become Jean's mistress, after all, than to continue in this way. Still, she applied the sticky rash-producing salve to her skin.

One day, as Irene stared out the window, as usual, she saw several prisoners being driven through the street. They were chained together at the ankles and clearly had come from a hard day's labor, as they were barely able to walk and were covered with dust and mud.

Suddenly, she gasped. In the back of the group she recognized a familiar figure. His carriage was stooped and his head was not held as high as she had always seen, but she could still tell it was David. He stood out from the rest. His clothing was not the tattered rags of the other prisoners, and he had a gleam in his eye that said he had not yet given in.

As the prisoners continued down the street, Irene saw David's back. The shirt he wore was slashed open and she could detect red welts beneath.

"How could they whip him? Have they absolutely no humanity?" Irene said to herself. "I hate them! I hate them! I don't want to stay here another minute. I've got to get away—I've got to help David!"

Irene resolved to discontinue using Susan's ointment.

I'll have a much better chance of escaping once I am out of this room, even if it means becoming Jean's mistress.

CHAPTER 25

Kay, Luciano, Demetrius and Fitzgerald departed Garsland and traveled hard for three days, searching for groups of refugees to recruit for their army. They headed west, towards the Valley of William Etté.

"Is this where Nan and Irene lived?" Fitzgerald asked, looking down at the once beautiful community.

"I think so," Kay said, consulting a map.

"Yes, I am sure you are right. I came here when I was a young man," Luciano said. "Although, I hardly recognized it in this deplorable state."

The town appeared abandoned. Walls had fallen; homes remained charred from fire. The army from the Secret Valley had even burned some of the beautiful forest surrounding the city.

"I can't believe my comrades could do such a thing," Fitzgerald said, shaking his head. "It all seems pointless. I feel so ashamed."

"I'm glad we did not bring Nan with us," Kay said. "I think it would be too painful."

"Shall we see if anyone is down there?" Demetrius asked.

"No," Kay replied. "I doubt anyone would be left, except perhaps a thief or two looting the empty houses and dead bodies. We can do without that sort."

The group rode into the Valley, but skirted the city walls. Demetrius wanted to find the camp he was taken to after being wounded in battle. He thought it was probably about ten miles to the southwest.

Kay, Demetrius, Fitzgerald and Luciano rode on, driving their horses hard. Eventually they decided to rest briefly by a stream. Kay took off her boots and dangled her feet in the clear water, while the men watered the horses.

After their break, the four mounted their horses again, and were preparing to ride off when a voice called from the woods.

"Ho there! Go not one step further. You are surrounded by thirty armed men."

"Who seeks to detain us?" Fitzgerald called.

"That I will reveal once you disclose *your* identity, and provided I believe you are honest."

"We are merely travelers, out on an expedition."

"What are your names, where do you hail from, and what is the nature of your expedition?"

"I will tell you gladly, if I may see to whom I am speaking, and see some proof we *are*, indeed, surrounded," Fitzgerald said, testily.

A hail of arrows came in reply to this, which landed neatly at the feet of the horses on all sides. The horses reared up in fright, forcing the riders to dismount in order to calm them. Once the horses settled down, a tall man emerged from behind a tree. In his mid-twenties, he had broad shoulders, a strong, trim body and handsome face with wide-set green eyes and light brown hair. He was attired in clothing common to the bourgeois class in many of the towns in the Valley; a deep green tunic, over a pale yellow shirt, brown breeches and leather boots. He carried a quiver of arrows and a bow.

"Now," he said to the four, "I ask you again—who are you?"

"I am Sir Fitzgerald and these are my companions: Kay, Sir Demetrius Keats and King Luciano."

"And where be your homelands?"

"Kay, Demetrius, and I are former citizens of the Secret Valley. Luciano is the ruler of a kingdom called Tondlepen."

"The Secret Valley attacked us and therefore you are our enemies," said the man. "Give me one good reason why I should not take you all prisoner."

Demetrius spoke up. "We are in search of a camp, sir. I was taken there after being wounded in battle several weeks ago. The people there ministered to my wounds and were kind to me, even though I fought against them."

"Ah! I thought I recognized you," said the man. "The camp was my own and I had occasion to look in on you a few times, though you were out of your head with fever. Why do you return?"

"We came to seek your help against a common foe to both of us— the Black Lord."

"As of yet our only foe is the army sent from your homeland, the Secret Valley."

"But you see, we believe the Black Lord is the power behind Lord William and his armies," Kay said. "He means to take over everything. Lord William is only carrying out his orders."

"If this be true, it alters everything. But why are you acting against the Black Lord if he is in league with your master, Lord William?"

"He is our master no longer, we assure you!" Demetrius said vehemently. "We all left the Secret Valley. Kay and Fitzgerald were driven out and I found it impossible to return after learning the truth. Lord William told us the surrounding communities were full of barbarians who meant to kill us all and take our lands. Your treatment of me after the battle showed me the truth."

"If you are not lying, there would be many to help your cause. But what if you speak falsely?" The man paused, eyeing them carefully. "Perhaps you are scouting for more people to slaughter. I would be inclined to believe the latter."

"I swear I speak the truth," Demetrius said. "By Mirn, I swear it! If we wanted to deceive you, we would never tell you we were from the Secret Valley. We know full well that it would incriminate us."

"Aye, that seems to make sense."

"Ken!" a voice shouted. "Someone approaches."

"Who is it?" the man called back.

"A small band of soldiers—numbering about ten or more. They are wearing armor, but I can't recognize their coats of arms yet. Wait...yes, I think...it is! They are led by Sir Richard—the black heart of the Secret Valley!"

"They followed us here!" Kay cried.

"Or were part of a scheme against us!" Ken said. "Men—hide yourselves well. We shall observe how they treat our guests." Quickly, Ken retreated into the forest.

"We must hide!" Kay said. "Richard will kill us!"

"Leave the horses; run," Demetrius whispered. "Hide in the brush. He won't hurt me. I'll detain him. Go!"

Luciano, Kay and Fitzgerald fled, leaving their horses and provisions behind. They barely managed to hide themselves before Richard came within sight of Demetrius. He stopped his horse and gazed at his friend in shock.

"Demetrius?"

"It is I, Richard."

"My friend, I am so glad to find you again! You are looking much improved. How are you?" Richard asked, dismounting and striding towards him.

"Better. Only a scar is left."

"How did the monks treat you? I hope monastic life wasn't too boring for you."

"No, it was fine. As you can see, the good monks provided me with four horses and more provisions than I could make use of."

"We have been following your tracks all day. I am still in pursuit of those traitors, Kay and Fitzgerald and the two prisoners I brought to Lord William. I thought the tracks came from their horses." He paused, looking puzzled. "Demetrius, why are all of your horses saddled? And why do you ride this way? You are traveling away from the Secret Valley."

"I am not alone, Richard. I am with some friends. They hid themselves because we did not know who you were at first."

"Friends? Who?"

"Uh...a few of the monks, Richard. They saved my life. I owe them much. I am going to go with them for a short time..."

"Demetrius, you forget yourself. Your obligation is to Lord William. You cannot go traipsing off at will."

"But there are extenuating circumstances."

"Be that as it may, our country is at war. The penalty for desertion is death and I will not grant you leave. Why, the way you act distresses me greatly, Demetrius. One would think you do not wish to return with me...*us*."

"I cannot go back with you at this time, Richard. Could you not be persuaded to forget you saw me?"

Richard shook his head. "No, Demetrius. We need you. Lord William is anxious to finish what we've started. There are several bands of men in the nearby woods who escaped and we must cut them down before they organize themselves to attack us."

"I have never gone against your orders, Richard. But now I must." Demetrius gathered the reins of three of the horses and tied them to his own horse's saddle. He mounted and began to ride away from Richard, who stared after him in astonishment.

"Demetrius," he shouted. "I beseech you to stop!"

"I cannot. Forgive me, Richard."

"If you do not stop, I will count you as a traitor. I will charge you with desertion! Come back, or I... I will be forced to kill you! Do not force yourself into a dishonorable death!"

Demetrius stopped his horse and turned around in the saddle to face Richard.

"What do you know of honor, Richard? Or shame? I have felt much shame of late. I hold myself in contempt for having believed Lord William to be a ruler of integrity. Now that I know his true colors and realize I played a part in his foul scheme, I must do what little I can to atone for my wrongdoings. If you are a man of scruples you will do the same!" Demetrius turned and proceeded onward.

"Demetrius. Halt! Do not make me do what you know I must." Richard turned to his soldiers. "Men, battle formation! Bows at the ready...draw arrows...Fire!"

A hail of arrows flew through the air, but not in the direction of Demetrius. Before one of Richard's soldiers could send off an arrow, they were all struck down by arrows shot by the men hidden in the woods under Ken's signal. Their aim was impeccable, and not one soldier was left alive. Only Richard, who stood in front of his men, remained standing. He turned in shock at the scene, then jumped on his horse and galloped away.

"Eric, Paul, Daniel," Ken shouted. "Ride after him! But don't kill him unless necessary!" Three men leapt down from their hiding places in the trees, mounted their horses and sped away.

"You needn't conceal yourselves any longer," Ken called out. "Demetrius has proved you're of good character."

Kay, Fitzgerald, and Luciano came out of hiding and returned to Demetrius.

"Forgive the test," Ken said, "but we are extremely cautious of strangers here. Come back to camp with me and you can rest and eat. Then we'll talk about joining forces in your fight against the Black Lord. I fear we must work quickly. If what Sir Richard said is true, Lord William's army could be here in a matter of days."

"Excuse me," Kay said, "but since you know our names and our origins, might we know the same of you?"

"Of course. My name is Ken of Craig Manor, which, thanks to Sir Richard, no longer exists. I was the son of a wealthy aristocrat and a knight to Neil, the Golden King, a title which means little now. Come, we will talk more later."

He ordered his men to bury the soldiers, and take their weapons and horses. He led his guests deeper into the forest.

◆

"Pardon me, m'lord," the servant said to Jean Louis, who was reclining on a chaise and surrounded by the girls of his harem. "I have just come from the prisoner, Princess Irene. The rash seems to be gone."

The harem girls' smiles turned to scowls. Jean, on the other hand, smiled brightly for the first time in days. He summoned Silent Susan and told her to gather a basin of fresh water, soap, perfume and a change of clothing for Irene, and accompanied her to visit the Princess for the first time in eleven days. When he opened the door to the room, Jean found Irene gazing out the small window. She turned a tear-streaked face to him.

"Tears, Irene?" Jean asked. "What cause have you to cry on this, the happiest of days?"

"Just now, I witnessed a small boy trampled to death by the oxen he was driving. His body lays even now in the street—bloody and neglected—with no mother to grieve over him or holy man to say a prayer or bury him. I find the cruelties of this place deplorable!"

"Come now, do not fret over a mere slave. The boy is undoubtedly better off!" Jean said in a cavalier manner.

Irene stared at him a moment, then laughed shortly. "Yes, I suppose he is. Indeed, I envy him."

"Watch your tongue, Irene!" Jean said sharply. "I will tolerate no impudence. Here are fresh clothes and some water for you to bathe with. I shall await you in my suite. I have not even been there since I saw you last, but have been taking consolation with my ladies. My guards will be outside to escort you when you are ready, but don't dawdle." He strode out of the tiny room and down the corridor to his suite, whistling.

After Susan bowed and departed, Irene hurriedly sponged herself and dressed. Eager to have done with the wretched business, she slipped on the violet gown that had been left for her. It had a deep neckline, long sleeves, no back to speak of at all, and only laces to hold the garment on. The flowing skirt boasted a daring slit up the front.

"It fits his garish taste," Irene said to herself. "Well, I might as well play the part if I am to go through with this."

Irene took some black kohl Susan left her with and rubbed it around her eyes. She applied rouge liberally to her cheeks and combed her hair. After checking herself in a small hand-mirror, Irene knocked on the door to signal her escorts she was ready.

She waited several moments and, getting no response, knocked again. Still no guards entered, so Irene tried the handle and found the door unlocked. She stepped into the hallway; it was empty, but there was a commotion at the other end, outside Jean's suite. Irene crept down the corridor and hid in a side passageway to listen.

The guards and servants were arguing loudly amongst themselves. Irene could not understand why Jean didn't stop the fuss outside his suite.

"Now, shut up!" a guard shouted.

"Let's hear the whole story again, and don't interrupt this time!" another said.

"Alright," a female voice said. "I came to his Lordship's suite to deliver some fresh linens. I knocked on the door and didn't hear anything, so I entered. I opened the door...and there he was, just as he is now, lying on his back with his eyes wide open and blood everywhere! I screamed and everyone came running to find out why. Then, everyone started yellin' and carryin' on!"

All the guards and servants spoke at once.

"How do we know it wasn't *you* what killed him?"

"Yeah, she were the only one in his room!"

"I say, let's kill her!"

"Yes! Stab her with the piece of glass she murdered him with!"

Distracted, the servants didn't see Irene flee down the side hall. Her mind raced as she tried to figure out how Jean had died. Perhaps he flung himself on the bed in anticipation of her arrival, only to land on the jagged piece of glass she hid in the bedclothes earlier.

It must have struck a vital area to kill him so quickly. Now's my chance to get away while the household is in an uproar.

Irene came to a stairway and raced down the steps to a large entry room with hallways on either side. Seeing no one, Irene made a mad dash for the door, hoping it led outside. Before she got five feet away she ran straight into Silent Susan, who was rounding a corner with an armful of wood. The kindling went flying and Susan and Irene both landed in a heap on the floor.

"Thank Mirn, it was you and not a guard I bumped into," Irene whispered, helping the small woman to her feet. "You won't tell anyone you saw me?"

Susan shook her head.

"Thank you, Susan. Thank you for all you've done to keep me safe. Good-bye."

Irene went to the door, opened it and peeked into the empty street. Suddenly, she felt something tugging at her sleeve. It was Susan, holding a long, black cape for her. She motioned Irene to wait a moment and ran to the kitchen. In moments, the woman came back with cheese and bread, wrapped in a scarf. She wore a cape similar to Irene's.

"Do you mean to come with me?" Irene asked, astonished.

The woman nodded her head, "Yes."

"But it won't be safe; you'd be better off staying here."

Susan only stood there waiting with a determined look on her face.

"Alright," said Irene, "let's go."

The two ran into the dimly lit street. When she reached the battered body of the child she'd witnessed trampled earlier, Irene stopped to pick it up and carry it to an alley. She laid the small boy on his back with his arms folded over this chest and said a quick prayer. Then she fled down the street with Silent Susan close behind.

JOURNEY TO WIZARDS' KEEP

CHAPTER 26

Kay, Fitzgerald, Demetrius and Luciano sat huddled with Ken around a map of the surrounding forests. He had marked it to show the refugee camps' locations.

"There are at least 30 other camps in the near vicinity—each with perhaps 250 or so men. There are women and children too, but they are no good for battle, of course," Ken said. "More a hindrance, actually."

"I take exception to that remark!" Kay said, her eyes flashing with anger.

"Oh, come now, Kay. You may be a fairly good shot with a bow, but you can't seriously expect me to believe you could handle a real battle. Against men?"

Fitzgerald cut in. "Kay already faced Richard's men before, Ken, and saved our lives. She can out-shoot almost every man I know."

"Even so," Ken scoffed, "how many other women like her would we find? What is the point of even bothering?"

"The point is, Ken," Kay said tightly, "that women can fill many valuable back positions which might otherwise be taken up by men who can fight, as you so nicely put it, 'a real battle.' I agree with you on one point—women may not belong in the frontlines of this war, but in support positions, such as running for supplies or armaments, why, they might make all the difference between winning and losing!"

"And against an army the size of William of Dob's we will need every available person—male or female," Fitzgerald added.

"Well, there is no way you can convince me a woman's place is in battle, support or no. Now, shall we continue where we left off? As I was saying—" Ken's speech was interrupted as Kay angrily tore the map from his hands and flung it aside.

"No!" she said. "We shall not continue until we resolve this. I tell you, we must train the women."

Ken stood, his fists clenched at his sides. He seemed ready to lash out at Kay, but took a deep breath to control himself. "Very well,

Kay. I will give you a chance to have your way. I challenge you to an archery contest. If you defeat me — best of ten arrows — you may train your women's army. If not, you will follow my directions."

Kay was livid at his arrogance. "You seem to forget it was *our* idea to form this army! Who appointed you General?"

"Without my aid, you will never find the other refugees soon enough to build your army," Ken replied coolly. "Go ahead, leave our camp if you wish, but you will find little success."

"Nor will your camp against Lord William's army," Demetrius broke in. "We both need each other and if a silly archery contest is how we will settle the debate, let us have it! Frankly, I think *I* know who will come out the better." He winked at Kay.

She shot back a grateful smile. Demetrius had saved her from becoming a total shrew. *How well he knows my temper!* Speaking aloud, she said, "I accept your challenge, Ken. However, it grows too dark. First thing in the morning?"

"Agreed," he answered shortly.

"Then let us continue to discuss how we will gather the various camps together," Kay handed the map back to Ken. Taking her seat again, she smiled sweetly.

◆

The next morning dawned bright and clear and when Ken came out of his tent, he found Kay already waiting. On her back hung her quiver of arrows and she held her bow loosely in her hands.

"Do you always sleep so late?" she inquired brightly.

In reply, Ken merely grunted. He was, unfortunately, not at his best. After the others had left to sleep, Ken had drunk several liberal helpings from his whiskey keg. Now, his head was pounding, his mouth was dry, and his eyes were a bit blurry. Damn! He had forgotten about the early time for the archery contest. He was about to beg off, but something in Kay's dancing eyes made him stop. Instead, he walked over to the stream and plunged his head into it. The shock of the cold water made his skull feel like it would split open, but it had the desired effect.

His head now clearer, Ken walked back to the tent, dripping water. Passing Kay, who watched all this with barely concealed amusement, he fought a tremendous urge to shake water all over her. Back in his tent, he reached for a mug and swallowed the remaining whiskey.

Hair o' the dog. Grabbing his bow and quiver, he again exited.

As Kay and Ken approached the field where the contest had been set up, Kay kept up a cheerful stream of talk, knowing it would irritate her opponent. He gritted his teeth but said nothing. The area

156

was crowded with people eager for entertainment. Kay spotted her friends and waved cheerily. Ken glowered as they walked to the shooting line.

The targets, crudely drawn with charcoal on two birch trees, were at the far edge of the clearing. The trees stood about two feet apart, and were of similar size, but one grew a good foot farther behind the other. Noting this, Ken said, "Perhaps you should take the closer tree, my lady. 'Twill give you the advantage."

Kay immediately responded by taking a step back from the shooting line. "I wouldn't want to give you an opportunity to say you were at a disadvantage m'lord...after I beat you." Loud laughter greeted this remark, and Ken scowled again.

"Would you like the first shot?" Kay asked sweetly.

"Ladies first," he said through gritted teeth.

Kay drew an arrow from her quiver and tested the string again for tautness. Placing an arrow to her bow, she pulled back and took aim. Everyone grew quiet. Kay let loose her arrow and it shot cleanly into the second ring painted on the tree, two marks from the bull's-eye. The crowd made approving noises, but Kay frowned.

"You can warm up a bit, if you like," Ken said.

"Shut up and shoot. You haven't won yet."

Ken drew back, aiming with care. His head still ached, but his eyes were no longer blurry. His shot flew with great power and hit one ring closer to the center than Kay's. The crowed cheered.

Kay did not even glance at the smirking Ken, but prepared for her next shot. Remembering what her grandfather taught her about visualizing her goal, she thought of nothing but...

"A bulls-eye!" Fitzgerald shouted. The crowd gasped in astonishment and cheered wildly. Kay's bull's-eye unnerved Ken, whose next shot was only a third ringer. Kay followed with yet another bull's-eye, to which Ken finally responded with a bull's-eye of his own.

By the ninth arrow, Kay was in a position to win. She badly needed one more bull's-eye to seal the victory. Kay drew back her arrow, when her string snapped, sending the arrow wildly into the field.

"Oh, what a pity," Ken said, and neatly shot his arrow into the dead center, which evened the score. "I guess I win."

"No. We're exactly tied now—we each get one more shot," Kay replied.

"Yes, but your bow is broken. I haven't got all day."

Fitzgerald came running up with another bow. "Use this, Kay. It's a little heavier weight than you are used to, but..."

"Thanks, Fitzy. Shall we continue?" she asked Ken.

"By all means. Your shot."

"No, you go first, please. I wish to get the feel of this bow."

"Very well." Ken took a particularly long time to aim and shot only a third ringer! Kay smiled. All she needed was better than that to win.

She took careful aim and let her last arrow fly. It shot through the air and... missed the tree completely. Kay stared in disbelief. Everyone cheered and thronged around Ken. Kay slipped through the crowd and walked back to the camp, fighting tears.

◆

Sometime later, Ken found Kay by the river, idly throwing rocks in the rushing water. He sat down next to her, but she didn't even acknowledge his presence and continued tossing stones.

Finally, he spoke, "Good match, don't you think?"

"Good for you, anyway."

"Oh, come now, you did fine!"

"What, fine for a *girl*, you mean?" Kay shot back.

"Fine for any person. I know plenty of men who couldn't shoot four bulls-eyes."

"What's your point?"

"My point is—I'm sorry I was so rude to you earlier. And, I must confess that had you not broken your string and had to use Fitzgerald's bow, you...you would have beaten me."

Kay turned to Ken in surprise as he continued. "So... I will accept your idea of having women in our troops—but only if you train them. And only if we can be friends."

Kay smiled. "Gladly. On both counts."

◆

Irene and Silent Susan hurried through the streets, trying to be inconspicuous. Susan led Irene through mostly deserted side streets. They ran on for some time. Irene was amazed at the old woman's agility and stamina. Finally, they came to rest in an alley. The two slumped to the ground behind some crates and tried to catch their breath.

"I... I really don't even know where to run!" Irene gasped. "I just had to get far away from that...that horrid place. I don't know if any of my friends are still here...I have no idea how to find David, and I'm so scared! Everything is just horrible!" She began to cry. Silent Susan patted her shoulder, all the while keeping a careful eye on the entrance to the alley.

When all her tears were spent, Irene sat for a while, thinking. Finally, she spoke. "It is always so gloomy here. How can one even tell if 'tis dawn or dusk?"

Susan mimed the sun going down. Irene nodded.

"Ah—then it will soon be quiet. I think we had best find a place where we can hide by night. Tomorrow we can search for David and maybe the others, if they're still alive. What do you think?"

Susan shook her head and pantomimed one of the great beasts.

"Yes, Susan, but they are on patrol day and night, so we will take our chances and try to blend in by day. At night we'd surely be more conspicuous. Come. Perhaps if we head back to the old temple, it will be deserted again, and we can sleep there." They headed towards the place she had been separated from her friends.

Irene was right. The temple seemed empty, and no one had bothered to repair the service door, so the two had no problem getting in. They explored until they found a small room off the main sanctuary. It had once been a dressing room for the high priests and many robes still remained there. Irene and Susan shook off the dust as best they could and put them on the floor in thick piles for a bed.

"How long until sunrise do you think, Susan?"

Silent Susan held up seven fingers, indicating seven hours. Irene nodded. "Good. Let us eat and try to sleep, for I am so tired," she said. They ate some of the bread and cheese, lay down and were soon fast asleep.

◆

Irene woke early, and for a moment could not remember where she was. In the dim light, she noticed the old woman sleeping nearby and memories flooded back to her. *I wonder if anyone has noticed our absence and is looking for us.*

Suddenly, Irene realized why she had awakened. Outside, she heard the cracking of whips, the shuffling of shackled feet and the cries of the foremen. Irene climbed up on a bench and tried to peer through the window, but it was so dirty, she could hardly see. She spat on the edge of her sleeve and rubbed it on a pane until it was clean enough to look through. Hundreds of slaves were being driven through the city—a sight Irene had often seen from Jean Louis' home. Before, she had only watched out of boredom. Now, she searched desperately for David.

Time wore on and, still, Irene stood, watching group after group. Her legs began to ache from standing on her toes for so long, but she ignored it.

Finally, the parade of slaves came to an end. Irene sighed with disappointment and climbed down from the bench. Maybe tomorrow. As Irene went to lie down again, she heard another group being herded to work. Irene almost ignored it, but finally dragged herself up again to look. Her heart skipped a beat when she spotted David! Again, he was easy to pick out of the pack, even though he appeared even wearier than before.

Irene wanted to open the window somehow and try to signal him, but she knew that would be a mistake. She jumped down and shook Silent Susan awake.

"Susan—he's here. Outside, I mean. David. The friend I told you about—the one Jean sold. Oh, hurry, hurry! I must follow him to see where he is being taken!"

Irene and Silent Susan ran from the room through the sanctuary to the back door. Cautiously, Irene opened it a crack. The alleyway was deserted and in the distance, she could still see David and the others being driven along. Irene and Susan slipped outside. Gathering their cloaks around them, they hurried after the slaves, careful to stay back and well out of sight.

◆

"Well, Your Majesty, supplies are ready for the troops. And every townsperson volunteered space for them," Nan said over breakfast with Gar and Stephon.

"How long do you think it will be before they get here?" Stephon asked.

Gar frowned, thinking. "It is at least a four days' journey to the woods surrounding the Valley of William Etté and I expect it will take some doing to get the refugees all organized and back here. So, it might be a few days yet until they're here."

"I hope the Black Lord doesn't attack before then," Stephon said.

"Yes," Nan said. "But since we do seem to have some free time, I plan on spending it learning some of those dances from your fairies, Gar. It has been too long since I enjoyed myself." She paused. "Oh. I'm sorry. That sounded terribly selfish, didn't it?"

"Not at all, dear girl, not at all," Gar replied. "It has been too long since *many* of us had a good time. Here's an idea. What do you think to having a party?"

"What a wonderful idea, Gar!" Nan bubbled. "I'll be happy to arrange the entertainment."

"How about a costume party?" Stephon asked.

"A masked ball? Yes, that could be fun. And we'll invite the whole township to attend. 'Tis the least we can do after all the help they've given. Fairies! Come hither. Send out a royal decree declaring a party in three day's time. The entire town is invited here to a masked ball—costumes are compulsory."

Nan stared in astonishment at Gar. "How can they possibly get everything ready in only three days?"

Gar waved his hand in dismissal. "It will be no problem for my fairies, Nan. In fact, they could do it in two. I am being generous with three days." He looked at the fairies. "Off you go then!"

The fairies bowed deeply and floated out of the room singing in excitement:

A party, a party—it's time for some fun!
We'll have food and drink and invite everyone.
With music and dancing to last through the night,
And costumes for all—what a wonderful sight!

◆

Ken and the others firmed up plans for gathering the various groups of refugees together. "I think 'twill take three days at the most, Fitzgerald," Ken was saying. "My men will guide you to the camps. Then you can make your case to have them join you."

"They'll join sure enough. They'll want revenge on Richard and his army," Fitzgerald replied. "When do you think we can start training?"

Ken started to reply, but stopped when he heard a commotion outside. He lifted the flap of the tent to see what was going on and hurried out. Fitzgerald and the rest followed. Ken knelt over the body of Paul, one of the men sent in pursuit of Richard. He was gravely wounded, and trying to gasp out his story.

"Richard led us straight to his camp. Eric and Daniel were killed. I managed to escape, but Richard and... his band have sworn revenge. They may be here...any day. I...I..." He gasped and slumped over, dead.

Ken pressed his friend's head to his chest, tears stinging his eyes. "Good work, my friend—you did your best." Releasing Paul's body to rest on the ground, he stood up and addressed some of his men. "Bury him quickly. If what he says is true, our time runs short. Richard's army could be upon us before we can get organized here."

Kay stepped up to Ken. "The solution is obvious. We must send even more people out to find the refugees. Rather than rendezvous here, we should all meet at Garsland. Richard will not find us there."

"Good idea, Kay," Ken said. "Geoffrey! Samuel! Isaiah! Prepare to leave immediately for the refugee camps, and tell the others. In the meantime, we will start to break camp here."

Suddenly everything was a flurry of activity as people ran to attend to their duties.

◆

Irene and Silent Susan managed to trail David and his group without being caught. Through the cobblestone streets they went, just keeping David's group in sight. When they reached the brick-pits, Irene and Susan hid behind a half-tumbled down building to wait and watch.

"I'm sorry to drag you out here, Susan," Irene whispered. "I realize it isn't safe. But I had to know where they were taking him." Susan nodded. "And now that I know, I wish I didn't. What a horrid job!"

As Irene saw David stamp the hay into the mud to make the proper consistency for the bricks, tears welled in her eyes. He seemed so tired and his day's work had barely begun. Irene wished there was some way to let David know she was there. Then she remembered the whistle David had used to signal her. Carefully, she sounded the five notes. David did not seem to notice. A little more loudly, Irene whistled again. This time he did hear, and raised his head from his work to glance in Irene's direction. Irene peered over the wall, so he could see her. His look of amazement was all Irene needed to know she had been seen, and she ducked back down. She heard David return the whistle in answer to her call. Happiness flooded through her, replaced immediately by worry.

What now? I cannot possibly rescue him by myself. And I have no one to help me but Susan. How could she be of assistance? Or even tell me of a plan if she had one?

CHAPTER 27

Within an hour, Ken's men dismantled the camp and they were on the road to Garsland. Kay rode up and down the line, calling out words of encouragement to the others. Suddenly, Kay was cold all over. Everything around her became dim, sounds faded away, and she felt as if she were going to faint. Her horse kept walking along with the rest of the group, but Kay didn't notice. Through the dimness, a scene was coming into focus. Kay strained to make sense of it, but the more she tried, the harder it was to see. Finally, she shut her eyes and made herself breathe deeply and relax. The picture came into view.

Kay saw a camp—Richard's camp—not far behind them. Kay could clearly hear Richard's voice: "I'll get them this time! That fool of a soldier led us right to them. It won't be hard to turn Demetrius back to my way of thinking. As for Fitzgerald and Kay—their deaths will mean little in the long run."

"Kay, are you alright?" Luciano's voice brought her back to the present. "You are pale as a ghost."

"Yes...I'm...I'm fine. Where's Ken?"

"Up front. Why? What's wrong?"

"I... I need to talk to him." She spurred her horse on to catch up with Ken. She found him leading the train of people and talking with one of his men.

"Ken," Kay called out, "I must speak with you at once."

"Of course, Kay," Ken led his horse off to the side and fell in beside Kay. "What is it? More plans for your women soldiers?"

"No. I... I don't know how to tell you this, but I've had some sort of...vision."

"What do you mean?"

"Well, I saw a picture in my mind of Richard and his soldiers. They're behind us. And not just the few we saw him with. He's got hundreds with him now! We've got to take a side path, or maybe double back, to throw them off the track."

"But that would take too much time. We've got to get to Garsland."

"I know, but we are nowhere near ready to fight. We must take evasive action."

"On the basis of a dream? Don't be ridiculous. Go back to the end of the line and make sure everything there is all right."

"Ken, please listen to me. This wasn't just a dream. I've never been so certain of anything in my life!"

"And you've never had a 'vision' before in your life either, have you?"

"No. But..."

"There you are. 'Tis only nerves. Now, please go back in line, Kay. I'm very busy."

Kay tried to protest but Ken rode on ahead. Kay frowned and went back to the rear, unable to shake off her unease.

◆

All morning long, Irene and Silent Susan sat behind the fallen building and watched David toil away in the brick pits. Once, he fell in exhaustion, but managed to stagger upright before the foreman could lay the whip on his back. Irene was hard pressed to keep back the tears when she witnessed such cruelty, but she could do nothing to help.

Finally, a large wagon rattled up the cobblestone street to the pit, and the weary slaves perked up. This was the food wagon, and it meant a break from the work—if only for a brief respite.

Each slave got a bowl of grayish, sticky glop and a hunk of coarse bread. From the slaves' expressions, Irene could tell the meal offered little in the way of flavor, and she could only hope it held some nutritional value. Irene saw David eat his as rapidly as possible—as if to lessen the ordeal.

"Oh, I wish I had something to give him!" she whispered. Irene felt a nudge and turned to see Silent Susan holding a piece of cheese from their own meager food stores. Irene smiled gratefully and crept closer to the mud pit, hugging the wall of the ruins. About ten feet away from David, she softly whistled the code and tossed the chunk of cheese over towards him. It landed next to him and he covered it with a foot, but not fast enough, for the foreman saw it and from where it came. He rushed over to Irene, and hauled her up from behind the wall. Susan darted away and ran.

Meanwhile, David stuffed the cheese into his mouth and moved deeper into the crowd of slaves. Irene fought, but the foreman held her tight. He dragged her over to the cluster of men.

"Awright! Where is he?" he barked, snapping his whip. "Where's the one wot got the food? Speak up, ye bloody bastards—or I'll horsewhip each an' every one of ye! Which one got that bit o' cheese?"

The slaves parted and David stepped forward. "It was I," he said in a shaky voice.

The foreman hauled Irene over to him. "Ye know this wench?"

David looked at Irene and shook his head. "No. I've never seen her before."

The man shook Irene roughly. "What ye be doin' hereabouts, anyways?"

Irene tried to collect her wits. "I...I... uh..."

"Well?" he roared.

"I... work for Jean Louis. Yes, that's it. I work for Jean Louis de la Grande Pomme. I buy his slaves for him. And... uh...I heard you had a particularly fine specimen here. I thought perhaps I would like to purchase him—at a fair price, of course."

At the mention of Jean Louis, the nearby slaves gasped, and the man released Irene's arm. He looked her over, noticing her fine clothing and elegant cape.

"So I came down here with my hand-maiden, Susan, to observe for myself this man of yours," Irene finished boldly. Silent Susan, hearing her name mentioned, hurried over, and bowed to the foreman.

"Well...uh...wot did ye throw that bit o' cheese for, then?" he asked suspiciously.

"I heard a rumor you fed your slaves poorly. A rumor now clearly confirmed! I dare say, had you not stepped in, there might have been a riot over that bit of food!" Irene was enjoying herself now—the lying came so easily. "Wait until I tell my master how you treat your property!"

The foreman glanced nervously from Irene to the slaves and back. "Ah, now, missy, it ain't all that bad. They gets their food and drink alright. And we don't whip 'em. Much."

Irene now drew herself up to her full regal height. "You may well find yourself at the *other* end of a whip when I tell the Black Lord of your conduct!"

The man appeared startled, and his eyes narrowed. "The Black Lord himself, ye say?" he asked.

"Yes, the Black Lord himse... Ouch! What are you doing?" Irene cried out as he grabbed her arm once again.

"Ain't nobody ever seen the Black Lord, much less talked to him. Ye be lyin'!"

Irene realized, too late, the trap she had fallen into and struggled again with the large man. He laughed and began to drag her away. Suddenly, he released her and clutched his head. Moaning, he fell to the ground and Irene could see blood gushing forth, as well as the brick that had done the job so well of freeing her. She grabbed Silent Susan's hand and ran. Guards set out after her, but they, too, were struck down by bricks hurled by David and the other slaves who wanted an opportunity to pay back a little of the harsh treatment they received daily.

The women ran back through the alleys and streets to the temple. They rushed in and didn't stop until they were safely in the cloakroom. Irene threw herself down, saying, "Stupid! Stupid! Stupid!" to herself over and over again.

A noise from the sanctuary caught Susan's ear. She shook Irene to get her attention and motioned towards the door, a finger on her lips. Irene raised her head and listened. Her eyes widened in fear as the sound of footsteps came closer.

"No. Oh, please, no," she whispered.

Susan looked for something to use as a weapon and spied a heavy brass candlestick. Nearly as big as she, the old woman lifted it and stood at the ready. After long moments, the steps halted outside the door. Silent Susan remained by the entrance, candlestick raised high.

The door slowly began to open. Irene felt a scream rise in her throat. Suddenly, it turned into a cry of joy as she stumbled forward into David's arms. Tears spilled, and she clung to him, calling his name over and over.

Silent Susan lowered the candlestick with relief. She watched David try to comfort Irene, but the strain of the past days was too much for him, and he fainted dead away in her arms.

◆

In the land of Gar, the whole township dressed for the masked ball. Kay, Irene, and the others were not far from Nan and Stephon's minds, but the excitement of the party seemed to override their worries, at least for now.

Choosing the costumes had not been easy for Stephon or Nan, as they were guests in Garsland, and had no access to materials. Gar, however, graciously put his fairies at their disposal and allowed them a small sum of gold to purchase what they might need.

After much consideration, Stephon decided to go as a masked highwayman, as a nod to his former profession. He chose all black, with a mask and matching satin cape edged in sequins. Under his direction, Gar's fairies sewed it and Stephon was pleased with the result.

Nan asked the fairies to make her into a forest maiden and was thrilled with what they created—a deep forest-green dress with cut out petals of material on the skirt to mimic leaves. It fit tightly over her slender torso, yet allowed freedom for dancing. The bodice was low cut, but not overly so, and Nan thought she had never seen so lovely a dress. It floated around her as if by magic. A matching green mask completed her outfit.

King Gar was resplendent in silver, with shiny black boots that came just above his knees. He wore an embroidered mask and a black satin cape, and while the mask might have hidden his identity, his silver crown, which he refused to part with, loudly proclaimed it. He greeted his guests as they arrived at his ballroom.

◆

Irene sat, half-dozing, against the wall of the small room of the temple. David lay asleep with his head in her lap. On the other side of the room, Silent Susan also slept on a pile of robes.

Over and over the events of the past few weeks played through Irene's mind. It seemed unbelievable that a little more than a month ago she had set out, happy and content, with her best friend Nan on a picnic. Now, her entire happy life in the Valley of William Etté seemed like a dream that begins to fade upon awakening.

If anyone had told me then where I would be today, I never would have believed it. Eventually, Irene fell into an exhausted sleep.

All was quiet, save the gentle breaths of the slumbering trio. Suddenly, Silent Susan opened her eyes. Why had she awoken? She glanced over at Irene and David, still sleeping. She strained to hear. Nothing. Nervously, the old woman got up and went to the door. Again, she listened carefully, and again she heard nothing. But something felt wrong. Quietly, she opened the door and made her way into the darkened sanctuary, shutting the door securely behind her.

Susan walked a little along the side of the room, stopping every now and then to listen. She thought she detected sounds above her, so she headed towards the stairs. As she reached them, an approaching light drove her back into the shadows. One guard carried a torch, and another followed. Silent Susan wedged herself between two pillars and held her breath as the two men walked by her without noticing. Susan recognized them from the brick pits. Unless she did something, Irene and David were doomed! She darted out from behind the pillars and ran up the stairs, making as much noise as possible. As she hoped, the two guards rushed back in pursuit. Susan had enough of a lead that she was able to get almost to the far back rooms upstairs before being spotted.

When the men saw who it was they stopped.

"It's only the old hag," one said.

"Shall I get her?" the second asked.

"Naw. If she's here, so are the others. We've got bigger things waitin' downstairs. Come on."

The two returned to their search of the temple. When they came to the door of the cloakroom they listened carefully. Certain they heard snoring, they burst in, torch and weapons held high.

"Don't make a move or it'll be yer last!" cried the one.

Irene and David stared in terror at the men, knowing it was useless to resist.

CHAPTER 28

"Bring the prisoners forth!" an imposing figure in a black robe, seated on top of a high dais, commanded. Guards brought David and Irene out from two small holding cells on one side of the otherwise bare, torch-lit courtroom to the foot of the dais.

"What bring these two to my court?" the black-clad figure asked.

"Treasonous acts against the Black Lord," a tall man in the back of the room said.

"State the nature of their crimes."

"The man, a worker in the brick pits, partook of food not in his daily allotment. He ate cheese we determined was stolen from one of the Black Lord's loyal subjects."

"And the girl?"

"She threw him the cheese. She claimed to be a slave trader of Jean de la Grande Pomme, but we discovered she was the intended mistress of his lordship until his untimely death. We now believe she is Jean's murderess. She was in league with a servant from the house of Jean who, unfortunately, managed to escape."

The man looked Irene and David over before speaking. "For your heinous crimes you shall suffer. The man will be returned to the brick pits to work day and night without food or water until he drops dead. The girl will be offered to Jean's harem. They can dispense with her as they see fit. The escaped servant is to be found in the time of one day. Take them away."

"Wait!" A hissing voice, which seemed to come from everywhere, reverberated throughout the room. At the sound, everyone in the room froze.

"I am intrigued by these prisoners," it continued. "I have been watching them since their arrival. The man shows intelligence. I can use him. But do not take him to the Chamber of Mirrors. His mind is of use to me in its present state. However, he will require some...persuasion. I will enjoy that."

"The girl's true identity is Irene, Princess of Cabbage. I want her. The entrance to my private domain is open. Take her to my gate and leave her there. Alone." The voice faded away.

"David!" Irene cried as armed men pulled her from the room.

"Be brave, Irene!" David called back.

The guards dragged Irene to a carriage waiting outside and threw her in. She immediately tried to scramble out, but there were no door handles. The horses jerked the carriage forward and drove past the brick pits before turning onto a bumpy road, which descended deeper into the cavern. Soon Irene could see no buildings, only craggy rocks, which slanted steeply up from the road on either side.

◆

Guards took David to an empty chamber. They told him to strip. Too weary to fight, he obeyed. Another door opened and four servants brought in a large wooden tub filled with steaming water. They motioned for him to get in the tub, and again, David did as they ordered. Two men with cakes of soap began to wash David. After a while, he relaxed a bit from the warmth and gentle motions. The servants scrubbed David from head to toe, assisted him out of the bath and wrapped him in large, thick towels. Silently, they led him to another room.

There, two elderly men dressed David in fine clothes, the likes of which he had not seen since he left his hometown years before to become a faux bandit—fine broadcloth trousers, stout boots, a warm silk shirt and a brocade vest. While he admired himself, two more servants entered, carrying trays laden with plates of hot food. They set the food on a table, politely bowed and gestured for David to take a seat.

Trying to act nonchalant, David strolled over to the table and sat down. He picked up a chicken leg and started to bite into it, when he suddenly stopped and dropped the food back on the plate, staring at it suspiciously.

"'Tis not poisoned, I assure you, m'lord," one of the servants said.

Still, David paused.

"Eat—I pray you."

The same ominous voice that they had heard before filled the room. Now, David was even less certain he wanted to partake of the meal. He hesitated. None of the servants spoke, but they were clearly nervous, and the room was filled with tension. David stared at the good food, his mouth watering. He was so hungry, but he didn't want to obey the Black Lord, as he was certain that was to whom the evil voice belonged. He glanced around the room and his eyes fell on a large mirror. For a moment, David thought he saw a face in it, but when he looked again, it was gone.

Once more David heard the voice, gentle and soft, coaxing him. "Go ahead. You must rebuild your strength, you know. It won't hurt you to try a little." The voice kept softly wheedling David to eat. "Go on...go on..."

David shut his eyes tightly, and tried to think of something else. But the smell of the food was too much for him. With a soft moan he opened his eyes and began to ravenously eat.

The Black Lord began to send ideas and commands into David's mind, so subtly that David was unaware of them. Soon he began to believe the thoughts were his own.

◆

As the carriage rumbled on, Irene heard a high piercing siren, which soon became so loud and shrill that she had to put her hands over her ears. Looking out of the window, she noticed the soldiers in her escort, as well as their horses, wearing protective coverings over their ears, but they offered her no such protection. The noise grew louder until Irene's ears ached and she huddled in the bottom of the carriage holding the seat cushions over her ears.

The escort came to a halt and guards pulled Irene out of the coach. An enormous iron door stood open in a wall. Through it Irene could make out a path, which led to another cavern, which was the source of the shrieking sound. Steam poured from the opening, making everything a glowing red haze.

The soldiers carried Irene to the inner cavern and deposited her on a rock pathway, which was warm and damp. The air was hot and moist and Irene found it difficult to inhale. The soldiers hustled back to the carriage.

The door swung closed behind her with a resounding bang, leaving Irene alone in the midst of the vapors and luminescent red light. She sat on the warm stones, pulled her knees to her chest and covered her ears in an attempt to block out the screeching wail.

"Welcome, Irene, Princess of Cabbage." The same voice from the courtroom now seemed to be coming from inside Irene's head and was even louder than the piercing shriek. Irene curled into a ball. Her eardrums throbbed in agony.

"I would very much like to meet you. Simply follow the path and you will come to the large, black castle in which I live. You had better hurry. I have cooled the rocks temporarily so you can walk on them, but I am sure you feel the intensity of the heat increasing. I advise you to hurry before your feet are burned, or you are permanently deafened by my sentinel's horn. Once inside the castle walls you can no longer hear the wailing which is causing you such pain. Make haste!"

The voice faded away. Irene clutched her hands to her ears and began to run down the pathway. She had no desire to meet the Black Lord, but the hot stones and the shrill noise left her no choice but to head to the castle for the promised relief. The steamy air made breathing difficult as she ran, and she became light-headed. Except for the smooth stone path, the terrain was completely rocky and jagged. Rivulets of red, hot lava flowed down into larger streams alongside her. Irene's head ached and she felt quite dizzy, so she stopped for a moment, panting.

Irene felt a rush of air above her head. Looking up, she saw huge black wings, a beak and red eyes. An enormous flying creature followed her, grasping at her with its claws. Behind it flew three more of the red-eyed birds. Irene screamed and batted at the bird with her hands, but one huge claw grabbed her right wrist. It yanked her along until her feet barely touched the path. She screamed in pain, trying to pull free from the claws. The talons only held her more tightly, tearing her flesh.

The bird pulled Irene towards a black structure in the distance. Its high walls of onyx were so highly polished, the light from the lava and flames reflected all across the building in a demonic dance of light.

When the princess saw the castle, she doubled her efforts to free herself. The bird lifted her a few feet off the ground, but abruptly dropped her. Irene fell in a heap on the path, gasping for air. To her horror, she saw the other three birds coming towards her. She reached for stones to throw at them, but her aim was poor. The birds landed in a circle around her, and began to peck at her. Irene pulled herself into a tight ball, crying with pain. With a thud, one of the birds fell over dead. Irene peeked from beneath her arms to see it had been pierced with a spear. A second spear found its mark in another bird, and the last bird took to the air and flew away. Overcome with heat and exhaustion, Irene fainted.

A creature with a human body, but the head of a reptile, gray and expressionless, came towards Irene. He lifted her in his arms and carried her up a hillside to a large rock on a level spot. The creature laid Irene down, held his hands up and the rock rolled aside. He picked up Irene again, hoisting her over his shoulder, and carried her inside. He raised his hand and the rock slid back into place.

CHAPTER 29

The late afternoon sun beat down on Kay's neck, making her head throb. She longed for nightfall. As she rode on, she became more certain that the band of soldiers, women and children stretched before her were in grave danger. She was deeply troubled by her vision.

"Fitzy!" she called. "I'm going to go back and do a little scouting around. I'll return soon."

"Do you want company?"

"No, I'll be fine, thanks."

Kay rode away from the group at a fast clip, keeping her eye on the road ahead. After riding hard a few minutes, Kay stopped and sat astride the black stallion for a moment, thinking. She looked to the left. She could just make out a narrow path that went up the hill. Spurring her horse on, she took it. Reaching the top of the rise, Kay dismounted. She spotted Ken and the refugees to the northeast through the trees. Kay traced the road with her eyes back towards the southwest. The road was clear but she couldn't see beyond the bend.

Kay remained on the peak for some time, looking for any sign of Richard or his men, but all around her appeared calm and serene. Satisfied, she was about to ride to catch up with Ken when she heard an ominous, low rumbling. She turned and saw soldiers—hundreds of them. Swearing an oath, she galloped back as fast as her stallion would go. She flew past Fitzgerald, Demetrius, and the others until she found Ken at the front of the line.

"Ken! Ken!' she gasped. "Behind us—Richard and his army!"

"How many?"

"I don't know. I spied a hundred or more through the trees. Richard must have gotten word to Lord William, who sent most of his fighting force!"

Ken shouted orders to hasten the mass of people. It was improbable they could outrun Richard and his men, but without weapons and preparation for a battle, they had no other options.

◆

Richard stopped his horse and used his spyglass to look into the distance. He spotted a rider far ahead of his army rushing up the trail at a fast gallop. Even at that distance there was no mistaking the familiar mop of golden hair.

"What is it, Sir Richard?" a soldier asked.

"The rider up ahead of us through the trees will lead us to what we seek. I am certain it is Kay." Richard took sword in hand and raised it high above his head. "Men! Onward!" Two thousand soldiers and horses sprang forward.

◆

Ken and Fitzgerald drove the band of refugees as fast as possible, but it became clear they could not keep up the pace much longer. There were women and children in the group, and too many were on foot. Fitzgerald and Ken tried frantically to think of some way to escape Richard's army. If they turned to fight, their tiny band would be slaughtered in a matter of minutes.

Hearing of the coming attack, Demetrius pulled off to the side of the road until all the others past him. He withdrew the orb from its pouch. It was a deep black-blue, with purple veins running through it. It appeared angry, as if upset it had not been used in so long. Instinctively, Demetrius softly stroked the orb, "Don't worry, you will get plenty of use soon enough." He closed his eyes to concentrate, breathing deeply.

The orb began to change color. It went from black to purple, to lavender, to rose, and finally to bright red. The glow lit Demetrius' face as he bent over it, and it warmed the palms of his hands.

Suddenly, the sky filled with black clouds. A brilliant flash lit up the landscape, thunder rumbled...and then it was as if the very seams of heaven split open to empty as rain poured down. Demetrius' horse whinnied nervously as the rain, driven by fierce winds, drenched both it and its rider.

Up ahead, Kay heard the thunder and stopped her horse. She turned and saw what appeared to be a wall of rain that began where Demetrius sat and stretched back farther into the distance towards Richard's army. Trees swayed in the wind.

The orb! Demetrius must be trying to slow them down. I'll go back to help him. She wanted to tell Ken her plan, but he was too far ahead of her. Kay sped back to Demetrius, slowing down as she approached him, afraid of disrupting his concentration. Now soaked, Kay sidled her steed up to Demetrius. The roar of the storm was almost deafening, and rivers of rainwater were washing out the roads.

Uprooted trees fell and settled into the mud. Straining to see through the darkness and downpour, Kay thought she could discern Richard's army struggling through the mess. They looked to be still a mile or so off.

We need to make our escape soon, she thought, glancing over at Demetrius, who still held the glowing orb. His expression was a mask of concentration. *Why, he doesn't even know I'm here! I had best try to rouse him now.*

Kay reached over and touched Demetrius' arm. A shock went through her body and nearly threw her off her horse. *My word! How can I get through to him?* Kay began to call his name, over and over, screaming at the top of her lungs.

Meanwhile, the muddy roads and the downed trees temporarily stalled Richard and his army. He pulled out his spyglass. Ahead through the downpour he could dimly see two figures on horseback.

"Aha! Demetrius and that traitor, Kay. I shall soon have them." He turned to the soldiers who struggled to move the trees in the road.

"Enough! 'Tis no use!" he shouted. "We will double back a bit and split off. Only the front hundred troops. Send the rest back."

A sergeant came forward. "The front hundred, sir? Won't we need more to capture the entire camp?"

"Time enough for that later, Sergeant," Richard answered. "Something far more useful to us is just ahead."

The sergeant began to direct his men.

Kay looked down the road at Richard's men. What she saw filled her with fear. The soldiers had doubled back and divided. The two groups moved towards her and Demetrius through the forest on either side of the impassable road.

Curses! They will find it easier to climb over fallen logs and brush than walk in the muddy road. I've got to get Demetrius out of this trance!

Again and again, she called his name, while keeping an eye on Richard's men. They were advancing slowly, but steadily. Seeing her shouting was having no effect, Kay grabbed her knife in desperation and, hesitating for a moment, sliced a short cut across the rump of Demetrius' horse. The animal shrieked in pain, reared up and bolted, throwing Demetrius from its back. Kay jumped down off her horse to help him. He sat in the mud, alert and frantically searching for the orb, which had fallen from his hands into the deep muck.

As quickly as it had clouded over, the sky cleared and the rain stopped.

"Kay, help me! The orb, I've lost it!" Demetrius cried as he searched through the mud.

"Not now, Demetrius—we've got to get out of here! Richard's men are within a half mile...or less!"

"I can't leave without the orb!" Seeing it was useless to try and argue, Kay joined in the search. Soon, Kay and Demetrius could hear the men as they stomped through the underbrush.

She grabbed Demetrius' shirt and yanked his face to hers. "Demetrius, if we wait any longer it will be too late! We must flee now! We've one horse between us. The soldiers are on foot. We stand a good chance of getting away, but only if we go now!"

They stared at each other. Then Demetrius nodded. "Very well, Kay, we'll leave." He stood up and took the reins of Kay's horse. He mounted the steed and pulled Kay up behind him. As he turned the animal around to begin their escape, a volley of arrows flew through the air around them. One nicked their horse, causing it to shriek and gallop away. Kay lost her grip on Demetrius and fell back down onto the muddy road.

"Bull pizzle!" she cried in frustration.

"Halt! Or you shall be killed!" a voice called.

Kay saw she was nearly surrounded by Richard's men, although they were a good twenty yards off. Desperate to escape, she tried to climb out of the mud. But the more she moved, the more she slipped and became hopelessly mired. She grabbed some rocks to throw at the men, anything to slow them down. Stuck as she was, Kay could hardly throw them ten feet, and the soldiers only laughed at her efforts.

Kay reached for another rock, when she noticed a light shining through the mud. *The orb!* Kay quickly hid it in her vest pocket and ceased to struggle, realizing she was about to be captured, but also hoping the orb might somehow help her.

◆

Oblivious to the coming danger, everyone at the ball in Garsland was having a marvelous time. Stephon found a willing dance partner in a half-fairy named Marguerite.

Nan was the object of much male attention, and never at a lack of someone to attend to her needs. One tall man with dark good looks was, in particular, quite attentive and as the evening wore on, and as she consumed more of the potent punch, Nan found herself attracted to him.

"What is your name, kind sir?" she asked as he brought her another cup of punch.

"Ah, fair maiden," he said, smiling, "we are not to reveal ourselves until midnight, as you well know."

Nan pouted prettily. It had been some time since she had flirted with a man, and she was enjoying herself immensely. Thoughts of Fitzgerald were far away just now.

"But it does not seem fair!" she continued. "All you townspeople know each other and can easily guess who is behind what mask. As for me, I have never met anyone, really, except for Gar and his fairies."

The man bent to kiss Nan's hand. She pretended to be shocked at his presumptuousness, but her giggling gave her away.

He smiled. "Yes, 'tis true what you say. And all of the town can pick *you* out as one of the strangers to Garsland. Let us take a little stroll, shall we? Then perhaps you can persuade me to tell you my name."

"Oh, but I don't want to miss any dancing," Nan said, coyly.

"Don't worry; there will be plenty of time for that." He took her hand and led her away from the crowd. After a few steps, Nan stopped.

"Really, I *do* think you should tell me your name before we go one step farther."

"Very well. I am the most honorable Turner Blackstone. I hail from Hayward Fields—just south of here." He held out his arm and Nan took it, smiling.

◆

Irene felt a cool hand at the back of her neck, raising her head. She drew back a bit, startled by the liquid on her lips.

"It's only water," a deep voice said. "Drink it. Your throat must be parched. Not too fast. Just take little sips. That's better."

Irene lay back after taking her fill, and opened her eyes slightly. She gasped and recoiled at the hideous creature before her. She wanted to scream or flee but was frozen with fear.

"What is it? What's wrong?" the creature asked. "You needn't be afraid. I want to help you."

Irene looked again at the repulsive, gray lizard face. His whole head seemed to be covered by a hard shell. He leaned closer to Irene in concern, but she turned away. On the cave floor, she spied another head just like his on the ground, and thinking it was decapitated from its body, began to scream. The creature looked to see what caused Irene's reaction and burst out in laughter.

"That's why you're so afraid! I'm so sorry. In my concern for your health, I forgot to take it off." Reaching up, he put both hands firmly on the sides of his head and lifted the lizard's likeness off, revealing a very human face.

"This just serves as a sound barrier for those high pitched noises in the cavern. I can still hear relatively low toned noises with it on...even your scream, but it protects my ears. Luckily, we don't need the devices where we are now...the noise can't penetrate these cave walls."

In relief, Irene studied the handsome man kneeling beside her. He had high cheekbones, an elegant nose, a neatly trimmed beard on a firm jaw line, intelligent blue eyes, and long blondish hair. Irene found herself smiling.

"That's better. It's good to see you smile," the man said. "Would you like more water?"

Irene shook her head. She examined her wrist, remembering the talons of the bird, but there was not a single mark where it had grabbed her. She looked at the man with a puzzled expression.

"You're surprised your hand is unhurt," he said. "I'll explain to you later. For now, please rest. I'll come back in a bit with something to eat."

Irene had a thousand questions, but was too spent to ask them now. She closed her eyes wearily and soon fell asleep. It seemed to be her first good rest since arriving in the land of the Black Lord. After sleeping for many hours, Irene was rudely awakened by a voice.

"I know where you are, little princess. You are out of my reach for now, but I will have you in time. There is no hurry. I am patient."

Irene sat up in fear, her heart pounding. The handsome youth came over to Irene and placed his hand on hers in reassurance.

"Anton!" the hissing voice came again. "Ungrateful wretch! What do you hope to gain by this folly? You will bring me the girl at once, if you do not wish to suffer any punishment. I am prepared to take harsh measures this time. Very harsh! I advise you to obey!"

Anton waved one hand in the air and muttered something Irene didn't understand. The voice faded away. Seeing Irene's panicked expression, Anton said to her, "Don't worry. His power can't reach us as long as we stay in this cave."

"Who are you?" Irene asked.

"I am Anton."

"Yes, I heard the Black Lord say your name, but how is it you are here in his domain and safe from him? How long have you been here?"

"Much of my adult life."

"Why?"

"It is too long a long story to tell now. Here, I brought you some of my clothes and a basin of water to wash yourself. I hope they will suffice, as I have nothing else for you. When you've dressed, please join me in the next chamber. I've prepared a meal, unless you'd like to continue to rest."

"No, I am feeling much better, thank you."

"Good. I'll go see to the food." He turned to go, but Irene stopped him.

"Please. One moment. Tell me, how is it that my wrist is not hurt? I saw...I *felt* the bird's talons tear into me."

Anton hesitated and smiled a little. "Here in the land of the Black Lord, things are not always as they appear." He left the room.

CHAPTER 30

Irene washed and changed into the clothes Anton left her. They were far too large, but she cinched the belt to hold up the trousers, and rolled up the cuffs and sleeves on the shirt. Much refreshed, Irene went into the other room of the cave. Anton squatted by a fire, cooking some sort of meat. The smoke from the fire rose to the cave's ceiling and out a small hole. Irene also spied what looked like potatoes roasting in the coals. Her mouth watered at the sight and smell of the food, and she realized how long it had been since she last ate.

"And only stale cheese at that," she murmured to herself, remembering.

"What's that?" Anton asked, looking up. His face broke into a broad grin as he looked at Irene. "You look marvelous! You should always wear men's clothing."

Irene frowned slightly, not knowing if she should take this as a compliment or not. For a moment they stood awkwardly staring at each other. Then Irene noticed black smoke.

"Oh! You're burning the meat!" she cried. Anton snatched it off the fire and examined it closely.

"Just a bit—it's not too bad." He took a small knife, and scraped off the burned portion. "Sit down. The yams are ready. Sorry I don't have any butter to go with them." He laughed.

"That's alright." Irene nudged a yam out of the coals and onto the cool cave floor. Tossing it from hand to hand to avoid burning her fingers, she dusted it off, and split it open. She inhaled the heavenly aroma that rose from within and sighed with pleasure. Anton handed her a piece of meat on a stick. His hand lingered on hers briefly and their eyes met.

"You...you're quite beautiful," he said softly.

Irene blushed and glanced away.

"I beg your pardon. I didn't mean to embarrass you."

"Oh, no, you didn't. But somehow, sitting in this cave after nearly losing my life to those horrid birds, and knowing the Black Lord is waiting for me like a hungry spider...it really was the last thing I expected to hear."

"Well, I meant it."

"Well...thank you." Irene smiled at Anton, and turned her attention to the food. Anton did likewise, but she noticed he kept stealing glances at her.

◆

The ball continued in Gar's castle and all were having a delightful time. Turner of Hayward Fields led Nan down the garden path to a back gate. They walked slowly and along the way, Turner stole more than a few kisses, which, in her tipsy state, Nan readily gave him. Finally, at the gate, he paused.

"Why are we stopping here?" Nan giggled.

"Oh, I want you to meet some friends of mine." At that instant, the gate door flew open and two men threw a sack over Nan. She tried to scream but Turner whacked her over the head with a stick, knocking her out.

"Hurry," he said to the men. "We can't take the chance anyone will see us."

The men dragged Nan outside the wall. "We know what to do, sir," one of them said. They heaved Nan onto the back of a cart, covered her with rubbish and drove off into the night. Turner smiled at a night's work well done. *Another hundred sovereigns, and the Order of the Holy Snake gets another 'convert.' She'll not be missed.* Chuckling, he made his way back to the party.

◆

Demetrius' horse ran wild for several miles before he finally got it under control. By then, he knew that Kay was Richard's prisoner and there was nothing he could do to help.

"Not without the orb, anyway," he muttered to himself. So he pressed his horse on to catch up with Fitzgerald and Ken. After a half hour, he found them, still on the road to Garsland.

"Ken! Fitzgerald!" he cried. "Kay's been captured. We must go back and save her!"

"How did it happen?"

"She came back to help me and my horse bolted and... what does it matter? We need to go back! Now!"

Fitzgerald and Ken exchanged looks. Demetrius waited.

"No," Fitzgerald finally said softly.

"No?" Demetrius cried. "You're insane!"

"He's right, Demetrius," Ken added. "If we go back, the army would slaughter us. It's probably what Richard is hoping we'll do."

"But...Ken! You don't understand, Richard hates Kay—he'll kill her!"

"Then it's a loss we must accept, Demetrius, much as it hurts. Kay would understand. She would even want it that way, I'm sure." Ken turned his horse back to the road. Fitzgerald took the reins of Demetrius' horse and led him aside his own. Demetrius sat, stunned, unable to react. He thought only of his dear friend, Kay.

◆

Kay, meanwhile, could only think about whether Richard was indeed going to carry out his threat to brand her with a hot iron. He waved it before her—red hot and smoking—Kay could feel the heat from a foot away. She decided to act as nonchalant as possible.

"I've been branded before, Richard, by the gypsies. 'Twill be no new experience."

"Not the way I intend to do it, Kay."

Kay feigned a yawn. "Really, Richard—you used to be such a lot of fun. You're simply too dull for words now."

"Would you prefer it if I turned you over to my men? Many have not had a wench in some time, and I have little doubt *that* would be a new experience for you!" Richard laughed, as he returned the poker to the fire.

Kay felt her face burn. "At least they'd know what to *do* with a woman, Richard! You wouldn't have the foggiest notion, I'm sure!"

With an angry cry, Richard slapped Kay across the face knocking her off the stool. For a moment, the only sounds were those of Kay's and Richard's breathing—hers heavy from pain, his from anger.

Then Kay broke the silence. "Well, your wrist isn't limp at any rate."

Richard screamed for his guards, and ordered that Kay be taken to a small tent on the other side of the camp. Alone, Kay found a tub of water and some rags to clean most of the mud off of her. Once done, she sat down to wait.

Now what?

◆

The fire was dying down as Irene and Anton finished their meal. For a long while, both were silent, each wrapped in their own thoughts.

Then Anton spoke. "You cannot stay here much longer."

Irene turned to him in alarm. "I thought you said we are safe from the Black Lord here. Why must I leave?"

"We *are* safe from his magic powers, but it does not mean he can't find some other means to force us out. He's letting us catch our breath right now."

"But soon the game will continue, is that it? We are nothing more than...than...mice to him! And he's the big black cat waiting by the mouse hole for us to come out. He said earlier he knew David and I were here. He's been playing with us all along, hasn't he? I might as well die now as later—why don't we just leave?" She began to cry.

Anton reached over to Irene and held her. "Please don't cry, Irene. It isn't entirely hopeless. I'll think of something, I promise." He rocked Irene back and forth and continued to murmur reassurance to her as she poured out all the grief and fear bottled up inside her. Finally, she lay silent in his arms.

"I'm sorry to let go like that, Anton. It's just been so very hard," she whispered.

"Shh...I know. Rest a bit now, and I'll try to think of something."

Irene closed her eyes and leaned against Anton. The fire was almost out, and only a few coals gave any light to the cave. As Irene dozed off, Anton tried to think of a way to get Irene safely out.

◆

Nan slowly opened her eyes. Her head throbbed, and although tempted to close her eyes again, something within told her she must find out where she was and what had happened.

The last thing I remember, she thought, struggling to sit up, *was that nice man, Turner, taking me for a walk in the garden.*

Nan looked around. She was in a small room, plain and nearly empty except for the bed in which she lay, a chest of drawers upon which sat a washing bowl and water pitcher, and a plain, wooden chair. On the wall above her bed, she spotted a large cross with something on it. She peered at it more closely and gasped in horror at the snake entwined on it.

Moonlight streamed in through the small barred window, illuminating the whitewashed walls of the room. Her head still aching, Nan eased out of the bed, and stood, weaving slightly. She noticed for the first time her ball gown was gone and a rough woolen robe had replaced it.

Where is my lovely dress? What manner of clothes are these? Where on earth am I?

Nan walked unsteadily to her door and found it unlocked. She exited the room and turned down the hallway. The stone floor, cool to her bare feet, made her shiver. No one else seemed to be stirring in the building as she made her way down a flight of stairs. She thought she heard some music in the distance and decided to follow the sound. She went down another long passageway lit by torches and her heart began to pound in fear as she came closer to the singing. Finally, she stood at the door, which she knew would open into the chanting. Her hand trembled on the wrought-iron door handle, which was shaped like a snake. She withdrew it again, afraid.

The doors suddenly opened and two robe-clad figures grasped Nan firmly on the arms. They pulled Nan towards the front of the room, which realized was a chapel. On either side of the aisle sat rows of veiled women, chanting. Their outfits were similar to Nan's, but of much finer cloth. As she passed them, she could make out part of what they were saying and went cold with dread.

"We thank Thee, oh most High...that Thou should bring us another eager convert...pray she will be found worthy...and join her sisters in the happiness of the Sacred Order of the Holy Snake," the women droned in unison.

Nan wanted to scream, run, fight, but she felt utterly helpless. *This can't be happening—it has to be a nightmare! Surely I am not about to be incarcerated in a convent for the rest of my life!*

But Nan knew she was not dreaming. She had been sold into service to a religious order; a common practice. Fathers would often make a tidy sum selling off excess daughters, and thus avoid having to pay any marriage dowry.

Nan also knew that, unlike those women who go willingly into an order, "sold converts" were called "lay sisters," and held a much lower position in the convent. Usually they wore a slightly different garment and instead of spending the day in contemplation and prayer, they did the work which enabled the order to keep operating—the washing and cleaning and cooking. Although allowed to attend one religious service a day, the life of a sold convert was little more than that of a drudge, and all this ran through Nan's mind as she arrived at the altar.

The head religious figure—the Abbess—stood on the steps above Nan. She wore a wooden cross similar to the one Nan had seen on the wall. On a table next to her lay an even smaller cross, and the maroon collar of the "lay" sister, to mark Nan as one of the lesser sisters in the order. Nan was made to kneel before the Abbess, and the choir began to sing again.

"With this collar, oh most High...bring peace and joy and love to our new sister. And grant that she shall live a long and healthy life, to serve her sisters and Thee for the remainder of her days."

"No..." Nan whispered as the maroon cowl, lavender veil and heavy cross were placed over her head. "Oh, no, please!" But as much as she wanted to run, she could not move. Everything seemed to be running in slow motion and she felt as weak as a baby. The two nuns forced Nan to stand for the charge by the Abbess, who stood with her hands over Nan's head.

"Be faithful, be kind, be true, be strong and...be silent!"

The ceremony completed, Nan was escorted to her room. As she sank onto the bed, she heard the door lock behind her.

◆

The masked ball in Garsland reached a fever pitch as the hands on the giant hall clock moved closer to midnight. Stephon went up to Gar, sitting on his throne.

"Gar, pardon me, have you seen Nan? I can't find her anywhere and she's been missing for some time."

Gar frowned, thinking. "I believe I saw her with that man over there," he said, gesturing towards Turner of Hayward Fields. "Why don't you ask him?"

"Which one?"

Gar pointed out a tall, well-dressed man standing alone by the refreshment table. Stephon hurried over.

"Excuse me, sir, but have you seen my friend, Nan? She's missing and Gar said perhaps you would know," Stephon said all in a rush and stood anxiously awaiting an answer.

Turner took his time in replying, filling his punch cup again before speaking. "Nan? Which one is she? So many fair maidens here tonight, and, as you are aware, we are not supposed to reveal our identity to each other until midnight."

Stephon hurriedly explained Gar had seen the two together earlier. "Nan has red hair and was wearing a green gown. You must remember!"

"Hmm. I don't recall anyone by that description. Gar must be confused." Then, in a conspirator's whisper, "He has been drinking quite a bit tonight." His tone turned cool. "No, my good man, I am certain you must have the wrong person. I do not know this Nan you speak of." He strolled away.

Stephon stood by the table, frustrated and worried. It wasn't like Nan to disappear. His concerns were interrupted by Gar standing on his throne, hushing the orchestra and crowd.

"It's nearly midnight!" he cried. "Get ready to reveal yourselves, if you haven't already done so to that special someone."

The township laughed and began to count out the final strokes of the big clock. On the last one, the revealing would take place.

"Eight...nine...ten..."

The ballroom doors flew open and Demetrius, Fitzgerald and Ken rushed in.

"Your Majesty, quick!" Fitzgerald shouted. "We've no time to lose! Richard's army is coming to destroy us all!"

PART TWO:
JOURNEY TO THE KEEP

CHAPTER 31

Everything erupted in panic. Women shrieked and fled to their homes to gather their children, pack what they could, and prepare to escape. Men gathered around Ken, Demetrius and Fitzgerald to take their orders, collect weapons and set up a perimeter of defense. Within an hour, all the men from the ball, as well as the newly arrived refugees, were in position, awaiting Richard's army.

In fact, however, Richard's troops were nowhere close to attacking. While a small band of soldiers had followed the fleeing refugees to the edge of town, they set back at once to rejoin the rest of the army, now camped several miles away.

Most of the camp was asleep by this time, except those on guard duty.

Kay was dreaming of a handsome man caressing her. She smiled in her sleep and rolled over. The stroking became bolder and, as she started to wake, Kay realized she was not dreaming!

Her eyes flew open and she saw a man lying next to her on the bear-skin rug of the tent. He had one hand under her neck and the other was traveling all over her body. Before she could scream, his lips were on hers, cutting off any sound. Fiercely she struggled, trying to hit him, but he grabbed both her wrists together in one of his large hands and pinned them firmly above her head.

Dear Heavens! Am I to be raped? Is Richard making good on his threat?

Tears sprang to Kay's eyes and she tried again to scream, but it only came out muffled. Her head swam, and she found it hard to breathe. The man was now half on top of her; his lips moved to the small of her neck. Her mouth now free, Kay gasped for breath as he fumbled at her shirt. She cried out, but he paid no attention.

If I don't do something soon, 'twill be too late!

Kay summoned all of her willpower, relaxed her body and said in a cool tone, "Is that the only way you can have a woman, sir? By forcing her against her will?"

189

Her words had the desired effect. The man stopped cold. Slowly, the man removed his hand from Kay's wrists and the other from her breast. She lay still until he rolled off of her, then sat up and scooted away from him, gathering her clothes about her. They stared at each other across the small tent.

He was not bad looking; in fact, one could well call him handsome. But he was unshaven, and appeared bleary-eyed from too much drink. Though she couldn't place him, he looked familiar to Kay.

After a moment, he said, "Ye belong to me. I bid the highest for ye, and if I wants ye—I'll takes ye. Make no mistake about that, Kay."

Kay gasped at her name. He knew her! He wasn't just some drunken soldier who had wandered in her tent. As his words sunk in, her surprise turned to anger.

"You mean...I was...auctioned off?" she sputtered.

The man smiled, his white teeth showing bright in the dim tent. "Aye, missy, and I paid nearly three months' wages for ye. So, now ye'll kindly shut yer trap and let me get me money's worth." He reached for her again.

Kay scurried over to the far wall of the tent. "I'll not be any man's property! Paid for, or not!"

He laughed, caught her by a leg and dragged her over to him.

Kay tried to fight him off but he was much stronger than she.

Again, he pinned her down as he kissed her forcefully, and caressed her body as if he did, in fact, own it.

Kay thought she would faint.

When her lips were finally free from those of the stranger, she said, "Of course, if that's the only way you can get a woman—by purchasing her—I don't wonder you act so rough."

The man sat up, pulling Kay with him. Gripping her, hard, by the shoulders, he growled, "I've had plenty a wench come to my bed eagerly, ye little brat. I won't force ye now—but there'll come a time, and soon, when ye'll want me as much as I want ye!"

"Never!" Kay hissed in his face.

"Don't make promises ye can't keep, Kay." He got up, pulling Kay along with him.

"Where are you taking me?" she asked, suddenly afraid.

"To my tent. Ye belong to me whether ye like it or not, Kay and ye will sleep in my tent even if ye won't sleep with me." He grinned at her. "Yet."

"No!" Kay cried, pulling away from the man. He only grabbed her and slung her easily over his shoulder like a sack of grain. Kay beat her fists against his back and received a stinging slap on the buttocks for her trouble. They passed Richard's tent and Kay saw him standing there, grinning.

"You'll soon lose that which you value most, Kay!" he laughed.

"Richard! I'll get for you this if it takes the rest of my life! Do you hear me?" But he had already entered his tent, still laughing.

The man came to his own tent and ducked in, closing the flap behind him. He unceremoniously dumped Kay on the rugs. She immediately scrambled to her feet and tried to push past him, but he caught her and kissed her again. This time, however, his kisses were gentle and soon Kay's head swam, her body tingled, and her knees became weak. She relaxed and moaned slightly as he kissed her along her neck. He slowly took off her vest and then began to untie her shirt. Suddenly, she pushed herself out of his arms. "No! You promised—you said you wouldn't force me," she said in a shaking voice.

He laughed. "I won't have to force ye soon, Kay—ye'll want me. I told ye that."

"And I told you, no!"

In response, the man calmly took a piece of rope and cut off two short lengths. He tied Kay's hands together then forced her to lie down while he bound her feet together.

"Just a precaution. I don't want to wake up and find three month's wages gone."

"Please let me go," Kay pleaded, near tears. "I'll pay you well—six months' wages!"

"Ye be the only payment I want." He pulled a robe over her and lay down beside her. Kay edged away, but it did no good. He brought her back close to him and closed his eyes.

"Wait. Who *are* you? Why do you want me so much? A... a good looking man like you could have any girl. Why me?"

The man slowly opened his eyes and stared at Kay intensely. A shiver ran through her. He smiled. "And not five minutes ago ye accused me of only being able to get a woman by raping her."

He shut his eyes and pulled Kay tighter to him once more. Kay tried, unsuccessfully, to squirm away. "But who *are* you?" she persisted. "It isn't fair you know who I am but I can't know who you are!"

"If I tell ye, dammit, will ye shut up and leave me to sleep?" he barked. Kay nodded. "My name is Seamus. Seamus of O'Connell's Way in the Secret Valley. Now go to sleep."

Kay felt far from sleepy. All at once, she remembered exactly who the man was. Her mind flew back to one of the rare balls held in the Valley. Seamus had repeatedly asked her for a dance and she had turned him down. When she finally relinquished and promised one to him, he had been so happy—but she had danced with Fitzgerald instead.

As if reading her thoughts, Seamus chuckled softly and gripped Kay even more tightly to him. "Ye may have refused me then, Kay," he whispered, "but never again. Ye be mine now and yer precious Fitzgerald can't save ye."

Together they lay on the rugs of the small tent. After a while, Kay heard snoring and knew he was asleep. She allowed tears to slip down her face.

Mirn help me! What am I going to do?

◆

"We needn't rush into battle," Richard said to his top officers as he sat cross-legged on the rugs inside his tent. "Now that we know where they are, we'll let them sweat a bit before we attack. Day after tomorrow, we shall break camp and divide our troops. One half will proceed southwest to make a large arc on the western slopes of Garsland. The other half will travel northwest to make a like arc to the east of Garsland. The army will rendezvous around the town and close the two arcs into a circle. The morning mist will give us cover until we are nearly upon them. Questions?"

"Yes, sir," a burly-looking lieutenant said. "What if the sky opens up and blocks us with a torrent of rain and hail, like today?"

"I think it highly unlikely such an aberration of nature should repeat itself. Now, I advise you to get a good night's rest. Garsland will soon be ours."

◆

Kay lay next to Seamus in the small tent, unable to sleep. Seamus' muscular right arm held her securely about the waist as he slept. To her chagrin, Kay found she almost liked the feeling of a strong man lying beside her.

How can I be thinking thoughts like this when all I hold dear is at risk? I would rather die in battle than be a slave and plaything to this man. But what can I do? Richard's seasoned soldiers are almost certain to defeat the inexperienced peasants in Garsland. If only I could get the orb to them—to Demetrius—they might have a chance.

Kay gasped. *The orb! Where is it? I put it in a pocket of my vest, but where is the vest?*

She raised her head and looked around the tent. She saw a bundle of clothes in a corner but, in the dark, she was not sure it was her vest.

How could she get it? Seamus hadn't moved his arm from her for hours and showed no signs of doing so.

Carefully, Kay tried rolling away from him. As she did so, Seamus stirred and made a guttural sound. His arm pulled her tight once more. Kay lay still, thinking. Suddenly, she began coughing loudly, and thrashing around in order to wake Seamus.

"What is it?" he asked.

"Help me! I'm choking!" Kay gasped out between coughs.

Seamus whacked Kay on the back, but she continued to cough and soon was gasping for air.

"Water!" she managed to sputter.

Seamus looked skeptical but his attitude softened when he saw the tears in her panicked eyes. "Alright, I'll get ye some water. Stay put."

"I can't...go far...with these," Kay indicated the ropes binding her hands and feet. "Please, hurry!"

Seamus nodded and took an empty whiskey flask to fill with water from the stream on the other side of camp. Kay kept coughing until she was sure her captor was too far away to hear her. Then she inched her way on her hands and knees towards the clothing she had seen in the corner. She found it was indeed her vest, but the orb was not in the pocket.

She scrambled back to the bedclothes and searched through the still-warm rugs, as well as Seamus' discarded coat and boots, without success. She sat back in frustration when her eye caught a pale, yellow glow coming from outside the tent. Scooting forward, she pulled back the tent flap and there, on the ground, was the orb.

Seamus must have kicked it outside when he left. Kay grabbed it in her bound hands.

Crawling back inside the tent, Kay clutched the orb to her breast, gratefully. Suddenly, it became too hot to handle, and she dropped it. A small beam of light shot out from the orb, and burned a hole through the top of the tent.

"Oh no!" Kay said in a hushed voice as she grabbed the glowing ball once more. The light beam changed directions and burned a hole in the sole of one of Seamus' boots.

"Oh, Mirn! Please, stop!"

Then, quite by accident, Kay turned the orb in her hands and the light beam burned right through the rope binding her. In an instant, her hands were free. Kay immediately aimed the orb at her feet, and again, the light burned through the ropes, freeing her. The orb turned dark and cool again.

Kay quickly donned her vest and boots and secured the orb in the vest pocket again.

She peeked out of the tent. Finding no one about, she ran as fast as her legs would carry her. She was thinking how lucky she was there were no guards in sight when she heard racing steps behind her. She pushed herself to the limit, but soon two strong arms grabbed her, and she was rolling on the ground with someone. Kay struggled to get away, but was no match for the man she wrangled with.

"Thought ye'd get away, eh?" Seamus taunted. "Crafty one. Water it was ye wanted? Then it's water ye'll have!" Seamus hoisted Kay over his shoulder and walked with long strides as Kay hit his back and kicked. He carted her around the perimeter of the camp, singing a bawdy tune:

"There once was a girl named Kay,
A virgin, or so they all say.
She's now in the army,
And keeping quite warm-y
By giving her virtues away!"

"Keep kicking, girl! I like a wench with fire!" Seamus said, laughing.

"Unhand me, you uncouth braggart!"

"Ah, no. Ye need to be taught a lesson. There's the water ye wanted so much!" He dumped Kay in the shallows of the river.

"You bastard!" Kay screamed when she came up to the surface. "It's freezing!"

"Come on out of there and I'll warm ye up," Seamus smirked.

"No, thanks. I'd rather catch pneumonia! What's to keep me from swimming away?"

"Don't try it. I can out run ye and I can out swim ye as well. Come out."

Kay deliberated for only a moment. The river was cold. She came to shore. Seamus wrapped his shirt around Kay's shoulders, took her hand firmly and walked her back to his tent. By the time they were inside, Kay was shivering.

"Take off those wet things," Seamus said.

"You wish!" Kay said through chattering teeth.

"Do it! It's for yer own good. I promise not to be making any advances on ye tonight...I can't afford to miss the sleep with the battle coming. Here. I'll even turn around while ye get undressed."

As much as Kay hated to admit it, she knew she could not stay in her wet clothes all night. Quickly as she could, Kay peeled off her garments, taking care that the orb remained deep inside her vest pocket. She did her best to spread her clothes out so they would dry a bit and dove under the rugs. Seamus joined her, and true to his word, he did not touch her again all night. He did, however, take the precaution of binding her feet and hands again. Kay lay shivering for some time before the warmth from Seamus' body took the chill off of her, and she finally fell asleep.

◆

In Garsland, the townspeople armed themselves with swords and crossbows, and stationed themselves around the perimeter of the village. All through the night they waited for the inevitable battle, but none came. By morning, the weary soldiers badly needed rest after reveling half the night and keeping watch the other half. Ken became impatient and urged the citizens to leave Garsland and travel northward, but they would not leave their beloved village.

Tempers became short the next day. Fights broke out between men over trivial matters, and by the time the sun set, nearly everyone was moody and restless. That evening, some of Ken's men broke into the store of liquor in a tavern and soon became drunk and unruly. Ken and Fitzgerald looked on in dismay. The townspeople were exhausted from lack of sleep, and one by one, they left their posts, or fell asleep, convinced Richard and his men were not coming after all.

Demetrius and Fitzgerald, who had served with Richard, knew this was not the case. They tried to convince everyone the battle would surely take place soon, but few believed them. Finally, Gar, Stephon, Fitzgerald, Luciano and Demetrius gave up and went to the tallest tower of Gar's palace to keep vigil. They scanned the landscape two at a time, while the others dozed.

When the sky was at its darkest, Fitzgerald and Demetrius noticed three strange stars out of the south...they were quite large, and shone bright blue in color. They hung in the sky, like beacons, keeping watch over the scene.

CHAPTER 32

"Anton, we must flee from this place—and soon," Irene pleaded.

"I wish we could. It is, however, a bit tricky."

"I cannot stay in this cave knowing the Black Lord lies in wait for me."

"Patience, Irene. His magic cannot reach us here. I have lived here a very long time and he has never been able to break the bonds of my dwelling."

"How can that be? I was told the Black Lord's power is enormous."

"Yes, he is strong. But there is one element even he cannot defeat. Goodness. He abhors it. He shrinks from it. You see, he can only conquer those who fear him. He uses illusion to convince men their lives are in danger and when men fear, their only concern is survival. They will push anyone aside for the sake of their own life, and in so doing, they become vulnerable to the Black Lord's evil influence."

"It seems so simple then to defeat him."

"Ah, yes, but he is crafty. He has a thousand ways to infuse men with terror—then they are his."

"But, how do you know all this? Have you seen him?"

Anton did not reply, but stared into space as if he were remembering.

Irene asked again. "Please, Anton. Tell me. How do you know so much about the Black Lord?"

"It's a long story, but for now, let me just say yes, I know him. Better than anyone. Now, please, you must get some rest while I make plans."

"You should sleep, too. I have been here, what...two days now? And I have never seen you sleep."

"I rarely sleep."

"How is that possible?"

"I cannot afford to. Not truly. It is the price I must pay."

Irene slept for what seemed a long time. When she awoke, lights filled the cave and she sat up, her heart racing. There was a gaping hole in the roof and flickering light poured in from a fire above. In panic, she called out Anton's name, but there was no answer. She raced about the cave, calling for Anton, but he was gone. Cautiously, she hoisted herself up to the opening and looked around. There, in the distance was the black onyx castle. Anton stood near the entrance. He beckoned to her, smiling. All at once, the fire and molten lava died down.

"Irene, come to me! Do not be afraid. All is safe. The Black Lord is not here," he called.

"Where is he?" Irene shouted back.

"Far away. Come here. I want to show you something."

"I don't...."

"Don't worry. You are safe with me."

Irene hesitated. Anton was acting strangely, and his smile seemed somehow different. Irene felt something on her hand. She looked down to see a large spider on it. She screamed and brushed it off. She saw, to her horror, the entire cave was filled with spiders. She pulled herself out of the hole and ran to Anton.

"Spiders! In the cave—hundreds of them!" she gasped.

"Never mind, you are safe now." Anton slipped his arm around Irene's waist. "Come. I want you to tour the most magnificent palace ever built."

"We're not going *in* there, are we?" Irene asked, pulling back.

"I told you, the Black Lord is gone. It is perfectly safe."

"You are certain?"

"Trust me."

Anton took Irene's hand and guided her inside. The castle had walls of black onyx, stretching twenty feet to the ceiling, from which hung several chandeliers. Numerous staircases swept at odd angles away from the main room to other parts of the building. All was cold and silent.

"Where is the Black Lord?" Irene asked.

"He's gone."

"Where? How?"

"Why? Do you want to meet him?"

"Of course not. I just don't feel safe here. Let's leave, Anton."

"But don't you find this all beautiful? Come, I'll show you the rest."

"No. I don't want to see any more. I'm frightened. Please, let's go."

"It's all perfectly safe."

"Anton..."

"Call me Anthony. I don't like Anton. Say it. Anthony."

Irene stared at Anton, perplexed. "Why are you acting so strangely? What has happened to you?"

"Nothing. Now say my name. I want to hear you say Anthony."

"Anthon..." Irene broke off. "I can't...I don't understand what's happening."

"I find you very attractive. I've been alone for so long. I need you, Irene. I think I'm falling in love with you." He pulled her closer. "I know things seem strange to you, but you are in no danger. I'll protect you."

"Yes, but...I just don't know who to trust anymore."

"You can trust me; I saved your life, remember? I'm sorry if I seem odd to you. I haven't been around people for many years. I guess I don't quite remember how to behave."

"I think I understand."

"I've been so lonely. You can't imagine how horrible such solitude can be."

"I'm so sorry. It must be terrible, being trapped here all these years. And," Irene smiled shyly, "I have a confession. I think perhaps I'm falling a bit in love with you, too."

Anton laughed with delight and grabbed Irene about the waist, lifted her and swung her in a circle. When he set her down, he looked into her eyes longingly and kissed her. The kiss was like nothing Irene had ever imagined. It overpowered her and left her feeling weak and dizzy. Each kiss seemed to take all her strength from her, but at the same time she could not get enough of them. The strength of the emotions running through her frightened her however, and abruptly she pulled away.

"No, please stop."

"Why? I love you, Irene. I need you."

"Not here—I'm frightened."

"I told you, there is no reason to be afraid."

Anton began kissing her once more. This time Irene was too weak to fight him off. Anton moved a hand to her shirt and began to tug at it as he eased her down to the floor. Irene wanted to stop, but her head swam with desire. She was only vaguely aware of what Anton was doing, but something felt deeply wrong; she no longer had control over her feelings. She was half undressed and there was something undeniably evil in her feelings. She struggled to regain control and as she pulled back from Anton and looked up at him, she gasped in horror. His once beautiful blue eyes had turned the color of blood.

When Anton saw Irene's panicked expression, he laughed—a sound that suggested something more animal than human. All this was more than Irene could bear and, mercifully, she fainted dead away.

CHAPTER 33

Irene opened her eyes. She shivered and sat up on the cool, onyx floor. She was still inside the Black Lord's castle and fully clothed. Had it all been an illusion? She needed to get back to the cave and find Anton. She rose and went to the door, but found it locked. She searched for another exit. Five stairways led from the main hall to the upper floors. Irene chose one and began to climb. To her dismay she found it led nowhere, ending as it reached the ceiling. She returned to the hall and tried another set of stairs. These ended in a small, windowless room with a lighted torch on the wall. The empty room stank of something vile.

Irene turned back again and when she got to the main room, she heard a voice some distance off. Someone was crying for help. Irene thought the voice sounded like Nan! She followed the voice down a narrow hallway. The ceilings of the hall became lower and lower the farther she walked until Irene was forced to stoop down. The voice came from behind a door at the end of the hall. It was definitely Nan's voice calling for help. Irene grabbed a heavy ring on the door and pulled. As it scraped the floor, Nan's voice ceased. Irene stepped into a frigidly cold room. It was empty.

"Nan? Nan, are you here?"

Silence. Irene turned to leave when a fluttering sound above her made her glance up. There were the huge birds that had attacked her before, roosting in the rafters. Irene fled the room.

The hallway was now flooded with light coming from the main hall. Sweet music of a flute and mandolin drifted to Irene's ears. As she entered, she saw a hundred lit candelabras floating in the air. A man stood smiling at her—Michael of Yorkshire, as handsome as she remembered him.

"Michael! Thank Mirn it's you!"

The tall, blonde man smiled and held his hands out. As Irene took them, he began to sway with the music, pulling Irene into his arms.

Irene thought it was hardly the time or place to dance, but she was unable to resist the lilting melody.

The pair swept the length of the room and back again. Irene searched Michael's face. It was vacant and dreamlike. She pulled a hand free and waved it in front of his eyes, but he didn't appear to see. Irene tried to get away, but he held her tightly. She shut her eyes to gain control of herself, but her feet would not stop dancing. Soon, she was so dizzy, she had to open her eyes again. To her horror, the face she was looking into was no longer Michael's. The man holding her so tightly now was Jean Louis!

Irene screamed and broke free from Jean's embrace and raced up yet another stairway. Laughter echoed behind her. The stairs led to a dim hallway, with many doors, but Irene couldn't open any of them. She finally huddled on the floor behind a small table, trying to sort out what was going on.

None of this can be real. This horrid place is playing tricks on me! Jean Louis is dead; Nan escaped; Michael can't possibly be here.

Irene heard footsteps and tried to conceal herself. A tall, slender figure appeared at the top of the stairs.

"Irene, are you there?" Anton called. "Please! Answer me."

Irene tried not to make a sound. She knew that somehow, Anton had something to do with this awful place.

"Irene. There's no time to lose. We must leave this place now. Where are you? This is no trick. I can guess what has been going on since you entered this castle. You probably can't tell what is real anymore, but I'm real, I swear to you. Please, Irene. We have to get out of here, before the Black Lord comes back."

Anton was close to Irene now. Her only chance was to catch him off guard. She sprang to her feet and bolted past him before he realized what was happening. She raced back down the stairs to the main room, now empty. Seeing the front door open, Irene made straight for it. As she was about to run through the door, a man stepped in front of her. Anton! His red eyes stopped her in her tracks and before she could turn to go the other way, the Anton who had been chasing her crashed into her. They both tumbled to the floor.

In shock, Irene looked from the Anton on the floor to the one still standing. They were alike in every way, except their eyes.

The blue-eyed Anton beside her slowly stood. "Brother, I cannot let you do this," he said.

"I don't see how you can stop me," the other Anton replied, cocking his head.

"What do you want with this skinny girl? She means nothing to you, and a great deal to me."

"I know. That's half the reason I want her."

The two men sized each other up. They seemed to be trapped in each other's gaze. The one nearest Irene gestured for her to get up.

201

"Irene," the blue-eyed Anton said calmly, "leave. Now. Wait for me outside."

"But, Anton, what..." began Irene.

"Go! I can't keep this up for long!"

Irene darted past the red-eyed Anton and escaped outside, stopping a safe distance from the castle. She anxiously waited until Anton finally appeared. He stepped out of the castle, turned around and held his hands to the huge doors. They slowly swung shut. Then he turned wearily and walked to Irene, sinking to his knees beside her. Irene assisted Anton back to the cave—it was as it was before, no spiders, no gaping hole. That, too, had been an illusion.

"In some ways I am still stronger than he is," Anton said as he slumped on the cave floor. "But I fear his power will soon be too much for me."

"Who *is* he?"

"That is my twin, Anthony, better known as the Black Lord."

"Your *brother* is the Black Lord?"

"Yes, I was going to tell you about him today. I think he sensed it. He fooled me to get me out of the cave and then lured you to the castle. I'm so sorry, Irene. I should have been prepared for his tricks."

"How did he come to be the Black Lord?"

"Have you ever heard of necromancers or wizards?"

"Yes, but those are only stories, aren't they? I've seen some old men who call themselves wizards, but they seem only to do common magic tricks."

"Long ago, there were true wizards—many of them, with great power. I know this, Irene, because *I* am a wizard, as is my brother. We are the last. At least, I think we are. There may still be a few old ones left; they went into seclusion. They wished to live out the rest of their lives at a place called Wizards' Keep."

"But how is it that your brother is so evil? I always heard wizards were good."

"Yes, we are pledged not to interfere with the lives of mortals at all, but Anthony refused to take that oath. He couldn't. Something...happened to my brother and me in the womb. I inherited all the potential for good, and Anthony, all the traits of evil. He worships the dark side. Worse, he wants to rule this land and make mortals like you his slaves."

"But can't you defeat him?"

"It's doubtful." Anton sighed. "He is as strong as he is evil. If I fight him directly, I could very well die. By staying here, I can at least ensure he doesn't leave the cavern. If he did, believe me, the land above and its entire people would soon be his. As it is now, he can only direct some mortals to do his evil work for him."

"And they're doing a good job of it," Irene said, thinking of Lord William. The two sat silent for a moment. Irene had an idea. "What about the old wizards? Can't they help you?"

"I don't know. When a wizard becomes old, his power begins to dwindle. In any case, I can't leave and go to Wizards' Keep to find out if they will help. I am all that is keeping Anthony from going above to wreak havoc. Plus, the old wizards might be dead by now. The last time I saw any of them, they were well in their fifth century. And most sorcerers don't live past 630 or 650 at the most."

"That old?" Irene exclaimed. She paused, and then peered at him closely. "Anton—how old are *you*?"

"167."

CHAPTER 34

Fitzgerald galloped towards Gar's palace from a scouting mission, jumped off his horse, and ran up the circular staircase to the tower where Gar, Stephon, Luciano and Demetrius waited.

"They're here! Richard's army is beyond the hills preparing for battle," he said, gasping for breath.

"How many are there?" Demetrius asked.

"I don't know—a lot. Maybe twice as many soldiers as we have."

"And twice as well trained," Demetrius said grimly.

"Well, let's sound the alarm," Gar said. "We have a war to fight."

"Right," Demetrius said. "Fitz, help me get the soldiers assembled. Gar, Luciano, and Stephon, stay here and keep watch. Ring the bell, if you see anything."

Demetrius and Fitzgerald managed to roust the sleeping soldiers and tell them to ready for battle. The men shook off the effects of the liquor, grabbed their weapons, stationed themselves at their posts, and waited.

◆

In another part of the forest, Kay stared at the old hag stirring the ashes of a dying fire with a stick in one hand. In the other, she held a club. Seamus had told the woman to smack Kay if she made any move to undo the ropes that tied her hands and feet. Kay still had the orb, safe in her vest pocket. If only the old woman would turn away long enough for her to retrieve it, perhaps she could escape the ropes as she had before.

Kay heard a distant whooping sound and recognized the war cry of Richard's army.

They must be attacking. Oh, no. It would take all the powers that be to help Gar and his village now.

The old woman walked over to the cliff to observe the action in the valley below. She kept looking back to check on her captive, but it was the chance Kay had been looking for—a few seconds was all she needed to fumble the orb from her pocket. It glowed bright red, which Kay found impossible to keep covered. The old woman spied the light.

"Hey, now, what ye got there? Put it down, or I'll club ye!"

"Whatever power you may have, don't fail me now," Kay beseeched of the glowing orb.

"Didna' hear me?" the woman yelled, still near the edge of the cliff.

Suddenly, a breeze came up. It was gentle at first but then, violently, swooshed up debris into the old woman's face. She stumbled back a few steps, dropping the club. The wind pushed harder, forcing the woman back to the edge, where she wavered for a moment, struggling mightily to regain her balance, before falling backwards, screaming as she fell.

The wind died down immediately and the orb changed appearance again. A grey, muddy matter oozed out of the sphere. Startled, Kay dropped the orb, and tried to get the gray mud off her hands. Some fell onto the ropes, and to Kay's surprise, her bonds dissolved where the gray stuff touched it. Quickly, she rubbed the mud on the rope around her ankles, breaking free. Kay pocketed the orb and started running towards the battle. Halfway down the hill to the road, she came upon three pack horses tied to a tree. Kay tore off the baggage, grabbed the reins of one and jumped on. She kicked him mercilessly to reach the battle.

Kay could barely stay on without a saddle, but she gripped her knees tightly and hung on to the reins and the horse's mane until her knuckles were dead white. Low branches scratched her face, but she didn't even notice. The horse tripped on a rocky patch in the road, but Kay regained control and resumed her reckless speed.

Soon, Kay saw both armies up ahead. Her horse stumbled on a jagged rock and Kay lost her grip and flew onto a bed of moss and ferns. Getting up, she winced at a twinge in her ribs, but at least she escaped serious injury. The horse limped away. Kay let him go, knowing he could be of no more use to her.

Holding her side, Kay began to run. Through the trees she caught glimpses of the back of Richard's army kneeling in rows with crossbows. At the bottom of the hill, she got a cruel surprise. The army had destroyed the only bridge over the river, which was both swift and wide. Kay stood in agony, knowing she wasn't a strong enough swimmer.

She looked back to the battle. Garsland was being crushed. Flames rose from the village. The bodies of slain men and horses dotted the countryside. Kay nearly cried in frustration. She took the orb from her pocket and held the ball to her heart.

"Please. Oh, please, if ever I needed you, it's now," she pleaded. "Do something. Anything! Stop this massacre, I beg of you!"

She felt the orb grow cold in her hands and looked down to see it glowing deep blue. Then a blue light shot out of the orb and spread towards Garsland, widening like a mist until it covered the entire landscape. Kay stared in astonishment as the blue haze reached the soldiers and everything froze in place. Even the flames became still and solid, as if made of glass. The river stopped flowing and was smooth as a pond. She quickly swam across to the other side.

On the battleground, Kay walked around in amazement. Men were statues. Arrows hung in the air waiting to fall. Swords, mere inches from bodies, were stopped from their fatal thrust, and horses were impossibly positioned on a single hoof. All stood frozen as Kay rapidly made her way through the blue mist. Along the way, she grabbed a bow and quiver of arrows for herself.

Outside the center of town, Kay came across Demetrius. He lay on his back. Above him, a frozen, grim-faced soldier stood ready to plunge a knife into her friend's neck. Kay knelt beside him, wondering what to do. She touched his shoulder and murmured, "Oh, Demetrius," and at once, he was revived. He blinked once, twice, and quickly scurried out from under the threatening man, who remained frozen.

Kay and Demetrius soon discovered that all they had to do was speak someone's name to free them from the spell. They went through the village calling the names of the soldiers and townspeople as they came upon them. Brought back to life, the villagers assisted in identifying people. Soon, all the refugee soldiers and citizens of Garsland were released from their frozen state, while their enemies remained like statues.

Fitzgerald suggested their soldiers move most of Richard's soldiers into the path of arrows. Some objected to this, but others said it was only practical, since Gar's castle did not have a dungeon and they couldn't take the men prisoner. With Gar's approval, they set to the task. There would be few of Richard's soldiers left alive to pursue them.

The blue mist was fading, and the townspeople decided it would be best to abandon their home, at least for now. They started packing their belongings to leave.

Demetrius, meanwhile, located Sir Richard, who was standing frozen on a hillside. He gathered several of Ken's soldiers and positioned them around him. Demetrius called Richard's name, and as he sprang to life, the soldiers took him prisoner.

The villagers and soldiers took the south road out of Garsland. They traveled as long as daylight lasted before stopping to make camp.

Kay could barely see Garsland from her vantage point, but she watched as the last of the blue mist faded away. The orb stopped glowing at the same moment. She glanced down in her hands at the orb, which was now black. Then it turned the color of granite. Slowly, flecks of dust began to drift off of it. Kay tried to protect it from the breeze, but when she opened her hands again, she was holding only ashes.

It must have used up all its magic.

She shook her hands and watched sadly as the ash floated away. "Thank you," she murmured.

◆

"But why can't I go? You said you can get me out of here," Irene pleaded.

"Yes, there *is* a way," Anton said. "In fact, now that Anthony has made it clear he wants you for some purpose, I think it best you leave soon. But you can't go to the Wizards' Keep."

"But we need them to help. The Secret Valley's army is too strong for us. Why can't I go?"

"Irene, I don't even know if they're still alive, and besides, no mortal has ever been there. Go back to your friends, tell them they must leave this land and live somewhere else."

"No. We can't run and let the Black Lord succeed."

"If you attempt to fight Anthony, you all will either die, or end up serving him for the rest of your miserable lives."

"Anton, I could never be happy in a foreign land knowing my homeland is in such darkness. We must try to defeat him. The old wizards may be our only hope."

"No. It would be nearly...it would be nearly..." Anton closed his eyes and grimaced.

"Anton?"

"Impossible...there are...too many...risks..."

Anton was breathing hard. His face became flushed and his temples pulsed. He moaned.

"What is it? Anton, are you alright?" Irene asked, becoming frightened.

"NO! No, you won't have me!" Anton screamed.

Perspiration ran down Anton's face. His skin turned red and he tore his shirt from his body, as if it were on fire. He began shouting angry words in a language Irene didn't understand. He screamed as if in agonizing pain. Irene felt both horrified and helpless. Anton's veins stood out on his body, and his skin had turned red as blood. The hair on his arms and chest started to burn, giving off a sickening odor.

"Help me!" Anton pleaded through his pain.

Irene looked around frantically. She grabbed a vessel of water from the corner and poured it on Anton. Large blisters erupted on his skin wherever the water touched. He screamed and fell to the ground. Irene knelt beside him.

"Anton! Oh, good Mirn, I've killed him. Anton! Please don't be dead, please." As Irene bent over the young man, his skin gradually became less red, but he lay very still. Irene took the torn shirt and began dabbing at Anton's face.

"Anton. Oh, please don't be dead. I promise I'll do whatever you say, just don't die on me. Please. I'll never forgive you!"

"Never?" came a weak voice.

"Anton! You're alive!"

"Will you please stop rubbing me with that thing? It hurts like Hades."

"Oh! I'm sorry."

"There's a small flask...on the shelf over there. There's oil in it."

Irene leaped across the room and grabbed the flask. She returned to Anton and held the flask to his lips. He smiled through his pain.

"It's not to drink," he murmured.

"I'm sorry. What do I do?"

"Put some on your hands and rub it into the blisters, please. Gently...ah...that's better." Anton reached up and gently touched Irene's worried face. "Don't look so concerned. I'm alright."

"What happened? Was it...him?"

"Yes."

"But how could it have been? You said he couldn't touch you here; that you were safe in the cave."

"Clearly, he's getting more powerful. The more slaves who come under the Bridge, the stronger he seems to get."

"Anton? I'll do what you said. I'll go back to my friends and persuade them to leave. I don't know if you heard me through your pain, but I said I'd do whatever you told me if you lived."

"I heard you."

"So, if you'll just get me out of here, I'll tell my friends we must flee."

"No. I've changed my mind. I think you should go to Wizard's Keep. Anthony is becoming too strong. He nearly killed me that time. Once he does, he'll be free to go above ground and he'll take over the land in a matter of days. He must be stopped."

"Anton, are you sure? Completely sure?"

"Yes."
Irene hugged Anton.
"Ow!" he cried, grimacing.
"Sorry."

CHAPTER 35

After Anton recovered from his brother's attack, he and Irene sat huddled near a small fire. Irene pressed him for more information.

"But, Anton, how am I to find the Wizards' Keep?"

"All I know is that you must go south, into uncharted and uninhabited land. There are, sadly, no maps to guide you. They don't want to be found."

"I wish you could come with me."

"I do, too." Anton put an arm around Irene, who shivered despite the fire. "But I must remain here to prevent Anthony from going above ground."

"I'm so frightened for you. He almost killed you. Maybe I should stay here, instead, and help you."

Anton smiled slightly. "Actually, Irene, your presence hurts more than helps me. You...break my concentration."

"Oh," Irene said in a small voice. "I'm terribly sorry."

Anton smiled even more, drew Irene closer to him, and bent down to kiss her on the side of her face. Slowly, he moved along her jaw-line to her full lips. Between kisses he said, "I'm not sorry. 'Tis most pleasurable."

Irene closed her eyes and sighed with happiness. Anton pulled her down next to him and, as Irene lifted her face to meet his kisses, she momentarily forgot the terrors of the Black Lord and the worries of finding Wizards' Keep.

◆

Nan stood over a huge pile of potatoes, slowly peeling one. She knew she should be working faster or she was likely to receive another beating, but she didn't care. All she could think about were her friends; she didn't know if they were alive or dead. Though the convent was several miles outside of Garsland, the sisters had heard of the battle and seen the rising smoke from the fires.

They must all be dead, or they would have come for me by now. A tear slid down her freckled face and dripped onto the potatoes. *I might as well be dead, too.*

Her shoulders ached—not from the work, but from the beatings she received for breaking rules...for talking, for working too slowly, and for trying to escape. Nan tried to run away the same day she was entered into the Order of the Holy Snake. She slipped out a back door in the kitchen and ran through the garden, not knowing quite where to go, but not caring. She just wanted to get away. They caught her as she was climbing a wall.

Stupid robe. If it hadn't been for this cumbersome thing I would have made it over that wall. She reached for another potato.

Sister Angelique came in and surveyed the still heaping mound of vegetables. She sighed and shook her head. "You had best hurry, Sister Nan," she said sternly. "You still have much more work to do." The chapel bell tolled and, with a firm nod of her head, the nun left the kitchen for prayers.

Nan nodded in affirmation. She knew better than to try and answer. Lay sisters could only speak during the single church service they were permitted to attend. *And then only to read the responses.*

"Sister Angelique is hardly an angel, eh?"

Nan dropped a half-peeled potato and whirled around. Sister Frieda, another lay sister, was standing behind her. Nan stared at her with her mouth open. Sister Frieda laughed.

"It's fine—no one's around, I checked," she said. A short, chubby nun, Frieda's brown eyes flashed merrily, and her mouth always appeared to be on the verge of letting loose a giggle. "It's OK, I tell you. They're all in another one of their dreary services."

"We might still get in trouble if one of the other lay sisters heard and told." Nan whispered.

"They wouldn't dare," Frieda replied, airily. "They know I have ways of getting even." Nan continued to stare at Frieda, who laughed again. "Will you shut your trap and quit'cher staring? You'd think I'd come from the moon or something!"

Nan blushed. "I'm sorry...it's just that—well—you're so...so... un-nun like!"

Frieda laughed until tears came to her eyes. "I ain't no more a nun than you! My parents sold me into this gawd-awful place three years ago to pay off family debts. Believe me, I ain't here for salvation!"

Now it was Nan's turn to cry, but the tears didn't come from happiness. "I... I guess I was brought here by some gentleman I met at a ball. His name was..."

"Turner Blackstone," Frieda finished for her. "You're one of several he's sold to the sisters, honey."

"I have to get out of here...I have to! Will you help me?"

"There's no way out, Nan. Don'tcha think every lay sister tries to run a couple times the first month or so? And all they get out of it are beatings. I hear you already got the rod a couple a times."

Nan sank to the stone floor, crying soundlessly. Frieda walked over and patted her on the shoulder. "Oh, honey...Nan, don't cry—it doesn't do any good. Really. You might as well get used to life here."

"Never!" Nan said fiercely. "I am going to get out of here if it's the last thing I do. I don't care how much they beat me."

"OK, honey, OK. I'll do my best to help you. Now stop crying. We gotta get these damned potatoes peeled before that devil-in-a-habit Angelique returns!"

Nan giggled through her tears, and hiccupped. "Oh...I guess we'd better."

"That's the spirit," Frieda said, picking up a knife and setting to work.

◆

Kay opened her eyes and, for a moment, she could not remember where she was. Then, in the dim morning light, she saw Luciano lying next to her. Farther off were Demetrius, Fitzgerald, and Stephon. Yesterday's battle and events came flooding back to her.

It's over. Or is it just beginning?

Trying not to awaken any of her friends, Kay rose and stole away. Most of the camp still slept, except those on guard duty. Kay went over to one of them.

"Where is Sir Richard being held?" she asked.

The guard pointed, too weary to even speak. Kay nodded her thanks and walked through camp to find Richard sitting on the damp ground, closely watched by two guards. He looked dirty and disheveled. Knowing how much the vain man prided himself on his appearance, Kay could not resist making a comment.

"Well, look what the cat dragged in!" she said, brightly.

"You'd be the catty one for sure, Kay," Richard replied looking at her with hatred in his eyes. A guard struck Richard a swift blow to the head. He fell over since his bound arms gave him no way to balance himself.

"Pick him up," Kay ordered, suppressing a smile. The man pulled Richard upright.

"Now, you listen and listen good, Richard. I once worshipped you. I thought there was no finer man or soldier alive than you. But I see you clearly now. You're nothing but a thug. Though you outnumbered us three to one, we still beat you because our cause is just. You can't stop us; Lord William can't stop us—no one can stop us. As soon as we can get an army together, we'll crush what's left of yours and the land will be safe."

"You will never win with an untrained band of peasant men and misfits, Kay. If it hadn't been for that freak occurrence back at Garsland, you'd have been slaughtered like the pigs you are!"

The guard, a resident of Garsland, struck Richard again, harder this time.

"Say the word, Kay, and I'll gladly run him through," he said, eyeing his prisoner with disgust.

"No. He's still of use. We don't know how many survivors of the army there are, but they'll be much less likely to attack once they learn we hold their leader. You see, Richard, they still worship you the way I once did." She began to move away.

"Kay, wait," one of the men called. "We took his weapons—what do you want us to do with them?"

Kay examined the assortment and found that Richard had carried a lance, a sword and three small daggers. Her face lit up at the sight of one of them. It was a small, but beautiful, gold and steel dagger with a jewel-encrusted grip. Lord William, himself, had presented it to Richard after a victory over a surrounding kingdom. Kay picked it up. It was not only handsome but also extremely deadly. She smiled.

"Take the rest of the weapons to Ken; I'll keep this one."

Richard bit back a cry of protest. Kay grinned, knowing how upset he was. *A perfect moment,* she thought as she strolled away.

"Excuse me, Kay, but none of us has seen Ken. We think he may have fallen in battle."

Kay stopped short and turned around, shocked. Ken, dead? No one had said anything and she was ashamed to realize she had not thought to find him in the hours after the battle as they fled Garsland.

"Then...take them to Demetrius and Fitzgerald," she stammered. "And send eight men back to the battlefield to search for Ken's body. The least we can do is give him a hero's burial. I'm...I'm going to the river to bathe." She hurried away before they could see the tears welling up in her eyes. Was Ken really dead? Kay remembered every detail about him—his handsome face, his laugh, his bravery. The tears began to overflow, and Kay angrily wiped them away.

That's part of being a soldier—death. I have to accept it.

◆

Kay went down to the river. When she located a quiet spot she quickly disrobed.

She placed the knife upon the riverbank within easy reach and stepped into the cool water. She had found some soapwort along the bank and made a bit of a lather from it to wash. She longed for a hot bath and perfumed soap, like those she had enjoyed back in the Secret Valley, but she knew those days were gone—at least for now.

After getting out of the river, Kay used her vest to dry herself off a bit and then quickly dressed in her skirt, shirt and boots. She tucked Richard's dagger safely into her right boot.

Walking back to camp, her thoughts were on what the group's next step should be. Because of this, she was unprepared for the hand that suddenly clasped over her mouth as she was dragged into the brush away from the main trail. Kay struggled but could not break free. Strong arms turned her around and she saw, to her horror, Seamus standing before her.

"Now, Kay, I shall finish what I should have before," he said.

Kay stood frozen to the spot, unable to move a muscle. She knew immediately that he intended to rape her and possibly kill her afterwards.

He smiled at her distress before releasing her, abruptly, causing her to stumble back a few paces.

"Take your clothes off, Kay," he said to her as he began to unfasten his own shirt. He said it as calmly as if he were inviting her to sit down for a cup of tea.

"Oh, no," Kay whispered, looking wildly around for an exit strategy.

"Oh, yes," Seamus said, now tossing his shirt aside. "And don't even think of trying to run. I can catch ye easily, and 'twill go harder on ye if I have to. I intend to make this very pleasurable…for meself, at least!"

With no choice, Kay began to slowly disrobe. She continued to examine her surroundings, however, still trying to find an escape route.

"That's better, Kay. I knew ye'd see reason." By now, Seamus stood before her, completely naked. Kay averted her eyes as she removed her vest and shirt as slowly as possible. Her face was burning with shame. Before she could reach for her skirt and boots, however, Seamus impatiently came over to her and pulled her close. He began to kiss her along the side of her face and down her neck.

"Touch me, Kay," he said. She shuddered, but hesitantly reached out and put a hand on his chest. "Lower," he commanded as he continued to kiss her shoulders and stroke her body.

She did as she was told, biting her lip to keep from crying.

Seamus pulled her down to the ground and pushed her onto her back. He pulled up her skirt and climbed on top of her. He was now kissing her breasts. He held her firmly, but released her hands. She began to stroke the nape of his neck with her left hand and moan softly. He murmured his approval.

Kay continued to caress him with her left hand as she slowly pulled her right knee up and reached carefully down towards her boot with her other hand.

"Oh yes, Kay—kiss me now," he said huskily, lifting his face back up to hers. "Kiss me."

Surprised, he gasped as Kay thrust Richard's dagger deeply into his side.

"This is my only kiss for *you*, Seamus!"

Kay shoved the man off of her using all of her strength. As she pulled the blade out, blood gushed. Without a second look, Kay grabbed her clothes and fled.

CHAPTER 36

"Now, the first step is for you to get back to the main part of the city. Do you think you can do that?" Anton and Irene lay together on the floor of the cave. The stone was cool against her skin, but she didn't mind with Anton's warm arms around her.

"I think so. But what if he sends those horrid birds after me?"

"You must remember they are created out of your own fear. They don't exist, but he will make you think they are real if you let him."

"They seemed real to me. I swear I could feel their talons grabbing me."

"It was nothing but an illusion. As long as you remember that you'll be safe." He handed her a key. "With this, you can exit through the underground sewer gates. Follow the river south until—"

"Anton—I'm not sure I can do this," Irene interrupted. "I don't know if I can control my fear."

"Yes. I thought of that." Anton sat up, reached into his pocket and brought out a small vial of white powder.

"What is that?"

"It doesn't matter. What *does* matter is that it will block out your fears and enable you to believe what I tell you." He shook a small portion of the powder on the palm of his hand and held it up to Irene. "Open your mouth."

Irene obeyed and Anton poured the powder onto her tongue. Instantly, she regretted it. It was bitter. She started to spit it out, but Anton put his hand over her mouth and told her to swallow. Tears welled in her eyes as she tried to do as she was told.

"Alright now?" Anton asked after a moment. Irene nodded her head. "Now, look into my eyes."

She stared into Anton's blue eyes and, although she felt like drifting off to sleep, she was completely alert at the same time.

How strange I feel.

"Listen to me, Irene. Concentrate on my voice, alone. When you leave this cave, everything that ordinarily would frighten you will not. You will know all of the evil creatures coming at you are illusions and cannot harm you. Hear what I say, Irene, and know it to be true. You will be safe if you remember."

Anton continued to speak but Irene no longer truly listened. Still, she understood everything—as if she felt each word inside her body, instead of hearing it. She slowly shut her eyes...

◆

Irene opened her eyes. She lay on the cave floor.

Funny, I don't remember falling asleep.

She glanced around. Anton sat on the ground near her, smiling.

"Are you ready to leave now?" he asked.

"Of course," Irene replied calmly. She wondered why she had ever been afraid. She got up and smiled at Anton, who also stood. He held out his arm and she took it. Together, they walked to the hole at the top of the cave.

"Thank you for everything, Anton," Irene said, as if thanking him for a dinner party. Anton behaved just as formally.

"You are quite welcome, Irene. I do hope we shall meet again."

Irene smiled and nodded. "Goodbye." She released his arm and climbed up and out of the cave.

Walking down the stone path, Irene hummed a little tune to herself. She saw the black castle where she spent such terrifying moments but, even as she remembered, she was completely calm. When she reached the bottom of the hill, she turned away from the castle and continued walking. The smooth black stones began to heat up, but Irene was not afraid.

It's only an illusion, she thought, and her feet were not burned.

The screeching of the evil birds that had pursued her before sounded above her, but Irene remained unafraid.

They're not real...they can't hurt me.

The creatures dissolved before they could grab her.

Irene walked on, the castle growing smaller in the distance.

Then the earth shook and Irene found it difficult to keep walking because the stones in the path kept tipping and shifting. She found it hard to keep her balance. Her heartbeat accelerated and sweat broke out on her brow. She tried to remind herself it was an illusion, but she was becoming afraid.

Hail rained down on her, and she cried out in pain.

"Help me, Anton!" she called as she fell. The stone slab she sat on tilted and Irene slid downwards. Before her loomed a gaping hole, within which appeared to be the faces of demons. She screamed in terror and tried to clutch onto the stones around her.

"Anton, help!"

"Irene!" the voice said, urgently, "All is illusion—remember! It isn't real—it isn't real."

The voice kept repeating the phrase over and over and Irene found herself speaking the same words out loud: "It isn't real...it isn't real...it isn't real..."

Suddenly, everything was silent. Irene sat on the cool stone slabs. Everything was calm.

"It *isn't* real," she said to herself, listening to the echo of her voice. Then she stood up and ran deep into the cavern, towards the center of the underground city.

◆

Turner Blackstone of Hayward Fields came out of his hiding place and looked around. The battle appeared to be well over and he was anxious to find out who won.

Not that it matters. I shall be of use to whatever side won. One always wants to be on the side of the victor.

He walked to the town's center. When he saw the smoldering ruins of Garsland, Turner was surprisingly moved. Although Turner lived in nearby Hayward Fields, his childhood was spent in Garsland, and he thought of it as his home.

"Ah, me," he said to himself. "The poor peasants must have died horrible deaths."

He began to notice, however, a good many of the bodies around him were enemy soldiers, not townspeople. In fact, the corpses of the soldiers outnumbered the townsfolk at least three to one.

Amazing. But if we are the victors, where is everybody?

Turner climbed a stairway of a burned building to get a better view. He saw nothing to the north or the west—nary a bird flew in the sky. To the east, he saw only the sunrise.

When he looked to the south, however, he spotted smoke.

Campfires, no doubt.

He headed south. Along the way, he looted a few valuables from some of the bodies in and around the city, reasoning the dead had no more need of them.

It was half a day before he came across the first group of survivors of the battle. Women tended to some of the wounded men, cooked food over small fires, or cared for their children. As Turner approached, two guards rushed up, swords drawn.

Turner had a weapon he took off a fallen soldier, but he didn't draw it. Instead, he greeted the guards cheerfully. "Hail, good fellows—well met! Could you be the brave lads who fought so fiercely by my side in the heat of battle?"

"State your name and origins," a guard barked.

"Why, Turner of Hayward Fields," Turner said, bowing. "It took me some time to catch up with you. I only recently returned from our glorious battlefield."

At least that is no lie, he thought smugly.

"What took ye so long?" the other guard asked. "Why didn't ye join us after the battle, when we evacuated the town?"

"Why, I just today awoke. You see, I suffered a nasty blow to the head. Knocked quite unconscious early in the fight, don't you know? I'm sure you all thought me dead. When I came to and saw we were the victors, I rejoiced and made my way straight here."

"Huh," the guard said. "Well, perhaps ye'd best have your wound looked at."

"Oh no," Turner quickly replied. "It's nothing, really—hardly even notice it now. What I would like is something to eat and directions to our leaders."

"Food is over by the fire. What's left of it, anyway. And our commanders are in the next encampment...about a twenty minutes' walk." The guard studied Turner as he went over to help himself to food.

To the other guard he muttered, "If he took a hit to the head, 'twere a mighty small one, if you ask me. He's not even dirty. Doesn't look like he came within fifty feet of the battle!"

◆

When Turner reached Kay's camp, he found her discussing security with Fitzgerald and Demetrius.

"I...thought I saw some of Sir Richard's men in the woods when I went to bathe in the river. We should tell Ken to double the guard and let's make ready to quit this place and move on as soon as we can."

"We haven't been able to locate Ken—no one's seen any sign of him," Demetrius said.

"Oh, yes, that's right. I'd...I'd forgotten. Well, aren't the men we sent to search for him back yet?" Kay snapped the question to cover her upset nerves.

"No, not yet."

"Well, we won't leave 'till we've found some trace of him, alive or...or otherwise." Kay sighed heavily. "Is there anything to eat? I'm starving."

"I just had a tasty meal at the last encampment."

"Who the blazes are you?" Fitzgerald asked, as they all turned to see who had spoken.

"Turner Blackstone of Hayward Fields, at your service. I recovered from a near fatal blow to the head and have only recently caught up to my fellow townspeople."

"I remember—you were the man with Nan at the ball," Stephon said. "Have you seen her? We still can't find her."

"Oh, no, I'm sure you're mistaken. Remember we were all masked. How can you believe it was I?"

"By your coat and leggings. I never forget a man's attire. In fact," Stephon frowned, "why are you still wearing your ball clothes? Most of us changed soon after we heard Richard's army was approaching."

"Oh...uh, I didn't have time to get all the way back to Hayward Fields. I was afraid I would miss the fight entirely. So, I simply stayed in my fancy clothes."

"And did you see Nan? I'm—*we're* so worried about her," Fitzgerald said.

"Oh, I don't recall. I vaguely remember talking with her, but after we parted company...I can't really say."

"Oh dear," Kay said. "We were so hoping you could help. She's a dear friend and there's no sign of her."

"I have no idea where she could be."

"Well, if you remember anything—anything at all..." Fitzgerald said.

"Of course," Turner said, smoothly. "You'll be the first to know."

"Well. What say we get something to eat?" Kay said. "I, for one, am quite famished."

"A few of my fairies have cooked up a little something for us," Gar volunteered. They headed over to help themselves.

CHAPTER 37

It was quite late by the time Nan and Frieda finished their assigned kitchen duties following the evening meal. As they worked, Nan had cautiously whispered her tale and the pressing need to return to her friends. Frieda nodded at Nan compassionately, her usually upturned smile pulled into a concerned moue.

"I've had a plan in the works for a while, now, Nan. It may be time to implement it," she mused under her breath. "I must speak to Marcus."

During the three years Frieda had been locked up within the walls of the Order of the Holy Snake, she had befriended the eunuch, Marcus, who did all of the heavy work and general upkeep. Marcus survived a horrific accident as a child, thanks to the sisters' medical assistance. His parents, unable to pay for the care, gave Marcus to the convent. After all these years, he was an accepted part of the community. He stayed out the way of the women, watching for things that needed to be done, taking care of them without any direction. When Frieda asked him about it, he muttered, "I likes it that way—no nagging or scolding for me."

The order was almost entirely self-sufficient, growing fruits and vegetables and raising chickens, goats, and pigs. There were often more eggs and milk than the women needed. Many of the lay sisters were accomplished bakers; they produced outstanding pastries and breads, as well as cheese from their goats. It was one of Marcus' duties to take these items to the market square and sell them. The income was used, in part, to purchase more lay sisters.

Marcus, however, long ago figured out he could skim a certain percentage of the profits for himself. Since the nuns never left the confines of the convent, they were not present for the sale of their goods. Therefore, their bookkeeping was dependent entirely upon Marcus' grunted: "It was a good day," or "A poor showing at the marketplace," as he handed over the day's gold. He had been careful to keep his take modest, but over time, he had amassed a tidy treasure hidden under a heavy barrel in the tool shed where he had a straw bed and little else in the way of material goods. The sisters did not give him much except his rough shirt and pants made of woven flax grown in the convent fields. Marcus and Frieda had developed a cautious, secret friendship and talked of a life together outside the Order of the Snake.

Frieda whispered fiercely to Nan, "Girl, go wash your face, and get some rest. Perhaps there is help for us..." She bustled out to the shed.

◆

As the famished group approached the table, Gar took note of everyone's appearance. Kay's clothing had definitely seen better days. They were dirty and her shoulder seam was ripped. Demetrius' garb also had not recovered from the mud bath when Kay had tried to wake him from his spell with the orb. Perhaps he would ask his fairies to whip up some new clothes for his friends. Stains of blood and perspiration seeped through the clothes of all of the warriors.

All of them, that was, but for Turner of Hayward Fields.

Surely this man had not seen even a glint of a sword or arrow. Not a hair was out of place, not a spattering of mud on his knee, not a drop of blood or trace of sweat upon his brow. Gar frowned, mulling this over as they sat to dine.

Gar's fairies had created a feast seemingly out of thin air. Kay gasped as they presented dish after dish, each more amazing than the last.

"Oh, Gar, if I weren't full, I would keep eating—it all tastes so good!" she said as another delicacy appeared.

Stephon patted his belly. "I feel as though I'm the fatted calf awaiting slaughter, but what a pleasant preparation, I must say."

Demetrius and Fitzgerald exchanged glances at this unfortunate comment. Both men were thinking about the certainty of more death as the war to defeat the Black Lord continued.

"Well, I know this much," Turner declared with a loud belch. "A man could get used to being attended to by fairies!"

"I, for one, will sleep well tonight," Fitzgerald said. "Gar, do you think your fairies could stand watch this evening? We must do some scouting today, and tomorrow we should gather our thoughts and decide how to proceed. This past battle is certainly not the end. We lost many men, and our numbers are even fewer now."

Gar nodded and appointed fairies to the task of keeping watch over the camp that night.

◆

Fitzgerald woke first the following morn. He sluiced his face with water and surveyed his tattered clothing, sighing as he noted the various rips and stains. For one always used to looking his best, wearing such stained and dirty clothes was a true hardship. He heard a fluttering sound and looking up, saw a smiling fairy above his head, holding a fresh shirt and trousers.

After a battle, although things are messed
A man will feel fine when his clothing is pressed!

"Why, thank you, good fairy! A man does feel better when outfitted right!" Fitzgerald quickly disrobed and stepped into the clean trousers. He pulled the shirt over his head, still chatting with the fairy. "I'll be glad when we can put this all behind us. I'm sure you and your fairy friends will be glad when you can fly through the forest without fear. What I wouldn't give to be able to fly about like that myself. 'Twould give me a better shot at my opponent," he laughed.

Lacing his boots, Fitzgerald continued to muse aloud, "This magic of yours must be potent. It's certainly mysterious." He looked up at the magical creature hovering above him. "How *do* you fly, anyway?"

In an instant, everything changed!

In a sensation rather like falling slow motion into a pool of water, Fitzgerald felt himself being sucked through what he could only describe as a vortex. When everything stopped spinning, he found himself behind a statue that stood before a small iron door, three feet high and three feet wide. To his horror, he realized he was back in the temple crypt in the land of the Black Lord! Before him was the poem showing him why he was sent back.

Herein lies the land of 'Gar,'
It's all uphill, but not too far.
Behind this door exists a sea,
But first you must unlock with key.
The key was lost in dungeon dark,
Which never heard the song of lark.
One key only fits this lock,
We will not answer if you knock.
But if the key you hold does fit,
Prepare to meet some souls with wit.
We make merry, drink, and sing,
And dance thrice daily with our King.

And if, by chance, you see us fly,
Please do not ask the reason why.
'Tis our secret, ours to know,
And if you ask us, back you'll go.

Oh, no—how could I have forgotten? Fitzgerald searched his clothing for the key, but realized he had not yet transferred it from his dirty clothes to the new ones. His heart sank.
What do I do now?

◆

Nan and Frieda crept wordlessly through the halls of the convent, eyes shifting this way and that as they listened for any signs of movement from the nuns asleep in their cells. Fearful of making any noise, the girls carefully lifted the heavy wooden paddle securing the massive entry doors from the inside and gently placed it against the wall. Opening one door only the smallest sliver, first Frieda, then Nan, slipped through into the bracing cool air in the convent courtyard.

There, Marcus prepared his cart for a trip to the market. With the slightest of glances, his eyes directed the girls to a wooden crate placed at the bottom of the cart. Nan climbed in and Frieda lowered the lid. Then Frieda climbed into a burlap sack placed next to the crate and Marcus loosely tied a rope around the opening to secure it. He piled loaves of bread atop them and surrounded them with canisters of milk, round cheeses wrapped in cloth, and baskets of eggs.

Marcus roused the sleeping extern sisters to open the outer gates. Drowsily, the two nuns lowered the drawbridge. With a grunt, Marcus flicked the reins and directed the horses to begin the day's journey to the marketplace. The sisters watched him exit, and again raised the drawbridge so they could return to their warm beds before morning prayers.

After moving down the road a mile or so, the cart stopped and Nan heard the milk canisters and egg boxes being moved. The cart shifted, and Frieda's voice exclaimed, "Oh, Marcus, at last! I thought I would expire from the stench in that sack." A crescent of light cut through the darkness in the crate, and Nan blinked as Marcus lifted her out and put her on a carpet of pine needles on the forest floor. They were well away from the convent.

"M'ladies, we are off to Garsland!" The two tore off their veils, positioned themselves on the plank next to Marcus, and the creaky cart bumped on down the path.

◆

Kay awoke with a start. She felt uneasy for some reason...as if something was amiss. Mentally, she began reviewing the night before: *The fairies kept watch as we slept. If anything were wrong, they surely would have sounded the alarm.* Kay saw her friends safely sleeping near the fire. *Well, I might as well get up now. Fitzy must have wakened early, too. I don't see him.*

Kay found a bucket of water and began scrubbing her face and neck. Looking down, she spied a tattered shirt and trousers, which she readily recognized as Fitzgerald's.

What in the world...where did Fitzy get other clothes to wear?

After a battle, although things are messed
A man will feel fine when his clothing is pressed!

Kay smiled at the fairy flying above her. "Yes, dear fairy, but you must see I am not a man, battle worn though I am--oh! Are you talking about Fitzgerald? Where *is* that man; do you know?"

A man should not wonder
about magic and such.
He'll end up down under
And suffer too much!

Kay felt a jolt of anxiety. "What do you mean? Did Fitzy get in trouble by talking to you? Oh, no! Gar? Gar! Where are you? Wake up!"

Gar emerged from behind a tree, sleepily rubbing his eyes. Kay ran up to him. "Gar! Fitzy is gone. One of your fairies said something cryptic about him going 'down under?' What does it mean?"

Gar shook his head and walked to the fairy. They held a whispered, but heated conversation. Finally, Gar turned back to Kay.

"Damned those fairies and their constant rhymes! 'Tis almost impossible to get a straight answer out of them. Kay, our friend appears to have inadvertently made a trip back to the Black Lord's realm. We'll need to mount a rescue mission. My fairies' magic can help, but we will need some volunteers to retrieve him. Of course, we can count on you and... yes, Stephon. I think Turner of Hayward Fields could offer support below as well—he's a large man. Any more people and I fear you would attract too much attention."

Gar motioned to three fairies, which handed fresh clothing to Kay and Stephon. Turner and Stephon had been roused by the noise, but hadn't yet quite comprehended the dire situation. Fitzgerald's disappearance was quickly explained to them.

"Gar, how do we go back to the land of the Black Lord?" Kay asked. "The Bridge of Doom won't appear again for a year's time."

"Before we talk about re-entering that place, let's discuss your exit strategy. Once you find Fitzgerald, you must use one of these golden coins. Fairy Bluebell, tell these brave souls what to do," Gar commanded.

Dressed all in blue, a rather defiant-looking fairy spoke:

Don't waste these coins as money
They won't buy you a thing.
But, if you use them wisely,
A special wish they'll bring.
Hold one tightly in your grasp
Say the place you wish to be,
In a flash, you'll find you're there
As quick as one, two, three!

Kay frowned. "Gar, why didn't you tell us about these coins earlier, so we could rescue Irene and David?"

"First, Kay, they're exceedingly rare. Plus, we're...not quite sure they'll work in the Black Lord's kingdom." At Kay's expression, he quickly added, "My fairies are *mostly* confident they will work—it's just never been tried before."

Kay gulped. "I see. But if they do, after we rescue Fitzy can't we can wish to be with Nan and Irene, to find them and then bring them back, too?"

The fairy flew right up to Kay and shook her head vehemently.

Heed this warning, we do plea!
Do not use the coins in haste.
One trip alone is all you get—
This magic, do not waste!

Kay stared into Bluebell's eyes and nodded her head in understanding. This was a one-shot deal. If they lost a coin or used it frivolously, that would be the end of their rescue opportunity. Kay looked at Stephon and Turner.

"Do you men understand the importance of what she said? These coins only have enough magic to get us back after we find Fitzy."

Stephon and Turner both nodded; though from their demeanor it was clear neither man was happy to have been conscripted into this rescue mission.

CHAPTER 38

The sun shone bright on the three fugitives from the Order of the Holy Snake as they continued to Garsland. Soon, Nan peered ahead with a pounding heart towards the river's edge where she could nearly make out the lines of the fortress. As the wagon approached, Nan blanched at the number of bodies in the fields. When they reached the castle of Gar, Nan shook her head with sorrow. No lovely pinkish glow emanated from the spires and turrets. The red carpet in the courtyard leading to the silver door was covered in mud and dried stains of blood.

They got out of the wagon to explore. All seemed deserted. No birds sang and no fairies were flitting about. Nor were there any citizens. After searching for some signs of life, they concluded only the shell of Garsland remained.

"My friends, what has become of you?" Nan murmured. She turned to Frieda. "Oh, Frieda, I am so sorry. I convinced you to leave the safety of the convent to join me here in these ruins. What have I done?"

"Oh, Nan, anywhere is better than that old nunnery!" Frieda replied, patting her friend's shoulder. "We were already plotting our escape; you just got us do it a bit sooner, is all. Marcus has revealed to me he is not a eunuch; it was only a ruse to get the sisters to allow him to stay," she giggled. "We want to make a life together. Now, dry your eyes and let's set up camp for tonight, and rest a while. We'll feel more cheerful after a good meal, too. Tomorrow, we can figure out what's next."

So the three travelers built a fire, washed in the river, and ate some of the nuns' cheese. When Nan went to lie down, she noticed something looming over the southern hills; three bright blue lights...but she was so tired she thought she imagined them. Stars, in the middle of the day? She drifted off into a lovely nap.

◆

Irene ran through the Black Lord's city. Suddenly, she gasped as strong arms pulled her into an alleyway. She fought back, jabbing her elbow into the ribs of her captor.

"M'lady, stop! It is I, David!"

Irene turned to see her friend but, having been fooled by the Black Lord before, she no longer trusted anything, so she continued to try to free herself. David held fast.

"Irene, 'tis me, truly! Please stop your struggles so we do not bring the beasts upon us. We need to use our energy to escape from this cursed city!" he urgently whispered.

Irene ceased fighting and took a closer look at David. No longer bedraggled and weak from working in the brick pits, David wore fine clothing and appeared rested. Was she safe with him? Or was this just another of Anthony's illusions?

"Please, Irene, allow me tell you what happened since we parted. After they took you away, I was taken to a chamber where I was bathed and dressed in these fine clothes. The Black Lord's servants tempted me with an amazing feast, but even as I ate, I plotted my escape. 'Twas not easy, but I slipped away. The Black Lord's attention was elsewhere recently and the whole city seemed to be unguarded and silent. Then, the air was filled with smoke and lightning as though a mighty battle was being fought. The servants were all at the windows staring at a place where a red light glowed overhead. I took a chance and slipped out the doorway and have been hiding in the shadows ever since."

David peered around the corner, and then led the way back into the street. "We should hurry, to miss the patrol. We must find an escape out of here."

Irene remembered Anton's advice to head south. She held up the key. "This was given to me by someone who helped me. He said it would unlock a gate somewhere near the sewers and lead to freedom."

David nodded. "Let's go."

Still wary, because nothing in this evil land seemed to be reliable, Irene followed.

◆

Kay turned to Gar and said, "I think I know how Fitzgerald was sent back, Gar. He asked the fairies something we were warned not to, am I right?"

Gar nodded. "Which is how you will return, too." He motioned for a silver-garbed fairy to come forward. "Crocus, here, has volunteered to make the trip with you," he said, handing her a gold coin as well.

"Please watch out for her as she watches out for you. Now, ask this fairy clad in grey, how she comes to fly this day."

Oh, drat! Gar thought, *now I'm rhyming!*

Kay, Stephon, and Turner all chanted together: "Dear fairy, tell us how your magic makes you fly." In no more than a moment, the three felt as though they were being swallowed by the air. They landed with a thump by the statue in the catacombs.

Kay, Turner, and Stephon looked around themselves in a daze. They heard a pebble skitter down the hallway behind them. The men turned, wielding their swords, and confronted a stunned-looking Fitzgerald, who held a torch. Kay threw herself into his arms with a cry of joy. But before they could even speak, Crocus said:

I counsel thee to use your charm
If you are to escape from harm!

Everyone began talking at once. Kay motioned for them to be silent. She understood the fairy wanted to return, but she had other ideas.

"I know we came to rescue Fitzgerald, but this may be our only chance to find Irene and David and free them from this place. Who is with me? If there's trouble, you can use your coin at any time to wish yourself back to Garsland."

Stephon rubbed his coin between his thumb and forefinger before nodding his head. Turner shrugged and also nodded.

"But, Kay," Fitzgerald whispered, "I do not have the key for the door! I left it in my other pants. We cannot escape the way we did before. I fear we are lost."

"No, it's alright, Fitzy. We have another plan." Kay unbuckled her scabbard and sword and motioned for him to put it on. She reached into her pocket and said, "Here is our escape." She showed him a golden coin and quickly explained to him that if he held it and wished to be in a place, he would be instantly transported there. "But Fitzy, we must try to find Irene and David and bring them with us. I believe it is their only hope."

With the fairy flying before them, the four moved as silently as possible to the stairs that led up to the main part of the temple. Kay had little idea where they would go when they left the temple, and doubted their chances for success, but she thought they must at least try.

◆

Irene and David continued to walk towards the center of the community, keeping a watchful eye for guards. Soon, Irene noticed her surroundings looked somewhat familiar.

"David, look at that building ahead. I'm sure it's the temple where we became lost from Nan and Kay." The two ran up to the abandoned building.

"Irene, wait!" David pulled her close to him and drew into the shadows of an alleyway. The sound of snuffling and stamping feet came behind them. "I think we are being followed."

The two ducked down behind some trash as four guards shuffled past. Then the two went around to the back of the temple. The rear door had been haphazardly repaired with some boards, but David pried them off, and together they entered the gloomy interior.

◆

Turner of Hayward Fields was truly confounded. Here he was, part of a rescue mission in the realm of the Black Lord, and he knew he should be terrified. Instead, he found himself intrigued. This temple through which they so carefully moved appeared to have once been filled with riches and treasures. If he kept his eyes and ears open, he might be able to find a few items left behind from the former days of glory. His fortune could be made! Plus, if he found himself at all in danger, he had this golden coin that he could use as his way out. He stood a little straighter and alertly scanned the walls and hallways looking for glints of gold or jewels.

Mistaking his motive, Kay reached over to pat Turner's shoulder. "Thank you for your vigilance, sir."

Fitzgerald nodded. "Good men in times of need will surely profit in times of peace."

Profit, Turner thought, *is exactly what I'm seeking.*

Just then, Stephon motioned for the group to stop. His eyebrows went up and a grin broke out on his face. He whispered, "I think I hear David's voice."

Everyone strained to listen. There it was—a slight humming and the sounds of careful footfalls on the temple floor.

Stephon, once again, whispered to the others. "When David is nervous—or thinking—he quietly hums like that. He thinks no one can hear. I am sure it is him."

"Yes, but he may be guarded. Move back around the corner and keep in the shadows," Kay whispered, extinguishing the torch. "Ready your weapons."

The group watched two figures come into view. The fine clothes on the one were a strong contrast to the overly large and plain garments of the other. As the two came nearer, Kay gasped.

"Irene, is it really you?" Kay rounded the corner and grabbed the princess in a fierce hug. "Your garb is not your finest, but your face is the fairest I've ever seen!"

Stephon clasped David's arm and clapped him on his well-dressed shoulder. "I feared I would never see you again, my friend!"

Both David and Irene were astounded and thrilled to be reunited with their friends. Irene turned to Kay.

"Kay, this key is supposed to help our escape, but I don't know what it fits."

"We don't need it, Irene. We have a better, faster plan."

The silver fairy scrutinized Kay.

Before another minute passes,
Peer into your looking glasses
All you see are not as seems
Darkness creeps into your dreams.

"I don't know what you're talking about, Crocus. But never fear. We are leaving right now," Kay said. She turned to her friends. "There are not enough coins for us all to escape individually. We'll need to hold tightly to one another and hope the magic will bring two back at once. Just think of Garsland and then say aloud you want to go there. Then, we'll catch up with our army."

Neither David nor Irene had heard of Garsland. So, Kay pulled out a gold coin, grabbed Irene tightly around the waist and closed her eyes.

"I wish us to be in Garsland," she said.

Fitzgerald gasped as the two girls disappeared in a faint puff of smoke. Stephon didn't hesitate, but held his gold coin in one hand and David's arm with the other. He spoke the same words aloud and they both vanished.

"You next, Turner," Fitzgerald said.

"Oh, no, please, you and the fairy go, Sir Fitzgerald. I would prefer to be the last, in case anyone is following. I would be far more able to disarm them than you."

Fitzgerald frowned at this slight insult, then shrugged. Crocus handed Fitzgerald her coin and held his hand. Once again, in a puff of smoke, they were gone, leaving only Turner of Hayward Fields in the corridor.

He smiled. *Why, if it is so easy, I'll just poke about a bit more before leaving. I am sure there are many riches to be had for those who would take the time to look.* Eager to find something of value, he began moving forward towards the altar of the abandoned temple.

◆

Nan and her friends were still napping, tired from their early morning escape from the convent. When Nan heard a faint rustling beside her camp bed, she opened her green eyes warily, then sat bolt upright. Could she believe what she saw? There, next to the fire, stood Kay, Fitzy, Irene, Stephon and David! A fairy overhead softly cried, shaking her head at the ruins of Garsland.

"My friends!" Nan cried out. "Is it really you? Oh, Fitzy!" She rushed into his strong embrace. Irene moved to join them and Kay added her arms to the group hug.

"At last our worries are over," Nan said.

"No, Nan," Irene said, "we are not out of danger! We need to make a plan immediately. The Black Lord may soon escape from his realm, below. If he does, he will begin a terrible siege. He wants to take over the upper world."

Fitzgerald frowned. "We must confer with Gar and what is left of our army. I fear we are not strong enough to take on this evil."

David looked around him. "Who's Gar? What was this place?"

Crocus stood in the air before him and said:

A place like none before
A place that all adore
Garsland was my home
From here I will not roam
Only good here abides
With fairy blessings as their guides
But evil soon will be revealed
In this place where all are healed.

She reached into a tiny pouch held at her waist and sprinkled glittery, silver dust on a small patch of ground. The charred earth glowed for a moment, then green, grassy tendrils began sprouting from the earth. The fairy slowly moved on and continued her work. Inch by inch, she began healing Garsland.

"This is Garsland, David," Fitzgerald explained. "When we first escaped the Black Lord's realm, we came to this fairy kingdom. It truly is a remarkable place. To see it so blackened and ruined makes me sick at heart."

Nan looked at Irene and shook her head, smiling. "Irene, remember, back in the Valley of William Etté, how we were so caught up in wearing the right clothes and fixing our hair so we always looked our finest? We are a sight now! Me in a nun's habit and you wearing oversized men's trousers and shirt! I wish we had a mirror to look at ourselves together."

The land around them was slowly growing greener as Crocus continued her work sprinkling the glittery dust on the ground. Suddenly, the air began to shimmer and a hundred fairies appeared around the encampment. Each began sowing more of the magic powder on the land and, slowly, the beauty of Garsland began to reveal itself once more. Everyone watched, entranced, as trees grew new leaves from charred stumps. Flowers bloomed right before their eyes.

Whumfp!

Everyone heard a loud thump and the screech of wheels braking behind them. "Bless those fairies," Gar muttered under his breath. "They can't drive a chariot worth a tinker's damn!"

"Gar!" Fitzgerald exclaimed. "How did you get here? Did you use a gold coin too?"

"Leave me some secrets, if you please, Fitzgerald. I came to check on you all. I see your party is intact—no! Where is Turner of Hayward Fields? Did he meet with trouble underground?"

The group looked around, realizing for the first time that Turner had not used his magic coin to return with them.

"We were so happy to see each other we didn't give a thought to him," Kay said, feeling guilty.

"Wait!" Nan broke in, "Turner of Hayward Fields—come to help rescue *others*? But...*he* is the one who sold me to the Order of the Holy Snake! At least, I think so. I shouldn't accuse him, I suppose, but on the night of the ball we were walking in the garden. And the next thing I knew, I woke up in the convent."

"Now, a few pieces of the puzzle fit," Gar said. "I've no doubt he was collecting his gold payment for Nan from the sisters during the battle, instead of defending his home. I knew there had to be a reason he showed no signs of having fought. Well, if he makes it back, we'll see he's dealt with properly!"

◆

Deep below, Turner warily approached the altar, which was covered with broken bones and mangled skulls. He was certain he had seen the glint of gold peeking out from under the altar's decaying mantle cloth. Shuddering, he reached under a long leg bone and moved the fabric just a bit to reveal what was beneath. His eyes widened. The surface was entirely gold! There was enough of the treasured ore here to make his fortune. Turner took his dagger and began scraping the soft metal from the altar to fill his pockets. Humming to himself, he was so enthralled in the task that he neglected to be watchful.

The beasts came upon him so swiftly there was no time for Turner to use his coin or think of any place of safety for the magic to take him. His howl of surprise was the last sound to come from his throat. Turner joined the dead sacrificed upon the altar with no one there to hear his cry and no friends to mourn his death.

◆

Nan introduced Marcus and Frieda to everyone and recounted how they all escaped the convent. Irene explained her clothing was given to her by Anton when she was fleeing his twin, Anthony, who is the Black Lord.

Gar instructed his fairies to create tents for everyone and better outfit Irene and Nan. The two girls then washed and changed—very grateful to be in lovely dresses again and feeling decidedly more feminine.

Meanwhile, the men gathered around maps that Gar produced. They discussed plans to move away from Garsland, while gathering more troops of citizen-soldiers willing to join them in the war.

David stepped outside the tent for a moment, unnoticed by the others. From a pocket inside his jacket, he pulled out a small mirror framed in black onyx and rubbed the handle between his thumb and forefinger like a worry stone. Hearing footsteps behind him, he quickly jammed the mirror back into his pocket and turned to face Fitzgerald as the tall redheaded man joined him.

CHAPTER 39

"A moment, if you please, David," Fitzgerald said. "I'm aware you have been through much as of late and, perhaps, it's presumptuous of us to even expect you to stay and help in our fight against the Black Lord. But I know I, at least, would like to hear whatever you can tell us about your time below. You may hold some knowledge that could help, even if you don't realize it. Won't you come back and share what you can about the Black Lord?"

"Indeed, Sir Fitzgerald. I will be more than happy to tell you of my experiences. But I... must attend to something first. Give me a few moments and I shall return."

Fitzgerald nodded and went back into the tent. David walked rapidly across the courtyard, seeking a place where he could be alone. Fairies fluttered about, continuing their healing of Garsland. The voices of Kay, Irene, Nan, and Frieda floated out of the other tent as they caught up on their respective adventures.

Damn it all, is there no place of privacy here?

Breaking into a trot, he headed over to the main gates of Garsland. Just outside, he saw a broken-down, low wall that had so far escaped the fairies' attention for repairs. He hopped over it and scrunched down to hide. He again reached into his pocket for the small onyx mirror and stared deeply into it.

"Master, I am here," he whispered.

◆

Demetrius Keats strode through the forest to where Sir Richard was held. Being the only prisoner held by the refugee army, just one bored man guarded the captive.

"I need to speak with the prisoner," Demetrius said. "Alone."

"I was told to never let him out of my sight," the man responded. "Kay will have my head if something happens."

"I'll take full responsibility. Why don't you walk to the main camp and get something to eat? Kay will be fine. Don't worry about her."

The guard shrugged and ambled off. Demetrius stood looking at his friend with compassion and embarrassment. Richard stared back, uncertainty in his eyes, before breaking the silence.

"I don't suppose you've come to free me so we can return to the Secret Valley together," he said.

Demetrius smiled ruefully. "No, Richard. I can't let you go. I'm here because I... because of our long-time friendship. I want to try and talk some sense into you—to get you to realize you're on the wrong side of this battle."

"The wrong side? The battle should have been one-sided! I can't for the life of me explain what happened! My men should have rolled over that tiny hamlet without any casualties. The fact that most of my troops are dead and I am captive is beyond belief!"

"Even if I told you the reason behind our victory you would not understand, Richard. I think it's a sign that the fates are on our side. That's what I want to talk to you about." He knelt beside his companion. "I need you to understand, as I now do, that what we've been doing under Lord William's leadership is evil. We haven't been destroying towns of warriors bent on our destruction—we've been killing innocent people who had no thought of violence at all! We in the Secret Valley were never threatened or in any danger. I can't understand why Lord William lied to us, or led us to become a community focused solely on warfare and slaughtering citizens of peaceful communities."

Richard was silent for a moment. He gazed deep into Demetrius' eyes and spoke. "Perhaps you're right, Demetrius. Maybe we were misled all this time. But what can we do now?"

"If we both went back to the Valley we might be able to convince Lord William to change his ways," Demetrius said, eagerly. "Or...or overthrow him somehow and start anew. I just know I no longer wish to be a soldier focused on killing and destruction. I want more out of life. And I hope you might want that, too."

Richard began to squirm uncomfortably. Demetrius was puzzled. "Richard, are you a'right?"

Richard laughed a little and glanced at Demetrius sheepishly.

"Well...it's...it's the call of nature, you see. I need to take care of some 'business.' So, if you'd be so kind as to free my arms so I can go off in the bushes, there. I promise I'll stay within sight of you."

Demetrius suppressed a smile and reached to untie his friend's arms. Then, he turned to undo the ropes binding Richard's feet. Seizing his opportunity, Richard grabbed a large rock nearby and smashed it into Demetrius' head. The blond man crumpled to the ground. Richard freed himself and bent over Demetrius. He was still breathing, and the wound to his head was bleeding considerably, but not dangerously. Richard glanced around to make sure he was alone.

"You'll wake with quite a headache, my friend. I'm sorry to hit you, but I must get back to Lord William. When I return, 'twill be with an even larger army to crush Kay and all her friends!"

Richard bent close to Demetrius and kissed him on the lips. "And if you stand with her, I will kill you, too," he said sadly.

With a final glance back, Richard ran north through the woods, hoping it would be some time before his disappearance was discovered.

◆

"Damnation!" cried Lord William, Son of Dob, as he paced his rooms. "Still no sign of Richard. The battle was planned for days ago. I should have had word by now. Guard!"

A guard entered the room and bowed deeply.

"Send for the most senior commander in my army at once!" William barked.

"Yes, sir!" the guard sharply turned on his heels and exited the room.

William sank onto a pile of soft cushions and stroked his beard, his mind racing. It seemed his entire world had turned upside down in the past weeks.

We have never lost a battle—not one! Richard is the finest leader of any army anywhere, and I cannot imagine he wasn't able to make quick work of that tiny Garsland. But why haven't I heard back yet?

William's musings were interrupted by a shrieking sound in the hallway. As the voice neared, he realized, with some horror, the babbling cries belonged to his wife, Lady Ruth, whom he had sent off to be killed. He rose to his feet as Ruth burst into the room and flung herself upon him, weeping hysterically. He stared in astonishment. Her clothes were in tatters, her hair hung filthy and lank, and it had clearly been some time since she had bathed. He held his head away and grimaced.

"Oh, my love, my husband!" she wailed. "I am home at last! The horrors I have endured—you have no idea. I was almost killed at the hands of bandits," she blubbered, her arms locked about William's neck. "I was nearly sent under something called the Bridge of Doom to become a slave! Then, my escort soldiers and attendants abandoned me, and poor Beth and I only managed to find our way home to you, my darling, by selling what was left of my jewelry."

William was dumbstruck. His careful plan to dispose of Ruth had failed utterly. He regained his composure. "There, there, my dear, do not take on so!" he said, disengaging her from around his neck. "You are safe here with me again."

Taking her hands, he led her to a sofa and sat her down. "I am simply horrified to hear of all this," he lied in a silky voice. "When I get my hands on the men in whose care I left you, I will have their heads, I promise you!"

And that, he thought to himself grimly, *is not a lie. How dare they fail in their duty to kill her?*

"Oh, William, my dear, dear husband!" Ruth said, leaning into him and resting her head on his shoulder. "I missed you so. Never send me away like that again, promise?"

"Of course, darling wife, do not fret. Go and get yourself cleaned up. Uh...did you say Beth returned with you?"

"Yes. I told her to go bathe, but I wanted to come to you at once. I knew it would ease your mind to know I was home safe and sound."

"Indeed it has. I am ever so glad you returned safely," William said, smoothly. He helped Ruth to her feet and ushered her to the door. "Now go and rest and we will talk more later. But do send Beth to me as soon as she is presentable. I wish to hear her version of these horrific events."

"Yes, my darling," Ruth said, lifting a dirty, tear-streaked face to her husband for a kiss. Gritting his teeth, William pecked her quickly on the lips and sent her on her way. Alone again, he could barely keep from screaming aloud. Why was everything going so wretchedly? He needed to speak to his master about this but was unable because, just then, the Captain of the Guard returned.

"You sent for me, sir?" he said.

"Yes. Send out a small company of soldiers in the direction of Garsland. We need to find out what happened. In particular, it is imperative we find Sir Richard."

"At once, sir!"

When the man left, William locked the door. Then he moved across the room to where a large tapestry hung. Pulling one edge of it up and securing it to the wall, he revealed a large mirror, framed in black onyx. He took a deep breath and stared into his own eyes. Shortly, William's image was not the only one in the mirror. Anthony, the Black Lord, appeared in the reflection, standing just behind him. Lord William knew that as long as he held his own eyes steady, the Black Lord's image would stay there. But as soon as William broke his gaze, his master would fade into the shadows.

"Why do you call me?" Anthony hissed. "I am quite busy, as you know."

"Yes, my lord. But I am concerned about recent events. My wife, sent off with soldiers instructed to kill her, has re-appeared, sadly, alive. My army has not returned from the battle with Garsland. I am in a quandary as to how to proceed."

"You fool! You failed me in the most elementary of instructions! The battle was a disaster, thanks to some wench who somehow got her hands on a wizard's orb. Your men are nearly all dead or deserted. But Richard remains alive and, fortunately, escaped the enemy's camp. He returns to you soon."

"I am so grateful for your ability to see all, my Lord Wizard," William said, still holding his own gaze in the mirror. "What would you have me do next?"

"When Richard returns, you will form a larger army and regroup. I will be able to keep you apprised of the enemy's whereabouts, thanks to a man I placed with them. The fools think he is on their side but he is loyal to us. We will crush them all in no time."

"Thank you. It will be done as you say." As William spoke, a knock at the door startled him and he broke eye contact. Anthony faded into the mist and William quickly covered the mirror with the tapestry again before going to the door. He opened it to find Beth standing before him, her eyes downcast.

"Well, well, well. Little Beth, come home at last. There is at least some consolation to my wretched wife's return." William chuckled as he pulled the trembling girl into the room, shutting and locking the door behind him.

CHAPTER 40

Following the account of David and Irene's experiences in the land of the Black Lord, Gar, Stephon, and Fitzgerald joined the rest for a meal. Plenty of bread, a variety of cheeses and milk remained on the cart Marcus stole from the convent. No one wanted to trouble the fairies for food—everyone could see how tired they were from trying to restore Garsland. While the grounds were slowly coming back to life, the castle was far from habitable.

"Ah, me," Gar sighed, looking about him. "I fear I have many more days of camping ahead. Perhaps I should just abandon my home and not bring my townspeople back at all. Especially if there's another battle ahead of us, as you seem to suggest, Irene."

"I don't suggest it, Gar," Irene said, firmly. "I mean to assure you! The Black Lord will soon be here. He has only to defeat his brother, Anton, to escape his underground lair and there will be nothing to save us. That's why we must leave as soon as we can to seek the Wizards' Keep. 'Tis our only hope. Anton is getting weaker. He fears he cannot keep Anthony underground much longer."

"And you have no idea where this Wizards' Keep is, Irene?" Kay asked. "Or how long it may take us to get there?"

"All I know is we need to travel south to an area generally uninhabited. Does anyone here have any idea what that place could be?"

Everyone remained silent. Then Gar spoke up. "Fairies and wizards do not mix, as you may know. But we have, or at least *had*, a fairy that once left Garsland in search of adventure. When he returned to us, he told fanciful tales of a land to the south with three tall mountains. They stood so close together, they were known as the Three Brothers. The fairy spent some time there and said it was where old wizards go to die. Nobody believed him, of course—quite ridiculous."

"No, Gar, that must be it!" Irene cried in excitement. "Anton told me the remaining wizards were old. Perhaps the Keep is in the Three

Brothers where they go live out their remaining years. Is the fairy still around? May we talk to him?"

Gar called a nearby fairy over. "Peony, we have need of Boe the Trumpeter. See if you can find him. If he's not anywhere about in Garsland, then you may need to go to the refugee camps and seek him there. Hurry. There's no time to waste."

The fairy rolled her eyes, and sighed.

Alas, I know right where he'll be.
I'll hear him first, before I see.
His trumpet sounds both day and night
Annoying everyone in sight!
But fetch him here for you I will.
Perhaps you'll keep his trumpet still!
I'll be back 'ere a new day break
And hope you've not made a mistake!

Peony zoomed off towards the refugee camps. The rest of the group stared in amazement.

"Boe, the Trumpeter?" Fitzgerald said. "Gar, you do live among the most amazing creatures."

"So, assuming the Three Brothers mountain range is where we need to head, who will go?" Kay asked. "I am willing, of course, and Fitzy, I'm sure we can count on you. Stephon, what of you? And David, perhaps you have undergone more than your share of trials already. I'm certain we all would understand if you wanted to remain behind. No one would think the less of you."

To her surprise, he shook his head. "No, I *very* much want to join in on this journey. You can certainly depend on me."

"I would be happy to go," Stephon said. "But the more of us who go, the more supplies will be needed. And what of Demetrius Keats? Or Luciano? They're still with the refugees. Perhaps I would be of more use with them, preparing for battle."

"You may be right, Stephon," Irene said. "Although, Demetrius may be willing to join us. Since we travel south towards the camps on our way, we can ask him."

"Good. I will remain in the camps to prepare for the coming fight. Also," Stephon smiled shyly, "I am hoping to spend more time with a certain someone." Kay and Fitzgerald exchanged amused glances. They had noticed how, when they were with the refugees, Stephon would often find an excuse to visit a lovely half-fairy named Marguerite with whom he had danced at the ball.

"Yes, Stephon," Kay said, still grinning, "I think you should stay behind. Besides, you already did your part, bringing David, Irene and Fitzy back from the land of the Black Lord."

"Very well, then—let's see," Irene said. "There's me, Kay, Fitzgerald, David and perhaps Demetrius. And if this fairy Boe can help show us the way, we will surely make a speedier journey than if we bumble around by ourselves."

"Wait, Irene," Nan spoke up. "You can't mean to leave *me* behind!"

"Well...yes, Nan. I didn't think you'd want to come on this part; you've been through so much."

"Well I do! I mean, no! I don't *really* want to head off into the unknown, but I don't want to be parted from you again—or Fitzgerald, either. And Kay, of course. And I have as much at stake in helping to defeat the Black Lord as anyone. My parents may yet be his prisoners. So, whatever it takes, I'm willing to do!"

"All right," Irene said quietly, "we welcome your help." She smiled at Frieda and Marcus and said, "No one expects you to join us, naturally. This is not your battle."

"Thank you, your Highness," Marcus said. "With your approval, we will follow you to the refugee camps and see what assistance we may offer there. Frieda has many skills, and I am a capable blacksmith. I can assist in making weapons if the means may be had to create a smithy."

"Then let us get a good night's rest," Gar said. "With luck, tomorrow Boe the Trumpeter will arrive and we will see what he has to say."

◆

Ta-tara-ta-ta! All the residents camping in the remains of Gar's palace, both fairy and mortal, were blasted awake at the crack of dawn. Stumbling groggily out of their tents, they saw Peony, the fairy that had gone off to find Boe the Trumpeter, and beside her, blowing a trumpet loudly, the proof of her success.

Ta-ta! Tara-ta-ta-ta-taaa! The horn blasted again. Peony rolled her eyes as if to say, "I told you so," then rudely pulled the trumpet from the lips of Boe and announced:

Here is Boe, your Majesty,
Though the need for him I cannot see!

Without another word she flew off, clearly relieved to be done with her mission.

Gar appeared less than pleased to be awoken quite so early, but seeing that everyone was now out of their bedrolls and waiting for him to say something, he stepped up to Boe and greeted him.

"Welcome good fairy, Boe. We sent for you because you have done what no other fairy here can claim. Or so you say. We need to know of the land of the Three Brothers Mountains."

Boe lifted the trumpet to blast it again but, catching the stern expression of Gar, changed his mind and cradled it in his arms before speaking.

'Tis true, I have been to that place.
Say, is that pudding on your face?

Irene looked at the others with dismay. Pudding? Good heavens! Was this fairy right in the head? Was this what Peony meant when she said earlier about making a mistake?

Gar, however, seemed nonplussed. "No, no. 'Tis only my beard. We will give you some time to recollect your journey, Boe. In the meantime, we will dress and eat." Turning to the rest of the gathering, he continued, "Let us meet in the largest tent in half an hour, everyone."

Soon, everyone crowded into the tent to question Boe. While they ate, Boe had entertained them with his trumpet. Nan feared she was getting the beginnings of a headache and was thankful when Gar convinced Boe to "rest himself for a short while." When everyone quieted down, Irene began.

"Good fairy Boe, the very existence of countless towns and kingdoms may depend on you. The Black Lord is intent on enslaving everyone within his reach and our only hope is to find the aging wizards at Wizard's Keep. We understand you may have been there when you journeyed south? When you were at the Three Brothers, did you actually see any wizards?"

Boe nodded enthusiastically.

I saw them, yes, indeed I did.
To hear more, you have but to bid!

He began to fly in a twirling fashion about the tent, which, because it was so crowded, required everyone to keep ducking as he flew by to avoid being hit in the head by his legs. Irene grabbed a limb as Boe swooped by and, holding him tightly, tried again.

"Yes, dear Boe. Please *do* tell all you know. I cannot stress to you the urgency of our mission." Irene pulled him down to ground level, and forced herself to smile to cover her anxiety. He smiled back at her brightly and continued:

They live up high above the trees,
In caves that glow bright blue.
I thought that they were very nice,
But one can be nasty, too!

"Oh, dear. Do you think you can find your way back? Would you take us?" Kay asked. "How long a journey would be for us mortals?"

Ha ha! That's right, you cannot fly!
And so by horseback you must try.
How long a trip? Well, if you dare,
The journey's not too hard to bear.
Perhaps five days if I do my sums.
Or longer, if the fat one comes!

And he pointed straight at Stephon, who look rightfully indignant, for he was hardly fat...just a touch stocky, perhaps.

"Why, you...you..." Stephon sputtered. David put a calming hand on his friend's arm and whispered to him to pay no mind as, clearly, this fairy was a bit addled.

Gar stood up, signaling an end to the meeting.

"Very well, Boe. As your ruler, I command you to accompany these good friends of mine to the Three Brothers Mountains. Take them to the wizards, if any wizards be left. Protect them as you would me and great shall be your reward when you return." Then, speaking to the others, "I advise you to leave immediately. My fairies rounded up some horses abandoned from the recent battle. You can go as far as the refugee camps today and see who else might join you."

"Are you not coming with us, Gar?" Fitzgerald asked.

"No. I have changed my mind about leaving. With the fairies' help we shall rebuild and restore my kingdom to her former glory. Hopefully, Lord William's army will think we all abandoned this area and leave us be. Tell the women and children refugees who wish to return to do so, and, as for the men, tell them I bid them to fight for our freedom."

CHAPTER 41

The fairies had collected enough horses for everyone, though Marcus and Frieda said they would continue on with the horse and cart they had 'borrowed' from the convent. Boe the Trumpeter flew alongside, often tooting his horn. Traveling at a respectable pace, they reached the outer edges of the refugee camps by mid-afternoon and the command center soon after. As they approached, Kay got a shock— alongside Demetrius and Luciano sat Ken! Spurring her horse past the others, she leaped off her mount and raced up to him.

"Ken, I am so glad you are alive! I was so...I mean, we were *all* so worried! How did you survive? Where were you all this time? We sent men out to search every day, but they couldn't find you!" she babbled. The two stood staring at one another. Ken smiled broadly, made a motion as if to embrace Kay, then checked himself and put out his hand instead. Kay looked startled, laughed and grabbed his arm with both her hands and pulled the handsome man in for a hug. Breaking their embrace, they stood grinning at each other while the rest of the group dismounted and approached. Fitzgerald and Stephon warmly welcomed Ken back and Kay introduced him to Nan, Irene, David, Frieda and Marcus.

When Ken finally told his tale, he said he suffered a blow to the head in battle, but when he awoke was in a small cottage with no idea how he got there.

"All I recall is seeing a fading blueish light outside the window as I came to. Nearby were food, drink and a chamber pot. I stayed there for days, alone, getting my strength back. When I was strong enough to leave, I found my way to the refugee camps. Luciano and Demetrius have caught me up on everything."

"Well, there is so much more to tell," Kay said. "Thanks to Irene and David, who just escaped from the Black Lord, we have a new plan to defeat him once and for all. It means a journey of several days to find the Wizards' Keep in the southlands and ask the wizards for help. This fairy, Boe, has been there and means to guide us. We'll leave at first light tomorrow. We had planned to ask Demetrius to join us, but now you are back, Ken, it might be better if you two take command of our army here. Perhaps Luciano can come with us, instead."

"Ah, no, Principessa," Luciano spoke. "I have been waiting for your return only to say goodbye."

"Goodbye? You're leaving us?" a stunned Kay asked.

"I have been so torn whether to stay and fight with you all, or return to my own kingdom. Demetrius and Ken both agree word must be spread as far as possible of the threat of the Black Lord. Perhaps he has already sent his assassins to Tondlepen, I do not know. But I hope to be able to warn my citizens and prepare for a battle if it comes our way." Luciano gazed lovingly at Kay. "Of course, nothing would make me happier than if you came with me, and became my wife—this time at your own will, of course!" he said, smiling sheepishly at the memory of his Mirror Self forcing a wedding upon her. "But I see you have a higher purpose here. So, my dear one, I will depart tomorrow as well...however, heading east, not south with you. I hope you can forgive me."

"Of course," Kay, stammered. "I think...it will be for the best. I will miss you, Luciano...so very much." With tears in her eyes, she flung herself into the large man's embrace.

◆

Late that evening, after everyone had retired for the night, Kay found herself alone, sitting on a tree stump and looking up at the stars. Suddenly, every sound from the camp around her seemed to disappear into a buzzing noise, and her head began to swim, as it had before when she had the vision of Richard's army. Determined not to fight it, Kay breathed deeply and tried to allow herself to be guided into a vision. She saw herself standing on a ridge overlooking a valley. Beyond, she saw what she immediately knew were the Three Brothers. Above each mountain shone a bright star, which before her eyes turned blue, and joined into one giant blue light, which dropped onto the middle mountain, disappearing behind the timberline. The vision faded, leaving her with just the view of the night sky again.

This is the way. I have been shown which mountain the Wizards' Keep is located on. I must tell the others! She stood and turned to find Demetrius approaching her.

"Kay, can we talk?"

"Of course, old friend. I am glad you are staying on to train our army. Next to Richard, I know of no finer soldier." The two sat down.

"Richard. Yes. Well, that's what I need to talk to you about. I asked everyone not to mention it, because I wanted to be the one to tell you. Richard escaped."

"What? Why didn't you tell me sooner? Why isn't anyone going after him?" Kay cried, leaping to her feet.

"Naturally, we dispatched soldiers as soon as his escape was discovered. The fault is mine. He tricked me and knocked me unconscious," he said, leaning in to show her his head wound. "It was some time before I came to and, by then, Richard had too much of a lead on us. He may well be in the Secret Valley by now. That's another reason I wish to stay behind. I, who am closer to him than anyone, know how he is likely to proceed."

"This is dreadful news!" Kay moaned. "We are now certain Lord William is in league with the Black Lord. With Richard back to lead the army, we will be at a huge disadvantage in the coming fight. Especially if the Wizards refuse to help us—if, that is, we can even *find* them. If they're even alive..." Kay suddenly broke down in tears. "Oh, Demetrius, I am so tired of running and struggling and... and... just everything!"

Demetrius took the crying girl in his arms. "I know, Kay, I know. It's not the happy, safe life we had in the Valley. But we cannot give up because there's no going back to that life. We know, now, it was a sham. I agree with Luciano. You and Irene and Nan all have a higher purpose. I believe you will succeed. Just know all our prayers go with you. Now, get some sleep, please. You will need all your strength for what lies ahead."

Kay nodded mutely, too tired to even reply. Giving Demetrius another hug, she entered the tent she shared with Nan and Irene and crawled into her bedroll.

Demetrius watched her go, wondering if, perhaps, he should accompany her and the others to Wizards' Keep after all. In his heart, however, he knew he was needed more here.

Turning to go to his own tent, he took one last look at the sky. Puzzled, he squinted his eyes to see more clearly. There they were again...three blue lights hanging in the southern sky. Demetrius remembered seeing them from the tower in Gar's castle the night before the battle.

'Tis an omen, surely. I pray it is a good one.

CHAPTER 42

Three days later, Kay stood gazing on the exact spot she had seen in her vision. She pointed it out to her fellow travelers: Fitzgerald, David, Irene, Nan, and Boe the Trumpeter.

"How long do you think it will take us to get up to the spot on the mountain I saw in my vision?" she wondered.

"I would guess at least another day's journey to cross the valley and reach the foot of the mountains. And then, to climb it...perhaps most of another day?" Fitzgerald replied. "Boe was right, about five days for us to reach Wizards' Keep."

"Tara! Tara-ta-ta-ta!" Boe blasted on his trumpet. Everyone else cringed. They couldn't decide which was worse, his repeated horn blasts or his often crazy rhymes.

"Boe," Irene said, patiently, "I thought we came to an understanding. You are only to blow your trumpet in case of a true emergency."

Boe scowled, but nodded in apology.

We are now so close, you see.
I could not help but sound the horn.
At the Keep we soon will be,
And then our victory will be born!

"Let us hope you are right, Boe," Nan said. "Forgive me for complaining, but I am weary of riding for hours on end. Still, knowing we are getting close to the wizards gives me renewed energy. Come on, let's hurry."

They all spurred their horses on and continued down a path to the valley floor. After a few more hours of travel, they were well into the wide valley. It was beautiful with a river, fields of what seemed like prime fertile land, and patches of dense woods.

"How peculiar that there are no inhabitants here," Fitzgerald said. "Surely this would be a most welcoming and prosperous place to set up a village. There's water, ample land, probably lots of good game to be had in the nearby woods. Yet, there's not a building or soul around."

"It seems unlikely we're the first humans to come here," Irene said. "Although Anton did say the area was uncharted and uninhabited. So that helps me feel we are on the right path."

"Perhaps the wizards make *sure* nobody stays," David added. He studied the sky. "It's well past the meridian. What say we take a break by the river to rest and water the horses and enjoy a bite to eat?"

"Good idea, David," Irene said, and the others nodded in agreement. Soon everyone was relaxing by the rushing river eating bread and cheese. David, however, seemed unusually antsy and kept pacing back and forth until finally Fitzgerald asked him what was wrong.

"Oh, nothing," David said. "I just am eager to stretch my legs as much as possible before getting back on a horse. You'll forgive me; I need to walk a bit. I won't be long." He headed briskly into a nearby grove of trees.

When he was far enough away not to be overheard, David pulled out the small mirror and stared into it. Within moments, Anthony, the Black Lord, appeared behind David's own image, his red eyes glowing.

"Master, we are so close. At what point shall I begin the killings?" David asked.

"Soon, my lad, soon. I am curious if this group of misfits can actually accomplish its goal of reaching the Wizards' Keep. I also must know if there are any wizards still living. It will make my plan much easier to achieve knowing they are not around to oppose me—old and weak though they may be. Keep checking in with me—you are to be commended for your loyalty."

"Yes, my lord. I live to serve at your command. I await your—"

"David?" Irene stood not far off calling to him. David immediately broke eye contact with the Black Lord and tucked the mirror away. "Who are you talking to?" Irene walked up to him.

"No one, Irene."

"I heard you clearly. And what were you holding?"

"What did you hear?" David said in an angry voice, grabbing her arm. Irene looked startled and afraid. Abruptly, David's face calmed and he laughed a little. "Sorry, princess. I'm just embarrassed. I was singing to myself—that's all. And I was admiring myself in this little mirror," he said, taking it out and showing her briefly before quickly shoving it back into his pocket. "We may be vagabonds, but one still wants to look one's best, don't you agree? Or do you think it terribly vain of me? It's just...I hate this scar Jean Louis gave me below my eye. Still, I would endure it all again for you." David took Irene by the arm and steered her back towards the group. "Was I taking too long? I'm sorry you had to come get me. Let's be off at once, shall we?"

Irene felt perplexed by David's actions, but put it down to anxiety about their mission. Still, a niggling little doubt remained as she and the others remounted their horses and proceeded on through the valley. She caught herself glancing warily at David off and on.

As nightfall approached, the weary travelers found a lovely spot in the foothills of the Three Brothers to set up camp. Kay and Fitzgerald went out to hunt; it had been some time since they had had much to eat except cheese, dried fruit and bread. Luck was with them and they caught two rabbits, which they skinned, cleaned and soon had roasting over a fire. The aroma tantalized everyone—they realized what a treat it was to taste fresh meat again.

After dinner, Irene, Nan and Kay were in their tent, talking softly. Irene was describing David's odd behavior.

"What do you think, Kay? Do you think he's telling me the truth?"

"I don't know. Such a handsome man could be excused for being a bit vain, I suppose. Was he really singing, as he said?"

"No. That's what puzzles me most. I am certain he was speaking, *not* singing. I hate to doubt him, though. He was so brave when faced with death at the hands of Jean Louis, and then he suffered greatly in the brick pits. It's just...something seems amiss."

"Well," Nan said, "all we can do is keep an eye on him as we head to the Wizards' Keep. Oh, Irene, do you think the wizards will help us? Will this horrible nightmare finally be at an end?"

"I hope so, Nan. I hope so."

◆

In the morning, the group inspected the center mountain. There appeared to be a narrow path leading up and into it, but it was hard to gauge how far they'd be able to ride their horses. After a couple of hours, they found their suspicions were correct. The path narrowed to such an extent and became so rocky, steep, and treacherous that they no longer could use the horses. They backtracked to a wide spot, tied the horses to nearby trees and bushes and debated whether one or more of them should stay behind with them. Fitzgerald thought perhaps Kay or Nan should remain, but they were having none of it.

"If you'll remember, Fitzy, *I* am the one who saw the vision directing us to this peak of the Three Brothers. I am certain the Wizards' Keep lies just beyond the timberline. I must go!" Kay said, somewhat heatedly.

"And I simply won't be parted from Irene again," Nan said. "My legs are strong from years of dancing, and 'twill be no difficulty for me to climb. Perhaps you should remain behind."

"No," Fitzgerald said. "At least one of the men needs to go with you ladies. Perhaps David can stay."

"No!" David, Irene, Nan, and Kay said in unison. There was an awkward silence. Then David spoke: "I think Boe the Trumpeter is the best choice. After all, his work is mostly done. He led us here, but the end is in sight. We don't need him now."

The others nodded in agreement. They instructed Boe to stay with the horses and blow his trumpet to alert them if there were any problems. With that settled, the three young women and two men began to move up the mountain. It was rough going, forcing them to climb over or around huge boulders, duck under brush and fallen trees, and pull themselves up walls of rock. Soon, everyone became dirty and sweaty. Irene and Nan were not dressed in the most suitable clothes for the arduous climb. Kay's garb was sturdier, being made of doeskin, but her ankle was bothering her again and, as she picked her way along more slowly to favor it, she soon fell behind. With Fitzgerald to help her, Nan and the handsome knight soon were well in the lead, with Irene and David not too far behind them.

Suddenly, the bright sky darkened and enormous clouds gathered overhead. Thunder rumbled, lightning flashed and rain poured down. Within minutes, they all were soaking wet and stumbling in the muddy, rocky path.

"Find shelter!" Fitzgerald yelled to everyone behind him. He pointed to a large group of trees and he and Nan ran towards them. David held Irene's arm to assist her over another boulder and then saw what appeared to be a small cave in the mountain that had escaped Fitzgerald's notice. He pulled Irene towards it and soon they were inside, protected from the rain, though the thunder still roared about them. David spotted some dry moss and sticks inside the cave, and used a flint to make a small fire.

"David, where is Kay? I don't see her!" Irene yelled over the storm. "Should we go back and find her?"

"She'll be fine. Of all you girls, she is the most capable," he shouted back.

"But I'll never forgive myself if she slips and hurts herself. I'll just go out a ways and call to her. Are you coming?"

"No—I'll stay here and keep the fire going."

As soon as Irene went out into the storm, David grabbed his onyx mirror and called to Anthony.

Irene peered through the rain for any sight of Kay. She saw her, limping slightly, but making steady progress, despite the downpour.

Irene shouted to her they had found a cave and pointed in its direction. Kay yelled back for the princess to go ahead and not wait in the rain. "I'll be there right away, Irene!" she called as she grabbed a nearby branch for support.

Irene nodded and hurried back to the cave. At the entrance, she saw David standing in the dim light, once again looking in the mirror and speaking.

I know he is not singing this time, and who would be so vain as to need a mirror now?

Slowly, she crept up closer to David, who, between concentrating on his conversation and the sounds of the storm, did not notice the girl. A few steps from David, Irene could not only hear David, but see to whom he was speaking! Horrified, she gasped aloud. David dropped the mirror in surprise.

"What are you doing?" Irene cried. "Why are you talking to *him*, of all people? What does this mean, David?"

The man gave her a look of pure evil. Irene felt her blood run cold. She wanted to flee but was held motionless with fear.

"What this means, dear princess," he said as he stepped closer, "is that it's time for you to say goodbye. I shall tell the others you attacked me and I had to defend myself. If they don't believe me, I shall kill them, as well. I have my orders." He lunged at Irene, grasped her around the neck and began to choke her. Her hands flew up to his and she tried to pull them off, but he was too strong for her. Irene kicked and slapped at him, trying anything to stop him, but he kept on until he was bent over her, slowly lowering her towards the floor of the cave, his eyes intent on hers as he continued to choke the life out of her.

"Tara! Tara-ta-ta-ta-ta!" the trumpet echoed in the cave.

Startled, David lost his grip on Irene who slumped to the floor. Boe the Trumpeter hovered at the cave's mouth, blasting on his horn for all he was worth. Quickly grabbing a knife from his belt, David threw it with deadly accuracy at the fairy. Boe fell to the ground. David turned back to Irene, who was coughing and trying to crawl away from him. As he reached down to her, he heard a voice.

"Stop or I will shoot you as surely as you stand there, David!" Kay stood over Boe's body with her bow raised and arrow poised.

David sneered at the girl. He reached for another weapon, but Kay did not hesitate, firing her arrow into his right shoulder. David howled in pain and fell back, striking his head on a rock. His eyes rolled back and he lost consciousness. Kay raced over to Irene, who continued to cough and gasp. "Irene, are you alright?"

"I think so," Irene croaked. "Thank Mirn you came when you did, Kay. Thank Mirn for Boe the Trumpeter! How did he come to be here at that moment?"

"He came up the mountain when the storm began. He was worried about us, poor thing. I told him to go ahead to the cave you pointed to. A good thing he did, for I fear my arrival would have been too late to save you."

Just then Nan and Fitzgerald, who had managed to hear the trumpet through the fierce storm, arrived. Nan screamed at the sight of Boe, who lay bleeding on the cave floor, and of David with an arrow in his shoulder. She ran to her friend.

"Irene! Irene, what happened?"

"David tried to strangle me, but thanks to Kay and Boe, he didn't succeed. Is he...is Boe dead?" she asked Fitzgerald, who knelt beside the fairy.

"No, but I fear he won't last. His wound is too grave and we have nothing with which to help him."

Irene cried out in despair and rushed to the dying fairy's side. "Isn't there some of that special sparkly powder that helped Nan? Perhaps it may save him," she said, frantically searching Boe's clothing. She found a small pouch tied to Boe's waist. After looking inside, she sprinkled some powder onto the fairy's wound. But it was too late. Boe was slipping away. Irene cradled him in her arms.

"Oh, Boe, thank you! Thank you. You saved my life," she whispered as tears fell down her face. Boe looked up at her with a wan smile.

'Twas nothing—just what I was told,
To keep you safe from harm.
My actions were both fast and bold,
And my trumpet called the alarm.

"You *were* fast and bold, and thank heavens for that wretched trumpet!" Irene said, laughing a bit through her tears. "We will never forget your bravery, dear, dear Boe." He smiled again and then gasped slightly.

Alas, I think 'tis time to go,
although I know not where.
My trumpet I shall only blow
On the other side of...here...

With his final rhyme, Boe the Trumpeter, softly exhaled and died. Everyone looked at each other with dismay.

"Brave little fairy," Fitzgerald said in a voice choked with emotion. He turned to glare at David on the cave floor. "Well, now. What to do with this treacherous villain?"

"He is in league with the Black Lord," Irene said. "That mirror on the floor is his means to communicate with him. I saw him—I saw Anthony's face in the mirror talking to David. And when David knew I had seen it he began to choke me. We have been betrayed!" She buried her face in her hands.

"All is not lost yet, Irene," Kay said, picking up the mirror. "We don't know what information David transmitted to the Black Lord. And he certainly is in no position to relay anything more."

At that moment, David began to stir and moan. His eyes fluttered, opened and he stared at everyone in the cave. "What happened?" he said. "Where are we and... how was I shot? Oh my stars, it hurts tremendously! Was I wounded in a battle?"

Fitzgerald stomped over to David and stood above him. "Kay shot you because you were trying to kill Irene!"

"What? Impossible! I would never do such a thing!"

"You deny you were talking to the Black Lord with this mirror?" Kay asked, holding it up. "Do you deny you have been his agent all along? What have you told him?"

"Nothing! I don't think...I don't even know how I got here—where are we? The last thing I remember is being in the underground world after Irene and I were captured and separated. They fed me, clothed me and... and... I don't remember what happened after that. You say I am a traitor? It wasn't me! I am not on the Black Lord's side; you must believe me!"

"Perhaps this all explains David's odd behavior," Irene said. "I knew something was wrong, but couldn't put my finger on it." Speaking directly to the wounded man, she said, "David, you must have been under some spell, and working against us all this time. Have you no memory of it at all?"

"None...I...ah!" David tried to raise himself up but fell back in pain from the arrow, still in his shoulder. "Can... can something be done about this?" he asked, gritting his teeth. Kay came over and inspected his wound.

"A good shot, I must say...it went clean through. Irene, bring what's left of the powder over here, please. David, this will not be pleasant." Working quickly, she took a knife and clipped off the arrowhead. Then, asking Fitzgerald's help to hold David down, she braced herself and as quickly as possible, pulled the arrow shaft out of the man's shoulder. He screamed in agony and fainted again. Kay took the fairy powder and muttered, "I hope I don't need any magic fairy words to use this." She sprinkled the powder into the wound, first on the front and then the back. Before her eyes, the wound ceased to bleed and began to heal over.

"Miraculous," Fitzgerald murmured, looking on.

"We'll let him and Irene rest here a bit and then continue," Kay said. "The storm has eased and we must reach the Wizards' Keep as soon as possible, don't you agree?"

The others nodded, but Nan pointed to the dead fairy and said, "What about Boe? Shouldn't we cover him or something? It seems terrible to just leave him there."

Fitzgerald looked around the cave. "We have no tools with which to bury him. There are lots of large stones here...let us at least cover him with them and create a kind of crypt."

Nan and Kay nodded and, while David and Irene recovered, they began to collect the stones to bury their fairy friend.

CHAPTER 43

"My lord! Sir Richard has returned," a soldier announced to William, Son of Dob, who was dining with his young son, Alex.

"At last! Send him to me immediately. Alex, stay here. It's high time you began to step into your role as my heir."

Richard came in, dirty and tired, bearing a grim expression. He strode up to Lord William and bowed briefly. "Forgive my appearance, Lord William. I met up with the soldiers you sent out to Garsland and rode hard with them to return. I wish I had better tidings to give you, but the battle was a fiasco. My men were nearly all killed..."

"Yes, yes, I know all about it," Lord William interrupted. "I am just grateful you are still alive. Tell me, did you see Sir Fitzgerald and Kay?"

"And Demetrius. He survived the earlier battle, but unfortunately, he has turned against us. He sides now with Fitzgerald, Kay and the refugees. I was held prisoner, but escaped. My plan is to get another army together as quickly as possible and pursue them. A rag-tag group such as that should be no trouble to finish off."

"And yet they defeated you once before," William said, sipping his wine.

"Strange things occurred which I cannot explain. But I assure you they will not happen again."

"Be that as it may, I want you rested and ready. Do not rush to go back into battle yet, Richard. Let us plan carefully how to proceed. I am sure we have time enough to take care of that little band of miscreants. We cannot afford another failure."

"But the longer we wait, the farther the group slips away, my lord. As my right-hand man, Demetrius will be preparing the refugees for battle, knowing, no doubt, my exact battle plan."

"Precisely. That is why we must wait and come up with a plan he will not expect. Now, go and clean yourself up, eat and rest. We will talk tomorrow."

"Father, is Fitzgerald my enemy now?" young Alex spoke up. "He was always my favorite knight. He would play with me and teach me how to fight."

"Yes, my son. Fitzgerald, Demetrius and Kay are all our sworn enemies. And if we take them alive, you will see them all hang in the courtyard. Richard—be on your way."

Richard bowed and left the room. Alex went back to his dinner and Lord William poured himself another glass of wine. Just then, Lady Ruth breezed in.

"Pardon the interruption, my dear, but I came for Alex. He must recite his lessons for me before bed," she said.

William stared at his wife with amazement. No longer the overweight, slovenly wife he was accustomed to seeing, Ruth was wearing a lovely gown and was groomed impeccably.

"You...you look different, my dear," he managed to say. He was rewarded with a radiant smile.

"Oh, William, you noticed!" she said, giggling like a schoolgirl. "Well, you see, when I returned, my dress was nothing but rags, and it wasn't until I cleaned myself and went to my wardrobe that I discovered I could fit none of my regular clothes. The long walk and difficult journey home had the benefit of making me lose quite a bit of weight. This dress is quite old, actually. I found it in the back of the wardrobe—'tis all that would fit! I am having my other dresses altered."

"Well, you look quite lovely, my dear," William mused as she took Alex by the hand to lead him from the room. "Perhaps...perhaps you would like to return when you're done with his lessons and join me for some wine."

Lady Ruth giggled and nodded as she left.

◆

After an hour's rest in the cave, everyone was ready to continue. There was some discussion over whether David should even be allowed to join them after he killed Boe the fairy and attempted to murder Irene, but as Kay pointed out, he no longer possessed the mirror to communicate with the Black Lord and he had been disarmed. They agreed that as long as they kept David in sight at all times, he was not likely to attempt anything. David still seemed somewhat confused by the situation, asking repeatedly if he had really killed the fairy.

The five began to climb the steep mountain once again. The rain had ceased, but now a strong wind was blowing. It forced them to go very slowly to maintain their balance on the uneven ground. Soon the wind blew so fiercely that trees crashed around them. Still, they climbed on. Then, the wind stopped abruptly and hail came down, stinging them badly.

"Someone doesn't want us to keep going!" Fitzgerald said, grimly.

"It must be the wizards," Irene said, gasping as she struggled along in her wet clothes. "Perhaps this is a test for us."

"Anyone else certainly would have turned back by now," Nan said. "I almost wish we could!"

"We don't have any choice but to continue," Kay said, as she slipped for the umpteenth time. "But look! I see light through the trees in front of us. It's the edge of the forest—the timberline. We're very close now—keep going!"

Kay was right. In just another hundred yards, they emerged from the woods to stand in an open field of rocks and boulders that stretched up to the snow-capped peak of the mountain. The weather was suddenly clear and sunny, whereas when they looked just a few feet back into the trees, the hail was still falling down. They waited a bit to catch their breath and surveyed the landscape.

"Now what?" Kay wondered, voicing what all of them were thinking as they gazed on the bleak surroundings.

"There!" Fitzgerald cried. "Over by that big reddish rock; do you see it? A blue glow."

They hurried over to the rock but the light was gone. Then Nan pointed farther up. "It's there. It's there!" And where she directed was the same blue, glowing light.

"It's leading us—come on!" Irene scrambled towards the blue light.

"Leading us off a cliff, if we're not careful," David said.

Again and again, the glow disappeared just as they were about to reach it, only to reappear again elsewhere on the slope. "Like trying to catch a rainbow," muttered Fitzgerald. But at last, it ceased its cat-and-mouse game and stayed in one place, glowing brightly in front of a huge boulder. When the five arrived, they stood, wondering what to do next.

"Can we get around it?" Kay asked. But after looking around a bit, they decided that wasn't possible.

"Perhaps we need to move the rock," Nan said. "But how could we? It's too big and heavy for even an army."

"I think...we have to *touch* the light," Irene mused. "I'm going to put my hands on it."

"No!" everyone cried. But Irene ignored them and walked straight up to it with arms outstretched. She reached into the blue glow and vanished.

"Irene!" Nan screamed, racing after her. As she touched the light, she, too, disappeared.

"Well, all in," Kay said. "Wherever that light sent them, we have to go, as well." She stepped up to touch the light, vanishing just as Nan and Irene.

"Very well, David," Fitzgerald said. "Let us go together." And before David could even respond, Fitzgerald grabbed his arm and pulled him into the light.

Fitzgerald felt a flash of heat, yet it was also a cooling sensation unlike anything he had felt before. It was as if the blue light passed directly through him and although he felt no motion of his own body he had the sensation of traveling—as if the world were passing him by at lightning speed.

Silence.

Fitzgerald slowly became aware that he was standing, still holding David's arm. Then he heard the sounds of his own breathing, felt the ground beneath him and a warm breeze on his skin. He opened his eyes and sharply inhaled. He was in the most beautiful place he had ever seen—an enormous cavern, covered in beautiful, multicolored rock formations. Giant clusters of crystals in every imaginable hue were all around. Glowing stalactites hung from the tall ceiling of the cave. To the right, a waterfall that kept changing colors before his eyes splashed into a pool. As his eyes adjusted to the dim light, he was grateful to see all his friends standing nearby, also marveling at the beauty of the cavern. Releasing David's arm, Fitzgerald walked over to Irene, Nan and Kay.

"Where are we?" he whispered, for it seemed a sacrilege to speak any louder.

"The Wizards' Keep, I am certain," Irene said. "No human place could be so lovely. It must be for wizards alone."

"You are quite right, Irene," came a booming voice that filled the cave. Nan squealed in fright and fairly leaped into Fitzgerald's arms. Kay and Irene looked around for the source of the voice.

"Will you...will you please make yourself known to us?" Kay asked. "You seem to know who we are. We would like to know you."

A crack appeared in the wall before them and the two sides began to separate. Behind the wall there was a room with three golden thrones, studded with precious gems. Upon each throne sat an old man. On the right sat a smallish man with curly grey hair, kind eyes and an impish expression. To the left was an enormous man who looked upon the intruders less happily. And in the center a tall, white-haired man with a long beard smiled. They were each garbed in robes of deep blue, and a blueish light seemed to hover and pulsate around them.

"You must be the wizards Anton told me of," Irene said.

"We are," the smiling wizard on the right, said. "I am Seever."

"I am Kaza. You are not welcome here," the fat wizard barked. "No human has ever been allowed in the Wizards' Keep. It is only because *he*," gesturing to the wizard in the middle, "convinced us to let you enter."

"I am Moor-ray," the bearded wizard said, in a soft voice. "Pay no mind to Kaza. He barely tolerates the company of other wizards, much less you mere mortals. And you are Fitzgerald, David, Nan, Kay and Princess Irene. We bid you welcome."

"Thank you," Fitzgerald said. "We have come a very long distance to find you."

"Yes, we know. We have been following the activities of you and your friends quite closely in recent weeks. Pity the fairy Boe was killed. We remember him from his earlier visit. Quite an amusing fellow."

David looked shamefaced. "They say it was I who killed him, though I have no memory of it and can only say in my own defense that I was under the influence of the Black Lord—a wizard who used me in a most foul way to do his bidding. "

"Yes, that is why we are here," Irene said. "To beg your help to defeat Anthony before thousands more are killed. Another battle is coming and without your assistance we do not have a prayer of winning."

"We have helped your kind enough already," Kaza spoke loftily.

"How have you helped us?" Kay asked, puzzled.

"Foolish girl! Do you really think *you* controlled the wizard's orb to free yourself? Or that you directed its rays to freeze the battle for your victory?" Kaza barked. "Or *you* had those visions? Bosh! 'Twas our magic going through you that made it all possible!"

"Be at peace, Kaza," Moor-ray said, calmly. "She would have no way of knowing it was us." Turning back to Kay, he smiled. "Yes, child, we have been watching and helping in small ways. It was we who saved your friend, Ken. It was we who froze the scene allowing your side to position the enemy into their fatal stances."

"That was my idea, actually," Kaza said smugly.

"Then you'll help us now," Nan said.

"No," Seever said, shaking his head. "We have decided we cannot interfere in a larger way. Anthony is too strong for us, and what will be, will be."

"But—so many will die!" Nan said, shocked. "And many others are still the Black Lord's captives, including my parents! Why won't you help?"

"We are old, child," Seever said. "We come here to live out our remaining years in peace and beauty. None of us has the energy or desire to wage battle. We are simply...too old."

The group stood stunned at the speech. After all they'd been through and all the loss they had endured, it seemed impossible to have failed, to have their plea so summarily rejected.

"And now you must return from whence you came," Kaza abruptly said. "We agreed for Moor-ray's sake alone to even speak to you, but you have heard us and now must leave us to our quiet life." He waved his hand and conjured up a giant blue ball of light. "You have but to walk into that light and you will be back by the place where you left your horses. We graciously save you the trouble of climbing down the mountain again. Now thank us and be on your way."

Nan, David and Fitzgerald all looked to Kay—surely she would speak up and convince them. But she stood there as shocked as the others.

Then a voice softly, but firmly said, "No."

Everyone turned to look at Irene. She was staring with determination at the wizards. Again, she said, "No."

The wizards exchanged glances of surprise.

"No? NO?!" Kaza thundered. "How dare you contradict me?! I can turn you into a rabbit, if I so choose, you impertinent little chit! Be off! We don't care about any of you or your little battles. Leave us...NOW!" The room shook and some crystals fell from the ceiling, shattering on the ground.

"Not without getting what we came here for!" Irene cried, stepping closer to the three wizards. "You say you are old and waiting to die. Well, good for you. But we are *young* and we have our whole lives ahead of us. And we want to live them! We want to marry and have children and contribute to our communities. We want to laugh and love and sing and dance and know that our lives *mattered* for something when we're gone. You can't just sit in here with all the power you have and not help us!

"Even if you don't have the same strength of power you had when you were younger, you've already shown us that you *do* have power. And, yes, you've shown us that you care, too, or else you would have let the residents of Garsland all die! You have to help us! You just have to! Because we want to live—we want to live!" Irene fell to her knees before them, breathing raggedly, fighting to keep the tears in her eyes from falling down her face. Emotionally exhausted, she whispered one more time: "We want to live."

There was a long pause as the wizards exchanged looks.

"The girl speaks the truth, Kaza," Seever said. "We do care. It was you, after all, who came up with the idea of freezing the battle."

"Rather brilliant of me, I know." Kaza sighed. "But do we really want to get further involved in this...and take on Anthony? A wizard a third our age with twice our power?"

"What he may have in power, he lacks in experience," Moor-ray said, stroking his beard. "It may be the last thing I ever do, but I vote to spend the rest of my power defeating him. I would go to my grave a satisfied wizard knowing I had done my best to stop him from taking over the upper-world. He has been held underground since we sent him down there eons ago and charged Anton to hold him. But Anton is getting weaker and we cannot ignore Anthony now."

"I, too, am reluctant to fight Anthony, Kaza," Seever said. "But I stand with Moor-ray. We must go to battle."

"Very well," Kaza grumped. "I cannot let you do it alone. I will join you both to help these foolish mortals."

Kay, Nan, Fitzgerald and David all cheered and threw their arms around Irene. "You did it!" Nan cried. "Now, at least we have a hope of victory."

"Hope, my dear girl," Kaza said dryly, "may be the only thing we truly have going for us."

CHAPTER 44

Realizing their mortal guests were both physically and emotionally exhausted, the wizards conjured feather beds with silk sheets—although Kaza muttered that cotton would be good enough. So relieved were the five, knowing they could count on help from the wizards, that they all fell into deep sleep.

The three wizards, meanwhile, began to debate ways they might prevail against the Black Lord. Kaza wanted to strike fast and bold, but Moor-ray and Seever suggested a more cautious, strategic approach. Not many wizards as strong as Anthony had ever been taken down. He was in his prime and had honed his skills for more than a century. They also did not know what special skills he might have mastered over these many years. The discussion went long into the night, ending with no firm agreement.

◆

Kay woke first. She looked around, still amazed by the beautiful hues of the cavern. She sighed happily as she remembered the wizard's promise to help them. She woke Irene and Nan.

"We'd better get started. We need to reach the refugee camps as soon as possible."

"I was dreaming of another ball at Garsland," Nan yawned. "But at this one I wasn't abducted. I was dancing with such a handsome man, and he told me I was the loveliest thing he had ever..."

"Oh, my stars—we must leave at once!" Irene interrupted, throwing back the coverlet. "I didn't mean to drop off for so long. How long did we sleep? So hard to tell if it's day or night in here."

David and Fitzgerald also began to stir. Fitzgerald smiled broadly, but David found it difficult to look anyone in the eyes. He got out of bed and walked to the waterfall, avoiding the others.

The crack in the wall parted once again, revealing the three wizards on their thrones. They all had serious expressions, except for Seever, who wore an impish grin.

Fitzgerald rushed over to them. "So, how does this work? Do you just wave your hands and we're all back at the refugee camps?"

"There are limits to what we can do," Moor-ray smiled. "Travel spells are a bit tricky and not always successful. Sometimes you end up with your head and torso in one place, and your lower extremities in another."

"Oh, let's not do that then!" Fitzgerald gulped.

"But what of the blue lights?" Irene asked. "Isn't that how you transport yourselves?"

Moor-ray laughed gently. "What you saw—the blue lights as you call them—are our eyes to things far away. It's how we monitored the last battle and from a distance, yes, we were able to help you in small ways. To be effective in the coming fight, we will need to be nearby. We can speed our journey, however. We have a conveyance which will greatly shorten our trip."

"What is it?" Nan asked.

"We call her Star Sail—a flying vessel. It is nearly invisible from the ground, and affords us a straight path to any destination at a much faster pace than a horse. We haven't dusted her off for many decades, but we trust she still works. Please prepare yourselves for our departure. We will ready the ship. There is a repast at our table."

Nan, Kay, Irene and Fitzgerald filled themselves with the generous meal the wizards left for them. David came to the table for a moment and munched on a piece of venison, but then walked away and sat on the floor, his back to the rest. He opened a satchel slung around his neck and withdrew Boe's shiny, silver trumpet, and gazed sadly at it.

"Come join us, David," Fitzgerald called.

"I...no, thank you," David said.

"Suit yourself."

Irene stared at David with concern and her hand involuntarily went up to her bruised neck. She was unsure if she could truly trust David again, but he seemed somehow...defeated. She would need to forgive him somehow. She was about to approach him when Seever hurried over to them.

"Star Sail is ready. We must board her at once. Oh, what an adventure! I thought I'd never see the likes of this again. I must say I am very excited!"

Seever led everyone out of the cavern to the mountain slope. They looked up and saw, to their astonishment, a wooden ship, swaying back and forth in the air as if it were bobbing in waves. A rope ladder hanging from it extended to the ground, and Seever ushered everyone to it.

"Hurry," Moor-ray called, leaning over the side of the ship. "I can't hold her for long!"

Nan nimbly climbed the rope ladder first, followed by Fitzgerald, Irene, and Kay. David hesitated, looking as if he might stay behind, but finally joined them. Seever ascended behind him, with amazing agility for one so old. Kaza climbed last, complaining as he struggled with the ladder, his weight causing it to swing wildly.

"Damnation! This is too much!" he shouted.

The ship was compact with two small masts and sails. It had a galley below and three roomy sleeping quarters. The wizards turned over Seever and Moor-ray's quarters to their five mortal companions. Nan, Irene and Kay took Moor-ray's large space, while David and Fitzgerald settled into Seever's room. Kaza grumpily agreed to share his with the other two wizards. Moor-ray pulled up the ladder and they sailed north towards their destination. The day was sunny and warm and everyone began to feel things might just turn out fine.

Although it wasn't apparent while traveling in Star Sail, when viewing it from the land below, the ship was sometimes disguised as a small cloud. Other times it would become transparent and blend into the sky.

Night fell and the stars came out. After a brief meal, Moor-ray sought out Irene and David. He wanted to hear everything they remembered about the Black Lord and his underground kingdom. After a lengthy discussion with Moor-ray, Irene and David headed to the upper deck to get some air. David was sullen and didn't seem to want to talk. Irene approached him.

"David. I know we haven't talked since the...um...incident in the cave, but I want you to understand I don't hold you accountable. I have seen the power of the Black Lord firsthand. Believe me, there was nothing you could do to control yourself. He is too—"

"Please, stop," David interrupted. "I know you are trying to make me feel better, but it's no use. I killed the good fairy Boe and nearly killed you! If I had somehow been stronger and resisted the Black Lord's power, I wouldn't have put you and the others in such peril. When we get to the refugee camps, I may leave. The best thing I can do now is just stay out of the way."

"No, David, you are wrong. We will need you. You possess cunning." She smiled at his shocked reaction. "You might not think this a respectable trait, but in the days to come, your unique skills may prove to be quite valuable. Please, David, I beg of you, put this unfortunate incident behind you and help us."

"I don't know. I... I will think on it. I can't promise anything. How can you ever trust me? Can you forgive me?"

"David, I..." Irene started to say she forgave him, but the words stuck in her throat. Something still made her doubt.

"I thought so," David said bitterly and went below deck. Irene watched him, worried.

I want to forgive him, but is he truly free of the grasp of the Black Lord?

CHAPTER 45

Since losing Irene, Silent Susan spent each day slipping from one hiding place to another seeking rest and food. Now, she heard the grunts and growls of the beasts on patrol and, finding herself back at the abandoned temple, ducked inside. Her nose wrinkled at an overpowering stench. Intrigued, and not unaccustomed to foul odors, Susan sought out the source. She pulled a bit of a candle from her pocket and lit it. Moving into the sanctuary, she came upon a body, ripped and torn, lying near the altar. She approached cautiously. A male lay stiff on the ground, dressed in fine clothing and slain, no doubt, by the beasts. She started to move away, but paused, thinking.

Perhaps there are valuables on the body I could use.

She checked his vest pockets and found only a blood soaked biscuit. She searched his trousers and rejoiced upon finding a small, gold coin. Then, Silent Susan noticed shards of metal all over the floor. She held her candle up and realized the shiny stuff was gold. It seemed the slain man had been in the midst of ransacking the temple before his death. Susan gathered up as much gold as possible in an improvised sack and bedded down for the night in the robe room she had previously shared with Irene.

Irene, I hope you are well...

◆

Ken and Demetrius discussed strategy for the coming battle. They took stock of what weapons and strong men they had and found they were sadly lacking in both. They tasked Marcus to forge what new weapons he could. They sent scouts to examine the nearby terrain and report back to them about any weaknesses or strengths in the territory which might be used to their advantage. They were in a heavily treed area, which could provide cover, and there were many canyons the enemy would have to traverse before it reached the small, ill-equipped army. Ken and Demetrius trained those who were willing to fight with archery and swords, but, compared to the highly disciplined soldiers of William of Dob, they knew this little army would be no match.

"Our only hope is the element of surprise. We must find a way to strike at them before they expect it," Demetrius said. "They will probably anticipate us using a nearby fortress to defend ourselves. The most likely place would be Garsland, even though they nearly destroyed it before. They know it is the only line of defense for many miles around. I suggest two things: we must return to Garsland and entreat the fairies to fortify the walls of the castle. And since there is only one logical road to take, we should station small bands of soldiers up in the trees throughout the canyons leading to the town to attack as they approach."

"I agree; the element of surprise may be our best hope," Ken said. "I pray the wizards get back in time."

"Yes, but at this point we can't count on them."

Demetrius and Ken rode to the castle to speak with Gar. He agreed that the low walls around his kingdom should be raised and fortified. He assembled the fairies and directed them to cease beautifying the grounds and put their efforts into creating strong, tall walls. They did so, but not without letting him know how they felt.

Although we need prepare for battle
And there is little cause for prattle,
We understand a pressing need:
A command for walls by king decreed.
Flowers, trees, and lovely garden
Will have to wait, please beg our pardon
Tall, strong walls are thought more practical.
And they are, of course, much more tactical.

"Yes, yes," Gar replied testily. "Just build up the damn walls, will you? It's for your safety as well as ours!"

◆

Star Sail continued towards her destination. Moor-ray remained at the helm, assisted by Fitzgerald. They estimated they would reach the refugee camps within a day. Kaza was clearly *not* on board with the whole enterprise. He had brought along a small pocket fiddle, called a Pochettes, which he played fiercely as they went along. Wizard Seever, however, seemed to be quite enthusiastic.

"I can't believe we are doing this! Although we are old, I believe there are ways we can defeat the Black Lord. Just give me time and I shall think of something. I am an avid historian and study the battles of old. There may be ancient tactics we can put into play. Oh dear, oh dear, I wish Kaza and I had brought *all* of our books along!"

Nan tapped her foot in rhythm to Kaza's music. She longed to dance, but the deck of the small ship did not afford much room. Instead, she went to the galley and brought Fitzgerald and Moor-ray some bread, cold meat and cheese.

"You must be hungry and tired," she said to Fitzgerald. "I don't think you've slept since we left the Keep."

"I do feel ready to drop. Perhaps I could sit down for a bit. I think I gave Moor-ray good guidance on how to find the refugee camps."

Nan guided Fitzgerald to a bench at the stern of the ship and entreated him to lay his head in her lap. Within moments, he was fast asleep. Nan stroked his hair as she viewed the land below them. Deer scampered over the ground, reminding her of the hills near her home. Would she ever be able to return there?

Kay looked at the contented pair and tried not to be too envious. She restrung her bow and inspected her arrows. The normally chatty girl was silent, filled with apprehension about the fight to come.

Night fell—another clear, starlit sky. Star Sail flew on, swaying gently. The only sound was the wind whipping through the sails.

Unable to sleep, Irene left Nan and Kay in the cabin and went up top to pace the deck. Even with the wizards, she was deeply worried.

Here we are, facing our destiny. What happens in the coming days will determine the future for us all. I pray we somehow come through this, although I don't see how. The wizards do not even have a firm plan yet.

Irene sighed and went below deck to try to sleep. David, who had been sitting silently in the shadows, gazed after her.

◆

Gar sent a few of his fairies to fly towards the Secret Valley to see if the army was coming. They reported back that the army was marching out of the Hooded Mountains. The plan was set. There was only one way into Garsland from the west, and that was through forested canyons. Demetrius and Ken thought the army would come through there, as they had before. The roads to the north were narrow, hilly and impractical for troops. There was a large river to the south and a good, wide road to the east, but it would take Richard's army many days out of his way to reach it. Demetrius felt his old comrade would want to attack as soon as he could.

Demetrius and Ken placed archers in the trees on both sides of the canyons to take out as many soldiers as possible before they reached Garsland. They built a barrier of boulders and fallen trees just past a

269

blind bend in a road. They hoped it would trap the soldiers so the archers could pick them off. They knew Richard's men would eventually get through but, with luck, it would reduce their numbers enough to be a fairer fight.

The newly fortified walls of Garsland were finished and all the remaining men and boys who could fight were sent there to await the battle.

Despite Kay's hope of using women for support positions, there had been no time to train them so it was decided to keep the children and women in the refugee camps, as far away from the fighting as possible. The camps were several miles from Garsland and near the east road, which they thought Sir Richard was unlikely to use. After the morning meal, families said goodbye to the men and watched them march off towards Garsland. A few older men with limited fighting skills stayed behind in the camps, just in case.

Demetrius and Ken rode back to Gar's castle by horseback. The soldiers followed.

"I don't suppose we can count on the wizards," Ken said. "I doubt they will get here in time to help."

"I'm still hopeful," Demetrius replied.

"But, you do know it is highly unlikely that you and I will come out of this...unscathed."

"Yes. The odds are not good for our side, but there is so much at stake and I can no longer live under the thumb of a corrupt leader." The two continued on in silence. Then Ken spoke again.

"Demetrius, may I ask you something?"

"Certainly."

"You know Kay pretty well, don't you?"

"Since she came to the Secret Valley at age twelve or so. Why?"

"Well, um...is she spoken for?"

Demetrius stared at Ken for a moment, and then began to laugh. "You like her!"

"Let's just say...she intrigues me. So, has she an agreement with anyone?"

"Well, since Luciano left, I guess there's no one in her life. Frankly, I was kind of glad to see Luciano leave. A nice enough fellow, but I did not think him a good match for Kay. We once thought she and Fitzgerald were fated, but nothing was ever announced and now that match appears to be over."

"Really?" Ken said eagerly. "Are you sure? Because I don't want to get in the way."

"Oh, Fitz has *quite* fallen under the spell of Nan. You can be sure of that. So, it's Kay for you, eh?"

"Yes. I have never met anyone like her. She can match any man with a bow and arrow. She has spirit and strength and doesn't back down. I think her strength is what I like most. God help the man who argues with her, for he will lose!"

Demetrius laughed. "Yes, I have personal experience with that! Well, best of luck, my friend."

CHAPTER 46

Star Sail had been flying now for two days. As the sun rose, Moor-ray took the helm, searching for signs of the refugee camps. Seever wanted to see what awaited them, so he sat cross-legged on deck and closed his eyes. A blue ball of light spiraled up from his body and headed north. After several minutes, the light returned to his body and Seever opened his eyes.

"Please, everyone," he called, "I need you all here."

Fitzgerald and Nan went below deck to get everyone. Kaza lumbered up last, devouring an enormous pink pastry. Seever looked at him with disdain.

"What?" Kaza said, shrugging. "I'm hungry."

"Everyone," Seever said, "I just viewed Garsland. The battle has not yet started. It appears the castle of Garsland is now fortified with a high wall—a very good thing. The volunteer soldiers are ready. Their families remain in the refugee camps."

"Good!" Kay broke in. "We have not missed the battle and there's a strong fortress from which to defend ourselves."

"There is more," Seever continued. "I tried to locate Sir Richard's army, but could not. Somehow, the Black Lord must be blocking my vision. We will be blind to their machinations until the last moment. However, I could sense this army is quite large, several thousand at least, and close to Garsland. I am certain the fight will begin soon."

"Oh, dear!" Irene said. "Moor-ray, you must make the ship go faster!"

"The ship can only travel as fast as the winds take us, child," he said.

"Look!" Fitzgerald exclaimed. "That craggy hill over there? We passed it not long after we set off to find the wizards. We are nearly at the camps."

"Yes, but we should head straight to Garsland now," said Kay.

Everyone agreed. Moor-ray directed Star Sail to the fairy kingdom.

◆

Demetrius, Ken and the refugee army arrived at Gar's castle mid-morning. The king came out to greet them, uncharacteristically donned in a subtle deep-blue tunic and matching tri-cornered hat.

"You are all most welcome. As you can see, my fairies did an outstanding job of erecting a high wall, complete with battlements, a sturdy drawbridge and, even, a moat. Oh, and they added a dungeon. I can't imagine what for, but they said if they were going to do it right, every fortress needs a proper dungeon."

"Thank you, fairies," Demetrius said.

A few fairies curtsied and tried to smile, but it was easy to tell they were nervous. They spoke in unison:

We hope this fortress meets your need
And truly wish you all Godspeed.
Never have we seen transpire
An aim so great, a vision higher.

Demetrius and his cobbled-together army entered the fortress walls where they were greeted by a sprightly march that was played by the instruments with no musicians. Much of the castle itself was still in disrepair, since efforts to fix things were put off while the new walls went up. The soldiers headed to tables inside, laden with food.

After eating, most of the refugees stationed themselves at the wall, though Demetrius selected thirty-seven young archers and sent them to the canyon to climb the trees. There was nothing to do but wait for the inevitable. The men tried to lessen their stress by sharing jokes and playing old country games with stones. Demetrius and Ken walked along the wall, encouraging everyone.

Suddenly, Demetrius thought he heard a voice call his name from high above. He turned around, trying to locate the source. Was he losing his senses? "Demetrius!" he heard again. He looked up and there in the sky, seemingly out of nowhere, he saw Kay climbing down a rope ladder to the main courtyard. Demetrius ran down from the wall and met her as she jumped off the last rung.

"Kay! I am so glad to see you. What is this marvel? How did you appear from out of the sky?"

"It's an invisible ship that flies. Oh, I have so much to tell you. The wizards are here! Three of them. They are going to help us."

Suddenly, a large anchor attached to a long rope plunged down into the courtyard, narrowly missing Demetrius and Kay. "Sorry!" a voice called. Irene, Nan, David, Fitzgerald and the wizards climbed down the ladder.

◆

All three wizards attempted unsuccessfully to view the movements of Sir Richard's troops. They couldn't overcome the Black Lord's blocking spell, but they all believed the army was drawing close. The wizards met to discuss how they might assist in the fight. Moor-ray was especially skilled in persuasion spells. He had hoped to use one to influence Richard. He might still be able to, but as of yet, he couldn't reach the knight. Seever was an expert in ancient potions. Kaza was a clever wizard with a talent in general spells, but had not used his powers much in a long time. Unable to come up with any specific role for himself, he vowed to jump in as he saw fit during the battle.

Seever walked out to inspect the grounds surrounding the new walls. He went to the riverbank and noticed a small plant with round, dark green leaves and purple flowers. He ran back to the castle in excitement.

"Quickly, your Majesty, I need help!"

"What? Is Richard's army here?"

"No, no. I need assistance to collect a plant called Tansinwort. I can use it against the enemy. Please, will you direct your fairies to gather as much of this plant as possible? Oh, and I will also need a hot fire, a cauldron, nose hairs from a weasel, bat urine, and goat's milk."

"How do you propose we do that?" the king frowned. "I suppose the fairies can collect the, what is it called, Tansinwort? The goat's milk is easy, and the fire and cauldron, but the rest?"

"It is all quite necessary."

"We will do our best." Gar began to give his fairies orders.

When the fairies gathered the necessary ingredients, Seever set to work mixing the potion. It took a deft hand to mix this potion correctly. Seever piled wood on the fire and the brew boiled rapidly. Gradually, the volume reduced, dried and left a powdery, purple substance in the bottom of the cauldron. Wrapping a scarf around his mouth and nose to avoid inhaling the powder, Seever scooped small amounts into leather bags and loosely drew the strings shut. He ended up with fourteen bags. He had hoped for more, but this would have to do.

◆

Stars came out on another clear night. Soldiers slept on top of the new castle walls. Archers in the canyons bedded down on the ground, taking turns to watch for Richard's army. A strong wind blew from the north, whistling through the trees.

Gar hosted a banquet of sorts in the main gallery of the castle for the wizards and invited guests. Demetrius and Ken updated those who had been on Star Sail on the strategy for the battle. The others headed off to bed, but Ken motioned Kay to stay for a bit.

"How are you faring?" Ken asked.

"Alright, I guess. I am so glad Irene convinced the wizards to come with us and we got back in time. It might make all the difference."

"That is not what I asked. How are *you* doing?"

"Oh! Well, I'm fine. I suppose. Apprehensive about how things might go—like everyone."

"How do you see your life after this is all over? If things go our way, that is. Certainly you can't go back to the Secret Valley."

"I don't know. I haven't thought about it, really. I guess I'll be homeless. But I've haven't lived in the Secret Valley that long. I guess I'll find a new home."

"I think if we can defeat the Black Lord there will be endless possibilities for the likes of you and me."

"We can only hope."

Ken drew closer to Kay and took her hand. Kay, startled, began to withdraw her hand, but then grasped Ken's hand firmly. She stared into his green eyes for a moment before reaching up to kiss him hard on the lips, then ran up the stairs to her room.

Gar gave Kay, Irene, and Nan a spacious, but mostly empty, room in the castle. Sleep did not come easily and the girls tossed and turned and chatted intermittently throughout the night.

"I wish I knew how I could help," Nan said. "I am not much good with weapons and such. I feel so useless."

"Why didn't I spend every spare minute teaching you two to use a bow and arrow?" Kay sighed. "Too late now." There was silence for a bit, and then she continued, "Do you remember when we all first met? I didn't know what to make of you two. I wanted so much to trust you even though you were the enemy. But, I also liked you both immediately and wanted to keep you out of Lord William's clutches."

"And we are tremendously grateful," Nan said. "I hate to think what our lives would have been without you. Irene and I are eternally in your debt."

"I am not seeking your gratitude. I just think...well, our friendship has been so unique, so strong. Don't you agree?"

"Indeed," Irene said. "I know we will remain steadfast friends, whatever comes."

The girls got out of bed and hugged one another, choking back their tears. Then the three returned to their beds to try once more to sleep.

CHAPTER 47

Richard's army reached the barrier in the canyon as the sun barely peeked above the horizon. There was little light to see by, but the archers in the trees did their best. After several soldiers were killed, the army abruptly withdrew. The archers cheered, thinking they had beaten back the soldiers.

Several minutes later, a dozen soldiers came back and launched fiery arrows into the trees. The trees ignited, forcing the men to leap down. Some fell to their death. The remaining few defending archers ran ahead to the castle to sound the alarm, sorely disappointed they had not killed more of their foes.

The battle cry of a trumpet woke the three girls. Kay rushed to dress in her doeskin. Irene grabbed Kay's quiver of arrows and helped Kay to strap it to her back, while Nan fetched Kay's bow. Kay ran to the high wall of Gar's castle. Irene and Nan threw on their clothes and tied back their hair.

"What should we do, Irene?"

"Let's find the wizards—maybe we can help them."

Having run off the archers in the trees, Richard's army moved on to the roadblock. They began to dismantle the trees and boulders.

Kay found Ken on the parapet, readying the archers. His expression was strained, but determined.

"Men!" he shouted. "This is the time all things can change for either the better or the worse. I entreat you to reach within yourselves and find a warrior's heart. We must not yield these walls. To do so will mean death, or a life of drudgery and despair. The future for us all now lies in your hands. Strike boldly and decisively and the day will be ours!"

The men cheered. Silently, Kay readied her bow and took her place near Ken, Demetrius, and Fitzgerald. Gar entreated his fairies to hide themselves inside the castle.

Nan and Irene entered the main courtyard looking for the wizards. Seever ran up to them. "I need the two of you—now! We must board Star Sail at once."

Moor-ray and Kaza were already aboard. Nan climbed the rope ladder followed by Seever. Irene placed her foot in the bottom rung but abruptly stepped back down.

Was that David she saw running into the castle?

Irene shouted up to Star Sail, "Go on without me!"

Kaza leaned over the rail, "Stupid girl! What are you thinking?"

"Irene, please," Nan begged. "You must come with us!"

Irene paused for a moment, then shook her head and waved the ship off. She ran after David.

Grumbling, Kaza used a spell to bring up the anchor and Moor-ray steered Star Sail towards the canyon. Seever approached Nan, his arms filled with small, leather bags.

"This is the potion I made yesterday, and if it works, it will be give our side a solid advantage. Now, take these little bags and loosen the strings. When I tell you to do so, toss them gently overboard so that they land upright and are open enough to release their contents into the air."

"I'll do my best, Seever."

"Never fear, I will help you. Go to the port side. I shall man the starboard side." He gave her half the bundles before he went over and readied himself.

Moor-ray was busy at the helm, so Kaza agreed to try to find Richard's whereabouts. He sat on the bench at the stern as his blue light shot straight up and traveled to the canyon.

◆

Irene sped up the stairs. She could hear rapid footsteps ahead of her. As she reached the second level of the castle, she spotted David darting into the room that she had shared with Nan and Kay the previous night.

What in the world is he doing? She crept down the hallway towards her room. She slowly opened the door and found David rummaging through Kay's things. *He is looking for the Black Lord's mirror!*

Irene raced into the room and tackled David, knocking him to the floor. The two struggled. David grabbed her and tried to hold her arms with one hand while reaching over to the mirror with his other. Irene saw he was inches away from grabbing the onyx mirror and, in desperation, bit his arm.

"Ow! Wait!" David shouted. "Stop! You don't know what you are doing!"

"Yes, I do! You are still in league with the Black Lord!"

278

"I am not. Truly! You must believe me!" he said, now straddling Irene and pining both her arms to the ground. Irene struggled to get free.

"Why should I believe you?" she said, glaring up at him.

"Have I done anything to harm you since I regained my senses?"

"No, but I still don't trust you."

"Would you trust me if I let you hold the mirror?"

Irene stopped her struggle for a moment and narrowed her eyes. "Why?"

"To prove I'm trying to help. You know my best skill is lying. You told me yourself my cunning could be of use. I think I can use this talent against the Black Lord. I don't think he realizes I am no longer under his power. If I can use the mirror to contact him, perhaps I can mislead him in some way."

"How do I know this isn't some scheme of the Black Lord's to get the upper hand?"

"Tie me up if you must. Just let me look into the mirror! If I betray you, pull the mirror away and contact will be broken."

"Very well." Irene used scarves to tie David's hands and feet. She gingerly picked up the mirror. She held it close to David's face as he tried to summon the Black Lord. Nothing happened.

"Wait," said Irene. "I think I heard you call him Master."

"I didn't remember that." He took a deep breath. "Master, I am here."

The Black Lord appeared in the mirror behind David's own reflection. "What news? Did you finish the killings?"

"Yes, my lord, I dispatched them all after we discovered the old wizards had all died. The Garsland refugees think I am the only survivor of a tragic journey."

"Very good. Where are you now? William informs me a formidable army assails the Land of Gar as we speak."

"I am in Garsland, my Master. The peasants are not well prepared. They are weak and many deserted, fearing Richard's army. Their defeat nears. But, I must warn you of something. William, Son of Dob, has been deceitful."

"How do you mean?"

"He wants to take the glory for himself. He will not bow down to you once he is victorious. He means to usurp you."

"How do you know this?" the Black Lord hissed.

"I intercepted a secret communication from Lord William to Sir Richard. It said once the battle is won, William plans to expand his empire."

"No. William has always been my most faithful servant."

"He has fooled us all, my lord. William is ambitious and self-aggrandizing. He seeks to defeat even you."

"That will not happen!" Anthony roared.

"Yes, Master, I, too, am deeply disturbed by this. It seems your real enemy is not the insignificant townsfolk of Garsland, but the ruler of the Secret Valley. How may I assist you?"

"Just stay at the ready."

"But...uh...since there is no real threat from Garsland and the refugees, should we perhaps call off the battle? Concentrate our efforts upon Lord William, instead?"

Irene now understood David's plan. If he succeeded, perhaps there would be no bloodshed today. She held her breath awaiting an answer.

The Black Lord sneered. "No. I wish the townsfolk of Garsland and the refugees to be completely wiped out. They are of no use to me."

"But..."

"That is all!"

The mirror went black. Stunned, Irene untied David's hands and feet.

"I thought, for a moment, this would all be over. I hoped you could persuade the Black Lord to abandon this fight. There is no way we can defeat him. We are doomed!" She began to weep.

"Oh, no, Irene, we may yet be victorious. We have the wizards, after all."

"No. I see now that ours is the futile attempt of a fly to defeat a fly swatter." Irene searched David's face. "Why are you even still here?" she asked bitterly. "This is our fight, not yours. Feel free to leave us and go back to your duplicitous ways. You make a better charlatan than soldier."

David, stung by this, said, "I cannot. I am bound by loyalty to you...and to the others. I actually can't believe I am even saying this, but..."

"This has all been for nothing...nothing!" Irene wailed.

David stepped forward and embraced Irene. She allowed it for a moment and, as she stepped back, David's hand dropped onto hers and the mirror she held. The second he touched it, David's face changed. He suddenly appeared haughty and malicious. Irene gasped, realizing the mirror still held sway for him. David made a sudden grab for it, but she snatched it away and threw the mirror against the wall, smashing it into pieces. She fled the room.

CHAPTER 48

Kaza repeatedly sent up his blue light to find Sir Richard, but he was unsuccessful. He had seen a young captain leading the soldiers in the canyon, but reported no sign of Richard. Star Sail flew into the canyon and Nan stood ready with the bags of Tansinwort dust.

"Whatever you do, do not inhale any of that dust," Seever called from the other side.

"What does it do?"

"It has properties to...wait! The men are below us. Nan, get ready. Wait until I tell you...and...NOW!"

Both Nan and Seever each tossed a bag over the sides of the ship. They landed below on either edge of the road with a 'plop' and purple dust rose out of them into the air. Strong winds wafted the dust straight into the path of the soldiers. As it hit them, the men fell to their knees, clawing at their eyes.

"I can't see!" a soldier screamed.

"It burns!" cried another.

As Star Sail made her way through the canyon, Nan and Seever dropped the bags every half a league or so. By the time the last one landed, only a few soldiers remained unaffected.

"That should slow them down," Seever crowed. "This potion was used in the battle of Coddleswood many centuries ago. If I remember correctly, they will be blind for several hours. This will give us quite the advantage."

"We must return to tell Demetrius and Ken," Moor-ray said, "so they can make use of this opportunity."

Star Sail returned to Gar's castle and the wizards explained that there would only be a few hours before the effects of the dust wore off. Demetrius, Ken and Fitzgerald took most of their men and rushed to the canyon. Kay wanted to go, too, but Ken insisted she stay behind.

"Some of Richard's soldiers may still make it here," he said. "We will need you to help defend the castle if it comes to that." He hugged Kay before he left. Nan rushed up.

"Kay, I don't know what happened to Irene! She was about to join us on Star Sail, but then she ran inside. Have you seen her?"

"No. It is not like her to turn her back on a fight."

Just then, David joined them. He told them what had happened between himself and Irene and of his failed attempt to stop the Black Lord.

"I hope I have placed holes in the Black Lord's confidence in Lord William, but I'm not sure."

"Where is Irene? Did you see where she went?" Nan asked.

David shook his head.

◆

Demetrius, Ken and Fitzgerald marched their army into the canyon. They fought off a handful of men who had been unaffected by the potion. After dispatching them, they found nearly all of Richard's soldiers kneeling on the ground. Blinded and writhing in pain, they were easily overpowered.

Ken ordered his men to tie the enemy soldiers up and take them back to the castle before their eyesight returned. "Put them in the new dungeons," he said. He turned to Demetrius. "We won! What a day. What a victory! Hardly a man lost, thanks to the wizards."

Demetrius, however, looked troubled. "I am not so certain, Ken. There is still no sign of Richard. Something is amiss. These soldiers...well, they don't seem to be well trained or outfitted. I don't even recognize most of them. And their numbers are not as great as I would expect."

"Then you think the fight is not over."

"Exactly. Richard is not done with us. We must return to the castle at once."

◆

While the army locked their prisoners in the dungeons, Kay, Nan, Ken, Demetrius, Fitzgerald, Stephon and the wizards assembled in the courtyard.

"Bad news," Kaza began. "I still can't see Sir Richard, but I can sense activity over the northern mountains. I fear they are headed here via the eastern road."

"No!" Kay cried. "That takes them right through the refugee camps. They'll slaughter all of those women and children. We must do something!"

"I knew there was something wrong," Demetrius said, grimly. "The first army was a diversionary tactic."

"Sound the trumpet!" Ken commanded. "Let the mounted soldiers take the lead. The archers and foot soldiers will follow."

Seever interrupted. "Wait. Give me some of your best archers to take aboard Star Sail. Richard's army won't expect an assault from above."

Ken selected several of his expert archers and asked Kay if she would be willing to go with them. She nodded and quickly went up the ladder.

"Kay, wait for me!" Nan cried, scrambling after her. Moor-ray began to follow, but then waved them on.

"Go ahead—I have an idea." He hurried into the castle.

The army headed out. David grabbed a sword and ran to catch up with the infantry, finding a place near Stephon. The horses galloped towards the east road, while more archers and foot soldiers ran as quickly as they could.

"Who would have ever thought we'd fight for real?" Stephon asked, nervously.

"Let's hope all our practice helps," David replied.

◆

Moor-ray went to the dungeon. The fairies, not quite understanding the imprisoned soldiers were the enemy, were giving them a soothing balm for their eyes. After a while, one of the soldiers remarked, "I can see a bit. The light is coming back and I can make out shapes."

"Yes, my eyesight is returning too," another said. This was followed by many mutters of agreement.

Moor-ray quietly entered the hallway near the cells and stood, thinking. *Since I cannot reach Sir Richard, a persuasion spell on him is not possible, but perhaps I can use one on these soldiers.*

Moor-ray sat on a stool and focused his mind. He placed his head in his hands and concentrated very hard, muttering an incantation over and over. Slowly, an amber glow grew around him. It became brighter and larger. Wafts of amber light stretched towards the soldiers, putting them in a trance. Moor-ray reached into their minds. He created a vision of what their lives would be if Lord William's army won; a wasteland, dead and colorless. He showed them that they would, in effect, be slaves to Lord William and the Black Lord. The land would be full of despair, devoid of joy or hope for them and their families.

After twenty minutes of this, an exhausted Moor-ray fell to the ground, gasping. It was hard enough to use persuasion spells on one man, let alone nearly two thousand. He couldn't be sure that it had worked. He could not hold the spell quite as long as he had wanted.

The soldiers slowly came out of the trance. Their sight was fully restored. "Let us out!" they clamored. "Please, give us a chance to fight! We must defeat our corrupt leader!"

The fairies seemed confused. Gar attended to Moor-ray, who whispered something in his ear. Gar nodded and turned towards his fairies. "Let them out and restore their weapons to them. Lead them to the battle!"

The fairies led the soldiers out of the castle and pointed them towards the east road. The men raced off to fight.

CHAPTER 49

Aided by strong winds, Star Sail soon hovered above the refugee camps. There was a strange fog engulfing the east road, just a quarter of a league from one of the camps. Suddenly, Richard's soldiers emerged through the fog. Hundreds of horses, in full battle regalia, rushed towards the outermost camp. Women and children screamed and tried to outrun the soldiers. A few older men with swords stood up to the soldiers, but they were cut down instantly.

Sir Richard brought up the rear, dressed in shining armor and astride a black steed. He stayed at the edge of the massacre, laughing as he watched the innocent citizens try to escape. Nearby, Lord William, Son of Dob, nodded with approval at the annihilation.

"Once we take care of these peasants, we'll move on to Garsland," he ordered. "And remember, I want to see Kay, Fitzgerald, and Demetrius die in battle or by my own hand."

Above, Seever regained the helm and Kay told the archers to prepare their bows.

"Draw arrows—aim..." she commanded, "release!"

On the ground, a hail of arrows seemingly came out of nowhere and struck the front regiment. Dozens of soldiers fell, to the confusion of those behind. Another volley killed more soldiers. Richard and William searched frantically for the source of the arrows, but could identify nothing. The archers on Star Sail shot off more arrows. They were now hitting their stride. Three more volleys took down even more men and now nearly a hundred soldiers lay dead. Richard's soldiers halted, not sure how to handle this invisible foe. But their captain refused to sound a retreat. He urged his men forward and so the slaughter continued. The scene became utter chaos as soldiers attempted to defend themselves against a foe they could not locate.

Ken, Demetrius and Fitzgerald led the front lines of their army. As they raced through the first refugee camps, they shouted at everyone to take refuge in Gar's castle. Women and children fled to Garsland. The refugees were very near sanctuary when enemy soldiers filled the road, advancing towards them. The civilians screamed and turned into the woods to take cover. To their surprise, Richard's converted soldiers ran right past them, completely ignoring them.

The small refugee army caught up to Richard's men at last and engaged the enemy. The clang of steel against steel rang through the air, as well as the screams of the wounded and dying. Casualties were high, mostly on the side of the refugee army. Kay and her fellow archers found it harder to accurately shoot Richard's soldiers because they were now mixed in with the refugee soldiers. They had to settle for picking off a few soldiers here and there. Richard's army relentlessly advanced towards Garsland.

Ken, Fitzgerald and Demetrius tried to hold the line, but it was clear they were losing.

Suddenly, over the clamor of the fight, they heard shouting from behind. They glanced back to see the soldiers from the dungeon coming towards them at full speed, swords raised above their heads. Ken turned to Demetrius in dismay.

"All is lost—we are hemmed in with no chance for escape!"

Many of the refugee fighters positioned themselves to face this new foe, but the soldiers refused to fight them. They sped past the refugees and began attacking Richard's army. Ken and Demetrius looked at one another in astonishment. They couldn't understand why these soldiers had joined their side, but, in the heat of battle, did not question it.

"Now we have a fair fight!" Ken shouted. "Fight on, men! Fight on!"

The battle waged for hours. Although Richard's army had far superior fighting skills, they were no match for the vigor in the army that opposed them. This army was fighting for more than territory. They knew if they did not win the day, everything they held dear would be vanquished.

CHAPTER 50

In the underground kingdom, Silent Susan ran into an alleyway, her bag slung over her back. The sound of the guards' feet came close behind her. She had been for running for so long and she was tired. She was resigned to become their next prey. She thought of Irene and hoped her friend and David had somehow escaped.

The beasts rounded the alleyway and snarled. Susan clutched the gold coin she had taken off the body in the temple and awaited the inevitable. Perhaps she could bribe the creatures with it. They came forward, snarling. One of them clawed at Susan, badly tearing the flesh of her arm. Susan sank to her knees, waiting for the deathblow. She closed her eyes, remembering Irene's kindness.

If only I could be with Irene once more.

She silently mouthed the name of her friend.

Irene...

Susan felt her body being pulled into some kind of vortex. *Is this what death feels like?* She lost consciousness. When she opened her eyes again, she was in a garden outside of a castle. There was sunlight. Trees. Color all about her. She gazed in wonder.

Oh, how beautiful. I had forgotten.

Just then, Irene burst through a door of the castle and ran into the garden, sobbing. Susan leapt up to intercept Irene's path. Irene stood a moment, stunned at the sight of her friend.

"Susan? Oh, Susan, I am so happy to see you! But how did you escape? How did you find me?" Susan just smiled and shrugged her shoulders, which caused her to wince in pain.

"You're hurt!" Irene took a handkerchief from her pocket and tied it around Susan's bleeding arm. Susan turned pale and collapsed to the ground.

Irene picked up Susan's small body and carried her inside the castle. After several minutes of searching, Irene found some fairies huddled in the great hall and begged them for help. The fairies placed Susan on a table and tried to work their magic. They sprinkled her with their sparkly dust, but Susan didn't respond. The fairies turned to Irene and shook their heads.

"Oh, please try again!" Irene pleaded. "Don't let her die. If it weren't for her, I would not be here now. Isn't there anything you can do? She must not die!"

One of the more senior fairies, dressed in a midnight blue cape, came forward. She held two small, white stones, which she placed upon Susan's eyes. Everyone waited in silence. Susan suddenly gasped and moaned.

"Oh, thank you!" Irene cried as she ran to get water and linens to clean and bind Susan's wounds. As the battle raged in the distance, Irene tended to her friend. She knew she should see if there was anything she could do to help her side win, but she couldn't leave. She owed Susan her life.

◆

The battle between Richard's army and the refugees waged on for most of the day, with each side gaining advantage, falling back, then gaining the field once more. Both sides suffered many casualties. Ken, Demetrius and Fitzgerald rallied their troops one last time to strike a decisive blow.

At one point, Demetrius battled so far into the fray that he was behind many of the enemy soldiers. He fought like a madman, knowing how much depended on his side's victory. After killing yet another soldier, he looked up, panting with exhaustion, and saw Sir Richard staring at him from a horse. The knight raised his sword and came galloping at Demetrius with intense hatred blazing in his eyes. As he came up on the tall, blond man, Demetrius nimbly leaped aside, spun, lashing out with his own sword, catching Richard's backside. Richard fell from his horse—hard—and lay still; the wind knocked out of him. Before he could recover, Demetrius was standing over him, his sword poised for a deathblow to the neck.

"Demetrius," Richard whispered, his eyes full of fear and love. "Has it come to this?"

Demetrius struggled with his emotions. He loved Richard, but the man stood for everything Demetrius now reviled. He knew he should kill Richard; knew he should end it here and now. The sounds of the battle faded into the background and all Demetrius saw was Richard's pleading eyes. He took his sword away from the man's neck.

"Only for you, Richard. Only because of everything we've meant to each other." He backed away. Richard scrambled up, jumped on his horse and fled to safety.

◆

Kay and the archers on Star Sail were key to the victory; Richard's troops never did figure out where the arrows were coming from. As quickly as they depleted their supply of arrows, Kaza used a spell to create more out of toothpicks he'd retrieved from the galley. He sat, chomping on a sandwich, happily making more arrows, as Nan ran them to the archers.

Below, Ken rallied the refugee army once more. "This is the time we all must strike without hesitation!" he shouted. "This is our moment! Victory is nearly ours! Forward!"

With a giant roar, the refugees made their final rush into combat. Sensing the end, many from Richard's army laid down their weapons in defeat. Others fled into the woods. On a far hill overlooking the battle, Richard and Lord William stood dumbfounded at their loss.

"How could this happen?" William screamed. "You promised me our army was unstoppable! Look at them—the cowards are running away! All, of course, but your regiments who have turned on us! What happened?"

"I have no explanation. There must be some higher power at work here, your Grace."

"This is a sorry sight," William growled. "The Black Lord will be displeased. *Most* displeased. I will be lucky if I retain my head. Or you yours, for that matter."

With a stormy expression on his face, William stomped up the road to his ornate carriage. He instructed the coachman to make haste back to the Secret Valley.

◆

Demetrius was taking weapons away from surrendering soldiers. He glanced back and saw a silhouette in the distance. He recognized Richard on his black stallion, staring at the ruins of the battle. Demetrius mounted a horse and rode to his old friend, certain he could convince him now to join his side, especially after sparing his life.

"Well done, everyone! Well done!" Fitzgerald said to some of his men. Ken nodded, adding his thanks to all.

"Where is Demetrius?" Fitzgerald asked Ken.

"He was just here…"

Fitzgerald scanned the surrounding landscape. He spotted Demetrius up on a hill with his back to them. He was talking to someone but, from his angle, Fitzgerald couldn't tell who it was. A sudden dread washed over him and he ran to a horse, mounted and galloped towards Demetrius. Fitzgerald drew nearer and saw his friend fumble for his sword, but not soon enough. Sir Richard caught Demetrius off guard and struck him with a single blow. Demetrius reached out to Richard with one hand before slumping forward and falling off his horse. Without a look back, Richard galloped off to catch up with Lord William.

Fitzgerald jumped off his horse and ran to Demetrius. His lifelong friend lay sprawled on the ground, a gaping wound to his chest.

"I tried to reason with him," Demetrius said, coughing blood. "I tried to persuade him to join with us. But he wouldn't hear of it. He..."

"Never mind," Fitzgerald said, kneeling. "We need to get you help." He looked around, wildly, hoping to find one of the fairies. "Help here! Please!"

"No, Fitz. I think I am done. Tell Kay and the others how much I admired them. How much I valued their friendship." He closed his eyes.

Fitzgerald took Demetrius' hand. "No. Please. Stay with me, Demetrius. We need you!"

Demetrius' hand pressed Fitzgerald's tightly for a brief moment, as if in answer, and then went slack and lifeless.

CHAPTER 51

The battle was won. The townsfolk and fairies set about collecting the dead and treating the wounded. Many of Richard's soldiers surrendered and were escorted to the dungeons where the fairies tended to their needs. The other soldiers who were turned by Moorray's persuasion spell milled about, alarming Gar's citizens, who had to be convinced that they were not the enemy. The men discussed returning to the Secret Valley to defeat their former ruler, Lord William, once and for all.

Irene, who had not left Susan's side, heard the sounds of the victorious soldiers returning and went to a balcony overlooking the courtyard. Spying her, Nan and Kay ran up to hug her. When she learned of Demetrius' death, Irene joined the others in their grief.

"What a kind and noble soul he was. I wish I had known him better, as you did, Kay."

Kay nodded mutely. Gar allowed them to place Demetrius' body in the chapel. The three girls kept vigil over him for many hours.

◆

The next morning was cool, but clear. The refugees, the townsfolk of Garsland, and the fairies gathered in a field at the west side of the castle to lay to rest the many who had fallen in battle. Demetrius was buried in a place of prominence, at the top of a small hill overlooking the river. The fight had left many orphans, widows and widowers. Children had been slain and their loss brought profound sorrow. Things would never be the same, but the citizens of Garsland knew they must somehow go on and rebuild their lives. Some citizens, whose houses were severely damaged, joined the refugees camping in fields. Gar and his fairies did their best to take care of their guests. Although victorious, no one in Garsland seemed jubilant. Too many had been sacrificed for anyone to feel real joy. A great sadness permeated the land. The cost of freedom had been very high indeed.

When Nan, Kay and Irene returned to Gar's castle following Demetrius' funeral, they found Seever awaiting them in the courtyard. The impish grin he normally wore was gone.

"I have sad news. Moor-ray is not well. He expended all of his energy with the persuasion spell that turned the soldiers to our side."

"Oh, dear. Is there anything we can do?" Kay asked.

"Sadly, no. There is no spell to help him; no potion we can give. All we can do is keep him quiet and let him rest. But I am afraid he won't recover. He is very weak and cannot perform even the most elementary spells. That is a sign a wizard is not long for this world."

"May we see him?" Irene begged.

"Of course."

Seever led them to the room where Moor-ray lay. He looked pale and drew his breath with effort. Kaza sat nearby, playing a plaintive tune on his fiddle. He stopped playing as the girls entered and sat quietly as they approached the bed to kneel by the wizard's side.

"Oh, Moor-ray," Kay began, "we cannot tell you how grateful we are for your help. Without you, we never would have won."

"Yes. Your magic made all the difference," Nan said, choking back tears.

Irene reached out to take Moor-ray's hand, "I am so sorry Moor-ray. It is our fault for asking so much of you. We never wished you to make such a sacrifice."

"I knew what I was doing," Moor-ray whispered. "I was fairly certain the persuasion spell would be the last thing for me. Do not grieve, dear girls. 'Twas the right thing to do. I have no regrets."

The girls each kissed Moor-ray and retreated from the room. Seever and Kaza remained by his side, waiting for the end.

That evening, after a meager meal, the girls returned to their room in the castle and fell into a deep sleep. The past week had been so very hard on them. They knew they needed to plan for the ultimate defeat of the Black Lord, but they were too exhausted to think about it just yet.

As long as he remained below, they would be safe.

CHAPTER 52

Something startled Anton out of his dozing rest; a feeling that all was not right. He waited a moment, then rose and climbed out of his cave. Things were oddly still. The pyrotechnics Anthony was so fond of were absent. Anton looked towards Anthony's castle. The onyx castle seemed almost peaceful.

"Anton."

He heard a plaintive voice. Again, louder. "Anton."

Was it Irene? It couldn't be. She had escaped from underground, but perhaps, Anthony managed to lure her back somehow.

"Anton, up here."

Anton turned to a craggy hill and saw Irene in a flowing white dress. Her arms were above her head, bound to the dead tree behind her. Anton blinked. He knew this was likely an illusion—a vision his brother cooked up to deceive him for his own amusement.

"Anton, please help me. I am so afraid Anthony will return."

Anton climbed towards Irene, although he feared that as soon as he tried to touch her she would dissolve into dust. He hesitated. Then one of Anthony's black birds descended on Irene, inspecting her as if she were a tasty bug. Irene shrieked as it pecked at her. Anton could no longer restrain himself. He ran up the hill and waved off the bird. Blood ran down Irene's cheek, mixing with her tears. Anton reached out to wipe her face. She was real. She didn't fade away when he touched her.

"Oh, Anton. Thank you."

Anton untied Irene's bonds. Irene embraced him tightly. Anton looked into her eyes and kissed her.

"Not so fast," Anthony's voice came from nowhere and everywhere. "I have plans for the two of you."

"Leave Irene out of this!" Anton shouted. "This is between you and me. You must let Irene leave this place."

"I think not," there was now a chuckle to the phantom voice.

Irene screamed as she suddenly rose into the air and flew towards Anthony's castle. She flailed her arms as if fighting off an invisible attacker. Anton raced after her.

She fell to the ground outside the castle door, where Anthony waited. He yanked her upright and forced her inside. By the time Anton entered, the grand hall was vacant. He paused, listening carefully before climbing the main staircase. He stood at the top of the stairs and waited.

"Over here," Anthony taunted, his voice echoing down the hall.

Anton hurried after the voice and approached an open door at the far end. He entered a grand room housed within a round tower. His brother sat casually in a high backed chair. Irene floated high above them. She was clutching at her throat as if being strangled. Tears streamed down her face.

"Let her go!" Anton demanded.

"Perhaps I will," Anthony calmly replied. "It all depends on you."

"How so?"

Anthony leaned forward, his red eyes blazing, "Let...me...pass!"

"You know I cannot let you go above ground," Anton replied, biting back his fear for Irene.

His twin shrugged. "Then she will die."

Irene gasped and kicked her legs as she struggled for air. Her eyes begged Anton to help her.

Anton had reached the limit of his patience.

He flew at Anthony. The two grappled with one another for a moment and then separated. Anthony conjured an amber sphere in his hand and unleashed it on his brother. Anton fell to the ground writhing in pain. He summoned a red sphere of his own and threw it at his twin. This stunned Anthony just long enough for Anton to fire off another ball of light, this time knocking Anthony down. Anton quickly held his hands, palms up, towards Irene and muttered an incantation to bring her down. She lay upon the ground, gasping.

Anthony was now back on his feet and hurled another amber ball at his brother. Anton ducked, but took a glancing blow that drove him to his knees in agony. Seizing the opportunity, Anthony grabbed Irene and pulled her from the room. Anton crawled to the door in time to witness Anthony dragging her up the spiral staircase to the battlements of the castle.

Anton half-crawled, half-stumbled up the narrow staircase after them. Irene screamed his name. When Anton reached the battlements, his twin was forcing Irene to the edge of the wall.

"One last chance, my brother." Anthony laughed. "Let me pass and I might release her."

"Please, she has done nothing." Anton was on his knees, still in pain. "Brother, let her be. I cannot let you pass."

"Your choice," Anthony calmly said. He pushed Irene over the wall.

"No!" Anton screamed.

Anton was not good at flying spells, but he summoned an old levitation spell from memory to follow Irene over the wall. His efforts were for naught. He watched her being dashed onto the rocks below. Anton continued downward, hoping against hope that she had somehow survived. When he reached Irene, she was slipping away, her eyes unfocussed and glassy.

"Irene, my love. I am so sorry. Forgive me," Anton said, tears in his eyes.

"Not...not...Irene..."

"What did you say?"

"Sorry...Anthony...tricked you. I'm...sorry. So sorry," she gasped and died.

Within seconds, Irene's face transformed. Anton found himself looking at an old hag—one of the many slaves from the Black Lord's domain. Anthony had transformed the old woman to appear like Irene.

Anton was relieved, but, at the same time, puzzled. *Why the cruel game?* He closed his eyes to concentrate on his twin. For the first time, he did not feel Anthony's presence.

Since he had come below to the land of the Black Lord, Anton had spent nearly every moment mentally connected to his twin to monitor his whereabouts. Now, the connection was broken. Anton knew Anthony was gone—he had escaped. Anton, in pain and weakened, struggled to the edge of the cavern and found the formidable door to the underground city wide open. He sank to his knees.

What will befall us now?

◆

A grey mist hung over the land the next day. People stirred slowly. Gar's fairies provided food for the castle's guests. Just as they finished their meal, Seever entered the room. The expression on the wizard's face made it clear—Moor-ray was gone.

Nan buried her face in Fitzgerald's shoulder, crying.

Gar stood. "I think I can speak for all of us. We are so very sorry for the loss of Moor-ray. He saved us all. I can never repay this debt. I proclaim today an official day of mourning. The fairies will hang black banners throughout the streets. We will erect a magnificent tomb for him. And, there will be a parade in his honor—nothing too flashy. It will be a sober and very tasteful affair, I assure you."

"We appreciate your thoughtfulness, Gar," Seever replied. "But we must take Moor-ray's body back to Wizards' Keep at once. Wizards must be buried as soon as possible and Moor-ray wished to be interred at the Keep."

"Very well. I understand. But the day of mourning still stands."

Gar's fairies gently placed Moor-ray's body in the center of an elaborately woven rug, took hold of its edges and flew it up to Star Sail.

"We will be back in six to seven of the sun's risings," Seever said. "We just need time to bury Moor-ray and say the proper funeral invocations. As long as the Black Lord lives, this land is not free from harm. We will return to plan the next phase of battle."

Seever looked sadly at the three girls. They rushed over to hug him tightly. Just before ascending the ladder to Star Sail, he turned and managed to muster his impish grin and a wink.

Kaza walked to the ladder and, as he was about to climb up, Nan, Kay and Irene encircled him in an embrace.

"Harrumph!" Kaza grunted. "Well. Guess it couldn't hurt." He awkwardly returned their affection. He slowly climbed the ladder and hoisted his large form over the side of the ship. Kaza hauled up the ladder and anchor, and in an instant, Star Sail blended in with the sky and was gone. Everyone below stood quietly for some time, each with his or her own thoughts.

◆

Later that day Ken gathered everyone together. "I know that no one wants to think about it, but what should we do about the Black Lord? Shouldn't we be strategizing on how to finish him?"

"I think plans can wait for now, don't you?" Irene said. "The Black Lord is being restrained by Anton. As long as he cannot leave his domain we are relatively safe."

"We must do something, and soon. But we also need time to rest and recover," Fitzgerald said. "Besides, I think we should wait until the wizards return before making any plans. If anyone knows how to defeat the Black Lord, it would be another wizard."

While they debated, they became aware of a low rumbling. The rumbling increased and the ground started to shake. Flowerpots toppled. Birds took flight. Everyone ran to the parapets for a better view. Several leagues to the north, they saw the earth rising; a mountain was forming before their eyes. Suddenly, the top exploded and lava poured out. A few moments later, a form slowly rose out of the volcano.

Irene screamed, "It's him! It's the Black Lord!"

Anthony sat astride one of his awful black birds. He hovered for a moment as if trying to get his bearings.

Ken and Fitzgerald took charge, ushering the peasants into the castle. Everyone in town panicked and searched for safety.

◆

The Black Lord flew north, away from the town. He circled slowly around, as if looking for something. Although Lord William had a full day's head start back to the Secret Valley, Anthony quickly caught up to the ruler's carriage. He and the giant bird set down in the road, blocking the way. William nervously looked out as Anthony approached him.

"My master," Lord William said, bowing his head. "Uh, what an honor. How may I serve you today?" He began to get out of the carriage, but Anthony held up his hand. Richard, on horseback nearby, slowly began to back up his horse.

"Oh, don't get out," Anthony said, his red eyes glowing. "Don't trouble yourself. You must be tired from your long journey and the battle. Oh yes, that battle," he turned to Richard. "The one your army should have easily won!"

"We didn't realize they would have the help of the wizards," Sir Richard said. "My own men turned on me. But I will get them back. I just need to—"

"Silence!" the Black Lord roared. The ground shook from his strong voice. He looked back at William. "What a miserable excuse for a leader. And you thought to usurp me. To take all for yourself!"

"What? No! I never!"

"A reliable source told me that once victory was secured you would turn your back on me."

"My Lord Wizard, I... I would never think of such a thing! You are the true ruler of this land. I am but your obedient servant." William stammered, sweat breaking out on his brow. "I would never betray you; you must believe me!"

"It is of little consequence now. As *I* shall have to finish off these pesky creatures in Garsland myself, I have no further use of *you*."

Anthony held up his palms towards the carriage and it levitated. Up it rose, higher and higher, and then began to spin, faster and faster. The doors flew open. Inside, Lord William clung to the seats to keep from being thrown out. Abruptly, the carriage came to a standstill. Anthony smiled cruelly and rapidly lowered his hands. The carriage plummeted to the earth and shattered into hundreds of pieces.

During all this, Richard, who suspected his own punishment would be shortly forthcoming, stealthily rode into the woods.

Anthony pointed at his black bird and spoke an incantation. The bird changed shape, becoming larger and longer, until it had transformed into a scaly, black dragon. Anthony climbed on its back, and with a rush of giant wings, the two took flight.

CHAPTER 53

Astride his dragon, Anthony flew to Garsland. When the castle came into view, he directed the giant beast to fly lower to let him take stock of what lay below.

The initial panic of seeing the Black Lord emerge from the mountain now past, Kay and the other archers assembled on the upper walls of the castle to ready themselves for battle. As Anthony took another pass, archers shot at the dragon, but the arrows, which could not pierce its skin, fell harmlessly away. Anthony made a low pass over the village, laughing as the dragon set fire to many of the surviving homes with its fiery breath. Citizens ran screaming from the town.

◆

Ken and Fitzgerald gathered the soldiers from the Secret Valley and found a few more men within the refugee camps willing to help defend the castle. They stationed themselves at the battlements, but they knew arrows, swords and broadaxes would have no effect on a dragon. The fairies and many peasants took refuge in the castle. No one spoke, except to utter a prayer. Nan and Irene walked among them, offering reassurance here and there. Ken sent Kay down to join her friends and see if she could be of help. She ran up to Irene and Nan.

"These may be our last moments together," she said, sadly. "I can't believe it. Why did the wizards leave? Without them we haven't a prayer."

"I know," Nan said in a shaky voice. "It isn't fair. I thought for sure the Black Lord would not prevail against such good people."

The three girls stood, looking at one another, trying not to cry.

"Good people," Irene said slowly, trying to remember something. She gasped. "Good people! The Black Lord cannot defeat good. Nan, that's it! That's *it*!"

"What do you mean? What are you talking about?"

299

"Anton told me that the Black Lord cannot defeat that which is honestly good. It's the only thing he fears. We *can* conquer him. I think...I think we must send out someone truly good to vanquish him."

Irene and Kay both turned to stare at Nan. "What is it?" Nan asked, "Why are you looking at me so strangely?"

"Nan, you are the best and nicest person I know," Irene said. "I have never even heard you say a bad thing about another person. You must do it."

"Do what?"

"Defeat the Black Lord. I believe you may be the only one who can save us."

"But how? I can't even wield a sword!"

"If I am right, you won't have to."

Kay and Irene grabbed Nan and ran with her out the front of the castle. On the way, Irene explained to Nan that their only hope was for her to stand up to the Black Lord and not be afraid. In fact, she needed to think thoughts of love and kindness.

"But Nan, he is cunning. He'll try to make you believe you are seeing things that are not really there to make you afraid. And if you are afraid, you will not succeed; you will be his. He will do anything he can to make you falter. You must remember it will all be an illusion. Please, Nan, be strong!"

"I don't know if I can do this."

"Yes, you can," Irene said, "I know you can. No matter what you see or hear, remember that he is deceiving you. None of it is real. Think on the good things in your life. Use them against him. You must control your fear, or all will be lost."

Nan gulped. "I wish I had your strength, Kay. And your resolve, Irene."

"I wish I could do this for you," Kay said. "But Irene is right. You are the only one. We have faith in you."

Kay and Irene each gave Nan a quick hug and pushed her on her way. Every fiber of Nan's body told her she should run. She felt as if she would faint. She forced herself to take a deep breath and climbed the stairs to the battlements. The Black Lord was still flying around the castle, sending amber balls of light at the few remaining soldiers. He laughed as they fell. Fitzgerald gasped in surprise when Nan walked past him. He ran and pulled her down beside him.

"Nan! What are you doing? Have you lost your mind? Go back inside—at once!"

"No, Fitzy. I can't. There is something I must do. I can't explain it now, but please let me go!"

"What about our future together?"

"There will be no future for *any* of us unless I do this," she said, fiercely. "You must let me go!"

Fitzgerald released her. Nan returned to the wall, knees shaking.

Anthony continued making wide sweeps back and forth over the landscape. Many of the trees, so recently renewed by the fairies' magic, were blazing like torches. Anthony glanced at the castle and started as he spotted a solitary figure, who seemed to be unarmed.

What can this be? Anthony directed the dragon to circle around to inspect this oddity. The dragon swept up to the front of the castle, and hovered in front of Nan. Nan felt the heat from the dragon's nostrils. She caught a glimpse of Anthony's horrific red eyes, and glanced away. She wanted to run, but stuck to her place, lowered her head and tried to think peaceful thoughts.

The Black Lord cocked his head. *Who is this girl? Well...no matter*. With a wave of his hand, he signaled the dragon to eliminate her. The fearsome beast took in a great gulp of air and exhaled fire. The blaze came at Nan. To her surprise, it seemed as if there were a wall between her and the flames. She remained unhurt.

Anthony was shocked to see the girl still stood. He sent an amber ball of light at her and watched it evaporate before reaching her.

Now Anthony was truly puzzled. He concentrated, closed his eyes, and reached deeply into Nan's mind. He searched for a memory he could use. When he found one, he nodded.

A furious Turner of Hayward Fields came racing across the parapet towards Nan at a dead run. His hands were outstretched as if to choke her.

No. It's only an illusion, she thought and stood fast. When Turner came within a few feet of her, his image splintered and fell away.

Anthony and the dragon still hovered in front of Nan. *This is going to be a challenge*. Once again, he reached into her mind.

"Nan," came a familiar voice. "Nan, down here. Help!"

Nan went to the side and saw her father below, dressed in rags with sores covering his body.

"Nan," he begged, "please help me. I am sick. If you just surrender to the Black Lord, he will take care of me. He will make me well again."

A tear slid down Nan's face, but she did not falter. She forced herself to turn away from her father.

"It is just another trick—my father is not there," she muttered.

"Nan, please. Don't you love me anymore? Please help me. I am so weary. So weary..." The voice faded and died away.

Anthony could not believe the determination of this spindly, insignificant girl. Once again he reached into her mind. He smiled as he found another memory.

"Nan!"

Nan looked into the courtyard behind her to see Irene and Kay, waving frantically. "Nan, we were wrong. We were wrong!" Irene shouted. "You cannot possibly defeat the Black Lord!"

"Run," Kay cried, "save yourself!"

For the first time, Nan couldn't be sure if this was real or not. She began to doubt. Anthony laughed—a low, throaty chuckle. Nan turned back towards Irene and Kay, who were still calling at her to retreat. She shook her head. *No, I mustn't waiver, even if I die.*

Nan closed her eyes. She concentrated and remembered the carefree days of her youth: the joy of dancing, all the happy times with Irene, her life in the cozy cottage with her brothers and parents, helping in her father's shop.

The happy memories sent a warm glow that spread throughout her body.

She slowly opened her eyes and smiled a small, secret smile. Staring directly into the red eyes of the Black Lord, she stood strong and did not retreat.

The dragon unleashed another blast of fire. Then another. And another. The flames could not touch Nan, who continued to smile at Anthony, and then to laugh a little.

Then, a strange expression came over the Black Lord—almost fearful. It appeared as if the wind had been knocked out of him. Both he and the dragon began to glow red.

Anthony screamed as he held his hand up to his face. The hand burst into flames, followed by the rest of his body and, finally, the dragon's. The fiery mess that was the powerful Black Lord and his dragon collapsed and fell to the earth, sending flames jumping into the sky. Black ashes rose from the pile and were carried away by a gentle wind.

CHAPTER 54

Joyous celebrations rang through Garsland following the defeat of the Black Lord. Townspeople, fairies, soldiers and refugees all danced through the charred remains of the village. Everyone had great hope for a future that, only a few days before, they could hardly even imagine.

Gar and his fairies invited all of the survivors to join them in the castle that evening to celebrate the victory and to honor their heroine, Nan. The unmanned orchestra played all night. The fairies set out much fine food and drink, and everyone danced throughout the night.

Shortly after the evening festivities began, Nan, Kay, and Irene came down the grand staircase into the ballroom. The fairies had outfitted them in magnificent attire. Nan was wearing an emerald green dress with a fitted silk bodice and a flowing skirt that seemed to be made of fine gauze. Her curly, red tresses were piled high on her head. Kay wore a light blue gown with a gold belt and gold trim around the neckline that hugged her shoulders. Her short, blond curls softly framed her smiling face. Irene was dressed in a pale pink, embroidered gown with a long silver surcoat. Her beautiful hair was pulled to the top of her head and hung down her back. As the three came down the stairs, the crowd began to applaud. Irene and Kay stepped aside, leaving Nan alone on the step. Everyone cheered long and loud for their savior.

After the cheering died down, Fitzgerald rushed forward and escorted Nan to the dance floor. He smiled as he held Nan, gazing into her beautiful green eyes.

"I am so proud of you, and so honored to be in your presence," he said.

"Oh, Fitzy, really. It's just me. I'm the same girl as before."

"Oh, yes. Only the girl who crushed the Black Lord and saved us all!"

"Really, Fitzgerald, you *do* need to get over that. And right now. I want us to live a normal life. No pedestals in our household, please."

"Our household? Are you saying? I mean...would you?"

"Would I marry you, do you mean? Well, I don't believe anyone has asked me yet. But I think my answer might be to your liking," she said coyly.

"Alright, then—would you?"

"Would I what?" Nan teased.

"Nan, you know what I'm trying to say. Could you...that is...would you marry me?" Fitzgerald finished all in a rush.

"Oh, Fitzy, yes. Of course I will!"

Fitzgerald kissed Nan as the other dancers swirled around them.

Kay and Irene watched their friends and exchanged glances. "I sense something significant just happened on the dance floor," Kay said, with a grin. Irene nodded.

Ken strolled up to Kay. "I don't normally dance," he said, "but, if you are of a mind to do so, I suppose I could be your partner."

"Well, now, *there's* an invitation 'tis hard to refuse," Kay replied tartly, crossing her arms and refusing to look at him.

"Oh. Sorry. Permit me to start again. What a lovely evening, Kay, and what delightful music. Would you care to dance?"

"Why, yes. I would," Kay replied, smiling.

The two made a pretty couple as they moved around the floor. Ken could not take his eyes off Kay. Despite herself, Kay blushed.

Irene stood by, watching the festivities. Her mind wandered back to the Black Lord's realm. *Where is Anton? What happened to him? Did Anthony finally kill him?*

Her thoughts were interrupted by David, who had quietly slipped next to her. He stood beside her for several minutes humming along to the music before speaking.

"Quite the grand party, isn't it? What a relief. I was pretty sure it was all over for us. Weren't you?"

"I confess I had a few doubts as to our survival." Irene replied. "I am so happy it ended well."

"So am I, so am I. Well..." he trailed off.

"David, I am sorry I didn't have more faith in you. Can you forgive me?"

David looked down, embarrassed. "No, you were right to be concerned. Whenever I held the mirror, it was as if I were falling into a black abyss and couldn't escape. I'm so sorry."

"Please. No more talk of the Black Lord. This is a night to celebrate. Let's dance!"

David held his arm out for Irene and they joined the others on the dance floor. The celebration did not conclude until dawn, when Gar and the fairies finally shooed the last of the revelers out the door.

CHAPTER 55

Two days after the ball, the soldiers from the Secret Valley who had fought for Garsland left for their home. Word had reached them of the death of Lord William, Son of Dob. They now wanted to be sure their homeland didn't fall into the wrong hands.

Most of the refugees made preparations to return to their towns, as well, though Gar had offered them citizenship in his small kingdom. A few accepted his offer, including Marcus and Frieda. They picked out a small parcel of land on which to build a modest home and smithy, financing it with the gold Marcus "accumulated" from the convent.

Kay, Nan, Irene, Fitzgerald, Ken, Stephon and David decided to wait for the wizards' return before making any plans. The fairies resumed their work to restore the castle and grounds to their former glory. The townsfolk lost no time in starting to rebuild their village. They cut out a large parcel in the center and began construction of a new town square. A local sculptor volunteered to carve a statue of Moor-ray to be placed in the middle of the square, to honor his sacrifice.

That afternoon, Irene went for a stroll in the nearly restored gardens of Gar's castle. In the midst of her walk, a male fairy, wearing loud, yellow leggings with a purple velvet tunic flew up to her. He bowed to Irene and said,

Silent Susan, silent no more
Asks for you, don't know what for.
You will find her at this hour
In the castle's far west tower.

Irene headed to the west tower, perplexed. *Whatever could he mean? Silent no more?* She found Susan sitting on a bench in a small room. Her arm was bandaged and in a sling, but otherwise she looked much better. Her filthy old clothes had been replaced with a sensible brown dress with fur trim at the collar. Susan smiled broadly and patted the seat next to her.

"Susan, I am so happy to see you up and around," Irene said, joining her. "You look quite well."

Susan gestured for Irene to lean forward, as if to share a secret. "Thank you," Susan said in a low and raspy voice.

"Susan, you can speak!"

"Whatever the fairies did to keep me alive also restored my voice. I have so much to tell you about everything that happened after we parted ways in the Black Lord's kingdom."

Irene smiled and settled in for a long chat with her friend.

◆

That same afternoon, a young man wandered into the outskirts of Garsland. Starving and weak, his tattered clothes hung on him. He headed to the first house he came upon—a small cottage owned by Marguerite, the half-fairy Stephon was now courting. The man staggered to her door and knocked.

"Stephon," Marguerite called, "is that you?"

Hearing no answer, Marguerite went to the door and, upon opening it, found the crumpled body of the young lad. Marguerite fetched water and held it to his swollen and dry lips.

"Where do you come from, sir? Were you injured in the battle?"

"What battle?"

"Why, the fight for Garsland."

"I know nothing of this. I have escaped from the Black Lord's kingdom. I was working when suddenly there came a mighty roar and rocks rained down from the sky. Everything was chaos. When we came out of hiding, there was a gaping hole at the top of the kingdom. It was too hot to approach, but eventually it cooled, so I climbed out. Some others are coming, but the climb is too steep and dangerous for most."

"We can help them," Marguerite said. "I will speak with Gar, the ruler of this kingdom."

Marguerite put him on a daybed and gave him some cold meat and bread, which he ravenously consumed. Marguerite hurried to the castle to find Gar. After hearing her story, Gar immediately called his fairies together and instructed them to rescue the poor souls. Then, Gar spoke with his townsfolk and the remaining refugees, and asked them to gather what supplies they could spare for the new guests.

The fairies began lifting prisoners out of the ruins one by one. They set them down at the lip of the mountain and the wretched men and women made their way to Garsland. Townsfolk met the ex-prisoners on the mountain slopes to help, giving them food and water and loading the weakest into carts.

Nan, Kay and Irene watched from the battlements of the castle as thousands of prisoners in dirty gray, torn clothing stumbled towards Garsland. As the mass of people reached the tent city, the three girls helped organize shelter and supplies.

As Nan assisted a woman and her young son to find a tent, she looked over to a distant hill. There stood a silhouette. It seemed familiar. It reminded her of her father. Nan squinted. A moment later, a woman and six young men came over the rise and joined the man. Nan knew at once this was no illusion—it was her family!

"Mama!" Nan screamed, as she rushed to them. "Papa!!" She threw herself into her father's arms. He stared at her incredulously.

"I thought we were to be parted forever, my daughter," he said. "I can't believe it. I have missed you so much."

"Oh, you're alive, you're alive!" Nan kept repeating as she embraced her mother and brothers. "Keep walking down the hill. I'll be right back with help."

Nan ran ahead to find Ken and Kay so that she could tell them her good news. They commandeered a carriage and horses from Gar. Nan soon crowded everyone into the carriage and took them straight to the castle. No tents for *her* family!

Irene and Kay worked all day helping settle the former slaves. Irene recognized many of her old friends and acquaintances from the Valley of William Etté and her home in Cabbage. She kept hoping her brother, or perhaps Anton, would show up but, throughout the day, saw no sign of them.

After the last of the Black Lord's prisoners were provided for, Irene and Kay headed back to Gar's castle. They were both too exhausted to care about dinner and went directly to their bedchamber. Nan was staying with her family down the hall. Kay and Irene barely laid their heads on their pillows before they fell asleep.

◆

At the first glimmer of morning light, Irene awoke from a dream in which she was chasing Anton, but he kept slipping away from her grasp. She felt certain that it was a message; that Anton needed her. She quietly dressed and went downstairs, sought out one of her favorite fairies for a favor, then saddled a horse and headed north.

Soon, she stood at the edge of the crater where the Black Lord's slaves had escaped. She peered with dismay at the steep fissure falling hundreds of feet to the ground below.

Oh dear. Perhaps I should return to Garsland and ask some of the fairies to lower me down. No. That will take too long. I will just have to try to climb down myself.

Irene began to pick her way down the steep, treacherous slopes. At one point, she lost her footing and slid several feet before slamming her side into a large rock. She was shaken, but got up and continued.

Irene finally reached the floor of the crater and gazed around the Black Lord's former kingdom. Most of the buildings were damaged by the mountain's explosion and the streets were filled with debris, rocks and the bodies of slaves. It was strangely quiet as she walked towards the Black Lord's private cavern to find Anton's cave.

When Irene came to a large, open square, she stopped and stared in amazement. Robed, dead bodies lay on their backs, arranged in a pattern as if they were spokes on a wheel. Irene could tell from their robes that these were the Black Lord's henchmen. As she got closer, she was puzzled to find these were not the gruesome, hairy beasts she had seen before. They were normal-looking people.

How strange. Why would they be wearing the robes of the beasts? She cautiously walked around them.

She found the door to the Black Lord's lair wide open. There was no longer any fire or glowing, hot rocks in the cave. All was cool and dark. Her footsteps echoed through the cavern as she made her way to Anton's home.

"Anton," Irene called softly as she neared his cave. "Anton, are you here? Please, Anton, answer me if you can."

She heard no reply. She began to climb up to the entrance. "Anton, it's me, Irene!" she called more loudly.

Still nothing. She moved nearer to Anton's cave, when suddenly something grabbed her foot. She looked behind her and saw one of the remaining beasts holding her. Irene screamed and kicked at the beast with her other foot, knocking him back enough for her to escape his grasp. She scrambled up to the entrance of Anton's cave.

"Anton!" Irene called, as the beast climbed towards her. "Anton! Help me!"

The rock sealing Anton's cave rolled away and Anton pulled Irene safely inside. He held up his hand.

"Beast of this ungodly realm, you are finished!"

The beast seemed to shrink and then implode. It shrieked a high-pitched yowl as it disappeared. Anton turned to Irene, started to speak and collapsed into her arms.

Irene cradled Anton and tried to rouse him. His face was ashen and his breathing shallow.

"Anton. Oh, please, Anton. The battle is over. Your brother is gone. We have so much to live for. You can't die. I need you. Anton!"

Slowly, Anton opened his eyes. He stared at Irene as if she were an apparition. Irene bent and kissed him. He touched her face and smiled.

"Irene...Irene," Anton said. "How did you...?"

"We must get out of here," Irene said. She retrieved the golden coin from her pocket she had begged from the fairy earlier. "I wish us to be in Garsland!"

CHAPTER 56

Lord William's remaining escort soldiers finally returned to the Secret Valley. They rode straight to William's castle and asked to speak with Lady Ruth on a matter of great urgency. The Queen, looking polished and confident, brought her son, Alex, to meet them in William's throne room.

A spokesman for the soldiers came forward and knelt before Ruth. "I bring sad tidings, your Majesty," he said. "William, Son of Dob, was vanquished, as well as much of our army."

Ruth gasped in shock but quickly regained her composure. She bade the kneeling soldier to rise.

"We will make a new beginning with a new ruler—my son, Alex. I will act as Regent until he reaches his majority in seven years. I will teach my son to be a fair and equitable leader." She took a deep breath. "As for our future, I declare we will no longer be a warring people, for this only brought us sorrow and hardship. We will support peace and goodness, and establish new relations with our neighboring kingdoms to repair the damage done under my husband's rule."

Alex was crowned the next day. The townspeople cheered him through the streets. While others celebrated, Beth of Coombs packed a satchel and left the Valley for good, hoping to leave her many bad memories behind. With a small bag of money stolen from Kay's room, she vowed to start a new life.

◆

The magic gold coin transported Irene and Anton to her room in Gar's castle, where she helped him to bed. The summer sun streamed through the window and birds chirped in the courtyard. Anton smiled up at Irene.

"I cannot tell you how many times I dreamed of this. I so wished to be with you again, but it seemed utterly impossible."

"Shh," Irene said. "You need to rest. We must get you well. It is my turn to take care of you."

"Irene. My dearest Irene..."

Irene waited until Anton fell asleep, and then set off down the hallway to fetch clean water, food and clothing. Kay met her at the top of the stairs.

"And just *where* have you been all day, Irene? I woke up and you were gone and I couldn't find you! Is this going to become a habit? Running off when it pleases you and not telling anyone?"

"I had something important to do, Kay, and I didn't want to bother anyone."

"Well, what was so important, I'd like to know!" Kay said in a huff. "Honestly, Irene. Nan is just in a *state* over your disappear—"

"Kay, listen to me!" Irene grabbed Kay's shoulders to get her attention. "I found Anton and brought him back here, to the castle. He's alive, but very weak."

"What? The wizard Anton? Here?"

"Yes, in our room. I need to get him some things—come help me."

While Irene went to the kitchen for water and food, Kay found a muslin shirt and trousers on a clothesline, and appropriated them. The girls returned to their room to find Anton fast asleep. At the sight of him, Kay stopped short and sharply drew in her breath.

"Sweet Mirn, he looks exactly like the Black Lord. Somehow, I thought he would be different. Well. Maybe he does look a *little* kinder."

Kay spread the word of Anton's arrival. Irene stayed to nurse him, refusing to leave his side.

◆

That evening, Kay felt a little in the way with Anton in the room, so she wandered outside to the riverbank. It was a warm night, with a clear sky. The moonlight reflected brightly on the water.

She kicked off her slippers, pulled her skirt up above her knees and waded out into the sandy shallows. She sang a simple tune under her breath and danced a folk dance from her childhood.

When Kay caught a movement out of the corner of her eye, she turned to find Ken standing by the river, smiling. She gasped, embarrassed. "I didn't realize anyone else was here. Sorry to have disturbed you."

"It's no bother," Ken said, as he walked towards her. "I enjoy watching you dance."

"I am only a little more graceful when I am on dry land," Kay joked, with a little bow.

Ken smiled. "I remember."

Not caring that his boots would get wet, Ken walked into the water until he stood before Kay. He looked into her blue eyes and lightly stroked her shoulders. They stood silent for a moment before Ken pulled Kay towards him into a tight embrace and kissed her. Her arms reached up around his neck. They stood kissing in the moonlight. After a few minutes, Ken picked up Kay and carried her to the riverbank. They lay there silently gazing at the stars and moon.

Ken finally spoke. "I want you to know, this is not some idle flirtation, although I have had my share of those. And sadly, I am not a rich nobleman. I have next to no prospects and, quite frankly, you should probably run for your life." He shifted to face her. "But I find something in you I truly care for. I believe you and I could have something unique. I think we would make good partners."

Kay frowned. "That sounds more like a business proposition than a proposal of love. Can you tell me you love me?"

"I don't think such flowery language is absolutely necessary."

"Well, I do! I want a life where the word 'love' is spoken often and with meaning. So, I ask again—do you love me?"

"Well, I think, in time...that is...such a thing might be possible. Oh, damn! What am I afraid of? Yes. Yes! I love you now and am not ashamed to admit it. I am in love with the stubborn, impetuous, headstrong, brave, insightful and lovely Kay!"

"And she is in love with you," Kay said softly. The two talked and kissed through the night as the moon slowly fell below the horizon.

CHAPTER 57

On the seventh morning after the defeat of the Black Lord, Star Sail came back to Garsland and anchored in the main courtyard of Gar's palace. Seever and Kaza were still grieving Moor-ray's death, but seemed glad to be with their friends again. When they learned how the Black Lord had been defeated, they congratulated Nan on her courage.

Irene asked Seever to come see Anton. Walking to the room, she explained how she brought Anton to Gar's castle.

"He seemed as if he was getting better," Irene said, "but today he is much weaker. I am very worried."

"Let me examine him and then, hopefully, I can tell you more."

Seever sent Irene away and examined Anton. Nan and Kay tried to distract her with a walk through the gardens while they waited for Seever to finish. After a while, the wizard came out of the palace and joined the girls.

"Well. Anton is...stable. I believe he will regain some strength in the coming days."

"Will he recover fully?" Irene asked.

"I can't say precisely, though I am optimistic. He asked to see you."

The three girls turned to enter the castle.

"He asked to see Irene *alone*," Seever said.

Irene went to their room and stayed for half an hour. When she emerged, her eyes glistened with tears. She smiled and seemed both happy and, somehow, profoundly sad.

It was all Kay and Nan could do to keep from asking what took place.

◆

The following day, Anton felt well enough to join everyone for the morning meal. Gar sat at the head of the table; Nan and her family took up one entire side. Nan's brothers, all with the same flaming red hair, were quite a lively bunch. They joked and jabbed at one another throughout the meal. They had voracious appetites and asked for seconds, thirds and fourths. After being half-starved in the land of the Black Lord, it seemed they couldn't get enough of the fairies' good food.

As everyone was getting up, Irene stood and bade them sit down again. "Please, everyone. I have an announcement. I know this will seem quite sudden, but Anton and I are getting married...today."

"Today?" Kay exclaimed. "Why the rush?"

"I want all of my dear friends to be present for the wedding. And although we haven't spoken of it, I know most everyone will be leaving soon."

"I protest!" Gar said, leaping to his feet. "Allow my fairies and me some time and we will whip together the most elaborate and gorgeous wedding ever. I am sure everyone is willing to stay a few more days." There was general assent to this.

"Thank you, your Majesty," Irene said. "We so appreciate it— truly. Anton is still weak, however, so we think it best that we have a simple ceremony. With your permission, we would like to hold it in the courtyard garden. Seever will officiate."

"This place is so magical, Gar," Anton said. "It is enough to marry in these beautiful surroundings. Irene hasn't said anything, but she is very worried about her kingdom and the fate of her brother. She wants to go home as soon as possible."

◆

A few hours later, Kay and Nan were preparing Irene for the wedding. Kay helped Irene into her dress from the victory ball. Nan brushed Irene's thick, lustrous hair and let it fall naturally. She placed a garland of small white flowers on her head.

Kay paced back and forth before finally blurting, "Irene, something is not right about this; I know it! Why the haste to marry? Has Anton bewitched you? There is something you are not telling us. I can sense it."

"Oh, my," Nan said, her eyes wide. "Irene, he hasn't put a spell on you, has he? Do you truly love him as you did Michael?"

"It's not the same kind of love I had for Michael, but yes, Nan, I do love Anton and he loves me. There's no spell. I really want to marry him, with all my heart. "

Nan and Kay exchanged glances. They could tell Irene was being truthful, but Kay still felt something was amiss. "Well, if this is what you want," she grumbled, "then of course we wish you great happiness."

Kay and Nan led their friend down the staircase out to the courtyard. The wedding ceremony was simple and brief, but it was clear to all the love between Irene and Anton was very real.

Gar insisted on at least providing the reception. The fairies whipped up a lovely feast and danced for everyone's entertainment. Later, the musician-less instruments performed so the guests could dance. Too weak to participate, Anton sat happily holding Irene's hand. Ken and Kay were side by side constantly and made no secret of their feelings for one another. Nan remained with her parents and brothers, looking longingly at Fitzgerald across the room. She hadn't yet told her family of their engagement.

Finally, Anton and Irene walked up the stairs to a beautiful room the fairies had prepared for them. Kaza stood in the moonlight under their window and played a slow and lovely tune on his violin as Anton and Irene shared their first intimate moments as husband and wife.

CHAPTER 58

The next day, Nan sat with her parents on a small balcony overlooking the gardens, waiting for Sir Fitzgerald. The knight approached and Nan's parents rose to greet him. Fitzgerald bowed stiffly and everyone took a seat. There was an awkward silence before Nan spoke.

"Father, Mother. Fitzy...I mean Sir Fitzgerald is really the most remarkable man. If not for him, I don't think I would even be here today. He is so brave; so honest. I just wanted you to get to know him. He has become a...very close friend."

"Well, that is nice," Liam said. "We can all use good friends. Tell me something of yourself, young man."

Fitzgerald cleared his throat. "Well, I grew up not far from here. Being a fit lad, I joined the army at age fifteen. By the time I was eighteen, I had been knighted. Aside from being a soldier, I sing fairly well and can dance. Let's see...oh! I love poetry and write a bit. Now that this war is over, I hope to use my head and not my brawn to better this world."

"All desirable traits," Liam said, approvingly. "But, you said you lived near here. Where, exactly, are you from?"

"Well, uh, I... I come from the Secret Valley, sir. Although I left as soon as I found out the real story behind—"

Nan's father and mother abruptly stood. "It was the army of the Secret Valley that took my family from our home!" Liam exploded. "Your army placed us in bondage in the Black Lord's Kingdom! I nearly lost all of my dear ones because of the likes of you. Come, Nan!"

"Father, please!" Nan pleaded, "You must hear him out. He left Lord William's army when he learned he truth—"

"No! I won't allow my only daughter to coerce with the enemy!"

"Father, please. I love him! I want to marry him!" She rushed to Fitzgerald's side and took his arm, defiantly.

Nan's father looked aghast. "Never!" he shouted. He grabbed Nan's hand and pulled her down the hallway, leaving Fitzgerald behind.

◆

That same day, a soldier dressed in the colors of the Secret Valley rode up to Gar's palace and asked for Kay and Fitzgerald. When the two came to meet him, they recognized him as their friend, Gregory John, a lad of intelligence and humor, who was a few years younger than Kay.

"I bring news from the Secret Valley," Gregory began. "Alex is crowned the new King, although Lady Ruth will act as Regent until he reaches his majority. Lady Ruth means to make amends to the surrounding kingdoms that her husband attacked. She asks the two of you to come home to help. You two have already established contact with many whom William and his army assailed."

Fitzgerald and Kay exchanged glances.

"I'm not sure, Fitzy..." Kay began. "So much is changed. I don't think..." she trailed off.

Fitzgerald cleared his throat. "Tell our Lady that, although we support her endeavors, we cannot return to the Secret Valley."

"Lady Ruth feared you would say that," Gregory said. "She bade me give you both a personal message." He paused, then turned to the handsome knight. "Sir Fitzgerald, Lady Ruth says her son Alex misses his father very much. She is aware you were the lad's favorite knight and she would consider it a tremendous favor if you would take him under your wing and teach him that men can be brave and honorable."

Smiling at Kay, he continued: "Kay, Lady Ruth says she realizes now you were her most stalwart supporter, even when she behaved badly. She says she misses your company very much and that you will find her much less of a handful these days.

"Should you return she will gift each of you with a home of your choosing; either a full suite of rooms in the palace or a house in the village. She would also happily welcome any spouse you bring. They would be accepted as full-fledged citizens of the Valley, with all rights and privileges granted."

"Well," Kay said, slowly. "This is all very generous. What do you think, Fitzy?"

"I don't know. If we return to the Secret Valley, we might do some good. But, I want to be with Nan and i fear she might not want to live in the land of her country's aggressors."

"Tell Lady Ruth we will decide within a few days," Kay said.

"Thank you," Gregory said. "For my part, I do hope you come back. Lady Ruth means to do the right thing, but our country sorely needs moral leadership."

Kay and Fitzgerald sat in the garden for hours, discussing the pros and cons of returning to their old home. What they didn't speak of, but remained a question deep in both their hearts, was whether or not Nan and Ken would join them.

As Kay and Fitzgerald walked back to the castle, David came riding out on a small, wiry black horse. He was dressed for travel and all of his belongings were slung over the horse's back.

"David, you are leaving us?" Kay asked.

"Yes. I never have been one to overstay my welcome. I think it is time I moved on."

"Where are you heading?" Fitzgerald asked.

He shrugged. "No idea. I will go wherever my nose leads me. I am sure I can find some mischief to get into," he grinned.

"What about Stephon? Isn't he going with you?"

"Alas, no. He wishes to stay here in Garsland. Something tells me a dark-haired lass named Marguerite has something to do with it. So, without him to play my partner in fake banditry, I might actually need to find a legitimate way to make a living!" He laughed. "Tell the others goodbye for me. This has been a wonderful romp."

David leaned forward on his horse and clasped both Kay's and Fitzgerald's hands. Kay thought she saw David's eyes become a bit misty before he turned his horse and trotted away.

◆

Slowly, more of the refugees and prisoners of the Black Lord headed back to their homelands. Some, feeling there was nothing to go back to, chose to remain in Garsland to start their lives anew. Frieda and Marcus exchanged wedding vows in a small ceremony.

"Not that I give two figs if we're wed or not," she told Nan, who acted as her bridesmaid. "I'm happy as we are. But then, again, maybe some of that religious stuff from the convent stuck!"

◆

Irene, too, prepared to leave. If, as she feared, her brother had not survived the war, she knew she must get home as soon as possible so that she might rule her tiny kingdom. In order to spare Anton the rigors of a long overland journey, Seever offered to take Irene and Anton on Star Sail back to Cabbage in the morning. Kaza, meanwhile, was debating whether to return to Wizard's Keep, alone, or to stay on in Garsland. The local children adored him and followed him around, begging him to perform little bits of magic for them. He grumbled about it constantly, but everyone noticed he did not stop walking into the village daily to be met by throngs of happy children. It seemed to have given him a new lease on life.

After the evening meal, Irene, Nan, and Kay took a walk. They knew it would be the last time they would be together for some time. Kay and Nan hugged Irene and told her they would soon visit. Nan, distressed, began to cry.

"Great Mirn, Nan," Kay said. "Don't take on so. You'll be able to visit Irene often—'tis not that far a journey from the Valley of William Etté to Cabbage, as you know."

"That's not it," Nan wailed. "My parents discovered Fitzgerald is from the Secret Valley and they forbid me to see him! And—I've wanted to tell the two of you something for days. The night of the celebration ball, Fitzy and I became engaged. What can I do? I don't want to turn my back on my family, but I love Fitzy so!"

"Well, we'll just have to convince them Fitzgerald is a good man," Irene said. "They'll come around. I'm sure of it."

"I wish *I* were. Once my father gets an idea in his head, he doesn't easily change his mind."

"Nan," Kay grinned as she wiped away Nan's tears. "After defeating the Black Lord, convincing your father you should marry whom you choose should be easy! Just be patient. It will all work out."

"I hope so." She paused. "My family leaves for the Valley of William Etté in the morning. I'll go with them, of course, but somehow I will marry Fitzy."

"Kay, what are your plans?" Irene asked.

"I... I don't know. Fitzy and I received an invitation to return to the Secret Valley and become ambassadors to mend fences with neighboring kingdoms. Since I have no other prospects, I might as well go back—even if Ken won't come with me."

"Oh, I think he will, Kay," Irene said, smiling. "I've seen how he looks at you."

Kay blushed. "Well. We'll see. He's something of a free spirit, you know."

"Oh! I need your help with something," Nan interrupted. "I must speak with Fitzy before we leave and my parents are watching me like hawks! Can you help me?"

"Of course! Give me a moment," Kay said. She crept down the hall and found the room Ken and Fitzgerald shared. She brought Fitzgerald to Nan and the two talked about their predicament before saying their tearful goodbyes.

CHAPTER 59

The next morning, Irene and Seever climbed the rope ladder to Star Sail, while fairies assisted Anton. As Irene's friends waved, the ship blended into the sky and sailed away.

Soon after, Nan hugged everyone goodbye and she and her family headed home to the Valley of William Etté. Fitzgerald watched from a window, not wishing to cause any problems.

He and Kay had decided to return to the Secret Valley. Fitzgerald thought it might be best for him to sever all ties with the Valley while he tried to win over Nan's family, but Kay convinced him they could make a more significant impact if they could show the people of the Valley of William Etté that their former conquerors were now a compassionate kingdom.

Kay explained her mission to Ken and asked him to join them. He shrugged and said that since he didn't have other plans, why not go with her? Kay was surprised at how relieved his answer made her feel.

Kay, Ken, and Fitzgerald broke the news to Gar that they, too, would be leaving his fairy kingdom. He planned one last splendid dinner for all of them.

"I respect your choice, of course, but I must say I really hoped more of you would stay on here with me," said Gar. "I have liked you all since the day you arrived in my garden those many weeks ago." He turned to Stephon. "Won't you please move into the castle?"

Stephon shook his head and put his arm around Marguerite. "We will come and visit often, your Majesty. But Marguerite's cozy cottage is just right for the two of us. We plan to wed soon. In fact, we will be happy to take you up on the wedding you offered to Irene and Anton, if that's agreeable to you and your fairies."

"Marvelous!" Gar said. "It will be a spectacle people will talk about for years!"

◆

Four Months Later:

Nan, Kay, and Irene wrote to one another often, but had not seen each other since they parted at Garsland. It was now autumn, and the trees in the Valley of William Etté were ablaze with colors of gold and scarlet. Nan kept busy helping her father and brothers rebuild his cobbler business. Shoes were in high demand after the war, and the business was growing rapidly as Liam's high quality footwear was much sought after. Nan even started her own line of dancing slippers, and taught dance to the town's children.

Nan missed Fitzgerald deeply and looked forward to the notes he secretly sent to her, tucked into Kay's letters. She longed to see him, or Irene, but her father was keeping her firmly under his thumb and would not allow her to travel. She lived for the letters from her friends.

Irene's brother never returned, so Irene assumed the throne in Cabbage, a duty she never wanted but knew she must take on. Rebuilding her tiny kingdom kept her extremely busy, but she and Anton, who was slowly regaining his strength, were happy. Seever stayed on in Cabbage to assist in Anton's recovery, concocting many potions to try to restore the wizard's health.

Kay, Ken, and Fitzgerald began their work to rebuild relations between the Secret Valley and the neighboring communities. They traveled often and enjoyed being ambassadors.

One chilly day, a messenger rode into the Valley of William Etté with a letter for Nan from Irene. Nan read the shocking contents and her eyes filled with tears.

My dear, dear friend,
I send sad news. Anton has died and his burial must take place soon.
Please, please come to Cabbage at once. I need you.
Love,
Queen Irene

Nan got permission from her parents to travel, packed a bag and set out on horseback.

Irene sent a similar message to Kay and Ken, who immediately left the Secret Valley. Nan reached Cabbage first. When she entered the castle, Seever greeted her.

"This is a sad time," Seever said as he walked Nan up to Irene's rooms. "Anton seemed to be doing much better. Indeed, his strength was gaining every day. He was so in love with Irene. I am afraid this will be hard on her."

"But what happened?"

"Anton was out walking with Irene in the garden and he suddenly tired. He sat down to rest and simply expired. That is how it is with us wizards sometimes. Our endings can be abrupt and unexpected. Anton was physically stronger, but he struggled to regain his abilities for spells. One day he could perform modest spells, but the next day he would falter. You see, once we lose our magic, we die."

Nan knocked softly and entered Irene's room. She saw her dearest friend staring blankly out of the window.

"Oh, Irene," Nan said, kneeling in front of Irene and taking her hands. "I can't tell you how sorry I am." Irene looked at Nan and, although there were tears in her eyes, managed a slight smile.

"Thank you for coming," Irene said in a calm voice. "I can't imagine going through this without my best friend."

"How are you doing?"

"Strangely, I seem to be managing. I somehow thought it would be harder."

She paused, granting her friend a tired smile. "We bury Anton in the morning. I do hope the others get here in time."

◆

On a cold, early winter morning, Irene laid her husband to rest in the royal family chapel beneath the palace. Kay, Fitzgerald and Ken arrived just in time for the burial service. Nan and Fitzgerald stood next to one another and held hands. Seever said incantations over Anton's stone coffin. Irene seemed heartbroken, but never shed a tear.

After the service, Irene asked Kay and Nan to come with her to her rooms. Servants brought tea and cake and then left the three friends alone. After a few moments, Kay spoke.

"Irene, we're so terribly sorry about Anton. Please tell us if there is anything we can do."

"Yes," echoed Nan. "Anything at all?"

"No. Just be with me."

"We will," said Nan firmly. "We'll stay as long as you need us."

"I must tell you something," Irene said. "That day in Garsland when Seever first examined Anton—do you remember Anton wished to speak with me...alone?"

Nan and Kay nodded.

"I went into the room and Anton looked so...defeated. He said he was dying. Despite Seever's hopes of a recovery, Anton knew in his heart he would not survive. He told me he loved me and his greatest regret was that we would never have a life together. I professed I loved him too, for you see, I truly did.

"Anton said he would return to Wizards' Keep with Seever and Kaza and live out his final days. He told me to forget about him and find a life with someone new—a mortal who could give me a normal life. He also revealed the wizard's line died with him. As far as he was aware, there were no more wizards after him. When I said I would marry him anyway, he became angry. He ordered me to leave—to make a new life. I knew he said this only to spare me the grief of his passing.

"I pleaded with him; begged him to stay, but he refused. He pushed me away when I tried to embrace him. I fell to my knees and implored him to hear me out. I told him my greatest joy would be to become his wife, no matter how fleeting our time together might be. I only wanted to love him. I wore him down and he finally agreed to marry me." She smiled, remembering.

"I believe I made him genuinely happy. I am glad he could find peace at last. His was an arduous path."

"Oh, Irene," said Nan, tears shining in her eyes. "I had no idea."

"There is more." Irene took a deep breath, as if to steady herself. "I am with child. If all goes well, I will give birth this spring. If it is a boy, he will be a wizard. If it is a girl, she will be mortal, like us. Seever has agreed to stay on to help me guide the child, if I give birth to a wizard."

CHAPTER 60

The next morning, Irene, looking pale, but in command of her emotions, joined her friends for breakfast. Nan and Fitzgerald sat together and couldn't help but steal short kisses when they thought no one was looking. When everyone was done eating, Irene stood up.

"Right, then," she said. "I think we are well past due in taking care of a certain matter. I can get a holy man here in a half an hour to do the honors." She looked directly at Nan and Fitzgerald.

"What do you mean?" Nan asked.

"Oh, Nan, for Mirn's sake. I think it is *high* time you two married. Don't you?"

"But...what about my father?"

"Do you really want to wait until he is convinced Fitzy is a suitable husband? You may be secretly engaged for a long, long time. We know how stubborn he can be."

"You are probably right." Nan turned to the knight. "Oh, Fitzy, this isn't the wedding I envisioned, but would you?"

"Of course! I would marry you here or in the middle of a desert— even in the land of the Black Lord! Anywhere!" exclaimed Fitzgerald. "Oh, my goodness—I am going to be a husband!"

Within the hour, Ken, Kay, and Irene witnessed Nan and Fitzgerald exchange their vows. Once they were pronounced husband and wife, Fitzgerald gave Nan a lingering kiss that made everyone break out in laughter. The two decided Nan should return to her home, for now. Unwilling to simply send a message to her parents about her marriage; she would go back and, at the right time, break the news. Her mother would probably come around, although she still wasn't sure about her father.

EPILOGUE

Five months after Nan and Fitzgerald's wedding, a late season snow fell softly on the hills of Cabbage. That year would be remembered as a hard winter followed by a reluctant spring.
In the very early morning hours, a newborn child cried for the first time.

ABOUT THE AUTHORS

KC Cowan has spent her life working in the media, as a reporter for KGW-TV, KPAM and KLX-radio, and as original host and story producer for an arts program on Oregon Public Television. She is also the author of two books: "The Riches of a City," the story of Portland, Oregon, and "They Ain't Called Saints for Nothing!" with artist Chris Haberman. She is married and happily lives in her hometown.

Sara Cole is an officer with Clackamas County Sheriff's Office, where she is the Crime Prevention Coordinator. Sara provides public outreach to citizens on topics such as Neighborhood Watch, ID Theft and Personal Safety. She also serves on many community coalitions, and is a board member of the Crime Prevention Association of Oregon. Sara is married and enjoys spending much of her free time with her two active grandchildren.

Nancy Danner is the daughter of a shoemaker and a teacher. Nancy is a teacher, and for many years taught in a blended class of hearing and hearing-impaired students. Nancy's love of music has her singing in church choirs, directing children's musicals, and writing songs for her students. Nancy's family includes two grown children, Sean and Clarice, a rescue dog named Hal, and a loving husband, Rodney.

ACKNOWLEDGEMENTS

Many thanks to my "Early Readers:" Kathy S. and Carolyn L. who gave me encouragement to move ahead with the book. Thanks also to my editor, Carrie.

KC Cowan